CW01024534

Healed

by the

Dragon

(Stonefire Dragons #4)

Jessie Donovan

Healed by the Dragon
Copyright © 2015 Laura Hoak-Kagey
Mythical Lake Press, LLC
Second Paperback Edition

Cover Art by Clarissa Yeo of Yocla Designs.

ISBN 13: 978-1942211235

To my editor, Becky Johnson

She always pushes me to be better and never allows me to be lazy. I'm grateful to have her and appreciate her putting up with my perfectionist tendencies!

Other Books by Jessie Donovan

Stonefire Dragons
Sacrificed to the Dragon
Seducing the Dragon
Revealing the Dragons
Healed by the Dragon
Reawakening the Dragon
Loved by the Dragon
Surrendering to the Dragon
Cured by the Dragon

Lochguard Highland Dragons
The Dragon's Dilemma
The Dragon Guardian
The Dragon's Heart
The Dragon Warrior (Feb 2017)

Asylums for Magical Threats
Blaze of Secrets
Frozen Desires
Shadow of Temptation
Flare of Promise

Cascade Shifters
Convincing the Cougar
Reclaiming the Wolf
Cougar's First Christmas
Resisting the Cougar

CHAPTER ONE

Finlay Stewart eyed his stack of paperwork and resisted the urge to toss it all into the bin. He loved being clan leader of Lochguard far more than he hated it, but there were times when he missed doing things on his own schedule.

His dragon laughed inside his head. *You had better hurry. She will be here in a few hours.*

She's not the reason I want to be done with the bloody paperwork. Our clan needs a new sacrifice.

Believe that if you wish. You can never lie to me.

With a growl, Finn took the next stack of papers and signed line one of about fifty. He wasn't about to be lectured by his bloody dragon.

Aye, Arabella MacLeod was due to arrive in the next few hours to start her trial foster period with his clan. But any clan leader would be anxious at the arrival of someone from a different dragon-shifter clan. Just because Finn enjoyed teasing the lass and riling her up didn't mean everyone else in Lochguard would feel the same, especially given the divide which still ran deep.

His dragon huffed. *You are clan leader. The others will come around.*

It's been nearly a fucking year. I'm impatient and tired of their bullshit.

They will learn.

With a sigh, Finn flipped to the next page of the sacrifice application for the Department of Dragon Affairs. Since the DDA hadn't been accepting applications for the last two months after the attacks in Manchester and London, Finn wanted to be first in line tomorrow when the requests reopened.

Yet as he signed his name for the umpteenth time, his mind wandered to the BBC interview with Arabella MacLeod. No matter how hard he tried, he couldn't forget one sentence she'd said: *A group of men held me down, poured petrol on half of my body, and set me on fire.*

Clenching his pen so hard it snapped, he cursed as ink spilled over his hand. Not wanting to ruin the DDA paperwork, he rushed to the toilet sink. As he washed his hands, he struggled to contain his anger.

The dragon hunters had fucking set Arabella on fire and he wanted to make the bastards pay.

No matter how much he'd argued the point with Bram Moore-Llewellyn, the leader of Clan Stonefire, Bram refused to plan any more attacks on the hunters for the time being. Visitation passes were just starting to be handed out to humans to visit dragon-shifter lands and Bram didn't want to fuck that up.

His dragon spoke up. *He's right. Humans are just starting to reach out to us, and like us. We can't risk ruining our positive image.*

He knew his inner beast was correct, but he didn't like it. *I'm used to how humans in the Highlands treat us. They would never turn us over to the hunters. We've saved their lives too many times in the past.*

His beast didn't disagree, and for good reason; memories were long in the Scottish Highlands.

Still, as he moved back to his desk and attacked his paperwork again, Finn vowed to make Arabella feel safe while she lived with Lochguard. If the dragon hunters thought her easy pickings and came looking, they would have to deal with the wrath of one particular golden dragon.

Finlay Stewart had yet to have any casualties on his own land while in charge. He wasn't about to let that change, not even if a whole fucking army of dragon hunters or the ridiculous Dragon Knights came knocking.

After all, Finn had a few tricks up his sleeve.

His dragon added, *Let them come. I'm bored of always sitting.*

We'll see, dragon. We'll see.

~ ~ ~

Arabella MacLeod watched as the Scottish countryside rolled by outside the car window. Deep down, she wished to see all of the crags and peaks from the sky, but despite her best efforts and her brother's help with training, she didn't trust her inner beast enough to shift into her dragon form.

Every time she tried, her nightmares returned.

The inability to shift had nearly cost her the foster position. Only because of her sister-in-law's support was she still going. What Melanie had said to Bram to allow Arabella to go, she had no idea.

Looking to the back seat of the car, her sister-in-law, Melanie, met her eye and smiled. Mel asked, "You nervous yet?"

Arabella's brother, Tristan, grunted from the driver's seat. "Why would you bloody mention that, woman? Now she'll get nervous for sure."

Arabella rolled her eyes at her brother. "Do I look paranoid to you?"

Tristan glanced at her and then back at the road. "You're a MacLeod, which means it's impossible to tell."

She smiled. "MacLeod's are also strong on the inside. If I say I'm fine, I am. I don't need you doubting me now."

Tristan grunted and fell silent. Arabella went back to staring out the car window when Mel said, "If anything happens, anything at all, don't hesitate to call us. I don't care if it's date night or I'm in the middle of a wild dragon-sex marathon, we'll answer for you."

Arabella shuddered. "I don't need images of my brother naked and having sex with anyone."

Mel laughed. "Too bad as he's quite good, you know."

Ara changed the subject. "If I'm in trouble, I'll call. Is that good enough?"

Her brother looked unconvinced, but Melanie answered, "I believe in you, Ara. In six months' time, no one at Lochguard will want to let you go."

Mel's unwavering faith was simultaneously comforting and disconcerting. "We'll see. If my fan group follows me to Scotland, Finn might be begging you to take me back before long."

Melanie laughed. "I think it's cute you have a group who are out to get justice for what was done to you, and will bother any politician who will listen. It won't be long before they have a law named after you to tighten restrictions when it comes to the hunters."

Arabella grunted, not wanting to discuss it further.

Grateful for the silence, Ara memorized the landscape until Tristan turned down the final road leading to Lochguard. Before long, the lake, or loch as they called it in Scotland, came into view. Loch Naver had not only given Lochguard its name, it was also beautiful. The late September sunshine danced on the surface. With the hills and peaks surrounding the long lake, it looked like a picture from a postcard.

As the clan's gates appeared in the distance, Arabella rubbed her hand against her trousers as a last-minute panic squeezed her throat.

The first few minutes on Lochguard's land would be critical. She wasn't sure she could handle looks of revulsion or pity. If they all looked at her that way, she may just beg her brother to take her back.

At least, the interview she'd done with the BBC two months ago had allowed everyone to see her face and scars already. It wasn't as if her appearance would be a shock. Or, so she hoped.

Her dragon's voice was low when she spoke. *We will have fun in Scotland. Stop worrying.*

Conversing with her dragon was still difficult for Arabella, but she pushed past her fear. *Thank you.*

Any time. I am always here, Arabella.

I know.

Her dragon backed off and left her alone again.

Arabella let out a sigh. Every adult dragon-shifter spoke of their inner beast as a lifelong friend. She wanted that, too, but after a decade of silence and pushing away her dragon, she wasn't sure if it would ever happen. She might spend the rest of her life with a cautious stranger hovering at the edges of her mind.

Tristan pulled to a stop in front of a set of stone and metal gates. The words, "LOCHGUARD" were spelled out in twining metal above the entrance. Below, in Mersae, the old dragon language, was the phrase, "Love, Loyalty, and Bravery".

Her brother opened his door to exit the car and Melanie followed suit. They waited patiently a few paces off.

Her brother and his mate had been extremely patient and understanding over the last year. The thought of not seeing them for six months brought tears to her eyes.

Stop it, Arabella. It's only six bloody months. You should focus on making new memories. With a deep inhalation, she blinked back the tears and schooled her face into a neutral expression. If she broke down and cried, there was no way her brother would let her out of his sight.

Having a protective older brother was both a blessing and a curse.

Her emotions under control, she opened the door and went over to Melanie and Tristan. She could just make out Melanie saying, "It's rude, Tristan."

Arabella interjected, "What's rude?"

Mel frowned. "You would think someone would greet us at the gate. But no one's here."

Glancing over to the gate, she saw nothing but the stone, metal, and wilderness. She looked back over to Melanie. "We're early."

Melanie opened her mouth just as a familiar Scottish male's voice shouted, "I'm here, I'm here."

The gate opened and Finlay Stewart slowed his pace to a quick walk.

Much like when she'd last seen him in person at Bram's mating ceremony, he was as handsome as ever. Tall, lean, with wind-ruffled blond hair and an ever-present scruff on his face, he was the sort of male who could have any female he wanted.

He was the kind of male who would never want someone like her.

Remembering him flirting with every unmated female back on Stonefire's lands, she managed to get past his attractiveness.

14

Yes, he was fit, but the male was nothing but trouble. She was going to stick to her plan to avoid him. She didn't want his cockiness ruining her first taste of freedom in more than a decade.

Finn approached and Ara schooled her face into borderline boredom. She would be civil, but she wasn't going to let him slip past her barriers like he'd done six months before. Arabella was stronger. Resisting the dragonman should be easier this time around.

~~~

As soon as Finn was notified of Arabella's arrival, he jumped up from behind his desk and rushed toward the front gate. The bloody woman was forty-five minutes early.

Knowing as much as he did of Arabella, she'd frown upon his not meeting them at the gate. Not only that, he didn't need her brother to hate him any more than he already did, especially given Finn's plans for the lass.

He half-ran to the front entrance and only slowed his pace when Arabella turned and met his eyes. There was a flash of relief, but it was quickly replaced with an unreadable expression.

His dragon growled. *She should never block us out.*

Give it time, dragon. It's been six months. The lass needs time to acclimate again.

With a huff, his inner beast retreated just as Finn approached Arabella, her brother, and her brother's mate. He looked to Arabella and winked. "Couldn't resist coming early to see me, eh, lass?"

Before she could reply, her brother growled. "I don't like you flirting with my sister. If I catch any word of you hurting her, I will fly up here and teach you a lesson."

Arabella's cheeks heated as she whispered, "Tristan."

His dragon piped in. *He embarrasses her. Send him away. That will not help our case.*

Hmph.

Finn resisted rolling his eyes at his beast's tantrum.

Arabella's brother pushed on. "No, the Scot needs to hear it because it's my only warning."

Finn cocked an eyebrow as Arabella turned toward her brother. Unafraid, Finn put every ounce of dominance and authority into his voice. "This is my land. If you're here to insult me, you can leave."

Tristan took a step toward him, but both Arabella and the human female stepped between them. It was the human, Melanie if he remembered correctly, who said, "Forgive my mate. To say he's protective is an understatement. I, for one, am grateful for you giving Arabella this opportunity."

The human then turned toward her mate and Tristan finally mumbled, "Just treat her well, Stewart."

"Of course. Arabella deserves the best I can give her."

The other dragonman's eyes narrowed at that, but Finn didn't care. He hadn't hidden his intentions from Bram and he sure as hell wasn't going to hide them from her brother.

Not that any of that mattered. Finn looked back to Arabella's eyes, which were filled with curiosity. *Good.* She wasn't bolting, which had been his fear all these months. "Now, if we're quite done with the protective male bullshit, you can fetch Arabella's things and follow me."

Tristan opened his mouth, but his mate whispering, "Leave him alone," shut him up.

As Tristan and his mate returned to their car, Finn moved to Arabella's side and placed a hand on her back. She didn't tense.

She merely looked up at him, a mixture of uncertainty and hunger in her eyes.

If he were to hazard a guess, she craved touch more than she let on.

He smiled down at her. "Come, I want to show you to your cottage. I helped decorate it myself."

Skepticism filled her eyes. "If it's filled with pink, fluffy bunnies and animal pillows, we're going to trade houses."

He grinned. "What about pink, fluffy unicorns? Are they more your style? And rainbow kittens. You seem like a rainbow kitten kind of lass."

She fought a smile and lost. "I'm the kind of 'lass' who will take every rainbow kitten I can find and pile them at your front door. That will improve your image as a dominant, scary clan leader for sure."

He leaned down a fraction and murmured, "Oh, I'm all for games of retaliation, Arabella. Start one with me and you won't stand a chance."

Her breath hitched. If it was because of fear, he would ease off. But there was no fear in Arabella MacLeod's eyes. No, there was a mixture of longing and fledgling desire.

Any doubts he'd harbored about the lass no longer wanting him, vanished.

Not caring how cocky his grin must be, he whispered, "That is all to come. For now, Arabella, let me show you to your new fluffy, pink paradise."

She broke his gaze and snorted. "If that's supposed to be charming, you're out of practice. It sounds quite creepy."

Her brother growled from behind, "Are we leaving anytime soon? I have my sister's belongings, but if you're going to stand there flirting with Ara right in front of me, not even my mate will stop me from beating your arse."

Rather than fight her brother any more, he gave Arabella a gentle push and they started walking. The sooner he settled Arabella, the sooner her brother would leave. Then he could really pull out all the stops.

Glancing at Arabella's profile, he barely noticed the scar across her nose or the healed burns on her neck. All he saw was the faint flush on her cheeks and her smiling face.

His dragon hummed. *We will make her smile every day. She deserves it.*

If Finn had any say in the matter, they would do exactly that.

CHAPTER TWO

Arabella had almost forgotten her nervousness because of Finn. As much as she hated to admit it, even to herself, the dragonman knew how to charm her.

Just thinking of rainbow kittens and retaliation made her smile wider.

Her dragon's voice was soft. *I told you, we will have fun in Scotland.*

Maybe. It's still early.

Before her inner beast could reply, Finn's Scottish accent filled her ear. "I see your flashing dragon eyes, Arabella. If your dragon ever wants to come out to play, I'll be first in line."

A year ago, a comment about her dragon coming out would have sent her into a panic, trapping her in the memories of the dragon hunters torturing her when she was a teenager.

After a year of hard work and coaching with her brother and clan leader, however, all Finn's words did was make her roll her eyes. "It's been what, five minutes since I came here? You're going to run out of lines real quick."

"Never for you, Arabella. I have a list a mile long."

At the huskiness in his voice, she glanced over at him. The heat in his eyes made her miss a step.

Then Finn turned his head and lifted his free hand. "Faye, I'm glad you received my message."

Ara followed Finn's line of sight. A tall, young dragonwoman in her mid-twenties with curly, brown hair smiled at them.

Arabella's heart rate kicked up. She knew she would be meeting other clan members, but it seemed too soon. She hadn't even had time to unpack yet.

The female stopped in front of them. After barely a glance in Arabella's direction, Faye turned her eyes to Finn. "Well? Are you going to introduce us properly, oh great clan leader?"

Finn laughed at the female's words and a small part of Arabella was jealous. Not that she had any claim on him, nor did she want to. Still, she hated being the outsider.

Rather than stand there, Arabella thrust out a hand. "My name is Arabella MacLeod. And you are?"

The woman's amber brown eyes met her gaze and simply stared. Ara wondered if she'd made the wrong step when the corner of the woman's mouth ticked up. She took Arabella's hand. "I'm Faye MacKenzie, your assigned Protector."

Arabella's tone was dry. "You mean babysitter."

From behind, Tristan's spoke up, "I rather like the idea of a babysitter." Her brother pushed between Finn and Arabella, met Faye's gaze and ordered, "Keep my sister safe from your clan leader."

Amusement danced in Faye's eyes. "Oh, aye? I'm taking orders from a stranger now, am I?"

Her brother blinked at the woman's words and Arabella bit her lip to keep from smiling. Arabella then said, "You don't have your scary reputation here, Tristan. I'm sure there are as many growly, broody dragonmen in Scotland as there are in the North of England."

Melanie pushed her way to Tristan's side. "That's all well and good, but this growly, broody dragonman is mine."

Faye grinned. "I have no intention of taking any male in the foreseeable future. Your mate is safe from me, Mrs…?"

Mel smiled. "I'm Melanie Hall-MacLeod, but please call me Mel."

Faye's eyes widened. "As in the author of *Revealing the Dragons*?" Mel nodded and Faye continued, "You looked different on TV. I loved your book, Mel, and all that it's accomplishing. Maybe someday you'll sign my copy?"

Melanie melted into her mate's side. "Sure, but not right now. I need to settle my sister-in-law into her new home. You'll take good care of her for me, won't you?"

Arabella opened her mouth, but Finn beat her to it. "Of course we'll take care of her. Now, before half the clan comes out to gawk, let's see Arabella to her new home."

Finn sounded irritated, but Arabella had no idea why.

Thankfully, Melanie took charge. "Yes, let's hurry. Bram and Evie are watching our twins and I'm a little anxious to go home."

Finn's voice sounded a bit more like himself when he asked, "Why? Because Bram will end up losing one of them during a nappy change?"

Mel laughed. "No, because I miss them."

Melanie's voice was full of love for her children. For a second, Arabella had a rush of homesickness. Her niece and nephew meant the world to her and had even helped Arabella become less afraid of her dragon. Six months without them was a long time.

Melanie placed a hand on her arm. "Don't worry, Ara, we'll bring them to visit, provided Finn says it's okay."

Finn sighed. "Are you lot going to make any more decisions for me and my clan? At this rate, I should just hand over the reins and take a holiday."

Arabella shot him a look. "Stop whining and take me to my cottage. I want to settle in."

From the corner of her eye, Arabella noticed Faye looking at her with interest. Before Arabella could ask the other dragonwoman a question, Mel walked ahead. "Right, let's go then."

The group fell into silence, the dynamic and ease from earlier with Finn was gone.

Which was as it should be. If she wasn't careful, Finn would find a way to convince her to care for him before breaking her heart. She had seen it happen several times back home at Stonefire with males who acted like him. She wasn't about to fall for the male's tricks.

~~~

Finn didn't often fall into a foul mood, but he was halfway there. The lot from Stonefire were giving him a headache.

Not Arabella, of course, but her overprotective brother and his mate. Melanie seemed kind enough, but the woman was as dominant as her male. Finn's best guess was that Bram had trouble controlling the pair.

Given Finn's tenuous position, he couldn't afford to let someone take charge. The slightest sign of weakness and a clan leader challenge would be thrown in his face.

Picking up his pace, the rest of the group matched him. Since it was late afternoon, most of the clan wasn't out and about.

If he were lucky, no one had witnessed the Stonefire couple challenging him.

His dragon chimed in. *You worry too much.*

Duncan is looking for any excuse to challenge me, and you know it. Until more of the clan is on my side, I need to be careful.

The Stonefire pair will leave and everything will be fine. We can talk more with Arabella.

His dragon's tone was more demanding than he liked. *Ordering me won't make anything happen. Besides, I need to finish the sacrifice paperwork. Faye will take care of her.*

With a disbelieving grunt, his dragon fell silent. It seemed everyone wanted to challenge his authority today.

They passed a few of the cottages on the edges of the clan and soon arrived at one a little off from the others. Finn forced a smile as they approached, stopped, and gave an overly dramatic wave toward the cottage. "And this, Ms. Arabella, is your new palace."

Faye merely shook her head, but Finn didn't care. They'd known each other their whole lives; if she guessed his intent toward Arabella, Faye would understand.

Arabella eyed the wild bushes in front of the cottage. "If you expect me to trim those, you'll be sorely disappointed."

Finn moved to the door and shrugged. "Do what you will. My garden is pretty much a wild forest at this point."

Opening the door, Finn quickly peered inside. He'd checked the place from top to bottom earlier to ensure it was safe, but he wasn't about to risk Arabella's life, especially given the growing hatred for her amongst the newly reformed Dragon Knights.

Not hearing, smelling, or seeing any threats, he flipped on the lights and motioned inside. "You lot can help Arabella settle in." He looked to Faye. "Once she's settled and the Stonefire couple are on the way home, let me know."

"You're not staying?" Arabella asked.

He very much wanted to toss everyone out of the cottage, pin her against the wall, and tell her he was staying. But not only did he have heaps to do, if he made a move too soon, Arabella would close herself off from him.

His dragon murmured, *We will pin her against the wall soon. I want her.*

Shut it, dragon. She's not a thing we can simply take. She must decide.

His inner beast huffed. *I still want her.*

Finn kept his voice nonchalant. "I have things to do, lass. Faye will help you with what you need, and I will be by to check on you later."

Tristan growled. "Maybe we should stay for a while."

Melanie let out a sigh. "No, Tristan. We have a six-hour drive home yet. Unless you can shift into a dragon and carry both me and the car back to Stonefire, we need to leave within the hour."

Tristan remained silent.

The urge to tease Tristan was great, but Finn resisted. "Right, then I'll leave you with Faye. When you wish to visit, let Bram know and I'll see what we can do. I can't have unsolicited visits at the moment, what with the hunters and Dragon Knights."

Mel nodded. "Of course. We'll allow Arabella to settle in and find her place inside Lochguard first."

"Then until next time, I bid you farewell." Avoiding Arabella's eye, Finn exited the cottage and walked toward his own.

HEALED BY THE DRAGON

~~~

Arabella was still trying to push aside her disappointment at Finn leaving when Mel placed a hand on her arm. Arabella met Mel's eyes as she said, "How about you and I make some tea while Tristan carries your luggage upstairs?"

Ignoring her brother's grunt, Arabella nodded. There were things she wanted to ask Melanie that Arabella couldn't ask in front of her overly protective brother.

Faye cleared her throat. "I'm going to wait outside and ring my team, if you don't mind?"

Arabella looked at her babysitter. "Okay."

When it was apparent that was all Arabella was going to say, Faye turned and exited the cottage.

Mel pushed her toward the kitchen on the far side just as Tristan took her first suitcase up the stairs. When they were alone, Mel asked, "We don't have much time, Ara, so if you want to ask me something, then do it quickly before Tristan comes back."

She looked away from Mel's gaze, her eyes roaming the kitchen counters as a distraction. "What happens if I can't last six months here? What will I do then?"

Mel patted her arm. "Then just call. However, if this is about Finn rejecting you, you are stronger than that. I'm sure there are a lot of hot Scottish dragon-shifters here to choose from."

Ara's heart rate kicked up and a hot flush crept up her neck. "Mate hunting isn't my main reason for being here."

"I know, dear, but don't rule it out. I think you can truly be yourself here, and if you can do that, you'll be turning quite a few heads here."

She looked into Mel's eyes. Kindness and love shined from her sister-in-law's gaze. How she could have ever hated the human in front of her, Arabella didn't know. Melanie was the closest thing to a sister she'd ever have.

Unsure of what else to say, Arabella mumbled, "Thank you."

Tristan's footsteps thudded down the stairs and Mel moved to the electric kettle on the counter. "Now, let's make some tea and get to work. We only have an hour or so before we need to leave. Twelve hours in a car, all in one day, must be a record for me."

Tristan appeared in the kitchen. "Believe me, I know. Staying still is not your strongest point."

Mel raised an eyebrow at her mate. "Says the dragonman who can't sit still through an entire movie without finding something else to do at the same time."

Tristan shrugged. "Dragon-shifters have more energy. Unless you want me to spend dinners away hunting in dragon form instead, you'll just have to put up with it."

Mel smiled. "Maybe once the twins are older, I can send all three of you away to hunt and give me a little peace."

Tristan walked up to his mate and pulled her close. "Or, we can just bring you with us. You're the one who likes studying dragon-shifters."

Mel grinned. "You got me on that one."

Arabella turned away as her brother kissed his mate. She'd spent a decade believing she would never have the closeness and regular touch of a mate. In recent weeks, however, she was starting to wonder if it were possible.

Her dragon's voice was cautious. *It will be if you allow me to help.*

She paused a second, and decided to risk a question. *I don't understand. What do you mean?*

Soon, Ara, but not yet. You're not ready.

Anger filled her body. *You're supposed to be on my side, bloody dragon.*

And I am. Just wait.

The kettle clicked off. Letting out a sigh of frustration, Arabella prepared the tea, wondering what in the hell her dragon could be going on about.

CHAPTER THREE

Arabella was alone. As she hung up several of her favorite framed pictures of doors, the cottage felt a bit more like home. Bringing all fifty-three of her door picture collection had been out of the question, but the ten on her wall would have to suffice.

She traced the outline of a faded blue door, crooked and slightly off its top hinge. The picture was from an old cottage in Ireland, but that wasn't what Arabella saw when she looked at it.

The crooked blue door was a portal to another land where dragons lived together in castle compounds and were the only race on the planet. They could fly and hunt freely, without fear of any predators. No, in Arabella's imaginary land, dragons were the top predators. Humans, and most especially dragon hunters, didn't exist.

Stepping back, Arabella glanced over her collection of doors. Each held a fantasy she'd used over the years to escape the terrible reality that had been her life.

She hoped to replace the pictures one day with actual memories. However, that day had yet to come.

There was a knock on the door. Arabella laid the hammer down and peeped out the hole to see Faye MacKenzie's smiling face. Her first instinct was to pretend she didn't hear the knock, but Arabella quickly pushed it aside. Even if it killed her, she would force herself to interact with people.

Opening the door, Arabella attempted to smile. "Yes?"

Faye raised an eyebrow. "Are you going to invite me inside?"

Stepping aside, Arabella motioned with a hand. "Come in."

Faye brushed past and strode into the living area. The dragonwoman's stride was confident in a way Arabella wasn't sure she could ever be.

After shutting the door, she followed and found Faye looking at her collection of doors. A stranger viewing her special escape mechanisms felt wrong, but she fought the feeling and waited to see what the other female would do.

Smiling, Faye looked at her and Arabella realized her amber eyes looked a lot like Finn's, both in shape and in color. Before she could stop herself, she blurted, "Are you Finn's sister? Or, maybe half-sister?"

Chuckling, Faye turned toward Arabella. "No, but you're not the first person to assume that. We're cousins, in fact."

The ease between Finn and Faye now made sense. "Your parents must've conspired with the names both starting with 'F'."

"Oh, don't even start with me on that. My older brothers' names are Fergus and Fraser. Given my parents' choice of overly Scottish names, I'm lucky my mum stood her ground or my dad would've named me Flora. Although I'm curious about you. MacLeod is decidedly Scottish, yet your accent is from Northern England. Do you know why?"

Arabella blinked. "Do you always jump from one subject to the next?"

Faye grinned. "Aye. It's a bit of a family trait. Just be glad my older brothers aren't here, too. Although I can easily bring them over, if you like."

29

Before she could stop herself, Arabella touched the burned side of her neck. The action made Faye frown. Her tone was a bit dominant. "We're going to have to fix that self-consciousness, hen, or you won't last long here."

Lowering her hand, Arabella studied Faye. "Why is that?"

"Lochguard is full of stubborn, clever dragonmen and women, but not all of them welcome the idea of a fostering. Show them any weakness and they'll pounce. Finn is determined to protect you, but he's clan leader and can't be everywhere."

Arabella's shyness melted, replaced with a growing hatred in her belly. "What exactly has Finlay Stewart been saying about me?"

Faye shrugged. "Not much, just that I'm to watch over you and report any ill treatment I see. I'd say my cousin is quite interested in you, Arabella MacLeod. Care to tell me what happened when he went to Stonefire?"

The dragonwoman's direct yet friendly tone unsettled Arabella. She had no bloody idea if it were sincere or not. Reading people was not one of her strengths.

Arabella decided to do what she did best and be blunt. "He quizzed me about security and the like. Most of the time, he was flirting with the single females."

Faye studied her a moment. "Aye, that sounds like Finn."

Even Arabella, a novice when it came to subtlety, understood Faye wasn't fooled. "I'm not completely helpless, no matter what Finn might say."

"I never said you were. But if you're to survive here, Arabella, I need to teach you a few things."

She didn't like the sound of that. "What things?"

Faye crossed her arms and tilted her head as she studied Arabella. Only through sheer force of will did Arabella manage not to fidget or lash out. If she alienated Faye MacKenzie, she would lose a valuable resource. So far, the dragonwoman was much more straightforward than Finn.

Just before Arabella mustered the courage to ask again, Faye answered, "For one, there is a rift in the clan. A little less than half don't like Finn's modern ideas on dragon-human relations."

"How is that my problem?"

"Well, they'll be watching you. A few of them may even try to scare you away. They aren't fond of any English dragon-shifters invading their territory."

Arabella clenched one of her hands. She was tired of being polite. "Why the bloody hell would they hate the English dragons? Stonefire hasn't tried to attack Lochguard in centuries."

"Aye, you're right. But memories are long. You forget we were the target of both the English humans and the other dragon clans during the Highland Clearances in the 18th century, when both wanted to steal our land. It's the reason there's only one dragon-shifter clan in Scotland instead of two."

"That was nearly three hundred years ago. And before you start on a long tirade of the level of injustices, my family has a tie. You asked why my last name is MacLeod yet I sound English. Well, my family was driven out of the lowland Scottish clan during the clearances, but I'm not about to blame a group of dead people for the pain of long-dead ancestors." Faye smiled, confusing her. "Why are you smiling at me?"

"You've a backbone, Arabella. You may do well here after all."

"You're changing the subject. You said I needed to know things, as in plural. Old history aside, why else should I be careful?"

Just as Faye opened her mouth, there was a knock on the door. Mischief danced in the dragonwoman's eyes. "That will be Finlay. He can tell you himself."

~~~

Waiting for Arabella to answer her door, Finn ran his hand through his hair. Why butterflies were banging around in his stomach, he had no idea. It wasn't as if the lass hadn't seen him worse off before.

Amusement tinged his dragon's voice. *Aye, but this time is different. This time, you can be alone with her without her family.*

His inner beast was correct, not that Finn would admit as much. *I'm more worried about her settling in. She doesn't do well with strangers.*

Faye is friendly and kind. Arabella will be fine.

Before he could voice any more of his concerns, his cousin, Faye, opened the door. Her voice was overly innocent. "Aye, cousin? Can I help you?"

"Why are you asking me that? Just let me in."

Faye smiled. "You said you'd be here in another hour. Since you're early, I'm just concerned something is going on and needs my attention. I am a Protector, after all."

Finn growled. "Stop your games, cousin. Move aside and let me in."

"Someone's grumpy." Faye laughed.

Rather than put up with his cousin's games, Finn pushed past her and walked into the living area. Scanning the room, Arabella was standing off to the side with her arms crossed over her chest. Careful not to stare at her plumped up breasts, he smiled and dusted off his charm. "Why, lovely Arabella, you're looking radiant as always."

His dragon snorted. *She won't like that.*

Arabella raised an eyebrow. "Still working on that list, Finlay? You should save yourself some time and toss it away."

Told you.

Ignoring his beast, Finn took two steps toward Arabella. When she didn't move away, it pumped up his ego. "And miss out on your gleeful responses? Never."

With a sigh, Arabella said, "Why are you here and what do you want?"

Finn took another step toward the lass, never breaking eye contact. "I'm here for you, Arabella."

Arabella's eyes widened a fraction. She quickly went back to a neutral expression, but it was too late. Her response gave him the courage to step even closer and lower his voice. "For the next two hours, you can do whatever you like with me."

He could hear her heart rate kick up. Never taking his gaze from hers, he whispered, "So, what would you like to do, Arabella?"

He waited to see if he'd pushed too far. But as he'd expected, she straightened her shoulders and stood tall. "I would like for you to leave so Faye can answer my questions."

"I can do that myself, lass."

She jabbed a finger into his chest and he resisted the urge to capture her hand in his. "You would spend half the time flirting, which just wastes my time. I'm sure the clan could use you elsewhere."

Faye's voice came from behind him. "Aye, cousin. You always go on about a never-ending list of tasks. You could tackle some of those."

Turning, he shot his cousin a warning glance. "Don't you have training to do? Last time I checked, you were in charge of a wing of Protectors."

Faye nodded. "Yes, but you're early. I can keep Arabella company for another half hour. You could settle a dispute or two during that time."

Finn steeled his voice and ordered, "I came early for a reason. Shay had some trouble with one of the other lads. You need to talk with him and work on nipping his temper."

His cousin remained silent for a few seconds out of pure spite before she nodded. "Right, then I'll go take care of that now." Faye looked to Arabella. "There's a list of phone numbers on your fridge, including mine. If you need anything, don't hesitate to call."

Arabella answered, "I'd much rather go with you and watch you train. I'm out of practice and could use the refresher."

Finn gave a minuscule shake of his head.

Faye smiled. "Sorry, Arabella. As much as I wish I could, not even I can disobey my clan leader without consequences. Finn wants some time alone with you, so you may as well get it over with."

Finn had barely growled, "Faye," before his cousin laughed and quickly exited the door.

Taking a deep breath, he turned toward Arabella. Rather than scared, she looked pissed off. "Now, now, Arabella. Is spending time with me really that awful?"

Glaring, she pushed against his chest. He ignored the heat that flared at her touch and focused on her words. "Why are you so keen to have me alone? If you think to charm me and make me one of your conquests, it's not going to happen."

Anger rushed through his body and he narrowed his eyes. "For someone who doesn't like people judging her, you're being bloody judgmental."

She pushed against his chest again. "I saw how you acted while at Stonefire, dancing and whispering into the females' ears. You had them eating out of your hand and the only reason a male does that is to get into someone's bed."

Trapping her hand against his chest, he leaned down. Not even her intake of breath could distract him from the anger raging through his body. "Think about it. Being all broody and bastard-like would've driven all of your clan away and then no one would've wanted to foster here. Charming a few lasses is worth it if it means I can further cement the alliance with Stonefire."

Arabella blinked. "You did it for the alliance?"

"Aye, I did. And I would do much more. But since you trust my cousin more than me, though who the fuck knows why, you can ask her how many hearts I've broken here. Maybe that will erase your judgmental bullshit."

As they stared in silence, Finn noticed the delicate, warm hand in his. Not only that, a faint smell of vanilla filled his nose.

His dragon growled. *She smells nice. And she's warm. I want her.*

Thankfully, Arabella replied faster than his inner beast. "Tell me yourself. How many, Finn?"

He didn't hesitate. "One, when I was a lad of eighteen." Her brows furrowed. Releasing her hand, he stepped back a few paces. "Believe it or not, I don't care, Arabella MacLeod. But I'll tell you this—if you truly wish to train and regain the skills you lost over the last decade, then I will be your trainer."

"But—"

"No. Faye would never admit it, but she has a lot on her plate. She's practically reinventing how my Protectors are trained.

She would never refuse you, but as her clan leader, I'm going to forbid it. If you want to train, you have to deal with me." He crossed his arms over his chest. "I need an answer and I need it now. What do you want, Arabella? This is your one chance to ask for it."

CHAPTER FOUR

Arabella clenched her hands at her side. "I've been here half a day and you're tossing ultimatums? Who the hell do you think you are?"

"Clan leader."

His matter-of-fact tone only made her blood hotter. "Clan leaders who rule through fear and ultimatums don't last long, Finlay Stewart."

Finn cocked an eyebrow. "So you know how I run my clan, now, aye?"

"I'd imagine this is your true self. Even if you've been hiding, the clan will find out soon enough."

Anger flashed in Finn's eyes, but Arabella wasn't afraid. If she didn't stand up to the Scot, he would feel entitled to boss her around the entire six months and she wasn't having it.

The dragonman moved toward her, until he was less than a foot apart. She swore she could feel the heat of his body.

Only his voice distracted her. "If you think I'm going to tiptoe around you and be gentle, acquiescing to your every whim because of a few scars, then let me be clear: it's not going to happen. You're stubborn, Arabella MacLeod, but I'm even more so. You train with me or with no one because I can't risk something going wrong. Or, in the worst case scenario, someone hurts you to get back at me."

She frowned. "What are you talking about?"

He stepped closer, and she stepped back only to come up against a wall. As he put an arm on either side of her head, his breath tickled her cheek. His heat and scent surrounded her, but before she could think too hard on why it made her feel safe rather than cause a panic, Finn whispered, "A section of the clan wants to oust me. They've tried everything from fabricating a scandal to fucking false claims of me impregnating every single female in the clan to ensure my place. Let's just say they're not happy about an English dragon-shifter living on our lands. If I'm not careful, they'll hurt you, Arabella. I couldn't live with myself if that happened."

Searching his amber eyes, she saw only truth. "Why wouldn't you just tell me this instead of pulling dominant alpha dragon bullshit and trying to order me around? Dancing around the truth and subtle moves aren't my forte, Finn. Tell me straight and I'm more apt to believe you."

He leaned a fraction closer. With her anger fading, she could no longer ignore his heat or masculine scent filling her nose.

Her dragon whispered, *He won't hurt you. Kiss him.*

I—no. I don't want to kiss him.

Liar.

Finn tilted his head to whisper into her ear, "I see your flashing dragon eyes, Arabella. Tell me what she's saying."

His neck was now just in front of her lips. Thanks to her supersensitive dragon-shifter hearing, she heard Finn's heart beating double-time.

She couldn't tell if it was all a game or if he really was interested in her.

Curling her fingers against the wall, she leaned a fraction more toward him. The scent of pure male mixed with wind and peat caressed her senses. She liked the way he smelled.

No. I can't do this.

Before her dragon could answer, Finn pulled away. The loss of his heat made her shiver.

As if the last few minutes never happened, Finn raised an eyebrow. "You may not want to discuss your dragon with me, but you will, Arabella. One day, I will know all of your secrets."

She cleared her throat. "And how, exactly, do you know that? Do you have a crystal ball you use to tell the future?"

His look grew heated. "No, but I don't give up easily on people and I have no plans to give up on you."

Blinking, Arabella tried to think of what to say. He surely couldn't mean he was interested in her. They barely knew each other.

Yet at the same time, his single-minded gaze was intense and a little unnerving. In this moment, he only saw her.

Then Finn put out a hand and wiggled his fingers. "So, how about a little training? I want you prepared in case Duncan and his crowd think to target you."

"Who is Duncan?"

"My main rival." He stretched his hand out a little further. "What will it be? If nothing else, think of it as a chance to kick my arse. That should make you happy."

Smiling at the image of kicking Finn in the balls, she placed her hand in his. "You finally have something I can't resist."

His grip tightened on her hand and a little jolt rushed down her arms. Somehow, she focused on his question. "Oh, aye? And what's that, lass?"

"The opportunity to send you to your knees."

~~~

At Arabella's grin, Finn felt like he'd been punched in the gut. Her whole face lit up with a smile. Add the amusement and a little too much glee in her eyes, and she was beautiful.

His dragon huffed. *You should have kissed her. I don't like waiting.*

But anticipation is part of the game.

I'm a dragon. I don't care about anticipation. I want to kiss Arabella and when she is ready, I also want to fuck her.

Pushing aside his beast's pulsing desire, he focused back on Arabella and grinned. "I think I'll have you on your back before that happens, lass."

He waited to see if she would bolt, withdraw, or who the hell knew what else at the innuendo. But his lass merely raised an eyebrow. "I take that as a challenge, and you should know that MacLeods take their challenges very seriously."

Tugging her hand, he moved toward the door. Arabella caught up to him and he glanced down at her. "Then I look forward to the challenge. I survived three days of hell to be clan leader, but maybe one wee lass has the power to send me to my knees in the end."

"I'm much more than a 'wee lass'. Before my life changed all those years ago, I had planned to be clan leader."

Unlocking the door, he glanced at her. When he didn't answer straightaway, her brows drew together. "What? You don't believe me?"

"Oh, I believe you." He winked. "I'm imagining you kicking Bram's arse and taking over."

HEALED BY THE DRAGON

In the ensuing silence, Finn opened the door before he finally said, "Enough talk. I want to see if you can walk the walk. Let's go. I may even give you a tour on the way, if you're nice to me."

They exited the house. After shutting the door, they headed in the direction of the nearby loch. He squeezed Ara's delicate female hand in his. When she didn't try to pull away, it pumped up his ego.

His dragon was hovering on the edge of his mind, but his inner beast's desire to do much more than hold the lass's hand was slowly filtering out. *Stop it, dragon. I can't train Ara with a hard cock.*

Then do as I wish. Kiss her.

Not now, you ruddy beast.

Using every bit of alpha dominance he possessed, Finn reinforced the walls between him and his dragon.

Satisfied his beast was contained for the moment, he looked around. The area was deserted, which wasn't unusual given the time of day. He would take advantage of their isolation to share a bit of his clan with Arabella. After all, he wanted her to grow to love Lochguard as much as he did. Revealing a bit of the magic might help to do that.

Pointing to the loch in the distance, he upped his nonchalant charm. "You probably saw Loch Naver on your way in. While the humans see it merely as a body of water, we have legends about that loch here."

Looking up at him, she tilted her head. "Well? Are you going to tell me or do I need to ask super nicely?"

"Just making sure I had your attention, lass, because it's quite a tale."

"It better live up to the hype, Finn."

41

Grinning, he tugged her a little closer to his side and leaned his head down to hers. "See the crumbling broch on our side of the lake?"

"You mean the half-destroyed tower-looking stone structure?"

"That's the one. Well, they say the Green Lady used to live there. She was a protective spirit who drew her powers from the loch. Some say she's the reason Clan Lochguard managed to keep their land when the Sutherlands cleared these parts of tenants in the 1800s to raise sheep."

Arabella gave him a skeptical look. "A magical spirit lady protected your clan? You do realize you're a dragon-shifter, right? And that, I don't know, it's more likely a group of dragons chased away the human landowners?"

"Where's the mystery in that? I like to think the Green Lady still resides in that broch, waiting to help the clan whenever we truly need it again. In fact, whenever a clan member turns eighteen, they visit it at night to experience the magic. I think you should try it. Maybe after you walk inside and feel the strange energy, you'll be a little less skeptical."

"Maybe, though I doubt it. I like facts more than feelings."

"I'll work on changing your mind, lass, just wait and see." Finn tugged Arabella's hand. "Come. As much as I like to tell stories, I only have about an hour left before my next appointment. If you want to train, we need to hurry."

~ ~ ~

Arabella gave one last look at the crumbling tower near the lake before following Finn's lead. While she didn't believe in magic or spirits, she was curious to see the inside of the structure.

The 'magic' of the place could probably be explained with a few cleverly hidden lights or speakers. She'd love to see Finn's face when she disproved his tale.

Blinking, she nearly missed a step. Her plan to steer clear of the Lochguard leader was not going well. While she had no choice but to allow him to train her, Arabella would find other ways to occupy her time. She still had programming work to do, for one. Also, she wanted to find out more information about the so-called rift inside Lochguard. While the Scottish dragon-shifter clan was similar to her own, it wasn't quite the same. She needed to figure out her boundaries.

As they walked, Finn would occasionally point out a few places of interest, such as his cottage, the main hall, and the central marketplace, but for the rest of the time, he remained silent. Glancing over to steal a peek, Finn looked deep in thought. Given his tendency to tease and banter, she sometimes forgot about the weight he carried as clan leader.

Then a dragon landed less than fifty feet away, catching her attention. The tall beast's purple hide glinted in the small streams of sunlight shining through the broken clouds in the sky.

As the dragon beat her wings to steady herself as her feet touched the ground, a twinge of longing squeezed Arabella's heart. In dragon form, Arabella's hide was nearly the same shade of purple.

More than anything, she wished to have the same sense of ease and familiarity as the purple dragon in the landing area. Yet despite her best efforts, Arabella had yet to shift of her own free will.

Her dragon's voice was gentle. *I am here. When you are ready, let me know. I will help.*

43

Much like in the past, Arabella remained silent rather than reply. Her inner beast was patient and ever since Arabella had ventured outside her cottage on her own a year ago, she hadn't forced Arabella to shift into a dragon. But a year without shifting would soon take its toll on her beast. The day was coming when she would shift whether she wanted it or not.

Tugging her arm, Finn pulled them behind a wall of rock, which blocked out the dragon landing area.

While wondering if he'd been watching her closely or not, the dragonman simply released her hand and took a few steps back. "Come at me, Arabella, and attack me with your best moves. I need to see what I'm working with."

Grateful Finn didn't bring up her gawking at the other dragon, she pushed her concerns about shifting aside. "I don't have any 'moves' as you put it. I spent a decade in near-isolation inside my cottage. I need to start at the beginning."

"I doubt that. I'll find a way to test you, though."

As the corner of Finn's mouth ticked up, she glared. "If you think to cop a feel to rile me up, I won't stop until I kick you in the balls, Finlay Stewart. Consider that your only warning."

The bastard grinned and Arabella tried to recall her training as a teenager. There had to be something she could do to unsettle the cocky dragonman.

She might have one move, provided she didn't bollix it up.

Taking a deep breath for courage, Arabella walked slowly up to Finn. When she stopped in front of him and placed a hand on his chest, his grin faded. His voice was husky when he asked, "What are you doing, Arabella?"

In a swift movement, she swung her leg, angled her foot and kicked the back of his knee.

Finn faltered a second, but instead of going down, he took hold of her arms, swirled her around until she faced away from him, and trapped her against his chest.

Being restrained and unable to see who was doing it made her stomach drop. She was trapped, just like during her capture as a teenager.

With her heart thundering in her ears, she was no longer in Scotland, but in a dark barn. The smell of manure and old male sweat filled her nose. A male held her against his chest, her struggles no match for his muscles.

Still, she tried. Her mother was tied in chains in the corner as another human male punched her.

No. She screamed for them to stop. If they didn't stop, they would kill her.

"Arabella MacLeod. Look at me."

It took a second for her to realize she was no longer restrained. Finn was crouched down in front of her, his eyes searching hers for answers.

Shame rushed forth. Arabella had worked so hard over the last year, yet the first man to restrain her in a friendly training session triggered her trauma. Maybe she hadn't been ready to leave her clan after all.

The dominance in Finn's voice caught her attention. "Arabella, are you with me?"

She averted her gaze and nodded. The next thing she knew, Finn took hold of her chin and turned her to face him. "Look at me."

Bracing herself for pity, she darted a glance and she blinked. There wasn't an ounce of pity in Finn's eyes, only intensity.

The dragonman's voice was pure steel. "If I'm going to train you, I need you to answer some questions truthfully. If you deflect, I will talk to Bram about sending you back to Stonefire."

Some of her unease was replaced with anger. "You can't do that."

"I can and I will. Now, tell me: what happened when you were captured by the dragon hunters? And no half-truths. I can tell when you're lying."

"How do—"

"I've had lots of practice. Now, there's no one here but you and me. Whatever you say will stay between us, so tell me what happened, Arabella. I need to know."

CHAPTER FIVE

Finn tried not to hold his breath. After playing his best hand with the threat of sending her back to Stonefire, all he could do was wait and see if it paid off.

Arabella freezing in his arms was a feeling he'd never forget. Whatever had happened to the lass hadn't been pretty. Even a few minutes later, he still fought the urge to shift into a dragon and find the humans who'd terrorized her.

His dragon hissed. *One day, we will find them.*

I agree, but not now. Arabella needs us.

Then heal her. We are the only ones who can.

He wasn't sure what to make of his beast's statement, but he'd think on it later.

Squeezing Arabella's chin, he murmured, "Tell me, lass. I need to know."

Her eyes searched his. At least, the terrified look in her gaze was gone.

Finally, her voice was low when she answered, "It's my fault my mother is dead."

"Then tell me what happened so I can judge whether to call bollocks or not."

Instead of fighting back, she merely turned away from him and Finn released his grip on her chin. He was losing her.

He tried to think of another way to approach the situation when Arabella's voice filled the small training space. "I was seventeen and wanted nothing more than to see the world. Like most teenagers, I was cocky and sure I could take care of myself.

"One day whilst flying with my mother to one of the hunting grounds belonging to Stonefire, I snuck away. I'd never seen any of the cities, only the towns and villages in the Lake District, and I wanted to see how the humans lived." Arabella glanced over her shoulder. "The reason I wanted to see a human city was because of my mum's passion. She was a bit like you, in that she wanted to mend relations between the dragon-shifters and humans."

Finn smiled. "Your mum sounds like a clever dragonwoman. No wonder you're drawn to me."

Arabella glanced at him. "I'm not drawn to you."

"If you say so."

"I'm ignoring your comment. As for my mother, she was brilliant without being cocky, unlike some dragon-shifters. She always said that after winning the stubborn heart of my dad, anything was possible, even making humans like us."

He grinned. "Judging by your stubbornness, you must take after your dad."

Fire flashed in her eyes and Finn resisted winking. His lass was coming back to him.

"If you keep interrupting me, I'll never get this story out. Can you stay quiet for two minutes?" He motioned with his hands for her to continue, and Arabella did. "Once my mother flew up to avoid hitting a peak, I snuck away and changed course."

Finn opened his mouth, but then Arabella raised her brows at him. Wanting to hear the rest, he closed his mouth and she spoke again. "While not a huge city, Carlisle was the closest on our way to the hunting ground. Earlier, I had researched directions and soon made it to the outskirts of the city.

"There were so many houses, more than a few clustered tightly together as I flew toward the city center. Compared to the small towns and villages near Stonefire, it was almost another world."

Arabella fell silent and his inner dragon roared. *She is retreating again. Bring her back.*

Give me a bloody chance, dragon.

If dragons could roll eyes, his dragon had just done it.

Forgetting his beast, he took a step toward her. He prompted, "And then what happened, Arabella?"

She met his gaze. "Then an electrical charge of some sort hit me. My wings wouldn't move and I fell out of the sky."

~ ~ ~

Even more than a decade later, Arabella remembered the air rushing against her hide as she plummeted toward the earth, unable to spread her wings to slow her descent. At the time, she'd been certain she would die.

Finn's voice broke through the memory. "You're still standing here, so stop with the dramatics and tell me what happened next."

She narrowed her eyes. "Ordering me about isn't going to make me share any quicker. Maybe I should stop there and make you wonder what happened next."

Finn merely cocked an eyebrow. "Aye, and I'll call Bram. You haven't told me the whole truth yet, so my order still stands."

Clenching her fingers, Arabella wished she had the moves to wipe the self-assured look from Finlay Stewart's face. She had a feeling not many people challenged him openly.

Of course, she didn't have any moves she could use to win against him. At least, not yet. Whatever it took, she'd find a way to pin Finn to the ground and make him answer some questions. It wasn't fair he knew so much more about her than she did of him.

Wait, why do I care?

"Arabella."

Frowning at Finn's steely tone, she answered, "Fine, I'll answer if you allow me to watch Faye train her Protectors. You're busy as clan leader and I'll grow old before you have enough time to train me properly."

The dragonman's cockiness slipped for a second. "You're bargaining with me?"

"Why not? You like to do it with me."

She braced herself for another dominant alpha order, but instead, Finn merely laughed. "I'm starting to see more and more of that hidden wannabe clan leader inside you, Arabella MacLeod. Life with you would never be boring."

Resisting a blush, Arabella forced her face to remain neutral. Nearly everyone on Stonefire called her the 'clan recluse'. She couldn't recall anyone outside of her family, her online friends, or Bram saying she was interesting.

She cleared her throat. "So what's your answer, then, Finlay? Do we have a deal?"

Grinning, he took a step toward her and put out a hand. "Shake on it, and I'll see what I can do."

A bit worried at what he wasn't telling her, she placed her hand in his. Squeezing her fingers, Finn rubbed the back of her hand with his thumb. The rough, warm strokes sent a little thrill through her body.

Luckily, before she did something daft like rub the back of Finn's hand with her own thumb, he tugged her close and whispered, "Now, finish your story, Arabella. I want to know you better."

As she struggled to ignore Finn's brushes against her hand or his breath on her cheek, her dragon chimed in. *Tell him. He will not judge or pity us.*

H-how do you know that?

I just do. He is what you need.

Blinking, she tried to make sense of her beast. Most dragon-shifters would press the issue, but Arabella was afraid. Of what, she wasn't entirely clear, but she had a feeling a few sentences from her dragon could make her confront something she wasn't ready to face. It was better to feign ignorance.

Tugging her hand, Finn released it. With the severed contact, it was easier to concentrate on her story. "As I hurtled toward the ground, my mother flew in. Placing her body under mine, Mum beat her wings as if her life depended on it and braced my fall. While not the best landing, it was rather more like a tumble, we were both alive with only minor injuries once the shock wore off.

"Of course, before we could do much more than blink, two hunters emerged from the nearby copse of trees carrying large guns. After shooting us both with high voltage blasts, the world went black."

Finn crossed his arms over his chest. "How in the bloody hell did they find those types of guns? They're illegal in the UK."

Arabella shrugged. "I don't know. And at the time, I was worried about bigger things, such as, I don't know, my life."

"I know, but it makes me wary that they still have weapons like that. You see, the Inverness hunters are rather disorganized and not much of a threat. We've never had to guard or protect against such dangerous weapons."

Remembering her brother's wounds from a laser gun nearly a year ago made her shiver. "They have worse weapons now, as I'm sure Bram told you."

"Aye, he mentioned your brother's run-in with death. Right now, however, that's not important. I want to know what happened to you. Tell me what happened next, Arabella."

The next stage of her story was the part that still haunted her in nightmares. Just thinking about what she had seen when she awoke in chains made her stomach churn in knots. She didn't want Finn to see her weaknesses twice in a day.

Maybe she should stop and test Finn's bluff. Would he really send her away?

Her dragon's voice was warm. *You can do this, Ara. I am here and I want to stay.*

As her beast hummed inside Arabella's mind, her panic faded. *Thank you. I want to stay, too. I will try.*

Glancing back to Finn's eyes, she couldn't read his expression. The lack of pity on his face gave her the courage to continue. "When I regained consciousness, my face burned. I tried to touch it, only to find myself not only in human form again, but chained to a large wooden post inside a barn." She touched the scar across her face. "They slashed my face while I was unconscious."

Finn's eyes flashed to dragon slits and he growled, "What else, Arabella? You're holding back from me."

"Bloody hell, Finn, I could tell this quicker if you stopped interrupting me."

He motioned with his head for her to continue.

With a gulp, she carried on with her story. "My mother was covered with bruises and cuts. At first, I thought she was dead. No amount of shouting would wake her up. However, the noise attracted the hunters. I risked breaking my wrists by shifting my arms. As I broke the chains, one hunter shot me with some kind of dart. Instantly, I became groggy."

Not being able to move or take control of her body had been the worst part. At least, until what happened next.

Her dragon hummed again, and memories of panic and sadness faded. With a deep breath, she pushed on. "That's when they took my mother and beat her in front of my eyes. A man had me trapped against his chest, but no matter how much I struggled, I couldn't break free." Tears prickled her eyes and she looked away. "I knew then, they would kill her."

Finn's voice was gentle. "Arabella." She met his gaze, his eyes flashing dragon slits. "Let me hold you, lass. My dragon doesn't like your tears."

A part of her longed to feel a strong pair of arms around her, yet another part was afraid. If she wasn't careful, she might wish Finn to care for her.

No, he was only offering her support as any good clan leader would do. Yes, if she reminded herself of that fact, she could revel in the strength of his arms around her and not read too much into it.

The first step was the hardest, but before she knew it, she laid her head against Finn's chest. The solidness of muscle under her cheek, combined with the heat of his body, helped to melt away her fears.

In Finn's arms, she felt safe.

At that realization, Arabella knew she was in trouble.

~~~

Finn never expected Arabella to say yes to his offer, but as the lass snuggled into his chest, he wrapped his arms around her and squeezed. A protectiveness he couldn't understand rushed through his body.

His dragon growled. *We will always ensure her safety. She is ours. Arabella belongs to no one.*

His beast grunted. *She will one day. No one will try to take her away.*

Laying his chin on Arabella's head, he breathed in her vanilla scent mixed with pure female and squeezed her tighter. After seeing her tear-filled eyes as she spoke of her mother's beating, he wanted to make fire dance in her eyes each day.

No matter what it took, he would convince the lass to allow him to do it.

Far sooner than he liked, Arabella raised her head and looked up at him. Every cell in his body wanted to see desire or tenderness in her eyes, but instead, all he saw was confusion.

In an odd way, the sight only encouraged him to try harder. His lass would need time to trust him. Finn needed to make sure he didn't fuck up.

Rubbing circles on her back, he wanted to see how Arabella would react. When she pushed against his chest, he forced himself to let her go for the moment. He would be holding her again soon if he had anything to say about it.

Finn noticed the position of the sky and knew his next attempt would have to wait. "Are you all right now, lass?"

She looked to the sky. "I'm fine." Meeting his gaze, she stated, "You need to go."

"Aye, but I can maybe cancel if you need me."

She shook her head. "No. Just show me back to my cottage. I have work to do."

Arabella was tweaking both Stonefire's and Lochguard's computer systems against outside threats. Since Finn had once been apprenticed to Lochguard's head IT person, he wanted to question her about her work. But if there was one thing he'd learned early on, it was that a clan leader put his clan above his personal desires.

Although, in this moment, he wanted to shrug them off and get to know Arabella better.

We will see her soon. Maybe then you will finally kiss her.

Shut it, dragon.

Flourishing his arm, he smiled. "Well, after you, my lady."

One second passed, and then another. Would they be able to fall back in the familiarity from earlier? Or, would Arabella become awkward and distant? He hoped like hell it was the former.

For a second, she merely studied him and his heart rate kicked up. Then she sighed, rolled her eyes, and Finn grinned. He motioned again with his arm. "So, is that a yes?"

She placed her hands on her hips. "If you're trying to be chivalrous, you're forgetting one very important thing."

"What's that?"

"I have no bloody idea where we are. If I go first, we'll be lost for sure."

He grinned wider. "Well, it's the thought that counts."

"Just hurry up or you'll be late for your meeting."

As he walked, Arabella matched his strides. "And I definitely wouldn't want to do that, or I'd miss all the fun watching you handle my cousins."

55

Arabella frowned up at him. "What the hell are you talking about?"

"Oh, didn't Faye mention it? You and I are having dinner with her whole family."

Arabella's step faltered. "What? Since when?"

Placing a hand on her back, he urged her to walk again. Once she started moving, he shrugged. "I planned it yesterday. The MacKenzies are not only my kin, but one of the friendliest, kindest families within the clan." He lowered his voice. "I mentioned enemies earlier and the MacKenzies are going to help me watch your back."

"I don't really have a choice, do I?"

"In this, no, you don't." When she looked away from him, he added, "Don't worry, Arabella. Ten minutes with the MacKenzies and you'll either strain your neck with head shaking or have a sore belly from laughing. I'm betting on the latter."

Her look was skeptical. After a few beats of silence, she answered, "Fine, but if I feel a panic attack coming on, you take me home, no questions asked."

Since he knew he wouldn't receive a better offer, he nodded. "Done. Now, we really do need to hurry. You'll have to survive without my charm for the rest of the walk home."

"I think I'll live."

Pressing against Arabella's back, Finn smiled wide. He couldn't wait for the evening. Dinner with the MacKenzies should help Arabella forget about her past. At least, for a little while.

CHAPTER SIX

Arabella tucked a section of hair behind her ear and tried to focus on her laptop screen. Finn was due to pick her up any minute and not even her work could distract her.

Dinner with the MacKenzies would be her first real test on Lochguard. It was also an opportunity to try to make friends, at least with Faye. Her plan was to spend the night talking to the other dragonwoman. That way, she could keep her distance from Finn.

She'd told him more than any other person outside her family about her run-in with the dragon hunters. Just because he hadn't shown pity earlier didn't mean it wouldn't surface eventually, especially since she had yet to tell him the worst part.

And if he pitied her when she did, a piece of her might break.

Yet even a few hours later, she still remembered the warmth of his embrace as well as his scent of male and peat. Alone, she couldn't deny how much she wanted to feel his arms around her again. Safety and peace were two things Arabella rarely felt in the presence of anyone, not even her brother or clan leader. Yet a flirtatious Scot who liked to push her buttons instilled the feeling without even trying.

Closing her laptop, Arabella gripped the device tightly in her fingers. She needed to keep her distance from Finlay Stewart. He was the wrong dragonman for her.

Her dragon piped up. *I don't understand. Why? You like him. He is nice. He will protect us.*

He will break my heart if I let him. I'm not strong enough for that.

You don't know that. Give him a chance. His family can tell you the truth about his character.

Arabella paused a second before asking what she really wanted to know. *You've spoken more to me today than in the past ten years. Why?*

Her inner beast simply stated, *Because you are ready.*

Before she could ask her dragon to explain, there was a knock on the door. She muttered, "Saved by the knock, dragon."

When the knock increased in tempo, she tossed her laptop to the other side of the couch and stood up. "I know your dragon-shifter hearing will hear me, so stop with the bloody knocking. I'm coming."

There was one last double knock before the noise ceased. The cheek signaled it must be Finn at the door.

Pausing at the mirror in the hallway, Arabella smoothed her hair. She never wore make-up, but the bright, emerald green blouse made her skin glow. It was the best she could do, not that it mattered. She was most definitely not trying to impress Finn.

With a deep breath, she opened the door and her heart skipped a beat. Finn, dressed in black trousers and a dark blue button-up shirt opened at the collar, held out a sprig of purple heather tied with gold ribbon. "For you, my lady."

Gingerly taking the heather, a rush of happiness warmed her heart. No one had ever brought her flowers before.

Then she remembered her plan to distance herself from Finn. Steeling her face into a neutral expression, she met his eyes, only to find them full of warmth and tenderness.

For a split second, she wanted to rush into his arms and thank him. However, she restrained herself and murmured, "Thank you."

"No worries. You deserve flowers every day, Arabella, and I'm determined to bring them to you."

A part of her wanted to believe him, but her practical side won out. "All this talk of flowers is going to make us late. Either we leave now to have dinner with your family, or I'm staying home. Take your pick."

"We'll leave, but first let me do this."

He plucked the heather from her hand, took something from his trouser pocket, and moved toward her blouse. Frowning, she took a step back. "What the bloody hell do you think you're doing? I was serious earlier about kicking you in the balls if you try to cop a feel."

He held up a safety pin. "Stop thinking the worst of me. I'm trying to pin the sprig of heather to your blouse."

"Oh."

One corner of his mouth ticked up. "May I have the honor of pinning it to your person?"

She battled a smile and lost. "Hurry up and make sure not to linger."

Grinning, Finn moved to the top opening of her blouse. The back of his fingers brushed her skin as he fastened the heather to her shirt. Each movement of his skin against hers sent a rush of warmth both to her face and between her legs. As Finn moved his head closer to see what he was doing, his scent surrounded her, which only made her body hotter.

With a pat, Finn met her eyes with a grin. "There you go. You can thank me later for not stabbing you with the pin."

His words broke the spell of his touch. "If you're quite done, we should leave."

Reaching behind her, his chest brushed her bicep. Hard and masculine, Arabella waited for the panic to set in, much like it had done every time a strange male had invaded her space to this degree.

But as he retreated, one of her coats in his hand, she felt nothing but peace. Finn arranged the coat over her shoulders. "The late September air is cool. You'll need this."

Unsure of what else to do, she replied, "Thank you."

"Right, let's go. I'd rather not upset my Aunt Lorna if I can help it."

As Finn guided her out the door and shut it behind them, she teased, "Big, bad Finlay Stewart is afraid of a middle-aged dragonwoman? That is something I'd like to see."

He frowned down at her as they walked. "You clearly haven't met Aunt Lorna."

"Well then, let's go. I want to see this female who can make you quiver in your boots."

"I'm not quivering in any bloody boots. Surely, you have an alpha dragonwoman in your family somewhere."

Arabella's smile faded. "No, I don't. I just have my brother."

~~~

Finn wanted to smack his own head. He'd known that, of course, about Arabella's lack of family. He needed to be more careful and think before he spoke. Too bad Arabella had a way of making him forget he even had a brain at times.

Picking up his pace, he was determined to keep the evening light. After his lass's revelations earlier, she deserved that much. "Don't let my auntie hear you say that, or she'll unofficially adopt you." He glanced at Arabella. "Unless, that's what you want, of course. Then I'll mention it myself to Aunt Lorna and she'll nose into your life quicker than you can say, 'stop'."

Arabella tugged her coat closer around her body. "Before you make plans of foisting me on some unsuspecting aunt, how about I meet her first?"

He didn't like the determined glint in her eyes. "Please tell me you're not going to conspire with my kin."

She put on a mock Scottish accent. "Oh, aye. I verra much plan to do that."

Laughing, he risked moving his hand from her back to her hip. If Arabella noticed, she didn't protest. "I dinnae think ye'll pass for a Scots, lass."

When she smiled at his exaggerated accent, his dragon hummed. *Kiss her soon. I want her.*

Stop it, dragon. She deserves some fun.

His beast huffed. *Soon?*

If I can work my magic, then aye. Give me time.

While smiling, Arabella remained silent, but he was fine with that. As his eyes latched onto the heather on her chest, a sense of possessiveness came over him. His male cousins would see the heather and recognize his claim. He only hoped his brash cousins wouldn't tell her the true meaning of the flowers pinned to her blouse.

Because if Arabella MacLeod knew he'd made a claim on her, she might push him away. But try as he might, he couldn't allow his male cousins to win her over. She was his.

They soon reached the MacKenzie household and he stopped a few feet from the door. Looking down at Arabella, he whispered, "I'm going to warn you, lass. It will be a bit crazy inside. Are you ready?"

Arabella took a deep breath and exhaled. "I suppose so."

Squeezing her hip, he murmured, "Don't worry. I wouldn't bring you here unless I thought you were ready."

She stepped away from him and Finn barely resisted frowning at the loss of warmth. Fire flashed in her eyes. "Since when are you making decisions for me? I'm twenty-eight years old, Finlay Stewart. I can make my own."

He forced his voice to remain serious. "Aye, is that so? And what decision will you make tonight, Arabella? Are you going to face the MacKenzies or hide away in your cottage?"

"I'm done with hiding."

She turned away from him and moved toward the door. She'd acted just as he'd wanted.

Before she could figure that out, he followed her. "Knock on the door, then. It's cold and I want some of my aunt's special reserve whiskey to warm my toes."

Without a word, Arabella knocked on the door four times and then whispered, "See? That's how a normal person knocks."

Just as he laughed, the door opened. Faye MacKenzie looked between them and grinned. "Right, you two. Come in before mum has a stroke. To her, three minutes late is the equivalent of a decade."

His aunt shouted, "I can hear you, Faye Louise."

Shaking her head, Faye stepped aside and looked to Arabella. "Welcome to the home of the MacKenzies. I hope you survive the madness."

~~~

Arabella blinked and tried not to let her confusion show as Finn guided her inside the cottage. Despite Finn and Faye's warnings, it couldn't be that bad. Could it?

Feet pounded down the stairs next to the entryway. Looking up, she did a double take. Two tall, muscled dragonmen with dark red, wavy hair near her own age stood on the steps with identical grins.

She blinked at the attractive set of twins. Was Finn's entire family comprised of models?

Finn growled at her side. "You can close your mouth now, Arabella."

One of the identical twins winked at her. "Forgive our cousin, lass. He's never accepted that we inherited the good-looking genes."

The other twin nodded. "We think he only became clan leader to draw the female eyes away from us."

Arabella studied the two dragonmen and noticed one had a scar near his left eye. "Since Finn is being rude, care to tell me your names? I'm Arabella MacLeod."

The male with the scar chuckled. "I like you, Arabella MacLeod." He straightened his shoulders. "I'm Fraser, the younger and more dashing of the MacKenzie twins." He pointed to his scar. "And more daring."

The other one rolled his eyes. "Yes, a scar is daring. Too bad you got it when you tripped over a rock." The male's blue

63

eyes met hers. "Forgive my brother. I'm Fergus, the cleverer half of the MacKenzie twins."

Fraser punched his brother. "Don't start that up again."

"You know it's true." Fergus hit back.

Faye muttered from the side, "The idiots."

Arabella blinked. She had clearly walked into a mad house.

As the brothers argued, Finn looked to her and whispered, "Let me take your coat, Arabella, before my aunt gets a hold of you."

Rather than ask why that mattered, she allowed Finn to take her coat. As soon as he turned to hang it up on a hook, one of the twins whistled. "I never thought I'd see the day, cousin."

Arabella focused back on the twins. Curiosity overcame her nervousness. "What the hell are you talking about?"

Mischief danced in Fergus's eyes. "And she has a backbone, too. Well done, Finn."

Finn touched her back and she frowned at him. "What are they talking about?"

Finn shook his head. "Later, lass. It's best not to keep my aunt waiting."

Arabella pointed a finger. "I will force it out of you, Finn. No matter how charming you try to be, I won't forget."

As the twins laughed behind her, Finn maneuvered her down the small hallway until they entered a cozy, warm kitchen. A middle-aged dragonwoman with blonde hair turned toward them with a frown. Her amber gaze latched onto Finn. "I don't care if you're clan leader or not, Finlay Stewart. Inside the walls of my house, you're just my nephew and I won't tolerate tardiness." Finn merely bobbed his head and the female looked at Arabella. Her expression softened. "And you must be Arabella MacLeod.

My nephew has told me all about you. I'm Lorna MacKenzie, but please call me Aunt Lorna."

"Yes, ma'am."

Lorna frowned, but then her gaze moved to the heather pinned to her blouse before looking to Finn. "Aye, so it's like that, is it?"

Finn smiled widely. "Auntie, Arabella's in a bit of a shock after meeting the twins. How about some of your fine whiskey to calm her down?"

Lorna waggled a finger at Finn. "I know what you're doing, but for the sake of Arabella, I'll ignore it for now." She turned toward Arabella and motioned with her arm. "Come, child. You can assist me while Finn helps the boys with the wood chopping. My boys are behind and winter will be here before you know it."

Without thinking, Arabella reached out and took Finn's hand in hers. He leaned down and whispered, "If it's me you want, lass, then say the word and I'll suffer my aunt's ire to whisk you away and steal a few kisses."

Releasing his hand, she shot him an exasperated look. "Again with the lines."

"Aye, and I'll never stop."

Amusement was replaced with heat and she forced her gaze away. "I think I'd like that, um, Aunt Lorna."

Lorna motioned again. "Then come, Arabella. I won't bite. I promise."

After one last glance to Finn, Arabella took a deep breath and walked around the counter to stand in front of Lorna. The dragonwoman was an inch taller than Arabella, but softer around the middle due to age. The blonde hair and amber eyes signaled she was probably Finn's blood relative.

Lorna assessed her and Arabella resisted fidgeting. She had little experience dealing with older, mother-like figures. Anytime she'd tried over the last year, memories of her mother's last moments had flashed into her mind.

Yet as eyes similar to Finn's stared down at her with warmth, some of Arabella's nervousness dissipated.

Lorna smiled. "You'll do, Arabella, you'll do."

Before she could ask what that meant, the twins each took Finn by a shoulder. "Come, cousin. You heard Mum. While you're here in the house, you're family and not clan leader. You're going to do your share of the work."

Finn met Arabella's eyes, a question in them. The coward's way would be to ask him to stay, but that went against her whole reason for coming to Lochguard. Arabella would never truly be free if she couldn't interact with strangers on her own.

Forcing herself to look to Fraser, she smiled. "Make him work extra hard."

Fraser winked. "Aye, we'll do that."

As the males left, Faye entered the kitchen and sat on one of the stools next to the counter. The young dragonwoman supported her head on her hands. "So, Arabella, what do you think of Finn?"

Arabella nearly choked. "Um, what?"

Lorna set a cup of tea in front of her and Arabella took it. Lorna scowled at her daughter. "Leave the poor dear alone. It's her first day here."

Faye shrugged. "She's known him longer than that. Besides, it's part of my job to protect the clan leader. I'm just making sure he won't be hurt. After all, he has more than enough on his plate."

Arabella put down her tea. "If you invited me here to grill me, then I'm going to leave. I only came because Finn asked me to."

Lorna placed a hand on her arm. The touch didn't bother her. In fact, the older dragonwoman gently rubbing up and down her arm reminded Arabella of her own mother doing the same when Arabella had been a child. Only when Lorna spoke, did Arabella snap back to the present. "Ignore my offspring and their antics. Finn came to live with us when he was fifteen and he's like a brother to Faye and the twins. Even though my children are younger than Finn, they're still protective, to say the least."

Faye snorted. "As if you're any less protective, Mum."

"Aye, I'm protective. But unlike you lot, I have manners. Now hush," Lorna replied.

Arabella could keep silent, but Lorna's words niggled at her curiosity. "Why did Finn come to live with you?"

Lorna stared at her a second before finally replying, "You might want to ask him yourself. It's not my story to tell."

Lorna's answer only stoked her curiosity further. Finn seemed happy-go-lucky, yet coming to live with the MacKenzies suggested something had happened to his parents.

He might understand Arabella's past more than she thought.

Faye pushing her stool back broke the silence. "The boys will be hungry, so let's set the table."

Lorna shook her head. "You mean you're hungry and want supper. Don't try to use your brothers as an excuse."

Faye looked sheepish and Arabella smiled, grateful the conversation had steered away from her.

When Lorna handed her a stack of plates and ordered her to lay them out, Arabella went to work. The menial task gave her time to think on all she'd learned. Maybe Finn truly did understand a thing or two about a tragic past. Once they were alone, she would find out what exactly had happened when he was fifteen.

Chapter Seven

Finn swung the axe and split the last log of the evening. The exercise had both kept his nosy cousins quiet and given him a way to cool his possessiveness.

At the rate he was going, he would be hauling Arabella next to him any chance he had.

His dragon, however, wasn't quieted by the sounds of chopping wood. *You may deny how much you want to check on Arabella, but I am a dragon and am honest. I want to see her.*

Soon. She'll be fine.

Not if they tell her the truth about the heather.

Stacking his split wood on the pile next to his aunt's house, his cousins each placed a hand on one of his shoulders. Finn merely raised an eyebrow. "Even if you two gang up on me, I'll still win."

Fraser smiled, his scar crinkling near his eye. "Oh, we learned that lesson last time. But we want to make sure you don't run inside to check on your lass before we had a chat."

"Chat about what?"

Fraser answered, "Does Arabella know what the heather means?"

"No, and you're not going to tell her."

Fraser shrugged. "If not us, then probably Faye. You need to tell the English dragonwoman what it means, because if she finds out on her own, I don't think she'll be pleased."

Finn's dragon preened. *They agree with me. It's three against one. You should tell her.*

This is not a democracy.

Fergus finally chimed in, "Judging by your eyes, your dragon agrees with us. If you don't tell her, then I fancy courting her myself."

Finn narrowed his eyes. "You touch her and I will kick your arse to the next county."

Fergus grinned. "It's about time you're consumed with finding a mate. I was starting to wonder if the rumors about you bedding every female you could find were true or not."

Fraser jumped in. "That's why you went to Stonefire, isn't it? Because you'd tried all the females here?"

Finn rolled his eyes. "Yes, that was my secret reason for going. I wasn't trying to ensure the future of our clan or anything."

Fraser shoved Finn's shoulder. "I don't know, cousin. With a few babies, you could breed a leader or two. But maybe change your last name to MacKenzie, aye? Then they'll be charming, clever, and good-looking."

Finn loved his cousins and the fact he didn't always need to act the part of clan leader around them, but the urge to see Arabella and make sure his aunt and Faye weren't giving her the similar treatment grew stronger. His lass was strong, but while she could handle his teasing, he wondered if she could handle it from others.

Luckily, Fraser and Fergus were prevented from saying anything else when the back door to the cottage opened and the light from inside outlined Faye's body. "Are you three finished yet? Supper's ready and I'm starving."

Shrugging off Fraser and Fergus's hands, Finn walked to the door. "We're all done. How's Arabella?"

Faye crossed her arms over her chest. "You worry too much, but I've been surrounded by alpha dragonmen most of my life and know my words won't be enough. Come see for yourself so I can eat."

He resisted arguing with his female cousin and pushed past her.

Finn entered the dining area. Arabella was sitting next to his aunt, but turned to meet his eyes. The sight of his lass smiling with mischief in her eyes soothed his dragon's fretting.

~~~

Arabella was smiling at Lorna's latest story of Finn as a boy when the very adult male himself showed up. The sight of Finn's hair mussed from the wind and wood chopping, combined with the way he zeroed in to her eyes as soon as he entered the room, made her stomach flip. To say the dragonman was attractive was an understatement.

Her dragon chimed in. *Yes. Give him a chance. You will like it. What?*

Don't be afraid.

Finn's voice silenced her inner beast. "Should I be worried about what my auntie told you in my absence?"

Lorna beat her to a reply. "Never you mind. Sit down so we can eat, or Faye's crankiness may move into the unbearable zone."

Fraser sat down across from Arabella. "Not even I will mess with my sister when she's hungry. Hurry up and dish the food before she starts grumbling."

Faye crossed her arms over her chest. "Says the male who moans at a paper cut. Males, especially grown dragonmen, are giant babies when they're ill or injured."

Fergus sat down in the empty chair to her right and Arabella resisted seeking out Finn's gaze. It seemed tonight's supper would be the ultimate test of how well she could do with strangers surrounding her.

Yet as she stole a glance at Lorna on her other side, Arabella felt safe enough. Despite only meeting the dragonwoman less than an hour ago, both woman and dragon didn't sense a threat. Arabella didn't think she would ever hurt her.

Finn's growl finally gave her the excuse to look at the Scottish leader. Instead of meeting her eye, he looked at Fergus. "That's my spot, cousin."

Fergus merely cocked an eyebrow. "Oh, aye? Care to tell me why?"

Finn narrowed his eyes. "You know why."

Rather than put up with the two males arguing, Arabella jumped in. "I'm perfectly capable of sitting between your aunt and cousin. Take the empty seat so we can start."

Finn looked at her and she drew in a breath at his flashing dragon eyes. She'd seen that look on her brother around Melanie, before they'd been mated.

No. It couldn't be. She'd never even kissed Finlay, and he certainly wasn't who she'd choose to be her mate.

Her dragon huffed. *Liar.*

Don't call me a liar unless you have proof.

Then kiss him so I can gloat later. You may lie to yourself but not to me. You fancy him.

Arabella clenched the napkin on her lap. She didn't like being called a liar.

Lorna's commanding voice broke through her anger. "Finlay, take the lass outside and talk with her in private. The tension in this room is riling up my own dragon."

Arabella frowned. "What are you talking about?"

Finn put out a hand. "Come with me, Arabella."

She could be ornery and refuse. Yet between her dragon's words and her own curiosity, the desire to know what the hell was going on was strong.

Standing up, she frowned as she went to Finn. She didn't take his hand. "If this is another game to get me alone and spit out flirtatious lines, then I'll turn around and come right back in. Your aunt went to a lot of trouble to cook the roast for us and I won't let you spoil it."

Finn clenched his jaw and turned. "Come."

She looked to Lorna, but the dragonwoman motioned for her to go.

Once they were outside, Finn turned toward her. The look in his eyes made her shiver. Somehow, she made her voice work. "Why are we out here, Finn? What's going on?"

He took a step toward her, their bodies now a few inches apart. "I don't want you sitting next to any other male, but especially not Fraser and Fergus."

The heat in his eyes made her heart rate kick up. She swallowed. "I don't understand, Finn. Why? Just tell me straight."

Brushing her cheek with his finger, he murmured, "I don't want to scare you, Arabella. I can wait as long as it takes. Despite what you might think of me, I can be a patient dragonman."

Each stroke of Finn's skin against hers made her heart pound harder. Between Finn's words and her dragon's, Arabella had a feeling she knew what they were both saying. Yet the human half of her wasn't ready to face it.

Then Finn cupped her cheek and some of her tension eased. His breath was a whisper on her lips. "If you really want to know the truth, then let me kiss you, Arabella."

Her voice was strangled. "Kiss you?"

Moving his free hand to her back, he rubbed in circles, his touch making her melt. "Aye. One kiss will tell you what you wish to know. Otherwise, you can just follow my order to stay away from other males and kiss me when you're ready."

She opened her mouth to protest when Finn pressed gently against her back. As her stomach made contact with his front, his hard cock pressed against her.

Instead of a panic, heat surged through her body. Her dragon whispered. *You are ready. Kiss him. I know you want to.*

Finn leaned down a fraction more toward her lips. "So, what will it be, Arabella MacLeod? Will you let me kiss you?"

CHAPTER EIGHT

Arabella MacLeod's heart thundered inside her chest.

Between Finn cupping her cheek and his hot breath against her lips, she should be terrified. Yet every instinct she possessed urged her to close the few inches between them and kiss him.

Her dragon's voice was soft. *You are ready. He is a good male and good dragon. Kiss him.*

Placing a hand on Finn's chest, Arabella searched his amber eyes. Why she was drawn to him, she had no idea. He was everything she had set out to avoid.

Yet he'd listened to the snippet of her past without pity. He also didn't coddle or tiptoe around her, but instead, liked to push her buttons.

If she kissed him, things would change. The question was whether she could handle it or not. If things turned south, she would have to run home and Arabella wasn't sure if she could handle the knowing looks back home; everyone knew she couldn't make it alone in the world.

Looking at Finn's lips, the urge to kiss the bloody dragonman only grew stronger. One kiss wouldn't hurt anyone, would it? After all, she was here to finally put her past behind her. A kiss would take her one step further away from hiding.

However, there was one thing she needed to know before she could convince herself to go through with it. "So, if I said to wait, you'd wait?"

Finn strummed his thumb against her cheek. "Provided you didn't go around kissing anyone else, yes."

"And if I did kiss someone else?"

Growling, he brought his face an inch closer. "Then I can't guarantee that male's safety."

Fingering the buttons of his shirt, she looked down at the strong male chest in front of her. Arabella had no desire to kiss anyone else. Everything underneath the fabric could be hers if she wanted. The only question was whether she wanted it in this moment or at a later time.

After a few more seconds, she looked back up and opened her mouth. However, before she could say anything, the door behind them swung open and slammed against something.

Arabella jumped and turned toward the sound just as Finn moved in front of her. Aunt Lorna stood in the doorway.

Finn growled. "Auntie, you'd better have a good reason for interrupting."

Lorna raised an eyebrow. "Don't growl at me, Finlay Stewart. I would scold you, but something has happened and that's more important."

Arabella gripped Finn's bicep and asked, "What? Is it the dragon hunters? Or even the Dragon Knights?"

Lorna shook her head. "No, this is internal. Someone broke into your cottage, Arabella."

Finn cursed. "Who reported it?"

Lorna motioned inside. "Come, and I'll fill in the details." The dragonwoman turned without a word and went back inside.

Finn brushed her cheek with a finger. "I'm not going to forget this, Arabella. We'll pick up where we left off soon enough."

As Finn took her hand and tugged her along, a small part of Arabella was relieved. She would have time to think out the situation with Finn instead of acting because of her hormones.

Her inner dragon was still on edge at being riled up and not kissed. Sending soothing thoughts to her beast, Arabella added, *Calm down. Addressing the threats is more important.*

If you say so. He will kiss you later, though. You need to let him.

As they went inside the MacKenzie's cottage, Arabella willed her cheeks to cool. No doubt, his cousins knew Finn's intentions, but she wasn't sure if she could take their teasing. Especially given that she hadn't figured out what the hell to do herself.

Would she have said yes?

Her dragon huffed. *Of course. By waiting, you will have to work up the nerve again.*

Rather than answer, Finn guided her to the living area, where Lorna and a strange male she didn't know stood. Faye and the twins were absent.

At the sight of the unknown, dark-haired dragonman, Arabella tried to pull her hand from Finn's, but he just gave her a squeeze and looked at the newcomer. "What happened, Grant?"

Grant's brown eyes darted to Arabella, full of interest, before looking back at his clan leader. "I was doing my patrols when I noticed a small fire in the English lass's yard. There was no one near or inside the house, but the door was busted open and the windows smashed." He looked to Arabella again and then back to Finn. "Someone also painted 'Send the English whore home' on the living room wall."

The living room wall was where Arabella had hung her pictures. While it was a bit childish considering how much worse the situation could've been if she had been home, the thought of someone toying with her former lifelines stoked her anger. She demanded, "Did you catch the bastards?"

Grant blinked. Arabella wondered if she'd crossed the line, then Finn squeezed her hand again and echoed, "Well, did you?"

The dark-haired dragonman shook his head. "No. Shay and some of the others are scouring the place now for clues."

~~~

Finn's heat from earlier at nearly kissing Arabella had transformed into a fire of anger. He didn't want to think of what would've happened if Arabella had been home this evening. Would his clan really have attacked her to get back at him? The thought squeezed his heart.

Still, he forced his mind to focus. He'd expected Duncan and his supporters to use an English dragon-shifter as an excuse to attack him. Without his wits, he couldn't protect Arabella. "I can't prove it, but I would bet my position the culprit is one of Duncan's. Go back to the house and look for anything that can lead to one of his supporters. Also, have someone pack Arabella's things and bring them to my cottage."

Since Finn was overly aware of everything about the female at his side, her whisper of, "What?" may as well have been a shout.

He ordered Grant, "Go." Once the Protector was gone, Finn looked down at Arabella. "I had hoped my clan would treat you well, but a few troublemakers want to flush you out. I won't risk your safety, Ara, so you're staying with me."

Tugging her hand, he released it this time. Arabella narrowed her eyes. "I appreciate the protection, but you can't just force me to move in with you."

"Aye, I can. Unless you want to go back to Stonefire?"

She took a step toward him. "You keep using that excuse against me. Would it kill you to ask for my opinion or at least give me some options? I'm finally in charge of my life again and I'm not about to just hand it over to you."

"And what about your safety, Arabella? You've let your training lapse. I also bet you haven't shifted into a dragon for quite some time. If I don't protect you, then who will?"

Arabella pointed a finger. "Don't bring my dragon into this. You bloody well know I'm working on that."

He should shut up, but Finn was past rational thinking. "Are you, Arabella MacLeod? I saw the hunger earlier today, near the landing area. If you truly want something that badly, you'd have it by now. You need to stop hiding behind the excuse of your past. A decade is more than enough to get over something tragic."

"What do you know of tragedy? You, with the winks and grins, flirting with every female in sight. Until you've been tied down and set on fire, then you can't say a bloody word to me about getting past it."

His dragon spoke up. *You're pushing her too far. Stop.*

No. She needs to hear it.

Shutting his dragon inside his mind, he closed the gap between him and Arabella. Taking hold of her arm, he leaned close to her face. "Just because I haven't been set on fire doesn't mean I haven't had my fair share of tragedy. Hell, I was forced to watch my parents be drained of blood right in front of me by a corrupt DDA employee, so don't say a bloody word about me not understanding. I got past it eventually. If you truly wanted to be free, you'll do the same."

Arabella blinked. "What?"

"Ah, not so cocky now, are you, lass."

Aunt Lorna's strong voice interrupted. "That's enough, Finlay."

Keeping his hold on Arabella's arm, he looked to his aunt. "Auntie, this is clan business and my call."

Lorna shook her head. "It may be clan business, but you're not treating her as if she were a normal member of the clan. The lass is right, give her options. She can always stay here." He opened his mouth, but his aunt cut him off. "Your inner dragon is making you hotheaded. Take a walk, Finn, and sort out the clan. Talk to the lass afterwards."

His dragon chimed in. *She is right. Arabella needs a break, and so do you. Don't lose her.*

That's the second time you've said that. She can take it.

Maybe, but I want her and she won't kiss us if you keep pushing right now.

With a grunt, Finn released his hold on Arabella and looked at his lass. "I'll be back later to finish this conversation. Don't run away."

Before anyone could speak or he could change his mind, Finn headed out the front door and toward Arabella's cottage.

~~~

Arabella stared at the door Finn had just exited. Without him nearby, her temper cooled and allowed her to digest what he'd told her. *My parents were drained of blood right in front of me.*

While different from torture, it was no less tragic, especially given that the Department of Dragons Affairs, or DDA, was supposed to help protect the dragon clans. Having one turn against you in that manner would've been devastating. At fifteen, Finn had been even younger than she when he'd gone through his tragedy.

Even so, his past didn't give him the right to act like an arsehole.

Lorna's voice interrupted her thoughts. "Come, Arabella, let's have some tea."

She was about to say she didn't want any tea, but the look on Lorna's face brooked no argument. With a sigh, she followed the dragonwoman into the kitchen. Lorna would've made a fantastic clan leader.

As Lorna filled the kettle with water, she said, "Finn has a temper with those close to him, but then again, I think so do you."

She almost felt sheepish at Lorna's words, but refused to show it. "He still didn't need to pull his alpha dragonman bullshit."

Lorna turned and crossed her arms over her chest. "If Stonefire's leader had given that order, would you have fought him?"

She frowned. "Probably not, but Finn is different."

"He's not, my dear. You fancy him, that's clear as day, but he will always be clan leader first. If you're going to stay here, you need to accept that."

"I'm not about to say yes to his every order."

"I never said you had to. But in matters of clan security, especially when your life depends on it, you should. His rival is keen to take over. Don't give Duncan the opening he wants to take the clan away from Finn."

Arabella looked down at the counter as she traced shapes in it. When put that way, she nearly agreed with Lorna.

Looking back up, Lorna's eyes were firm yet understanding. Her mother had been like that, too, back when Arabella had been a hotheaded teenager. Her clan might have forgotten it, but back then, she'd been worse than Tristan with her stubbornness.

Her dragon spoke up. *Talk with her if you can't talk with me. I do talk with you.*

But not to confide. The Scottish dragonwoman is willing to listen.

Guilt rushed forth at her neglect, but Arabella wasn't about to digest that in front of Lorna MacKenzie's overly perceptive gaze.

Truth be told, Arabella did feel more at ease with Lorna than her dragon for one reason—Lorna hadn't been there with the dragon hunters.

Before she could convince herself otherwise, Arabella blurted, "Even if I listen in matters of clan security, I can't live with him, Aunt Lorna. I just can't."

"Why, my dear? He won't hurt you. The sprig of heather is proof of that."

Arabella fingered the purple flowers. "Just because he gave me flowers doesn't mean he won't hurt me eventually."

Lorna sighed. "I wasn't going to say anything, but since you're not from Lochguard, you should know something."

"What is it?"

The older female gestured toward her blouse. "Finn has never given a female heather before. In the Highlands, it is a sort of proclamation amongst dragon-shifters."

"What kind of proclamation?"

Healed by the Dragon

"Finn believes you're his true mate."

~~~

Finn wanted nothing more than to challenge one of his cousins to a fight. A mixture of desire, anger, and irritation pounded inside his head. If he didn't use up his excess energy, he would miss something and make a mistake.

Since any mistake could end up harming Arabella, he couldn't afford to make one.

His dragon spoke up. *This could be our chance to exile Duncan. Good can come from the bad.*

In no mood to talk with his dragon, Finn jogged the last stretch to Arabella's cottage.

Faye and Grant were in the front yard, arguing about something. Moving closer, he could hear Faye's words. "There's no way I'm going to risk Arabella and use her as bait. I want to catch Duncan as much as you do, but that's going too far."

Grant replied, "He's been sneaking by for the last year and I'm tired of his bullshit, Faye. This might be our only chance."

Covering the ground between them, Finn walked up to the pair. "No, Arabella MacLeod isn't an option. I'm guessing from your conversation that you didn't find anything."

Faye glared two more seconds at Grant before looking to Finn. "No. The paint used on the living room wall was black and could have come from anywhere."

Finn glanced behind him, at the smoldering ashes in the yard. "What did they burn?"

"Most of Arabella's belongings, including her laptop," Faye answered. "But no worries, I've already got someone looking for a new laptop and some clothes for her. But, Finn." He looked back to his cousin, who gave him an assessing look. "Maybe we should send her home until we can ensure her safety."

Finn's dragon roared at the same time as he stated, "No."

Faye motioned for Grant to leave. Once she and Finn were alone, she whispered, "Look, I know how you feel about her, cousin. As much as I'd like to keep her here since I like her, there are very few places in the clan she could stay and be safe."

"My place or your mum's," Finn answered.

His cousin blinked. "Aye. But I'm not sure if she'll agree to either. Mum's is a zoo and she's still trying to decide what to do about you."

Faye MacKenzie was too clever for her own good. "Oh, I'll convince her to stay."

"And let's just say it doesn't work. What then? She could run away or call her clan leader. Remember, the alliance is still new. If you do anything to hurt Arabella, Stonefire's leader will never forgive you."

"I still have time to convince her. If it becomes apparent we can't protect her, I won't have a choice but to send her away. However, I'll do whatever it takes to prevent that from happening."

Faye gave him a skeptical look. "She's been here nearly a day and you almost bit off Fergus's head at the dinner table. There's no way you'd survive her leaving."

Steeling his jaw, he ordered, "I haven't kissed her yet. While my dragon will be moody, I can still keep my wits about me."

"If you say so."

Finn decided to drop it. "Find out what you can here and then report back to me at your mum's house. I need to have a conversation with Arabella that can't wait."

Before his cousin could open her mouth to reply, Finn left. While Faye and her team were young, he trusted his handpicked Protectors to investigate the scene thoroughly and report back to him.

Finn had bigger things to handle at the moment.

He needed to do everything in his power to convince a stubborn dragonwoman to stay with him. The thought of Fergus and Fraser living in the same house as Arabella only made his dragon roar and claw, wanting to take control. He didn't even want to think what his dragon would do if Arabella left.

Finn hadn't lied; he could keep control of his dragon for the foreseeable future. Even if he kissed her, he bet he was strong enough to keep his hands to himself for a short while.

However, he'd been careful with Arabella up until this point in time. Not as careful as her clan had been with her, but more than Finn usually was with anyone else. From here on out, the gloves were coming off. He was in it to win, and he had a dragonwoman to claim.

CHAPTER NINE

Arabella sat alone at the table, picking at the plate of roast beef, potatoes, and cooked carrots with her fork.

She'd been barely a day in Scotland and she already had a big decision to make. Lorna's explanation about the heather only confirmed what Arabella had sensed earlier.

However, she still couldn't bring herself to admit the truth. To do so would give up any chance she had at true freedom. After kissing their true mate, a dragon-shifter would go into a sex frenzy. Finn and Arabella wouldn't be able to stop until she was pregnant.

She could barely take care of herself. Hell, she couldn't even shift into a dragon. There was no way she could handle a mate, let alone a baby.

There were rumors of dragons subduing their frenzies, but it usually didn't last long unless a dragon-shifter's inner dragon was strong. Finn's might be able to do it, but not Arabella's.

Of course, her dragon's weakness was all Arabella's fault. She was the one who had battered and chased away the once strong, beautiful beast inside. It looked like Arabella would pay the price. Her only options were to go home to Stonefire with her tail between her legs and live out her life as "poor Arabella", or kiss Finn and hope she could handle a male touching her in places she'd never been touched before without going into a fit.

While she'd been keeping her dragon at the far reaches of her mind, the beast finally broke through with a huff. *I am stronger than you think. Kiss him and I will stave off the frenzy.*

I wish that were true, but it's not.

Her dragon growled. *I am quiet, but strong. And I will prove it to you.*

She tried to think of what to say to that when the front door opened and Finn's voice traveled down the hall. "Arabella? Where are you?"

At his voice, her heart rate kicked up. So much for having time to prepare herself for the confrontation with Finn.

Still, she was done hiding. Unlike the last decade, she would face her current problem and see what happened.

Taking a deep breath, she shouted, "In here."

Finn appeared in the doorway, his windblown hair and light scruff on his face taking her breath away. Despite the no-win situation she was currently involved with, the male would always be handsome to her.

His amber eyes darted to her plate and back up. "Why haven't you eaten?"

Dropping her fork with a clang against the plate, she stood up. "I don't know, maybe because people attacked the place I was staying and I've been preoccupied."

When he took a step toward her, Arabella held her ground. "You need to take care of yourself, Ara. My dragon isn't happy when you don't eat or sleep properly."

It was on the tip of her tongue to blurt out what she'd learned, but Arabella wanted another minute to work up the nerve. Instead, she focused on something neutral. "What did you find at my cottage? Do you know who vandalized it?"

Finn shook his head. "I'm sorry, but your place is no longer habitable. Most of your things are gone too."

"My laptop?"

He nodded. "Yes, that too. You have every right to flee back home after this. What was done to your things was inexcusable and I will find the culprit." He took another step closer. "But know this before you make a decision: I want you to stay."

His words were steady and sincere, which only made her heart beat faster. Clearing her throat, she forced out the words, "Because you think I'm your true mate."

Surprise flashed in his eyes. "What?"

"Don't deny it. Your aunt told me the meaning of the heather. And yet you were going to kiss me without saying a word. Withholding information is nearly the same as lying, Finn."

He closed the distance between them. Before she could try to move away, he gripped her shoulders. "Says the woman who refuses to listen to her dragon. She would've sensed the same as mine."

"Don't try to push the blame to me. You knew and didn't say. I should've known better than to think you flirted with me because you wanted to. No, it's just your dragon instincts and your cock giving the orders."

Narrowing his eyes, Finn's voice was low when he replied, "Don't ever think you're not worth it, Arabella MacLeod. Even you know it takes time to sense a true mate. It was your wit and inner strength that drew me at first. To figure out you were my true mate only made me that much more determined to have you."

Finn's scent and heat surrounded her, his words only confusing her. "Lying to me won't get me to kiss you."

"I'm not lying." He nuzzled her cheek and she drew in a breath. "Few people know what it's like to have their lives turned upside down and come out stronger on the other side. You do, Arabella. You and I are more alike than you might think."

Somehow she made her voice work. "You're talking about your parents."

"Yes." Moving his head, he stared into her eyes. The dragon slits should frighten her, but they only highlighted his alpha dragon side, which made her heart beat faster in a good way. "You seem keen on proof, so let me kiss you, Ara. I can control my dragon for a time, allowing you to acclimate to the idea."

She remained silent, searching his eyes, looking for even a grain of deceit, but she didn't find it. Finn believed he could hold back.

Before she could stop herself, Arabella whispered, "But I don't think I can and I'm terrified."

She expected pity, but Finn's eyes only became more determined. "If your dragon has even a fraction of your strength, she can. What does she say?"

Not asking would be the easy way out, but the situation with Finn was too important, so she forced herself to ask, *Putting aside your instinct to mate, can you truly hold back? If you can't, I'll break.*

Her dragon's voice was firm, yet gentle. *Of course I can. Female dragons always make the males work for it. It's part of the game.*

What are you talking about?

Alpha females always make the males wait. Finlay Stewart is no different. I will drive him and his dragon crazy on purpose.

Arabella smiled at her dragon's smug tone. *I like you this way.*

Me, too. No more hiding. Kiss him.

Finn raised an eyebrow. "Well? I can't read your bloody mind, woman. What did she say?"

~~~

The second Arabella smiled whilst talking to her dragon, Finn's confidence at her accepting him ticked up a few notches.

As he expected, his female was stronger than she'd given herself credit for. It made both man and beast more impatient to finally kiss her.

Using every ounce of restraint he possessed, Finn kept his eyes trained on her gaze rather than her lips when she finally answered, "If I do this, I want to lay some ground rules."

He sighed. "What rules?"

Arabella lifted her chin. "Kissing is as far as you take it until I say otherwise."

Given her past and the decade she spent as a recluse, he had a feeling she'd never been with a male before. "For now. But if you string me out for months, my dragon will lose his mind."

"Fair enough."

Resisting the urge to nuzzle her cheek again, he asked, "Anything else?"

Her face softened. "I've only kissed one male before, so I don't know what the hell I'm doing. While I'll probably be shite at it, don't point it out. Just show me what to do."

Moving one of his hands from her shoulder to her cheek, he brushed the back of his fingers against her soft skin. "You'll do fine, Ara. Kissing you will be the best moment of my life." Her breath caught and he smiled. "And yours too, I bet. You'll never be the same afterwards, and not just because of your dragon. The ground will sway beneath your feet after just one kiss."

She narrowed her eyes and he grinned. Arabella's voice was strong again as she ordered, "Stop it with the lines, Finn."

"I bet your nervousness has eased a fraction, am I right?"

She hesitated. "Maybe."

"Good." Chuckling, he moved another few inches toward her lips. "Now, kiss me, Arabella MacLeod, and make me the luckiest dragonman in the world."

She rolled her eyes and he leaned closer. Her breath was hot against his lips as she replied, "I can't believe I'm about to kiss such a cocky male."

"Then kiss me, already, woman. Otherwise, I'll need to think of some more lines." He touched his nose to hers, the contact sending a little shock through his body. "Maybe I should compare you to the heather on your blouse. Yes, beautiful and delicate-looking, yet hardy and strong, just like you. Heather can be my pet name for you from now on." He stroked the skin beneath her lips. "What do you think, heather?"

Arabella growled, "No fucking way you're calling me that again," before standing on her toes and pressing her lips to his.

The second her soft skin touched his, he wanted to haul her up against his body and feel every inch of her tall, lean frame against his before stripping her clothes and fucking her senseless.

Sending a warning to his dragon to get it together, he focused on the innocent movement of Arabella's lips. It reminded Finn that she'd never been kissed properly before. He needed to make it good.

Cupping her cheek with one hand, he nibbled her lower lip before sucking the top one. When Arabella copied him, he couldn't help but smile. Arabella pulled away, her breath hot against his lips. "Don't you dare laugh at me or I will kick you in the balls, Finlay."

With a chuckle, he took her lips again. Since her mouth was partly open from speaking, he dared to taste her mouth.

Fuck. Arabella's taste was sweet nectar, and despite his desire to take it slow, he pulled her up against his body and took the kiss deeper. The second his lass stroked back against his tongue, his cock turned hard as stone.

Finn growled, loving the little moan he elicited from his lass. When Arabella actually ran her hand to the back of his neck and made contact with his skin, his dragon broke free in his mind. *She is ours. If you don't want to scare her, break the kiss now. The first taste is too much. I want her badly.*

Hearing the frenzy in his dragon's voice, Finn pulled away. Arabella opened her slitted dragon eyes and whispered, "What happened?"

Stroking her cheek with his thumb, he smiled. "My dragon wanted more and told me to stop."

She ran her fingers against the back of his neck, each movement like a brand on his skin. What he wouldn't give to have her fingers travel down his chest and grip his cock.

His dragon huffed. *Stop it. I want her. The images make it harder to hold back.*

I'm not doing it on purpose.

Well, stop it.

Arabella's husky voice snapped him out of his head. "Mine is actually demanding more." She tilted her head. "Kiss me again, Finn?"

He ran a possessive hand up and down her back. "For you or the dragon?"

She hesitated before whispering, "Both."

"Good, lass. Always ask me for what you want. Don't ever hold back with me." Nuzzling her cheek, he added, "But to avoid you calling me a liar again, just know that every time I kiss you, it will become harder to resist you. You're my mate, Ara. I want all of you."

As Finn waited for Arabella's answer, his heart pounded faster. Being truthful was new to him after so many years of flirting and hiding his true self. If she decided to back down and wait, he had no bloody idea how he'd handle it, let alone his dragon.

His beast did a mental stretch. *She will be fine.*

Maybe she doesn't want all of us.

Why not? We are brilliant.

A little modesty would be nice.

Modesty is for humans. We make Ara stronger. She knows it. She'll always want us.

For once, Finn hoped his dragon was right. While he'd only known Arabella a short time, a future without her would be lonely, and all of his plans to bring out her playful side would be for nothing.

And Finn lived for the day he could make Arabella laugh and play without her past weighing her down. The lass had better give him the chance to do it.

~~~

At Finn's words, Arabella's heart warmed. Part of her still cautioned that Finn was lying and would say anything to get her naked, but she pushed aside her old, paranoid and skeptical self. She would no longer allow that version of Arabella MacLeod to be in charge.

Her dragon spoke up. *Good. I don't like her. Now kiss him.*

She hesitated a second. *Are you also losing control each time? I'm not ready for a sex-crazed dragonman.*

I am strong and in control. I want another kiss.

She smiled at her dragon's grumpy tone. *We can't always get what we want.*

Huffing, her beast replied, *This will be my warning against denying me the kiss of our mate.*

Instantly, desire flooded her body, making every nerve sensitive. Wetness rushed between her legs at Finn's heat and scent. As her pussy pulsed, Arabella drew in a breath.

Finn's eyes turned concerned. "What's wrong?"

Her dragon was smug. *That is what I'm holding back. Give me a kiss, or I'll give you the full force. He is our mate and I want to fuck him until we carry his young. Then everyone will realize he's ours.*

Arabella blinked. Somewhat shocked at her dragon's demanding nature, she made her voice work to answer Finn. "My dragon."

"Is she not strong enough to hold back?"

"She is, but she's taunting me. All she wants is to fuck you."

Finn grinned. "Oh, aye?" He leaned close. "That can easily be arranged, for a price."

She frowned. "What the bloody hell are you talking about? I'm not about to pay you just to sleep with you."

"Oh, it's not money I want, Arabella. I want you to agree to stay with me."

"That again."

"Yes, that again. There's no way I'm allowing you to stay here with Fraser and Fergus under the same roof. Even when I'm not home, I'll have Aunt Lorna, Faye, and maybe one of the other female Protectors guard you."

Arabella had an idea. "Can they train me?"

His brows came together. "I'm the one who will be training you."

Using her newfound power over him, Arabella leaned against Finn's chest and he sucked in a breath as her hard nipples made contact. "But you'll be busy. It's a win-win."

Rubbing her fingers against the warm skin of his neck, Finn's voice was strangled as he replied, "If I agree, you'll move in with me, no questions asked?"

Deep down, Arabella knew moving in with Finn was a bad idea. If her dragon lost control over the frenzy, she'd be naked and in bed with Finn in two seconds flat.

Although, leaning against Finn's hard chest with his taste still in her mouth, the idea wasn't as frightening as it had been a few minutes ago. Her dragon had given her a glimpse of how desire could be a good thing. While she was inexperienced, even Arabella knew dragonmen treasured their true mates. "Will I have my own room?"

"You'll have an office, but you'll be sleeping with me." A small sense of panic crept up her back, but Finn's voice drowned it out. "Just to sleep, Ara. Nothing else as long as I can hold out. I give you my word."

Some of her confidence faded. Even if Finn could hold back, could she?

Her dragon chimed in. *For now. But once we have his hard cock pressed against our back, even you will want more.*

I—who are you?

Your dragon. This is the real me. Get used to it.

Finn brushed her cheek again. As soon as she met his eyes, the corner of his mouth ticked up. "You can even decorate it in rainbow kittens, if that will help."

She laughed, erasing most of her tension. "Maybe I should. Redecorating should include your wardrobe. I'm sure there are a few rainbow cat t-shirts online somewhere."

"No cat shirts, full stop."

Staring into his flashing dragon eyes, Arabella yearned to have this closeness every day, to be able to tease and argue. Finn would keep her on her toes, that was for sure.

And with a few words, she could have it.

Keeping to her new mantra of no longer hiding away, Arabella raised her chin. "Even without the cat shirts, I suppose so." She narrowed her eyes. "But if you expect me to cook and clean for you, Finlay Stewart, you're in for a surprise. I have my own work to do."

"Aye, of course you do." His lips were currently an inch away from hers. "How about a kiss to seal the deal?"

"I don't know. Your control is in jeopardy. Maybe I want to wait until you've had time to cool down."

With a growl, he pressed her even tighter against him. "Now, Arabella. Otherwise, my dragon will drive me insane."

She raised an eyebrow. "So I'm supposed to agree to kiss you to placate your dragon? Aren't you supposed to be a mighty clan leader?"

"I am with everyone but you. Around you, Ara, I lose my fucking mind."

Kiss him.

As soon as she gave a slight bob of her head, Finn's lips touched hers. Unlike last time, she knew what to expect and didn't hesitate to open to him.

And damn, as his tongue stroked inside her mouth, filling her with his delicious taste and heat, all she could think about was how much she wanted to feel his tongue on other parts of her body.

Her dragon spoke up. *Yes, it would feel good on our nipples. Or between our thighs.*

Before she could reply, Finn stroked harder and fisted her hair with one hand. He was trying to take control, but Arabella fought back, tugging his hair and twining her tongue with his. Finn's growl sent a shiver through her body, straight between her legs.

She moved her hands to his back and pulled him close. His solid, broad chest should terrify her and remind her of being pinned. Yet terror was the farthest thing from her mind. Finn's lean, hard body made her feel feminine in a way she couldn't remember feeling since she'd been a teenager.

Finn finally pulled away, gently kissed her lips twice, and then murmured, "You're a quick learner, Ara. You already have me wanting to beg for more."

Unable to judge whether he was telling the truth or spouting nonsense, she interpreted it as the latter to avoid discussing the future. "Then you can reward me with some dinner and get me a laptop, or you'll be dealing with cranky Arabella."

He smiled. "Oh, aye? I think cranky Arabella would be quite adorable."

Rolling her eyes, she pushed against his chest and he let her go enough to look into his eyes. "Can I add another requirement to living with you? You can stop with the cheesy lines. They're unnecessary."

Squeezing her hip, his eyes twinkled. "We already sealed the deal with the kiss, Ara. No add-ons allowed." He grinned. "Just wait until tomorrow. I've been saving my best lines for my future mate. I finally get to use them."

"Great. My eyes will soon be sore from rolling so much."

"Eventually, I'll have you laughing." Patting her side a few times, he released her. "We best take some of Aunt Lorna's leftovers and go home, lass. I need to touch base with my Protectors and sort a few clan matters out before bed."

Her dragon chimed in. *Yes, bed. We can tease him and drive him crazy, all without even taking our clothes off.*

No. He's the flirt, not me.

Her dragon tsked. *I am part of you and I want to try. I can wait until tomorrow, but no longer.*

She replied sarcastically, *Great.*

As Finn went to the kitchen and packed up some dinner, Arabella watched him in a new light.

The blond Scot was all but hers. Despite the fact they'd only kissed twice, the thought of another female kissing him caused her to clench her fingers. Whether it was her dragon's influence or not, Arabella didn't know, but she was already growing possessive of Finlay Stewart. If only he would tell her more about who was trying to take away his clan leadership, she could help.

She would ask tomorrow. First, she had to survive sharing a bed with the dragonman.

While it'd been months since her last nightmare, she hoped like hell one didn't come in her dreams later. Parts of her were still damaged and she wasn't ready to show those to anyone yet, not even Finn.

CHAPTER TEN

A few hours later, Finn frowned at Faye. "Convincing Arabella of that will take some doing."

"Aye, but if she's living with you, Finn, you need to let the clan know why. A gathering to show off the lass will help."

His dragon spoke up. *It's a good idea. Other males will know to stay away.*

Fine, I will try. But you need to restrain yourself. Ara doesn't seem like the type to kiss in front of just anyone.

We will see.

Faye's voice snapped Finn out of his head. "Cousin, stop with your dragon and listen to me. It's important."

"Aye, I'm listening. What is it?"

"We scoured the cottage from top to bottom, but all we found was a small piece of blue fabric, ripped from a shirt. It may or may not have to do with the break in."

"It's from the break-in. The cottage was pristine, and Arabella hasn't worn anything blue yet."

"Ask her to make sure. Even if it belongs to the intruder and not Arabella, I can't go through all two hundred cottages in the clan and look for a ripped garment. It's a dead end, Finn."

He tapped his fingers against his arm. "Now with Ara's safety on my mind, we're going to have to grow bolder and flush out the wannabe traitors. I'll think of some ideas, but I also want you and Grant to brainstorm together."

"I can brainstorm on my own."

"Grant stands up to you whereas most of the others are too scared or inexperienced. Learn to work with him, Faye. It'll do you good."

Faye sighed and waved a hand in dismissal. "Fine. Even though he's worse than Fraser or Fergus at getting under my skin, for you, I'll try."

"Good lass." He uncrossed his arms. "That's it for tonight. I'll meet with you tomorrow after I hear the last of the clan disputes and we can discuss your ideas."

She nodded. "Right. I'll also set up the gathering for tomorrow evening. Mum and I should have most of it planned before our meeting."

"Since it's your idea, you're also in charge of Ara's dress and getting ready. As much as I'd like to undress and dress her, she's not ready for it."

Faye's gaze turned sympathetic. "Don't worry, Finn. It'll happen sooner than you think. Anyone who can put up with the MacKenzies has the strength to tackle you."

"Gee, thanks."

Faye laughed. "You know I love you." She turned toward the door. "Until tomorrow, then."

As soon as he heard his cousin exit the front door, Finn let out a sigh.

Work had served as distraction for what came next. Spending the night in bed with Arabella without touching her would be the ultimate test of his self-control.

Going to the bathroom, he undressed and put on a pair of pajama bottoms and a t-shirt. Scratching at the material against his chest, he wished he could do without the extra fabric, but too much skin might set off his lass.

Arabella was strong, but not even Finn was naïve enough to think she could shed her past in a matter of hours, let alone days.

Careful not to make a sound, he slipped into his mostly dark bedroom. The moonlight from the window highlighted Arabella's sleeping face. He scrutinized her features and listened to her breathing, but as best he could tell, she was truly asleep.

Taking the opportunity, he studied the planes and curves of her face. The scar across her cheeks and nose was faint. It reminded him of her story earlier in the day, of how she received it. Even hours later, it still stirred anger in his belly for what they'd taken away—her innocence and a decade of her life.

As his eyes moved to the healed burns on her neck, he wondered at the rest. A few lines from her TV interview weren't enough for man or beast; if he could pinpoint her attackers, he might be able to repay the bastards for what they'd done to his female.

Arabella snuggled into his pillow and he smiled. The pillows were the ones he used every day and it stroked his ego to know she was covering herself in his scent.

Aware he had to get up in about five hours, Finn tiptoed to his side of the bed and carefully slid in next to Arabella. Holding his breath, he waited to see what she'd do. But not even her breathing changed from its slow, steady rhythm.

His dragon's voice was sleepy. *Hold her close. Her warmth will give me the strength to restrain myself.*

I would think quite the opposite. Touching her skin will make it harder not to kiss her and wake her up.

I never said skin. Now who's impatient?

Too tired to argue, Finn inched closer to his female and gently laid his arm over her waist. A few seconds passed before Arabella turned over and nestled against his chest.

As her breathing turned into a soft snore, he smiled and snuggled closer. When Arabella MacLeod was asleep, her past and stubbornness melted away to reveal her true instinct and desire. His lass felt safe in his arms.

Closing his eyes, Finn inhaled Arabella's sweet scent, which helped to calm his dragon. It wasn't long before he also fell asleep, dreaming of the lass he'd been waiting his whole life to claim.

~~~

Arabella awoke to an empty bed.

The faint sunlight streaming through the window told her it must be midmorning. She couldn't remember the last time she'd slept so late; usually she woke with the sun.

Looking to the empty side of the bed, the indent in the pillow and mussed sheets told her Finn had slept there, yet she'd never woken up. Maybe her dragon's desire to be near her mate had overpowered Arabella's usual light-sleeper tendencies.

Her dragon yawned. *I didn't do anything. You simply trusted him. Somehow I don't believe you.*

Giving a mental shrug, her beast continued, *It doesn't matter. Our male carries faint traces of our scent now. The other females will stay away.*

Since Arabella had yet to drink her morning coffee, she ignored her dragon, stretched, and rose out of bed. Trudging to the window, she saw the wild forest of a garden Finn had mentioned yesterday. His room must be at the back end of the cottage.

Looking to the left, the sight of some unknown peak in the distance caught her eye. While different in shape from her home in the Lake District, the barren beauty poking into the sky reminded her enough of Stonefire to smile. As long as she had mountains nearby, she felt right at home.

Footsteps echoed down the hall. Just as she turned toward the door, Finn appeared in the door with a mug in his hand. Holding it out, he said, "Good morning, sunshine. Coffee?"

Frowning, she took the mug. "Do I look like sunshine to you?"

Putting on a mock serious face, Finn gave her a once-over. Then he winked. "You are as radiant as the sun."

She resisted rolling her eyes and instead took a sip of coffee. The milky sweetness made her sigh. "As much as I hate to compliment you, this is good coffee."

"I was trained by Aunt Lorna. Bad coffee isn't tolerated in the MacKenzie household." He dropped his voice to a whisper. "Faye inherited her crankiness from her mother, and you don't want to talk with Aunt Lorna before she's had her coffee."

She took another sip. "At least you've been trained. That means we shouldn't starve."

He took the two steps between them and brushed a hair off her face, his warm skin sending a tingle through her body. His accent thickened as he murmured, "I was starved until I met you, Arabella."

She was about to reprimand him, but the heat in his eyes stilled her tongue. She half-expected his eyes to flash to dragon slits, but they remained round. It was his human-half talking.

To give herself a second to reply, she took another sip and then another. Once the spell of Finlay's words and gaze had broken, she cleared her throat. "So, any clue as to who was behind the attack on my cottage?"

Finn's smiled faded, replaced with a frown. "Not much. The only clue we found was a piece of torn fabric. You haven't ripped anything blue since arriving, have you?"

"No." She took a sip of her coffee, the strong, sweet brew clearing the sleepy fog from her brain. "So I know you don't have any proof, but do you have an idea of who did it?"

"Aye, Duncan Campbell, the male who wants my job."

"Tell me about him and maybe I can help think of a plan." Finn scrutinized her and she raised her brows. "I know all you see when you look at me is a runway model, but I assure you, despite the dazzling exterior, I have brains."

Finn cupped her cheek. "I know you meant to jest, but you could be a model, Ara. A few scars don't make you any less beautiful."

Shaking her head, Finn removed his hand. "Don't start flirting. I want to know about Duncan."

Finn opened his mouth just as her stomach rumbled. Moving to her side, he placed a hand on her back. "I'll tell you while I make you something to eat."

The thought of spending a normal morning with a handsome dragon-shifter cooking breakfast for her made her heart beat a little faster. "But don't you have things to do?"

"Aye, in about an hour. I worked for a bit while you were sleeping."

As he guided them out of the room, she looked up at him. "You should've woken me. I'm behind on my work."

"I bet you are, but I'm still working on getting you a powerful enough laptop to do what you need to do. All of mine were given away last year."

They entered the kitchen. Finn took away his hand to pull out a chair. Rather than tell him she could sit herself, Arabella sat down. "That's right. You used to help with the IT department."

"Aye, which is why I know what I'm talking about."

As Finn took out some eggs, milk, and bread, Ara moved the conversation back to where she wanted it. "Right, you're making me breakfast, so tell me about this Duncan bloke."

She watched as he broke some eggs into a rectangular container, added milk, cinnamon, and vanilla, and then whisked everything. "Duncan was the protégé of the old leader, Dougal. Everyone had expected Duncan to win the clan leader trials and carry on as before."

"So how do you figure into all of it?"

He took out a non-stick frying pan and turned on the front cooker ring. "Well, I'd been watching the clan slowly lose the goodwill and trust of the local humans. Lochguard has fared much better than most dragon clans because of our isolation. Loch Naver isn't exactly a top destination for tourism in modern times, and was bloody well impossible to get to in olden times."

He placed a piece of bread into the egg mixture, turned it, and put in the pan. As he repeated the process, Arabella asked, "How exactly was the old leader losing their goodwill?"

"Well, we used to openly take females as mates from the locals, and in exchange we not only protected the local villages, we also held yearly celebrations near the loch so the females' families could visit. That all stopped when I was fifteen."

"But isn't that when your parents died?"

Finn nodded his head as he flipped the French toast. "My father used to be clan leader."

Arabella blinked. "What? This is the first I've heard of it."

"I try not to advertise it, lass. I want to succeed on my own merits and not sail by because of my father's."

Her opinion of Finn rose a few notches. "So, there are humans living on Lochguard now?"

Finn looked her straight in the eye. "Can you handle it if I said yes?"

Taking a sip of her mostly cold coffee, Arabella thought about it. A year ago, she would've said without hesitation that she couldn't handle it. But thinking of her sister-in-law, Melanie, and Bram's mate, Evie, she'd learned firsthand how not all humans were bad.

Looking back to Finn, she answered, "Yes, I can handle it. So, are there?"

Taking the French toast out of the pan and putting them on a plate, he nodded. "A few. Most left when Dougal took over and he started harassing them."

"Where did they go? It's not as if they can move to the nearest city."

"No, they started their own offshoot holding. They call themselves Clan Seahaven, although they aren't technically a clan. The DDA doesn't recognize them as such since there's only about ten families." He looked over to her. "Seahaven's existence isn't public knowledge, Ara. You can't share it with anyone, not even your brother."

"You're trusting me with clan secrets?"

"Aye, I am. So don't let me down."

Wanting to hide her response from Finn, she looked away. She could hardly believe he was trusting her with something as great as the existence of a secret clan.

Her dragon spoke up. *As I said before, he is a good male. You should kiss him as a reward.*

Stop with the kissing requests. Bloody hell, I haven't even had breakfast yet.

Kiss him for that too. Maybe then he'll make us breakfast every day.

You're demanding.

I'm making up for lost time.

Finn's voice interrupted her internal conversation. "Tell me what your lovely dragon has to say, Ara. Is it about how wonderful I am?"

Arabella snorted. "You would become unbearable if I told you the truth."

He winked. "Then it is about me. Now, I just need to think of ways to woo your dragon."

Her dragon preened. *I like him. He can woo me all he wants. I may reward him later.*

Stop it.

Laying a plate of French toast in front of her, Finn added, "Tell your dragon that I think she's beautiful."

"Oh, for crying out loud, stop it. I can't handle it from the both of you."

He chuckled. "I can't wait for you to let your dragon out to play with mine."

~~~

Finn tried not to hold his breath. He'd brought up the topic casually on purpose.

Studying Arabella's face, there wasn't any panic. Aye, she was a little less relaxed than she'd been a few minutes earlier, but no panic. He could live with that.

He eyed her plate and then back to her face. "Eat."

"Someone's being bossy."

"That's the pot calling the kettle black, lass."

Arabella closed her mouth and picked up the knife and fork he'd laid on the side of her plate. She cut a piece and the second she put it in her mouth, her eyes widened. Her mouth half-full, she said, "It's good."

"Don't act so surprised. Remember, I had Aunt Lorna."

As he watched Arabella eat her breakfast, a sense of contentment settled over him. The last year had been hell, what with changing Dougal's former anti-human structures and rules as well as reforming his Protectors. Outside of his time spent with Arabella and his brief part in rescuing Bram's mate, he hadn't really done anything simply because he wanted to. Yet, watching Arabella eat his food with gusto, he wanted nothing more than to cook for her every day.

Arabella caught him staring at her. "While you're standing there, how about you tell me how you plan to handle Duncan."

Looking to her plate and then to her mouth, Arabella sighed and took another bite before he continued, "I'm working on that today with Faye. I hope to have an answer before this evening."

"After nearly a year, why the sudden deadline? If you're worried about me, I highly doubt this Duncan guy will attack me while I'm staying here."

"Aye, you're probably right about that. Still, I want to set things in motion before tonight. After the gathering, everyone will know you're mine. The news is bound to stoke some anti-human hatred amongst Duncan's circle of supporters."

Arabella frowned. "What gathering?"

"It'll only be a matter of hours before the whole clan knows you're staying here. I can't keep secrets from them. A gathering will tell everyone what's going on. A few should even grow protective of you because of their love of the clan."

"Did you ever think to ask me? My brother has spent most of the last decade deciding things for me. I'm not about to have you do the same."

"Ara, this is different. In matters of the clan, I am in charge."

"Be that as it may, if you plan to make me your partner in bed I should also have a chance to be your partner in everyday life. If you want my trust, Finlay Stewart, then start telling me what's going on."

His dragon spoke up. *She is right. Your mum and dad worked as a team. Give her a chance.*

Aye, and look how it worked out for them. Sharing duties cost both of them their lives.

"Finn."

Arabella's voice snapped him back to the present. "I didn't ask you because I know you hate them. The gathering back on Stonefire was proof of that."

Standing up, Arabella walked over to him and poked him in the chest. "Just because I don't like something doesn't mean I can't do it. In the beginning, I couldn't stand you. Yet I came to Lochguard and even kissed you. Don't coddle me, Finn. You never have and I'm not about to let you start now. If you do, true mate or not, I'll leave and never look back."

109

"I won't let you leave." Arabella raised an eyebrow. "I mean, I won't coddle you."

"Better. Don't do it again."

"I promise." He took her hand and pressed it against his chest. "So, we're having a gathering, Arabella. Would you do me the honor of accompanying me?"

"I'm not fond of your tone."

The feel of her skin and her proximity stirred both man and beast. Aye, he should be civil and have a rational discussion. Yet with Arabella standing close, his cock wanted to do the thinking.

Lowering his head, he laid his cheek against hers. "Then I have a proposition. We're going, but how long we stay is up to you."

Arabella's heart beat faster. "How so?"

He nipped her earlobe and she melted a little against his chest. Finn's voice was husky as he whispered, "If you promise to show me your naked body tonight, and I promise I won't touch unless you give permission, we can leave after our 'First Kiss' in front of the clan." He nipped again. "If you don't, then we'll postpone the kiss until the very end, after dinner." Moving a hand to her back, he pressed her body against him. "What do you say, Ara? The decision is in your hands."

~~~

Arabella was grateful Finn couldn't see her face. At the mention of seeing her body, she'd been mortified at first. Yet with each nibble on her ear, some of her nervousness eased.

The promise to look but not touch was a nice one, but while Finn had seen the burns on her arm and neck, he hadn't seen the rest of her scars. Apart from Dr. Sid back home and her brother and father, no one had, not even Melanie.

She hated the fact she was self-conscious, but the possibility of disgust entering Finn's eyes was too much.

Her dragon chimed in. *He will want us no matter what. You may ignore the way he looks at us, but I do not.*

Only because of his dragon driving him to mate.

Stop with the self-pity. You are better than that. If you would ever allow me out, I wouldn't care about the scars on my hide. They would make me look tough.

Finn rubbed her back and pulled back to look into her eyes. "What's taking so damn long, woman? You wanted a choice and I gave you one. If it's going to take this long every single time I ask a question, then nothing will ever get done."

She narrowed her eyes. "Excuse me if I don't have males asking to see my naked body every day. It's a bit of an odd request."

"That's still not an answer."

She growled. "Fine. You promise we'll stay about half an hour, and I'll let you see me naked. But no touching."

One corner of his mouth ticked up. "Oh, lass, I'll have you begging for me to touch you. You'd be surprised what a few words can do."

"Forgive me if I'm not entirely convinced. I've heard lots of your words, and none have inspired me to rip my clothes off."

He rubbed her back again, and the strokes sent heat rushing through her body. Finn's voice was husky when he added, "You've heard my extravagant compliments, but you haven't heard my dirty talk yet, lass. I'll have you in a puddle within minutes."

Confidence oozed in every syllable. Even Arabella's skepticism faltered.

Her dragon chuckled. *I can't wait. I've always wanted a dirty talking male.*

Deep down, Arabella thought she did too. However, she'd rather cut off her own arm than admit it to Finn in that moment.

CHAPTER ELEVEN

An hour later, Arabella opened the bathroom door and came face-to-face with Aunt Lorna. Blinking, Arabella managed to say, "Hi."

"Hello, child. Faye told me about the gathering and we have lots to do before it starts."

"Um, it's about five hours away."

Lorna waved a hand in dismissal. "And it'll fly by in no time. You deserve to be pampered, Arabella MacLeod. And while no doubt my nephew will do a fine job as mate, you need a motherly influence. I've volunteered for the job."

It was on the tip of Arabella's tongue to say she hadn't asked for one, but she held back. Lorna had not only been kind, she could be Arabella's ally against Finn, if she needed one. "What happened to Finn?"

"Clan leader stuff." Lorna took her hand. "Come. I have a few surprises waiting for you in the spare bedroom."

As the older dragonwoman tugged her down the hallway, Arabella tried not to smile. Lorna's enthusiasm was infectious.

Truth be told, she was glad it'd been Lorna and not Finn when she'd finally stepped out of the shower. Finn's words about dirty talk still lingered, and it was taking all of Arabella's self-control to restrain her dragon. Her beast had all but repeated, "Kiss him" over and over inside her head.

To think, she'd scolded her older brother for always thinking about sex. Her dragon would be doing the same once she had a taste. Arabella only hoped she could handle it.

Her dragon finally muscled out of her invisible cage. Since Finn wasn't around, Arabella allowed her to stay out. *This is your warning, dragon. Be nice or you're going back into the mental cage.*

I don't know why you put me in there. All I wanted to do was kiss our drop-dead gorgeous male. Why you resist, I will never understand.

Thankfully, Lorna stopped them in front of the door to the spare bedroom. "Close your eyes."

While her tone was pleasant, the thread of steel made Arabella close her eyes.

The older female took her shoulders and guided her into the room. A few seconds later, Lorna ordered, "Open your eyes and see your presents from the clan."

She did and she gasped at the array of items on the bed.

From the jeans and t-shirts to the formal dragon-shifter dress to the questionable pile of fancy lingerie, everything was beautiful and in the colors that best suited her skin.

While her brother and his mate had given her gifts before, no one had spent this much effort and time into picking out things that suited her. To think an all but unknown clan would help her made her suspicious.

Of course, the act still touched her. Blinking back tears, Arabella forced her voice to remain even as she spoke. "I appreciate the gesture, but I have a feeling you put this together. No clan would help out a stranger in this manner."

Lorna tsked. "I don't know how the English dragon-shifters act, but here in the Scottish Highlands, we always try to help our own." Arabella opened her mouth to refute the statement, but Lorna beat her to it. "You know secrets spread like wildfire.

Pretty much the whole clan knows you're Finn's by now. The only exception is probably old, deaf Angus, and that's because he sleeps until one p.m. every day." Lorna picked up the traditional dragon-shifter dress. "This is what you'll wear tonight."

The dark purple dress shimmered in the light. Unlike a few hundred years ago, the dress wasn't made of wool or cotton but rather some type of silky-looking material. She moved to touch it, but then resisted. "It's too much. I don't know a lot about fashion, but even I can tell that must've cost a fortune."

Lorna smiled. "A frugal lass? You are one after my own heart, Arabella MacLeod." She held out the dress. "But this is worth it. If you're to be a clan leader's mate, you can't wear bin bags for clothes. You don't want to make Finn look bad, do you?"

"You lay it on thick, Aunt Lorna."

"When you have children such as mine, you have to. The twins alone are responsible for three-quarters of my gray hairs."

"Yet they still live with you. Don't tell Finn, but they're gorgeous. They'll be mated before long."

"If only that were true, Arabella. I have a feeling they'll be with me until well into old age."

Arabella smiled at her exasperated tone. "Start burning the food and they might leave sooner than you think."

Lorna laughed. "Child, I like you more and more." The older woman moved in front of Arabella and offered the dress. "Try it on. I may need to take it in a wee bit. As much as I'd like to say Lochguard has magical elves who sew gowns overnight, this is just one we found lying around."

Touching the smooth fabric, Arabella convinced herself to take the dress. The purple was nearly the same shade as her dragon's hide. If she tried it on, would it trigger a memory?

Her dragon chimed in. *No, because I'm here. I can stave them off. You're cockier with each passing hour.*

It's not cocky if it's true.

Lorna gave her a shove and Arabella sighed. "I guess I'll try this on, then."

Arabella headed into the hall and went to the bathroom. Slowly, she undressed and tossed the dress over her head. Traditional dragon-shifter dresses only had one strap, and it sat atop on her non-tattooed arm, the one with the burns. Since the sight of her old injuries was ordinary to her, she smoothed the fabric and took a deep breath before looking up into the mirror.

The dark purple dress was a little big in the bust, but it fit her slender waist and hips fairly well. Unlike some of the latest trends, the dress was simple and unadorned with anything that sparkled. She almost wished it had some sequins or rhinestones; maybe then it would draw attention away from her arm and neck.

Her dragon grunted. *We are beautiful. Display your battle scars proudly. You are stronger because of them.*

Her beast reminded her a little of Finn, but she kept that thought to herself. *I will try.*

Don't try. Do.

Staring at the shimmery purple fabric, Arabella had a flash of the last time she'd shifted into a dragon, about eighteen months ago.

Out on one of her morning walks, her dragon had snarled inside her head before the shift happened. In a matter of seconds, her beast had roared aloud and Arabella had banged inside her mental prison to try to get out. She didn't want to be a dragon. If they didn't shift back, the hunters might find her and finish what they started.

Yet her dragon had kept her in that hell for six hours. By the time she'd shifted back to a human, she'd been mentally and emotionally exhausted.

With a sob, Arabella snapped back to the present. Wiping away her tears, she pushed aside the fear and hatred of the memory.

In retrospect, it was silly to think the dragon hunters would find her simply because she was in dragon form. Maybe she should try shifting before the gathering. Only then would she finally beat the hunters who killed her mother and destroyed Arabella's family.

Her dragon's voice was soft. *We can do it. We have time. I want to fly.*

Flying is a stretch. I might not remember how.

A dragon never forgets how to fly.

Pounding on the door snapped Arabella out of her head. Lorna's voice drifted through the door. "Everything okay in there, child?"

If anyone else called her child, Arabella would hate it. Yet when Lorna said it, it made Arabella almost feel like family. "Yes, but I have a request."

There was a pause. "What, dear?"

"Is Faye busy? I think I need to shift to ease my dragon."

~~~

Arabella walked beside Faye, clenching and unclenching her fingers, trying her best not to lose her nerve.

Yet she truly had never felt the desire to shift as much as she did currently. Hell, she'd kissed a male yesterday and survived. If she was ever going to take the step to have sex with Finn, she had bloody well better get over the lesser obstacle of shifting into a dragon.

Her dragon chimed in. *Good, I want to fly. Later, I want to fuck.*

Bloody hell. You're as bad as my brother.

We're twenty-eight years old and a virgin. I have a lot to make up for.

Faye glanced over to her and her voice silenced Arabella's dragon. "You sure you don't want me to call Finn? He'll come if you need him."

Raising her chin, Arabella didn't back down. "No. He's busy and I can't call on him for every little thing." Her bravado faded a fraction. "Although I'm sorry to take you away from your busy schedule. I'm sure you have things to do."

Faye waved a hand. "I needed a break from Grant anyway. That male drives me crazy."

She debated asking a question, but decided to risk it. "Do you fancy him?"

"No. He and I were friends once, but then he bollixed it all up a few years ago. I recognize his talents with regards to strategy and investigations, but otherwise, I talk with him as little as possible."

As Arabella tried to think of what to say to that, Faye took her hand and pulled her into a large open space which was surrounded by high, natural rock walls. "This is the private training area I usually use for my wing of Protectors. We'll shift here. Now, strip."

Arabella blinked. "In the open? Won't someone see us?"

"Don't worry, hen. I have Protectors nearby. They'll keep spectators away. It's just you and me. Since you didn't bring any clothes, you need to be naked when you shift or you'll be walking naked back to the cottage." Arabella hesitated and Faye rolled her eyes. "You're the first dragon-shifter I've met who is shy about nudity. Let me assure you, I've seen it all before, Ara, thousands of times."

I want to fly. Hurry up.

Don't you dare shift before I take off my clothes.

Then get to it. I'll give you sixty seconds. One, two, three…

Muttering, "Bloody dragon," Arabella kicked off her shoes. Taking off her socks, she hesitated. Then her dragon's countdown continued, *Fifteen, sixteen…*

She was fast learning her dragon didn't bluff. Rather than risk it, she unzipped her jeans and wiggled out of them. She was careful to keep her ankle turned away from Faye; the crinkly scars were mixed with soot that had never been cleaned from her skin. The result was a bumpy, half-colored patch of skin.

Her dragon's voice grew louder. *Forty-five, forty-six…*

Closing her eyes, Arabella lifted the hem of her t-shirt and tugged it over her head. She stood in her bra and underwear. The light breeze made her shiver.

Glancing over at Faye, the woman was already naked. "Don't look at me. Finish getting undressed. It's a bit nippy today."

Her dragon shouted, *fifty-seven, fifty-eight…*

Shit. Arabella slid the straps down her shoulders and just managed to unhook her bra when her dragon spoke up. *It's time! Let me out.*

Faye's voice carried over. "Just let your dragon take over. I'm shifting now, but I won't take off until you're ready."

The confidence and expectations in Faye's voice, of how she fully expected Arabella to shift without any problems, gave Arabella the nerve to take off her underwear and say to her dragon, *I'm ready.*

Letting down her internal barriers, her dragon rushed to the forefront of her mind. *Work with me. Imagine each part of us changing shape. The process will come back to you.*

Her beast sent images of their arms and legs growing into limbs and hind legs, wings sprouting from their back, and a tail growing from their tail bone. Arabella captured each image and replayed them inside her head. After about sixty seconds, the images started to become reality as her bones and skin stretched, causing a rush of pain and pleasure to course throughout her body.

With a shout, her body grew into the shape of a dragon. Soon, the shout became a roar and Arabella opened her eyes. Looking down and to the side, the tough yet thin purple skin of her wings glinted in the sun. *I did it.*

Yes, but we're still on the ground. I want to fly.

Give me a few minutes. I-I want to embrace my dragon form and chase away any fear.

Okay, a few minutes. No more.

A grunt from Arabella's side garnered her attention. A large, female dragon with blue hide stared back at her. It had to be Faye.

The blue dragon tilted her head in question. Arabella gave the universal dragon-shifter signal to wait by raising her wings up behind her and lowering the right one.

Once Faye nodded, Arabella studied what she could see of herself.

She watched as she moved her tail from side to side, the sensation of the air against her hide a long-forgotten memory. Remembering other stunts as a child, she laid her tail on the ground and ran it back and forth against the grass, the combination of the rocks and tickle of the blades urging her to roll around on the ground. Unlike when she was little, no adult would scold her from getting her hide dirty.

Her dragon harrumphed. *I want to fly, not roll around in the dirt. Dogs do that, not dragons.*

I remember you enjoying it well enough twenty years ago.

I am an adult now. I have more dignity.

We'll see about that.

Not wanting to trigger any memories, Arabella skipped the rest of her body. Looking to Faye, she nodded.

It was time to fly.

Faye jumped into the air and beat her wings until she was about twenty feet off the ground. Hovering, she stared at Arabella.

This is it, dragon.

Taking a deep breath, Arabella crouched and jumped. Her wings moved automatically, until she was at the same altitude as Faye. While her muscles were out of practice, Arabella would deal with the soreness at a later time. Raising one hind foot and shaking it twice, she told Faye to fly.

After giving her an assessing look, Faye maneuvered her body slightly away from Arabella and moved forward. While Arabella's movements were a bit clunkier, she followed.

At first, her concentration was on moving and not falling. A few minutes later, however, Arabella dared to look down.

Lochguard was below them. Various dragon-shifters were walking about in their human forms, not really paying attention to Arabella or Faye. To them, a flying dragon was as natural as breathing.

As much as she enjoyed the sights below, the views of the crags and nearby peaks were breathtaking. Maybe someday she could take a trip around the Highlands, and maybe even the Isle of Skye.

Her dragon chimed in. *Ask Finn. I want to tease his dragon. I also want to play chase in the sky.*

I thought you were an adult.

It's different with mates. I need to drive him crazy.

If Arabella had been in human form, she would've smiled. *One step at a time.*

You are fine. We're safe here.

Faye changed course and Arabella paid attention again. They were flying in the direction of the lake.

Giving a low roar, Faye looked over her shoulder and then pointed down toward the lake with a hind leg.

The choice was Arabella's: did she want to go for a swim?

Follow her, her dragon ordered. *My hide is a little itchy.*

She should tease her beast, but Arabella also yearned to swim in dragon form. Apart from flying, it used to be her favorite thing to do.

Folding her wings back, Arabella dove toward the water. Careful of her trajectory, she dove in and moved around in the water. The cool liquid against her wings and slightly sore back muscles felt good.

She stayed beneath the water until her lungs burned and then moved to the surface. Blinking, she cleared the water from her eyelids. Confirming Faye was swimming nearby, Arabella looked toward shore.

The small tower-like broch was in front of her. Scanning further up the shore, she spotted some men.

They didn't have any tattoos on their arms.

Dragon hunters. They had to be.

Flailing her wings, she tried to swim toward shore. But the longer she looked at the men, the less control she had of her body.

Her dragon shouted. *They can't be hunters. Faye would never allow harm to come to us.*

They are. Why else would humans come to the lake? Arabella tried swimming again, but failed. *Why won't you help me?*

Before her dragon could reply, Faye was in front of her, crooning gently.

Arabella ignored her and kept flailing. Faye quieted, dove into the water and surfaced under one of her wings. Arabella held on as the blue dragon swam toward shore. When the water was shallow enough, she stood and walked the last few feet to shore.

Staying in dragon form would make her an easy target, so she slammed her dragon into a mental prison and imagined her body shrinking back into a human female. Her wings merged into her back, her legs and arms shrunk, and her snout transformed back into a nose. Glancing toward the group of men, she was relieved to see they were still far away. Turning, she ran toward the clan gates, uncaring about her nakedness. All Arabella cared about was getting to safety.

CHAPTER TWELVE

Finn was listening to a dispute between two of the clan farmers when Fraser burst into his office. Before Finn could say a word, Fraser spoke, "The lass needs you."

The farmers, Callum and Archie, glanced at each other and then back to him, although Finn barely noticed. The lass Fraser had mentioned must be Arabella.

His dragon roared. *Go to her. She needs us.*

Looking to the farmers, Finn kept his voice calm and collected. "I've given you all of the possible solutions. Take a day or two to think about them and come back with a decision."

Callum frowned. "But I haven't finished my list of grievances."

Hurry.

"Come, Cal. I know every single grievance you would list. Hearing them again isn't going to change my mind. You have your options, aye?" Once the two older males murmured their agreement, Finn stood up. "Right, then if you'll excuse me, I need to attend to another matter."

The second he and Fraser were out of the room, he whispered, "Tell me what happened."

Fraser remained silent until they were outside and away from any prying eyes or ears. "Arabella ran naked through the front gate and kept going until she found a sheltered rock area to hunker down. Faye has tried talking with the lass, but she won't listen."

Picking up his pace, Finn demanded, "Tell me what you know."

"Not much, cousin. Faye said something about flying with Arabella before they went swimming in the loch in dragon form. Not long after, Arabella had a meltdown. I thought it more important to fetch you than to ask for more details."

His dragon's voice was laced with worry. *Why would she shift into her dragon without us?*

She has an independent mind. You know that.

Still, she should have waited.

Shushing his beast, he all but ran after Fraser until they reached one of the sheltered, open-aired spaces used for training the children. Faye stood at the entrance, with three of her Protectors shielding her and keeping the spectators away.

Since getting angry at who the hell knew how many males that had seen his female naked would accomplish nothing, he focused on Arabella's well-being. He wasn't about to allow her to regress.

A few feet from Faye, he ordered, "Tell me what happened."

The worry in his cousin's eyes eased some of his anger toward her. "You know the humans we allow to fish on the loch? She saw them and panicked. She kept mumbling something about dragon hunters." Faye took a step toward him. "Help her, Finn. The scars on her body alone tell me that whatever memory she's trapped inside must be awful."

"Keep everyone else away and make sure someone fetches a blanket, coat, or something for Ara to wear."

Faye bobbed her head. "I already did. Mum should be bringing them soon."

Schooling his face into a neutral expression, he walked through the opening. He finally found Ara sitting on the ground with her knees to her chest and her head on her knees.

Naked and curled up like that, she looked vulnerable.

His dragon spoke up. *Our mate should never be afraid or sad. Help her.*

Give me a bloody chance, dragon. Handling Ara is different than handling the clan.

I don't care. You're the one with the voice. Use it.

Walking toward her, he called out her name. When she didn't answer, he put every ounce of dominance he could muster into his voice. "Arabella MacLeod, look at me." Her head moved a fraction, but then stilled, so he tried again. "The human males weren't dragon hunters, Ara. They were just fishermen. Stop allowing the past to take all of your attention. You're my female and you need to pay attention to me." Her head lifted a fraction, but not enough. He pushed. "Snap out of it or I'll pick you up and carry you naked through the clan. Of course, I'll have to punch every male who looks at you. Do you really want to be responsible for me possibly breaking my hand in the process?"

With a growl, she looked up. While anger danced in her eyes, the tears squeezed Finn's heart. "Leave me alone, Finlay Stewart."

"So you're not trapped in a memory? Why didn't you respond to Faye?"

Arabella wiped her eyes. "Because it's humiliating, that's why."

Pushing aside his reaction to Arabella's tears, he took two steps toward her. "That's it? You're just giving up? Maybe you aren't the female I thought you would be."

"I never said I was giving up, but how can I face everyone now? I was known as 'poor Arabella' back on Stonefire and after today, it'll now be the same here."

Rolling his eyes, he crossed his arms over his chest. "Shall we bring in a violin to finish off your 'poor me' session?"

Arabella narrowed her eyes. "Stop being an arsehole."

"Oh, is that what calling you out on your shit is? If so, I'll take it. You're hiding, Ara."

"There's a difference between hiding and figuring what the hell to do about my future. A group of humans set off a panic. That is a huge red flag for me."

"And if I had mentioned the humans fished on our loch from time to time? Would that have changed anything?" Arabella hesitated, and he pushed. "I thought so. As much as I'd like to shout at you for going into loch without any notice or warning, I'm not going to. Instead, I'm going to give you a choice. Once some clothes arrive, you can either toss them on and walk with your head high out of this hiding spot and back to my cottage, or you can hide here until we chase everyone away and you can return to your clan. Which will it be?"

"I'm getting pretty fucking tired of your ultimatums."

He shrugged. "Then stop giving me reasons to use them."

Arabella stood up and Finn was careful to focus on her face instead of her naked body. She took a step toward him. "I hate you sometimes."

"Good. Hate means you care. When you're indifferent, then I'll start to worry."

Making a noise of frustration, she poked him in the chest. "You're a bastard."

He took her hand and pressed it against his chest. Leaning forward, he murmured, "You can call me a bastard a million times a day if it means I can have you naked and arguing in my bed."

Her voice lost a little of its heat. "Finn."

Leaning back, he stared straight into Arabella's eyes. The flashing dragon slits told him all he needed to know. "Having a disagreement with your dragon, lass? I bet she wants you to kiss me."

The firmness of her jaw told him he was right.

Releasing her hand, he asked, "What about you, Ara? If I looked down, would your nipples be hard little points? If I touched between your legs, would you be wet for me?" Her silence made him bold. "If nothing else, you've forgotten all about your pity session. Am I right, lass?"

~~~

Arabella wasn't sure if she hated or loved Finn in that moment. He always seemed to walk the line between the two emotions.

Her dragon huffed. *Stop fighting it. We both want him. He was right about you being wet and ready. Kiss the blasted male already and let him fuck us.*

Out in the open? I think not.

Then you want him to fuck us too. That is progress.

Exasperated with her beast, she focused on Finn. "I'm a big enough person to admit you made me forget the humiliation, but if you think I'm going to jump into your arms and let you fuck me until I'm pregnant, you have another thing coming."

The corner of his mouth ticked up. "I like that you're thinking of my cock inside you, lass."

Growling, she resisted the urge to stomp her foot. "Do you ever stop?"

"Give me permission to look at your body and I'll keep quiet," Finn answered. She raised an eyebrow and he added, "Well, for a little while, at least."

Arabella's heart rate sped up. "Somehow, I don't believe you."

His voice was husky when he replied, "Believe me, Ara, when I finally get to see your body, I'll be drinking in every sight and storing it into my memory."

Her dragon's voice was also husky. *Let him look at us or I'll release some of my pulsing need to mate out again.*

You and the threats, too. I swear you two are working together.

He and I want the same thing—to mate. We will wear down your stubbornness, or drive you crazy trying.

Looking back into Finn's eyes, she stated, "Look but do not touch. You try and I will shift and fly away."

"That was the wrong thing to say, lass. I'm itching to chase you in dragon form."

Fuck. His heated gaze made her entire body tingle. She wouldn't be surprised if she looked down and saw her skin had turned red.

Clearing her throat, she tried to sound stern but failed. "Have a look, but pity me, Finlay Stewart, and I'll never forgive you."

Without a word, Finn closed the gap between them until he was standing a mere foot away. She watched his eyes as they looked at her neck, then her shoulder. When he was finally staring at her breasts, her nipples tingled as if he had touched her.

If he was repulsed at the burn mark at the edge of her right breast, he didn't show it.

Her dragon huffed. *You could cover your body in mud and he would still think you beautiful. He likes our spirit, Ara. You should reward him for that.*

Finn moved to get a better look at her right side and she held her breath. The gnarled, healed tissue appeared in patches rather than a straight line. When she'd been set on fire, only parts of her clothes had burned the whole way through before the hunters had doused the fire. They'd been keen to torture her and break her, not kill her.

"Arabella." She looked up and he poked her belly. "Tag, you're it."

Then he jogged to the far side of the clearing, shucked his clothes, and simply said, "Catch me and I'll reward you," before shifting into a giant, golden dragon. The faint sunlight streaming through the clouds glinted off his hide as he jumped into the air and hovered just over the sheltered clearing.

When he brought his tail in between his hind legs and waved it back and forth, she narrowed her eyes. The bastard was taunting her.

Chase him. If you allow me, I'll teach him a lesson.

You'll just flirt.

That, too. But do you really want him to fly away? If he leaves, he may give up on us and we might never see him again.

For all the dragonman stoked her temper, the thought of never seeing Finn again, let alone smiling at one of his corny lines, made her stomach drop. She'd never felt more alive than she had over the last two days.

And not just because of the true mate pull. From day one, Finlay Stewart had made her forget her past whenever she was with him. *Fine, we'll chase him. But I have a few ideas of how to trick him.*

Good. Let me out and we'll try some of them.

Arabella hesitated a second, but then said what the hell. Finn would never take her somewhere dangerous. Her biggest worry would be avoiding his touch once they were both back in human form.

Since she was already naked, Arabella let her dragon half take control of her mind. As she imagined her body changing shape, she once again grew into a fourteen-foot-tall dragon. With a roar, she jumped into the air.

Flicking his tail, Finn turned and flew away. She followed.

He was fast, but Arabella was lighter. Focusing on her wing beats, she closed the distance between them.

Just as she was about to catch him, Finn turned at an angle and glided downward. He was headed toward the copse of trees.

I don't think so.

Use your tactic.

The next second, Arabella pretended to strain one of her wings and fell toward the ground, flapping one wing to keep from falling too fast.

As expected, Finn roared and dove toward her. Once he maneuvered under her supposedly injured wing, she nipped his neck and beat her wings. Taking advantage of his momentary distraction, Arabella dove toward the trees and gently landed between a few of them. Once on the ground, she shifted back to a human and hid between a group of large rocks nestled next to one of the trees.

Soon, Finn's golden hide descended from above about twenty feet from her hiding spot. Slowing her breath, she waited to see if he would find her.

As her heart thumped, both human and dragon halves wondered what he would do next. After all, Finn had promised a reward.

~~~

While still in dragon form, Finn scanned his surroundings for Arabella.

His ego wasn't overly fond of being tricked, but he appreciated her cleverness. For a lass who'd never been in the army, let alone trained as a Protector, she had a natural tactical instinct.

His dragon grumbled. *You are overly protective. I knew she was faking.*

Bullshit. You were just as worried as me.

At his dragon's silence, he finished his scan. He couldn't see anything, and there were too many scents to pick out his female.

To get a better look closer to the ground, he imagined his body shrinking back into a human. The familiar flash of pleasure and pain snapped right before he was a six-foot-three human male.

Studying the marks on the ground, he found where Arabella had landed, but didn't see any human footprints. He was about to turn away when he spotted the broken branch of a bush next to a rock formation. If he were trying to hide, that would be the place to do it.

Still, he wanted to surprise the lass as payback. Turning away, he wandered to the trees on the far side until he was invisible from Arabella's hiding spot. Having grown up in these woods, he easily made his way around the clearing in silence. Even if Arabella heard a few whispers of branches brushing against each other, she would dismiss it as nothing more than the wind.

When he was right behind the rock formation, he could see Arabella's back through the foot-wide opening facing him. Moving ever so slowly, he reached just to her side and brushed his fingers to tickle her.

Arabella jumped and hit her head as she muttered, "What the hell?"

Convinced she wasn't gravely injured, he chuckled. "Payback's a bitch, isn't it?"

Before she could reply, he walked around the rock formation to the opening on the other side and peered into her hiding place. Arabella gave him the two finger salute. "That was no bloody reward, Finn. I think I cracked my skull."

"Stop whining and come out so I can give you your proper reward."

For a second, he thought Arabella would be stubborn and remain in place. Then she sighed and wiggled out of the narrow opening of her hiding spot. "It had better well be a good one, Finlay."

"Aye, lass, it is." He held out his arms wide. "Me."

Arabella looked unconvinced. "That rather sounds like a reward for you and not me."

He grinned. "No, you didn't let me finish. I'll stand here and allow you to ogle and touch me to your heart's content and I won't move a muscle, except to breathe."

"A male who wants nothing more than to mate is going to resist a female touch? I don't think so."

"For you, Arabella, even if I go mad with desire, I will resist. Judging from your slitted dragon eyes, your beast is urging you to touch me." He leaned forward. "Oh, and I forgot to add that once you acclimate to my body, I plan to make you come with my tongue."

Arabella's eyes remained slits. "What about the gathering and your clan duties?"

"A good portion of the clan saw you chasing me. The chase always heats the blood and everyone will expect us to be away for a while." When she remained silent, he pushed. "Don't be afraid to take what you want, Ara. I'm not about to take advantage of your trust, flip you over, and pound into your pussy until the frenzy clears. You gave me the gift of looking at your body. This is me repaying the gift."

His skin tightened each second Arabella remained silent. Controlling his dragon was bloody difficult; if she didn't make a decision soon, he might have to push her away to avoid breaking his word.

If he did that, Arabella's fragile self-confidence might shatter.

His dragon chimed in. *I can handle her touch. Stop doubting yourself.*

Says the dragon who keeps pushing me to fuck her.

His beast huffed. *This is different. I want to play more with her dragon, but to do that she needs to trust us. I will be fine.*

Finn only hoped his beast's confidence would last. Acclimating Arabella to his body was the first step. *You better be, or we won't be able to taste her afterwards.*

His dragon remained silent, and that worried him.

Gathering his own training and experience from winning the clan leader trials, Finn watched Arabella.

HEALED BY THE DRAGON

~~~

Arabella was torn on what to do.

Her dragon, however, was not. *You already peeked at his chest and cock. I want to touch him. Don't you?*

Yes, but—

No buts. Have faith in his dragon. He already made you forget about your sadness. Let's make him a little happy.

Arabella smiled. *You're the worst, dragon.*

No, this is me playing nice. Wait until I don't hold back. We might break our male's penis.

Arabella couldn't help it, she laughed. When Finn raised an eyebrow, she shook her head. "Trust me, you don't want to know."

"If you're laughing about my cock, lass, it's not funny."

Emboldened by her dragon's words, Arabella decided to hell with hesitating. Walking up to Finn, she laid a hand on his chest and rubbed it in slow circles, loving the light bristle of his chest hair.

Looking up, Finn's eyes were slitted. She tilted her head. "Do you think you can still hold back?" She moved her hand a few inches lower and Finn drew in a breath. "I need to know."

His voice was strangled when he spoke. "Aye, as long as you keep your end of the bargain and let me lick between your thighs when you're done."

Yes, yes, yes, her dragon chanted.

Ignoring her beast, she straightened her shoulders. With anyone else, Arabella would say no. Yet Finn had done nothing but help and push her to be better. Not only that, she was already wet at the thought of Finn doing anything to her body with his tongue. "Only when I say I'm done."

"Aye, then get a bloody move on, woman."

Running her hand up, she moved to his shoulder and then the muscles of his bicep. Finn was built more like a swimmer, with lean muscles, but she didn't doubt his strength. Maybe one day she'd feel comfortable enough to let him pin her with that strength and drive her crazy with his caresses.

Moving around to his back, she placed her other hand on his skin and took in the breadth of his shoulders. Arabella had once had a weakness for a broad, strong back. As she rubbed up and down, she decided she still did.

Her dragon growled. *More, I want to feel more. Stop being a chicken. Go lower.*

Maybe I should slow down. I don't like your attitude.

You can lie to everyone but me. You're just as anxious as me to have Finn's tongue lapping at our pussy.

Rather than reply, Arabella focused back on Finn and moved ever so slowly down until she reached his firm buttocks. When she gripped the tight, round muscled cheeks with her hands, Finn sucked in a breath. Digging her nails into his ass, he croaked, "Lass, you're killing me."

Without thinking, she murmured, "Not yet," and her dragon cheered.

Yes, tease him. Don't make it too easy.

One second you want me to finish, the next you want me to draw it out. Make up your bloody mind, dragon.

Just stop talking to me and go for his cock.

Rolling her eyes, Arabella leaned close to Finn's back and took a deep inhalation. The scent of male and peat made her heart beat faster and her nipples tighten. For a second, she considered licking his skin to see what he tasted like, but decided against it because her dragon might end up losing control at the taste.

So little faith in me. I think you use me as an excuse.
Do you want me to argue or head toward his cock?
Cock. Definitely, go for his cock.

Smiling at her beast, Arabella released her grip on Finn's arse and moved back up to his shoulders before circling around to his front. One look at Finn's eyes, filled with heat, desire, and a little bit of dragon frenzy, nearly made her knees buckle. She'd never expected for a male to want her so much.

Finn's voice was husky as he asked, "Are you finished, Ara?"

"Almost."

Running one hand down his chest, she looked down at Finn's cock, erect for her.

Tease the tip. Drive him crazy. It will make everything better for us later.

How do you know that, dragon? You have as much experience as me.

Just call it a dragon's instinct.

Looking at the thick, swollen head, she noticed a drop of moisture. Curiosity won out and she rubbed the bead with her forefinger.

Finn's whole body tightened. "You don't know how long I've been waiting to feel your finger on my cock, lass. Don't stop."

His words bolstered her confidence, and Arabella wrapped her fingers around his hard length and tugged. Finn moaned, and Arabella did it again.

Finn whispered, "Arabella, love, please. Do much more of that, and I'll come all over your hand."

She didn't move her hand, but did look up into Finn's eyes. "Is that supposed to be a bad thing?"

"Och, lass, you are better at this than you think you are."

Blushing, Arabella looked back down at Finn's cock in her hand. She was far bolder with actions than words when it came to sex.

Her dragon huffed. *If you're not going to make him come, then let him lick us. If I can't fuck, I want an orgasm.*

You're going to be worse once the frenzy takes hold, aren't you?

By then, you'll enjoy it as much as me.

Arabella wasn't ready to think about the frenzy and what resulted. In the moment, she just wanted to have some fun.

After giving Finn's cock one more tug, she release him and whispered, "Kiss me and I'm done."

With a growl, Finn pulled her flush against him and kissed her. As his tongue invaded her mouth, Finn rubbed and caressed her back, her hip, and finally gripped her arse.

However, there was no panic. Each stroke of his tongue and hand only made her pussy pulse.

Finn broke the kiss. When his slitted eyes met hers, he ordered, "You can stand or lie on the ground, take your pick. But then spread your legs for me, Arabella, so I can devour you."

Chapter Thirteen

As Finn waited for Arabella's response—to stand or lay on her back while he devoured her pussy—it took every ounce of his self-control to keep his dragon from taking over his mind.

His beast growled. *I have better stamina. I can give her more orgasms. I should be in charge.*

I won't let her first time be with you.

Why? We are the same.

I want Ara to see human eyes as I lick her to orgasm.

Before his dragon could argue, Arabella straightened her shoulders. "The ground is damp, so I'm going to stand."

His dragon was confident. *I like the challenge. I may fight you for control.*

In this, dragon, I'll win. Behave or I'll toss you into a mental maze.

At his dragon's silence, he brushed the top of her breast and murmured, "Does that mean you're ready for my tongue, lass?"

"Y-yes."

Looking back up to her eyes, he confirmed the desire and curiosity in her gaze. Realizing he would be the first male to taste her pussy, stroked his ego, as well as his dragon's. "You'll like it, Ara."

"You seem pretty confident."

Smiling at her tone, he brushed the curve of her breast and traced her already taut nipple. "Let me give you a free preview of what's to come."

Before she could reply, he bent down and took her nipple into his mouth. After sucking her hard, he swirled the tight bud with his tongue. When he nibbled lightly, Arabella moaned and threaded the fingers of one hand through his hair.

Releasing her, he blew on her wet flesh and Arabella shivered. His voice was husky when he asked, "Well? Did you enjoy your free preview?"

Arabella cleared her throat. "Maybe. But if you expect me to beg you for more, then you're going to be waiting a long time."

He kissed the spot between her breasts. "You do know I like a challenge, right, lass?" Kissing her shoulder, he placed a possessive hand on her hip. "I think I can win you over."

The light, hesitant touch of Arabella's fingers on his back nearly made him groan, but he held back. He didn't want to risk anything spooking Arabella.

His dragon chimed in. *Enough talking. I want to know what she tastes like.*

Shut it, dragon. We need to make sure she's not afraid.

I smell her arousal. She is ready.

Arabella's voice silenced his beast. "I enjoy a challenge myself. If you can make me beg, then I'll owe you a favor. If I resist, you will owe me one."

Finn looked to her eyes. "That's a dangerous bet to lose, Ara."

She raised her eyebrows. "I don't plan on losing."

Grinning, he ran his hand up and down her hip. "In this, Arabella, you are in over your head."

"Then stop with all this talk and show me already. I'm getting cold."

His dragon hummed. *Maybe one day she'll give orders in bed. I would like that.*

Rather than go down that line of thought, Finn focused all of his attention on the female in front of him. "You have a deal." Leaning down, he placed a gentle kiss on the burned side of her neck. "I just need to work my way down your body." Nuzzling the scar at the side of her breasts, he murmured, "My beautiful lass deserves to be treasured."

"Finn."

Running his hand down her scarred side, he shook his head. "Don't try to scold me, Ara." He looked into her dark brown eyes. "You are beautiful."

~~~

Arabella's heart skipped a beat at Finn's words. Unless he was a bloody good liar, he really did believe she was beautiful.

Of course, her dragon stated. *We have always been beautiful. You need to believe it.*

As she stared into Finn's eyes, she truly felt it for the first time.

Then Finn's cocky grin broke the spell. "Are ye waiting for the Scots way to say it? Ye're verra bonny, lass."

At his exaggerated accent, she giggled. "When you do that, it's both sexy and funny."

"Och, aye?"

Shaking her head, Arabella warned, "Just don't get any ideas in your head of pulling out the Scots on a regular basis. I'll pretend not to understand you."

His accent returned to its usual rhythm. "Enough talking. What I have planned doesn't require any words, let alone a special accent to impress you."

She opened her mouth, but then Finn ran a hand down her chest, over her belly, and stopped just before the dark curls between her legs.

As his fingers lingered, lightly brushing her skin, Arabella's heart pounded harder. She'd waited a long time for this moment, when a man would touch her pussy, but as much as she wanted it, her stomach flipped with nervousness. Things would never be the same with Finn after this.

Her dragon spoke up. *Good. I'm tired of waiting. The sooner you accept he is ours, the sooner we can fuck him.*

"Arabella." She looked down into Finn's brown eyes. "I want you to watch me. If you look away, I'll stop. Are we clear?"

Some of her nervousness faded at his order. "Does this mean I get to give orders to you, too?"

Finn's eyes flashed to dragon slits. "Lass, I look forward to that day, because then you'll truly be mine."

Stop fighting him. It will feel good. Just obey for the moment. We can turn the tables on him later.

Liking her dragon's way of thinking, Arabella decided to tease him. Dropping her voice to a husky whisper, she replied, "Then make sure you're good enough to keep my attention."

Good girl.

Finn moved his free hand to her arse and rubbed slow circles on her right cheek, her skin warming with each pass. "I think I can do that."

He slapped her arse and she squeaked. "What the bloody hell was that for?"

Finn removed his hands and she instantly missed his heat. "I have your attention now, lass. Widen your stance and shush."

A few seconds passed and she realized he wasn't going to touch her again until she obeyed.

With anyone else, she would have called him a bastard and walked away. However, the slight sting on her arse combined with Finn's heavy-lidded gaze and slight heat of his breath on her belly only made her pussy pulse in anticipation.

Even if she couldn't say it aloud, she wanted his tongue so much she ached.

Her dragon chuckled. *You're finally being honest. Stop trying to lie to me because it won't work.*

Shut it, dragon. If I don't pay attention to Finn, then you'll never have an orgasm.

Her beast huffed and fell silent.

Moving her feet against the soft grass, Arabella widened her legs. Even then, all Finn did was look over her body. Would the man never get on with it?

Someone's impatient.

Last warning, dragon, or I'll lock you tight inside a mental cage and enjoy Finn all to myself.

You wouldn't dare.

Watch me.

A light breeze blew and Arabella shivered. Enough was enough. With a growl, she spoke up. "You're losing my attention, Finlay. Hurry the hell up."

The corner of his mouth ticked up. "That anxious for my tongue, lass?" She opened her mouth to reply, but then he ran the back of his hand down the inside of her thigh, his touch a brand on her skin. Finn leaned forward until she felt his breath on her lower belly as he continued, "Sometimes, waiting only increases your pleasure."

He traced the crease where her inner thigh met her hip and Arabella's knees nearly gave out.

Her dragon roared. *How can he be teasing us? He is male and should have no control.*

Ah, so the dragon doesn't know everything.

Her beast grunted. *I still know more than you.*

Finn removed his finger and she cried out, "Don't stop."

He raised an eyebrow. "That almost sounds like begging to me, lass."

Arabella clenched the fingers of one hand. "It wasn't. And I'm this close to walking away and leaving you hanging."

"Then stay with me. I want you to watch me as I make you come, not your dragon. Push her aside. I want Arabella MacLeod squirming as I lick and lap your pussy."

Her dragon sucked in a breath. *Oh my, I like him.*

Then shut it or he'll stop.

Her beast fell silent again.

Arabella placed her hands on her hips, but then Finn's eyes went to her breasts currently jutting out from her body. A slight flash of embarrassment coursed through her, but she fought against it. "She won't interrupt us again. I hope all of this is worth it. Get on with it already."

"With pleasure." He looked to the trees on her side. "You may want to hang on, though. I'm pretty damn good and your legs will probably give out."

Arabella wished she had a witty reply, but she had no idea if a male really could make her legs go wobbly. Reaching out a hand, she leaned against the tree. "I won't fall. Now, stop stalling."

Finn winked at her before he sat down on the ground and moved his hand between her legs. Never taking his eyes from hers, he traced the lips of her pussy. At the warm, rough touch, wetness rushed between her legs.

She wanted more, much more. Arabella had never ached for another person's touch as much as she did in this moment. With Finn, she wasn't afraid.

He continued to trace her opening, but never her clit. Instead, he circled around her pulsing bundle of nerves and back down to her swollen lips.

The combination of his touch and the desire in his gaze made her dragon roar, but Arabella fought it. She wanted to be in charge when she finally felt Finn's hot tongue.

"Arabella." He thrust a finger inside her and she moaned. "You're mine."

~~~

Finn's entire body was tense. Making Arabella yearn for his touch was part of the plan. As the scent of her arousal grew stronger, his dick fought for control of his brain, as did his dragon.

Then he plunged his finger into his female's pussy and his beast growled. *She is ours. Take her. After one orgasm, she will beg for our cock.*

Someone is confident.

She is our female. I burn for her.

Slamming his dragon into the back of his mind, Finn slowly moved his fingers. At Arabella's moans, he decided to up his game. "Is there something you need, Arabella?" He moved his finger again and she sucked in a breath. "If you're in a hurry, I can make you come with my finger."

"No," she shouted.

He grinned and she immediately scowled. "You're losing our bet, Ara. Just tell me you crave my tongue and I'll stop my torture and make you scream."

He saw the battle in Arabella's eyes, the desire mixed with fire. She wanted him, but didn't want to lose.

Removing his finger, he put it into his mouth and sucked it as he pulled it out, her taste driving his dragon crazy. Finn rather agreed with his beast; he would never grow tired of Arabella MacLeod.

Arabella's eyes flashed to dragon slits and she cursed. "Hurry up, Finn. Fuck me with your tongue or my dragon will lose her mind."

"Only if you ask for yourself as well."

Her voice was barely a whispered, but Finn's hearing was keen. "I want it, too."

"That's my lass."

He turned around and scooted back until he could thread his arms between her legs. Gripping her hips, he leaned his head back and stared up. "Holy fuck, Ara. You're perfect."

She shifted her weight, but he tightened his grip. Her pink pussy was swollen and glistening. The fact she not only wanted him, but trusted him enough to grant access to the most vulnerable area of her body warmed his heart.

He would make this good for her.

Raising his head, he darted his tongue out for a quick taste of her arousal and groaned. Only because of his ironclad control could Finn lightly flick and tease her opening. With each taste, his dragon demanded more.

146

Once the tension under his hands relaxed, he thrust his tongue into Arabella's pussy.

She moaned as he lapped and teased. She was so wet and tight. It made him glad he'd started with his tongue and not his cock.

With a slow lick, he moved from her entrance to her clit. Swirling and teasing the hard little nub, Arabella's hands covered his. Her voice was strangled as she spoke. "Please, Finn. I'm close."

Past the point of teasing her, he gave her clit a long, slow lick before sucking it between his teeth. Worrying her sensitive nerves with strokes of his tongue, he dug his hands into her hips in a possessive grip.

Then with a gentle bite, he mentally claimed Arabella. She yelled his name as if agreeing with him, and he moved to plunge his tongue into her pussy, loving the grip and release of her muscles. As her spasms slowed, he gently lapped her orgasm, the best fucking thing he'd ever tasted.

He slowed his licks and Arabella whispered, "Finn, that's enough."

Smug at her spent tone, he gave one last long lick before lowering his head, releasing her hips, and moving from between her legs. Looking up, Arabella's eyes were slitted and half-lidded. Some dragonmen would spout fancy words and promise the world. That wasn't Finn. "You lost."

"I don't care."

He rose on his knees and hugged Arabella's waist. "A dragonman could get used to this, you know." He rubbed her back in slow circles. "I bet I could get you to declare me the sexiest dragonman of all time if I went down on you again."

Arabella finally frowned. "Shut up and kiss me before I push your arse to the ground and fly away. No matter how good the next orgasm might be, smug Finlay is irritating."

With a chuckle, he slowly caressed up her body as he stood. When he was at full height, he pulled Arabella close and nuzzled her cheek. "Thank you, Arabella, for trusting me with your body."

~~~

Arabella's post-orgasm haze finally lifted at Finn's words. Whenever his cockiness slipped and was replaced with tenderness, the male wiggled his way a little deeper into her heart.

Truth be told, she'd been afraid. Touch had put her off for so long that the idea of a male touching her had scared her for years. With Finn, however, there was no fear; it was all fire and heat.

She drew on her growing trust for the dragonman in front of her and tilted her head. "Are you going to keep spouting sweet nothings or are you going to kiss me?"

Finn pulled her tighter against his body. "You asked for it."

Before she could reply, his lips descended on hers. He nipped her bottom lip and she opened. His tongue stroked hers as his hand wandered to her arse. When he slapped her, she growled and moved a hand to his hair. Tugging, he growled back.

They both fought for control of each other's mouths.

Then Finn pulled away suddenly and she demanded, "Why did you stop?"

"I need a bloody second, woman, or I'll take you right now. Is that what you want?"

Her male's patience was really starting to become saint-like.

Her dragon added, *And what about me? I want to ride him and fuck him hard, but I'm holding back.*

Barely.

I'm still holding back. I deserve praise.

You're cocky enough, dragon.

Finn's voice prevented her dragon from replying, "Well, Arabella, stop talking with your damn dragon and tell me, what do you want?"

Arabella searched his eyes. Part of her wanted him to take her, but another part was afraid her past would come between them. He still didn't know the whole truth.

Hugging him close and laying her head on his shoulder, she answered, "I can't take the frenzy yet."

He hugged her tightly and she reveled in the feeling of his strong body against hers. For once, she wished he wasn't clan leader and they could just stay here for as long as they liked without the world intruding.

However, all too soon, they'd have to return to Lochguard and reality. Once they did, Arabella wasn't sure what to do. The clan probably thought the worst of her after her breakdown earlier.

Of course, thinking of earlier reminded her of the evening plans. "Do we still need to go to the gathering?"

Finn stroked her back. "I'm afraid so, lass. The sooner I introduce you properly, the sooner I can start assessing friend and foe." He leaned back to look in her eyes. "As much as I'd like to simply introduce you as 'Finlay's female, so stay the fuck away', I think you might not go for it. What should I introduce you as?"

Arabella resisted shaking her head at her male's words. "So, no pretty words for the clan? That's new."

He grunted. "You're mine. I don't need pretty words to say it."

She raised an eyebrow. "Does this mean you're done with the flirty words?"

"I never said that, heather."

Arabella growled. "Call me that again. I dare you."

"Heather," he said with a grin.

Since Finn's hard cock was still pressed against her belly, Arabella leaned back and gripped it in her hand. Squeezing, Finn drew in a breath before she replied, "If you expect me to giggle and blush just because you gave me an orgasm, you really don't know me."

Squeezing him a fraction harder, Finn groaned. "What you don't know, Ara, is how fucking fantastic it feels to have your hand squeezing my cock. Do it again, lass."

Her dragon spoke up. *It's our turn to tease. Do it.*

Will it push you into the frenzy?

I can hold back. At Arabella's skeptical pause, her dragon added, *I can. I want to play.*

Raising her eyebrow at Finn, she ordered, "Only if you stay still." Pushing aside her embarrassment, she added, "And make sure to watch. You look away and I'll stop."

"Bloody hell, I've created a monster."

Ara smiled. "Oh, I'm saving my best tricks for later."

Finn's eyes flashed to dragon slits and warmth shot between her legs. Holding such power over Finn was more erotic than she'd ever imagined.

Not that she always wanted to be in charge, but once in a while, she wanted to bring the cocky male to his knees.

Her dragon cheered. *Just make sure to share the playtime with me. I want to drive him crazy, too.*

150

Eventually. For now, he's mine.

Her dragon bowed down to her possessive tone.

Tugging Finn's cock once, she asked, "So, do you agree?"

Never blinking, Finn answered, "Of course I fucking agree. I've been dreaming of this for months."

Rather than focus on Finn fantasizing about her, Arabella looked down. Using her free hand, she traced circles on the tip. A drop of moisture formed. Curious, she touched it with her finger and put it to her mouth.

The saltiness on her tongue made her wonder what it would feel like to have Finn come in her mouth.

Finn's strangled voice broke her thoughts. "Ara, you're killing me. I'm not sure how much longer I can last, love, so if you're going to play, then do it quickly."

"Ah, so you're not quite the sex-god with stamina you made out to be?"

Finn's eyes grew more heated. "You'll just have to wait until next time to find out."

The confidence in his voice sent a jolt between her legs. She couldn't wait, not that she'd admit as such to the male in front of her.

Her dragon chimed in. *Stop flirting and tease him.*

But I thought you liked flirting.

Not when we have our male's cock in our hand. I wish it was in our mouth.

For a second, Arabella was shy at the idea. Then Finn's lingering saltiness on her tongue gave her courage. When she knelt before him, Finn asked, "What are you doing, Ara?"

"Shush and let me try something."

Releasing Finn's cock, she ran her hands up his thighs and around to his arse. Gripping his tight cheeks, Finn's muscles tensed under her fingers.

Afraid she'd lose her nerve, Arabella kept her eyes trained on Finn's long, hard cock jutting in front of her and flicked her tongue to the tip. Finn groaned and clenched his fingers at his sides. With a deep breath, she looked up to find Finn's pupils round and dilated. His voice was husky when he asked, "I know you said no touching, but, fuck, Ara, I need to thread my fingers through your hair."

With a smile, she tilted her head. "Now who's close to begging?"

"I have a feeling your hot mouth will be worth it."

Trying her best not to blush, Arabella mustered up her courage. "If that's so, ask me nicely."

Finn growled. "Bloody stubborn dragonwoman."

Her dragon piped in. *Run your finger under his cock. He will beg then.*

Following her dragon's advice, she ran her forefinger up and down the underside of his erection. "Ask nicely, or I leave."

Through clenched teeth, Finn spit out, "Please, Arabella, queen of all dragon-shifters, let me thread my fingers through your hair."

She smiled. "Better."

Growling, Finn's eyes flashed to slits and back. "If you're waiting for me to beg, it's not going to happen, Ara. Only because it's you, can I even give up control for a few minutes. If I don't touch you soon, my dragon will break free, and you know what'll happen then."

He's talking about the frenzy, her dragon stated.

152

While a small part of her wanted nothing more than to fuck for days on end until she was pregnant, most of her wasn't ready. If she wasn't careful, she would push Finn too far.

She nodded. "Fine, but once you no longer have the frenzy excuse, I will torture you on purpose."

Finn threaded his fingers through her hair and tugged lightly. The slight pain made her wetter. His voice was gravelly when he replied, "Och, lass, after the frenzy, you can do whatever the hell you wish with me because by then, you'll be mine for good."

It was on the tip of her tongue to say he would be hers for good first, but she resisted. The thought alone scared her; she wasn't sure if Finn could remain in control if she said it to him. Dragon-shifter males were possessive to a fault. The instant someone claimed one with words, they became unbearable and cocky.

Finn sure as hell didn't need any more cockiness.

Her beast snarled. *Stop thinking so much. His dick is waiting. Play with it.*

Fine, but learn some patience.

Shutting her dragon into the back of her mind, Arabella moved one hand to grip his cock. Gently, she took him into her mouth just as Finn tightened his grip in her hair.

Twirling her tongue, his nails dug into her scalp. Taking the encouragement, she took him deeper and teased his taut, soft skin with her tongue down the length of his erection. When she took him as far as she could, Ara tightened her grip of her hand at the base of his cock and moved her mouth.

Working a steady rhythm, she grew accustomed to his size and reveled in the way a flick here or a twist there would elicit a groan or her name from Finn's lips. Also, for the first time, she burned to feel his hard length inside of her without fear.

Pushing aside panic about the frenzy and resulting pregnancy, Arabella concentrated on sucking, licking, and even nibbling. Judging by how tight Finn gripped her hair, he was close.

Her dragon hummed. *Good. His scent will be embedded in our skin. Everyone will recognize our claim.*

We haven't claimed him yet.

Isn't that what you're doing right now?

Forcing her beast to the back of her mind, Ara increased her pace until Finn grunted. "I'm coming, Ara."

It was a warning, but there was no fucking way she was pulling away. Squeezing him harder, Finn roared her name as he came with hot, salty spurts into her mouth.

When Finn's grip eased and he caressed her head, Arabella swallowed, gave one last, long flick with her tongue and pulled away. Taking a deep breath for courage, she looked up to Finn's face and sucked in a breath at the tender-yet-heated look in his eyes. "Stand up, lass."

Without a word, Arabella stood and Finn drew her against his body. Laying his forehead against hers, he murmured, "That was bloody fantastic, Ara. While your mouth is hot and tight, I can't wait until I can fuck your pussy with my cock and make you scream."

Despite her best efforts, her dragon broke free and filled her mind with Finn taking them hard from behind, the side, and any which way before adding, *I want all of that, and soon. I can't hold back much longer.*

Try. Two days isn't enough time for me.

With a grunt, her beast stated, *Just one more day, at best. Any more than that, and I will lose control.*

Finn's voice broke through her inner conversation. "Tell me what you're thinking."

Narrowing her eyes, she tried to pull away but Finn's hold was like steel. "Don't order me around."

Grinning, he lightly brushed his fingers against her side. "It seems to be the only way I can get you away from your dragon. She's become bloody chatty."

Since talking about the progress with her dragon could bring back memories of why her beast had been silent so long, Arabella changed the subject. She wouldn't let the damn hunters ruin this memory. "Before you start trying to charm my dragon, there's something more important we need to do."

His eyes flashed. "What, me licking between your thighs again?"

Slapping his chest, she growled. "No. Focus, Finn. And not with your cock."

He winked at her. "With you, I'm always thinking with my cock, Arabella. You're sexy, clever, and stubborn. Not a second goes by that I don't ache for you."

Unable to tell if he was joking or being serious, Arabella decided to ignore his remark. "You might have forgotten your leader duties, but I haven't. We have a gathering to attend."

Sighing, he kissed her nose. "And here I thought I'd convinced you with my wondrous, magical cock to do whatever I wished. I guess I'll have to keep trying."

The corner of her mouth ticked up. "Someone is a little proud of themselves. I'm sure other males have wonderful cocks, too."

He growled. "Don't be thinking of other males' cocks."

She laughed. "If it keeps you on your toes and knocks down your ego a few notches, I may bring it up on a regular basis."

Finn stared at her a second before his fingers fluttered against her sides and Arabella laughed. "Stop...it."

Tickling her for another minute, she was out of breath when he finally stopped and hugged her tightly against his body. "Bring up other males' dicks and I'll do it again."

She rolled her eyes. "How about you just shut up and kiss me before we head back?"

His hand caressed down her back until Finn gripped her arse possessively. "That I can do, love. That I can do."

As Finn kissed her, he devoured her mouth, and Arabella forgot all about her past with the hunters, her scars, or what Clan Lochguard would think of her when they saw her at the gathering. In this moment, she was being kissed by a male who could make her laugh one minute and heat her body in the next.

Woe betide any female who tried to flirt with him. Finlay Stewart was hers and she would make sure his clan knew it.

CHAPTER FOURTEEN

Arabella was eyeing the purple dragon-shifter dress on her bed when someone pounded on her door. With a sigh, she yelled, "Finn, I told you to leave me alone. I'm trying to get ready and I don't need your distractions."

An amused female voice answered, "The twins are keeping him occupied. We thought you could use some help getting ready."

Recognizing Aunt Lorna's voice, Arabella strode to the door and opened it. "Sorry, Finn kept knocking every few minutes and I got rather tired of opening the door only to slam it shut again."

Faye poked her head out from behind her mother. "I wished I'd been able to see that. The cocky bastard gets his way too often."

Lorna scowled at her daughter. "Faye Louise, you do realize your cousin is clan leader?"

Faye shrugged. "So? He's still my cousin."

Shaking her head, Lorna looked back to Arabella. "If you don't want our help, child, just say so." The older dragonwoman raised her arm and Arabella noticed the dresses hung over it. "We just thought it'd be fun to get ready together."

Arabella looked from Lorna to Faye and back again. Apart from Melanie and occasionally Evie, Arabella didn't have much female companionship. This could be practice for the gathering in a few hours.

Her dragon did a mental eye roll. *You don't need to justify every action. They're kind and fun. Let them in already.*

Someone's bossy.

I'm stuck inside a house when I'd rather be flying or fucking our mate. Whatever it takes to help me forget about Finn and the frenzy, I will do.

She didn't like her dragon's grumpy tone, especially since she sensed the tension underneath it. If nothing else, spending time with Lorna and Faye would help her forget about Finn, his talented tongue, and the way he'd made her come in the clearing.

Her dragon growled. *Stop it. Remembering our male licking between our thighs only makes me hornier.*

I could take a deep breath and you'd think of sex. Don't blame it on me.

With a huff, her dragon settled down and sulked.

Smiling at her beast's response, she stepped aside. "All I plan to do is toss the dress on and pull back my hair. That should take me about ten minutes, but you're welcome to come in."

As Lorna walked past, she clicked her tongue. "If I have any say in the matter, it's going to take more than ten minutes, Ara."

Once both dragonwomen were inside the room, she shut the door. "Do I dare ask why?"

Faye held up a case and winked. "We're going to send Finn to his knees."

Worry gathered in the pit of her stomach, but before she could ask anything, Lorna beat her to it. "Not that you aren't beautiful just as you are, Arabella MacLeod. But from what little I know of you so far, you enjoying teasing my nephew. Give us a little time, and we'll surprise him. You can make him speechless for once, which is a rare thing for Finlay."

Arabella eyed the case. The old Arabella would've just lied and said she didn't enjoy teasing anyone. She might have even told them to bugger off.

Yet after her afternoon with Finn, combined with the strength and confidence of her dragon, Arabella decided to be truthful. After all, Lorna and Faye would soon be her family.

Blinking, Arabella wondered when she'd accepted her future would be with Lochguard. Her dragon spoke up. *Of course it's here. Do you really want to leave Finn behind? He's so much fun to tease. I want to tease him more when he's naked.*

Rather than answer her randy dragon, she straightened her shoulders as she met Lorna's eye. "What do you have in mind?"

Faye whooped and lightly slapped her bicep. "You just made my day, Arabella." She lifted the case. "As for this baby, I call it the master makeover kit. But first, you need to get dressed."

Lorna picked up her dress from the bed and the older dragonwoman asked Arabella a question with her eyes—was she able to undress in front of them, or did she need to go to the bathroom down the hall.

Her heart rate kicked up. Finn seeing her body was one thing, but for anyone else to see her was another.

Her dragon's voice was grumpy. *Just undress. If we leave this room, we might run into Finn and then I'll want to kiss him. At least in here, his scent is barely noticeable.*

Drawing strength from her dragon, Arabella unbuttoned her jeans. "Just don't turn me into a complete tart. I don't want to give the clan the wrong impression of me."

Faye grinned. "Don't worry. We'll find just the right amount of sexiness and kickass." Putting down the case, she clapped her hands. "I can't wait. I never had a sister, so this should be fun."

As Arabella continued undressing, she fought the urge to run. Yet as she revealed more skin, the two dragonwomen barely paid attention. They were treating it as an everyday occurrence.

Once she was naked, a sense of accomplishment rushed through her body. It may only be with two dragon-shifters, but if she kept pushing her boundaries, Arabella might soon be like any other dragon-shifter on Lochguard, meaning she could talk with her dragon, shift at will, and not care two cents about being naked in front of others.

The only thing she really needed to do was survive telling Finn about the rest of her time with the dragon hunters. After that, she might finally be free of her past. The thought of visiting Stonefire and being whole again warmed her heart. She would never be 'poor Arabella' ever again.

And it was all because she'd taken the chance of fostering with Lochguard. Coming to Scotland had been one of the best decisions of her life, not that she'd tell Finn. His ego was already big enough.

As she pulled the dress over her head and tugged it down her body, the silkiness of the material caressed her skin. Once it was on, she looked in the mirror. Rather than noticing her scars, she saw herself as pretty for the first time.

Her dragon grumbled. *Not pretty. We're bloody beautiful.*

Smiling, Arabella turned toward Faye and Lorna. "Okay, ladies, do whatever it takes to render Finn speechless."

Healed by the Dragon

~~~

Finn paced his living room as he waited for Arabella. Faye and his aunt were helping her to get ready, but they were taking a bloody long time. Given the glint the two females had had in their eyes, he was fairly certain they had something planned.

A part of him itched to go check on Arabella again, but he knew she would hate him for it. The lass was growing stronger. He wanted to protect her with every iota of his being, but if he did that, she would hate him.

Truth be told, all he wanted to do was spend the rest of the next week with Arabella naked in his bed. The memory of her hot, wet mouth around his cock nearly made him groan.

His dragon growled. *Stop it or I won't last the night.*

I thought you could take anything.

I hadn't expected Ara to be so good.

In that, Finn could agree. *Maybe we can have more tonight. Can you last that long?*

His beast huffed. *I will try. Just keep the other males from touching her.*

Finn shouldn't have a problem with most of the clan, but glancing at his twin cousins on the couch, they were bound to give him a hard time.

Fraser noticed his look. "Have you reconsidered, cousin? A quick flight and a game of chicken might help your nerves."

Fergus added, "I could referee. I've been spending too much time at the computer and need to stretch my wings."

Finn crossed his arms over his chest. "Fergus, you always favor your twin."

"No, Finn, you just like to lose," Fergus stated.

161

"I wouldn't bloody well be the clan leader if I lost as much as you claim," Finn answered.

Fergus opened his mouth, but Fraser rubbed his hands together and beat him to the punch. "I can replace Fergus with someone else. So, if I find another referee, is that a yes?"

Finn's dragon chimed in. *It will help. Do we have time?*

No.

Steps sounded down the stairs and Finn nodded toward the stairs. "That sounds like our answer, lads. And don't try to find someone else to play chicken during the gathering."

Fraser gave an exaggerated look of hurt. "It pains me you would think the worst of me, Finn."

Rolling his eyes, Finn's voice was dry as he said, "Your antics are annoying. How I ever survived living under the same roof as you two for five years, I'll never know." He moved toward the stairs and added, "Now, stop your whining and come on. Arabella needs our support."

Without another word, Finn went to the foot of the stairs and looked up. His heart skipped a few beats.

Arabella's hair was half-swept up from her face and pinned to the top of her head. The bottom half of her long, dark hair cascaded over her shoulder and complemented the deep purple of her dress. The fabric hugged her small breasts and slim frame. Her tattoo was fully visible on her upper arm. If all of that wasn't enough to turn his cock to stone, the light make-up on her face brought out the deep brown of her eyes and the plumpness of her lips.

His female was sexy as hell.

Then she turned her scarred arm away and he frowned. "Show me all of you, lass."

Lorna spoke up. "That's not much of a compliment."

He raised his brows. "I could compliment her all day long, but I want to see her first so I can be truthful." He met Arabella's gaze. "Arabella appreciates the truth."

"Since when are you so concerned with the truth, Finlay?" Arabella asked.

He motioned with his hands for her to descend the stairs. "Since I know it makes you happy."

Despite the blush on her cheeks, Arabella kept her shoulders back as she moved toward him. "I'll remember that the next time you spout one of your lines. That might make you stop."

"I doubt it." He raised a hand to her and she took it. Curling his fingers around hers, he guided his dragon-shifter goddess down the last few steps. Once she stood in front of him, all he could think about was kissing the living shit out of her. Needing a moment with his female, he murmured, "Come with me."

Pulling her down the hall and into his study, Finn shut the door and kissed her. After a split second of shock, Arabella parted her lips and met him stroke for stroke as she gripped his shoulders. The fact she was as hungry for him as he was for her only made his cock harder.

His dragon growled. *Be careful or I won't be able to stop.*

With monumental effort, he broke the kiss to look into Arabella's eyes. The urge to rip off her clothes and fuck her was overwhelming, but somehow he managed to keep his tone light as he said, "That was me saying how beautiful you look, by the way."

The corner of her mouth ticked up. "I could wear a dress of weeds and I bet your cock would still go hard."

Rubbing his dick against her, he murmured, "True, but I'm not lying about how beautiful you look tonight. Say the word and

I can snake a hand up your dress and make you come with my fingers."

She smacked his shoulder. "Finn, stop it."

He grinned. "You can't blame a bloke for trying."

"You never stop trying. That's the problem." Arabella looked to the door. "Besides, we shouldn't keep the MacKenzies waiting."

"Oh, aye? Have you formed a coalition with Faye and Lorna against me, then?"

She gave a sly smile. "That's for you to find out."

He laughed. "If this is you after two days with my clan, I better prepare myself for the rest of my life. I have a feeling you'll always keep me on my toes."

Arabella's smile faltered. "There's still the threat from within your clan. I don't want my presence here to cause a rift, Finlay."

The fact Arabella hadn't dismissed spending the rest of her life with him only warmed his heart. He caressed her cheek with the back of his fingers. "Don't worry, lass. Duncan has been a pain in my arse for a while and I'll deal with him. However, most of the clan will love you, even if you talk in a funny accent."

Raising an eyebrow, she ran a hand across his chest. "I don't know what you're talking about. This is how to speak English properly."

As he took in Arabella dressed in her traditional dragon-shifter attire and added in her teasing him, for the first time in a long while Finn wanted to dodge his clan leader duties and be selfish; he wanted to whisk Arabella away for a weekend break and show her a good time.

Yet he knew he couldn't, and not just because of his clan leader duties. Between the dragon hunters, the Dragon Knights, and Duncan's supporters, taking Arabella anywhere outside of Lochguard would be dangerous.

With herculean effort, he stepped back and motioned toward the door. "You can debate how to speak English at the gathering. I have a feeling the Scots' way will win."

"Maybe we should ask Melanie when she visits since she's American and a little less biased."

Opening the door, Finn drew Arabella against his side and squeezed her hip. "I think not. She's mated to your bloody brother. Of course she'll side with him."

Amusement danced in Arabella's eyes. "You clearly don't know Melanie very well, do you?"

"We have our whole lives to fix that, Arabella MacLeod, provided we survive tonight."

Arabella glanced up at him. "You'll have to win my brother over before he'll ever leave you alone with his mate. You really can't know Melanie until you've spent an hour alone with her. That female is a force of nature."

Finn winked. "Winning over your brother should be a piece of cake."

She gave him a skeptical look. "The day you get along with my brother is the day I'll let you tie me up and do what you like with me."

His eyes flashed to slits. "Is that a promise, lass?"

Shaking her head, she answered, "It will never happen, so there's no point in promising anything."

"Oh, I can be quite determined, Arabella. Promise me the reward, and I'll find a way to make it happen."

Arabella sighed. "Fine. But getting along with my brother doesn't mean sharing a pint. I want to see you two together at a gathering, singing and drinking as if you were the best of friends."

He placed a finger under her chin and kissed her. "Consider it done." As Aunt Lorna's voice boomed down the hallway, telling them to hurry up, Finn sighed. "I can't believe my own aunt is cockblocking me."

Arabella grinned. "I'm glad."

"Glad? Why the bloody hell would you be glad? If nothing else, your dragon is probably roaring for my dick right about now."

She poked his chest. "Even if she was, I don't need your clan thinking any worse of me. We need to go to the gathering. If you had your way, we wouldn't, and rumors would start. I had enough of rumors back home. There are probably already a few because of what happened this afternoon, but I'll never change their minds if you keep me locked in a bedroom."

Finn blinked before clearing his throat. "I think the version of you, who had wanted to be clan leader, is back with full force."

Her confidence faltered a second. "Maybe. I have a few things I still need to do, but I'm working on it."

Caressing her cheek, he murmured, "Let me know if I can help in anyway, love."

Arabella nodded as Lorna's voice boomed down the hallway, "Finlay Ian Stewart, get your arse out here or I'll come in there myself."

Arabella smiled and whispered, "We should listen to her, Finlay Ian."

He rolled his eyes. "Great, now you're going to do the first and middle name scoldings, aren't you?"

"Maybe." Arabella tugged at his clothing. "Let's go, Finlay Ian."

Shaking his head, he opened the door and guided them back to the foot of the stairs, near the front entrance.

Faye spoke as soon as she saw them. "Finn, we're late. You need to learn how to keep your tongue and cock to yourself." Faye gave Arabella a once-over. "But at least you didn't destroy my work."

Finn sighed. "Of course not. I learned a long time ago not to cross paths with you and Aunt Lorna."

Lorna threw a cloak over her shoulders and looked at him askance. "I'm not sure about that. But rather than argue, let's hurry up. We don't want to keep the clan waiting too much longer."

After laying a cloak around Arabella's shoulders, he walked out the door and toward the great hall with Arabella at his side. Only because of his dragon snarling inside his head did he not wrap an arm around her shoulders and draw his little alpha goddess close.

Finn only hoped the evening would go well. Faye's Protectors were in place, as were the other Protectors stationed around the clan's perimeter. After what had happened back on Stonefire, when a child had been kidnapped during a clan gathering, Finn was being overly cautious. If anyone tried to take Arabella from his side, they would have to deal with him.

~~~

Despite Finn's comforting heat at her side, the walk to the great hall wasn't easy. Her stomach twisted a little bit more with each step. Public events had never been her favorite activity, even when she'd been whole and healthy. As much as she could be confident with Finn, it was going to take all of her energy to be strong in front of the entire Lochguard clan. She only hoped she could pull it off—not just for her, but for Finn, too.

167

Her dragon sighed. *I don't like this lack of confidence. What happened to your fuck-the-past mentality? We are amazing. Act like it.*

Her beast's tone stoked her anger. *If we're so amazing, why did you remain silent so long? If I'd had you around, I could've been strong a lot sooner.*

You wouldn't let me out. That's not my fault.

Arabella growled and Finn touched her shoulder as he asked, "Do I need to charm your dragon a wee bit to calm her down, lass?"

She forced her dragon into a mental cage. "No, she's in time out and doesn't deserve any charm."

Fergus slowed his pace to match theirs. Due to his sensitive hearing, he'd heard Arabella and jumped in. "I've found that time outs aren't very effective. A mental maze, on the other hand, occupies them for a bit. My dragon tends to be a little less growly when he's done with one of those."

Arabella blinked. "I've never thought of that."

Finn tightened his grip on her hip. "Don't give Fergus too much credit. It was originally my idea."

Fergus raised an eyebrow. "It might've been your idea, but I perfected it."

When Finn growled, Arabella rolled her eyes. "Does the 'who has the biggest cock' contest ever end?"

Lorna spoke up. "No, lass, it doesn't. You're starting to see why I have so many gray hairs."

Fergus looked toward his mother. "That's not fair, Mum. It's not as if Faye is the golden child of virtue."

Faye turned and glared at Fergus. "Say that again, brother, I dare you."

"Why, are you going to beat me with your tiny little handbag? I'm so scared," Fergus taunted.

While Arabella was getting used to the MacKenzies, spending time with them was still a zoo. Maybe she should invite her brother to Lochguard just to see how deep his frown could go.

Before Arabella could think of a witty reply to add to the discussion, Finn's voice boomed out, "Enough." The dominance in his voice stilled everyone and he continued, "Tonight I am showcasing Ara to the clan. Inside the great hall, I'm clan leader and she's my female. Given Duncan's hatred, I don't need any excuse for him to call me out on a challenge. What works in private won't work inside the hall. Understood?"

As the twins and Faye murmured, "Yes," Arabella had a feeling Finn had to remind them of his status on a regular basis.

"Good," Finn answered. "Since we're nearly to the hall, I want a few minutes alone with Ara. Go on without us."

The twins looked about to say something when Lorna placed a hand on each of their elbows. "Come, lads. Leave Finn to care for his mate."

It was on the tip of Arabella's tongue to say she wasn't his mate yet, but the MacKenzies were gone before she could.

Finn sighed. "Given my family, I'm surprised you haven't bolted."

Arabella smiled. "They're fun. Besides, I have a feeling they'll always help me out if I want to get back at you."

"Oh, is that right? They are my kin, so they should side with me."

Without thinking, she added, "We'll see. There's plenty of time to test out your claim."

Finn turned to face her and drew her closer. "Is that so, heather?"

169

Slapping his chest, Arabella gave her best glare. "Don't call me that."

Leaning down, he whispered, "Then promise you won't conspire with my family, and I promise not to use the nickname."

"That isn't fair."

He nuzzled her cheek. "No, what's not fair is the fact I can't take you home, undress you, and tease you until you beg."

Her dragon roared to be let out, but Arabella kept her trapped. "What, Finlay, is your cock controlling your brain now?"

The huskiness of his voice sent a shiver down her spine. "Aye, lass. And it very much wants you, and only you."

Heat flooded her body and her dragon roared louder. Arabella's breath was barely a whisper when she replied, "We can't. We need to attend the gathering."

Finn chuckled. "So, you admit you want to fuck me too?"

Her dragon finally broke free. *I want to fuck him.*

No, you promised you could last.

I don't care. I want him and his cock. Tell him to behave or I will take control.

Besides sex, is there any way to help?

Her beast huffed. *As long as he stops talking about sex and what he wants to do to us when we're naked, I can control the urges a little while longer.*

Fine. I'll try.

Her dragon grumbled, *I don't understand why you fight it. You like it when he teases you with words and his tongue.*

She paused a second and decided what the hell, her dragon would know if she were lying. *Most of the time.*

It's because he's fun. Still, tell him no fondling or sexy kisses until we're alone.

170

Finn watched her and she finally sighed. "I have bad news, I'm afraid."

"What did your dragon tell you?"

She blinked. "How can you tell it's my dragon and not me?"

Caressing her cheek, he answered, "Because I'm starting to get to know both of you. I'm fairly certain that whenever your dragon says something irritating or that makes you uncomfortable, you narrow your eyes."

She raised an eyebrow. "I don't know about that. I save my best glares for your shenanigans."

"Well, then let me educate you."

"Oh, so the big, bad male must explain things to me?" She rolled her eyes. "Can we just go inside, already? It's chilly out here."

Her dragon's tone was stern. *You still haven't warned him. Right now, a kiss is too much. Tell him.*

Shut it. I'm working on it.

Liar. Don't be weak. Just tell him straight or the frenzy will be your fault.

Finn stroking her cheek quieted her dragon. Then the dragonman leaned close enough she could feel his breath on her lips as he murmured, "You did it again, just now. Since your eyes were slitted, I know you were talking to your dragon. So, what did she say, lass?"

The fact Finn watched her so closely made her heart thump harder. Rather than let on she liked his attention, she shrugged. "Oh, just the usual. How you're a randy bloke who can't stop thinking with his dick."

Finn's eyes flashed to slits. "Mention my cock again, and I'll throw you over my shoulder and carry you off to my bed."

"No you won't. I'll escape first."

"Is that a challenge?"

As they stared at one another, Finn's scent surrounded her. Combined with the heat of his breath on her lips, Arabella ached to close the distance between them and kiss him. Yet if she did that, the frenzy would overtake her. She couldn't allow that to happen. At least, not yet.

Clearing her throat, she answered, "Maybe later."

He quirked an eyebrow. "That wasn't the answer I was expecting. What's going on, lass?"

She paused a second. Just as her dragon moved around and was about to speak, she spit out, "My dragon is close to losing control."

Finn leaned back a few inches and she nearly pulled him close again. "How close?"

Picking at the material of his kilt-like outfit, she murmured, "A kiss could set her off."

He cursed and stepped away. "If we don't kiss in front of the clan, Ara, they'll be offended." Releasing her, he ran a hand through his hair before assessing her. "Can't you help her control the frenzy? Just for the kiss? If it means I can't hold you close all evening, then no matter how much I hate it, I'll do it for you, lass. For all my talk, I won't take you before you're ready."

Studying him a second, she believed he was telling the truth; one word, and he would keep his distance. Sure, he would probably growl at any male who even looked her way, but he would restrain himself from touching her if she asked.

Remembering every interaction with Finn since arriving, it hit her that he'd always held back. Even with all the flirting and ridiculous lines, Finn always thought of Arabella's needs, no matter how difficult it had to be to control the mate-claim frenzy.

172

He didn't do it because he felt sorry for her. No, he did it because he cared for her.

Searching his brown eyes, Arabella was no longer afraid of Finn, of sex, or even the possibility of a baby. True, if given the choice, she would wait a year before trying to have a child, but neither she nor Finn would last that long. Each day she held back was another day Finn could lose control of both his dragon and his clan. He was strong, but every dragon-shifter had their limits.

Even if all of this was happening faster than she liked, Arabella knew that between Finn and the MacKenzies, she would never be alone again. They would help her if she asked.

Her dragon spoke up. *He is ours. Don't be afraid of him or the frenzy. You'll enjoy it.*

And how do you know that?

Call it a dragon's instinct. I just do. Besides, he will give us a child who will be strong, clever, and handsome. That is a good combination.

Arabella smiled. *I'm a bit worried about your priorities, dragon. But I do agree Finn is strong, clever, and handsome.*

Good. Then stop being afraid of the future.

Looking up at Finn, she made a decision. While she would always love her brother, Melanie, and her niece and nephew, Arabella was ready to start her own family with Finn and the MacKenzies. They would protect her no matter what happened, and she finally needed to become the strong female who could watch their backs.

Her first step toward doing that was to go into the hall, face the clan, and use her own stubbornness to restrain her dragon. For the first time in a decade, Arabella was confident she could do anything she set her mind to.

Still, she would never let Finn off easy. After all, where was the fun in that?

Arabella tilted her head. "Well, whether I can restrain my dragon or not depends if you're going to flirt with every female you see. Because if you do, between me and my dragon, I can't guarantee what will happen next."

A bit of the strain eased from Finn's face. "As much as I'd like to see you take on all of the single females of the clan, I'll try to hold back."

Arabella nodded. "You'd better or you might wake up one day with your cock missing."

Chuckling, he reached out a hand and then pulled back. The action made her sad; she never wanted Finn to hold back. His voice was stern when he replied, "Just remember, love, as possessive as you're feeling right now, I'm ten times worse. Flirt with Fraser and Fergus, and to hell with what the clan will think of me, I will punch them both in the face."

Sensing the steel underlying his tone, Arabella decided not to wake the beast. The gathering was important for her future here. Everything needed to go well. She raised her eyebrows. "Any other warnings I should know about?"

"Don't let anyone peek down your dress."

Staring down at her cleavage, Arabella shook her head. "There's not a lot there."

He growled. "It's perfect and it's mine."

Worry gathered in the pit of her stomach. Maybe her dragon wasn't the only one on edge. "Is your dragon under control, Finn?"

"Barely."

Shit. "You should've told me." She glanced toward the entrance to the main hall. "Then let's hurry. The sooner we're inside, the sooner your dragon should care more about the clan's welfare than me."

174

She looked back to Finn and his gaze burned into the depths of her heart. "Let's hope that choice never comes to pass, because I'm not sure the clan would win."

"Don't say that. You barely know me."

"But it's true."

Finn's behavior warmed her heart. He truly wanted her.

Her dragon stated, *Of course he does.*

Do you ever have doubts?

Not anymore.

I wish I could be as confident.

Give it another week or two and you'll be close.

She resisted the urge to smile. Arabella was starting to think she and her dragon were on their way to becoming great friends. Before much longer, Arabella might act like a real dragonwoman.

Arabella started walking. "Come on. We're already late. We can talk some more later."

Finn murmured, "Oh, I plan to do much more than talk, lass."

Resisting a shiver, they walked the last stretch to the hall in silence. Her beast tried to speak up, but as they entered the hall, Arabella pushed her dragon back inside a mental cage and turned her attention to the packed room.

Long tables lined the sides of the large space, leaving an empty area in the middle for people to mingle. Quite a few were already sitting down at the tables and eating.

Everyone was dressed in the traditional style, although some were more decked out than others. Combining the array of colors with the material draping at intervals from the ceiling, Arabella felt as if she'd just walked into a fairy tale. She'd only been to a handful of gatherings back on Stonefire, which made this one all the more special, especially with her male at her side. Finn made her forget her past so she could tackle the present.

As they neared the raised dais at the front of the room, the chatter died down. Everyone's eyes were on her.

For a second, Arabella's heart pounded so fast she thought it might explode, but then Finn squeezed her side, giving her courage. Keeping her shoulders back and head high, Arabella forced herself to smile at some of the clan as they passed. Some of the return smiles were genuine, while others were forced. The eyes of the forced smiles ranged from pity to disgust to skepticism.

Her break down earlier, when she'd run naked through the clan, probably hadn't helped things.

Her bloody dragon broke free again. *Do you want to stay with Finn?*

Of course, she stated without hesitation.

Then who cares if they pity you or not. It will be their loss.

We're that great a catch then?

Yes, we are bloody brilliant.

Arabella smiled at her beast's confidence. Taking a deep breath, she channeled her dragon and tried to exude the same amount of confidence. She was Arabella MacLeod and she'd survived being tortured by a gang of dragon hunters. Dealing with a few skeptical, Scottish dragon-shifters should be easy.

CHAPTER FIFTEEN

Finn had nearly made it to the stage when Duncan stepped into his path. The older dragonman's eyes were hard, but unreadable as they took in Finn and then moved to Arabella. It took every ounce of control Finn possessed to force a smile and keep his tone neutral. "Duncan."

Duncan looked back to him. "I've heard the rumors. Is it true you're going to mate the hideous female? That will reflect poorly on the clan."

Finn took a deep breath to calm both man and beast. Before he could reply, Arabella did. "The hideous female, as you put it, is standing right here. Although, I do have a name. I'm Arabella. Who the bloody hell are you?"

Duncan blinked and Finn wanted to cheer. Then his rival's eyes turned assessing before he answered, "Duncan Campbell, and you should watch your mouth, English dragonwoman. You may stand strong next to Finlay, but I saw you earlier. I could squash you with one hand tied behind my back."

Finn narrowed his eyes. "That's enough. If you can't be civil, you can leave, Duncan. A gathering is no place for your petty bullshit."

Duncan answered, "I'm not going anywhere. But if you mate the English and fuck up, I'll call you out on it. We don't need the alliance with Stonefire, nor do we need the humans coming and going on our land. Dragon-shifters need to shrug off humans and band together. Despite being English, at least Clan Skyhunter understands that."

Clan Skyhunter was the dragon-shifter clan south of London. "Well, it's a good thing you're not in charge then, isn't it?" Finn looked to the side and back, signaling he was done. "You're in the way."

Duncan stared for a few seconds before moving aside. As Finn walked past, Arabella said to Duncan, "And just to let you know, if you fuck with me, you'll need both hands to survive."

The older dragonman remained silent. As they walked away, the tension eased from the crowd. Finn lowered his voice and whispered, "You were bloody fantastic, Ara."

She raised an eyebrow. "He's just an arsehole. I've faced real monsters and survived. He, on the other hand, would run the other way at the sight of them."

The corner of his mouth ticked up. "I feel the same way." He lowered his voice further. "Fear only goes so far."

She smiled. "Oh, and charm goes much further?"

"Aye, it does." Putting out a hand, he bowed his head. "May I hold your hand, lovely?"

For a second, he thought she'd decline. He knew full well her dragon was on edge, but so was his.

His beast grunted. *Too many males are looking at her, especially after telling off Duncan. We need to make the claim.*

She's already ours, dragon. Don't fret.

Someone has to worry, or another male will steal her away.

Before he could think of a different way to convince Arabella to touch him, she placed her hand in his. Squeezing it, he pulled her toward the stage. "Come. The sooner I introduce you, the sooner we can dance."

"I never said I would dance."

"Oh, come on. If you're to be the clan leader's mate, you have to do things you don't like occasionally."

"Remember our conversation about asking me things? Dancing is definitely included in the list of things to ask me about first."

"You're resisting me on purpose, you bloody woman."

She battled a smile. "Maybe."

Laughing, Finn gently tugged her arm. "As much as I wish we could banter for hours, we both need to do our duty." He leaned toward her ear. "But I look forward to convincing you of the merits of dancing."

Arabella blinked. As they took the steps up the dais, Finn couldn't help but grin. Not only because he would soon tell his clan that Arabella was his, but also because having the comfort of Arabella's own brand of wit and charm helped eased his own tension. Sometimes, carrying the weight of a clan could weigh a dragonman down. With Arabella, the weight was barely noticeable.

~~~

Despite Arabella's cool exterior, her heart was beating a million times a minute. Her stomach was also twisting and turning in knots.

Her dragon sounded amused. *You just stood up to that bastard Duncan. Why be nervous now?*

After this, my future will be decided.

Her beast paused a few seconds before stating, *You want Finn. Everything else is secondary. Problems will arise, but we'll solve them. With me, you will always have an ally. I'm also pretty good at kicking arse.*

Arabella bit her lip to keep from laughing. *Modesty isn't in your vocabulary, is it?*

No. Modesty is a human idea that wastes too much time.

Biting her lip harder, Finn looked at her. "Are you plotting with your dragon against me?"

Shushing her dragon, she answered, "No. She was telling me her feelings about Duncan."

Finn grinned. "I can't wait to hear about that later, lass. The more I hear of your dragon, the more I like her." He stopped them in the middle of the stage. "Unfortunately, reality intrudes for now. Ready to face the clan, heather?"

Between Finn's teasing and her dragon's confidence, Arabella nodded, albeit with a quick glare to Finn for the ridiculous nickname. "As long as you don't call me that in front of everyone."

He winked. "And damage my alpha reputation? I think not."

"We can debate your alpha reputation later. Just get on with it already."

Her dragonman squeezed her hand and then turned them toward the crowd. After raising his free hand, the room fell mostly silent; only the clatter of a few knives and forks echoed in the great hall.

Finn's voice boomed. "Thanks for coming on such short notice. My dragon is impatient to claim what's his, and as you all know, ignoring your dragon for too long will result in a man walking about with a hard cock for days, unable to think straight." A few chuckles went through the room and Arabella used the pause to dig her nails into Finn's palms. If he felt it, he didn't show it as he continued, "But in all seriousness, I wanted to give the clan an opportunity to know Arabella MacLeod. Not only as our first foster from Clan Stonefire, but also as my future mate."

Murmurs rose up. Most of the looks thrown her way were full of curiosity. There were a few glares coming mostly from the older dragon-shifters. Those were the ones she'd need to watch carefully.

Finn raised his hand and the noise died down. His deep voice boomed again. "Even if my dragon didn't crave her, I would still choose Arabella MacLeod. She is strong, clever, and will be a great asset to our clan." He gave a stern look as he scanned the crowd. "Anyone who hurts her will be ousted. Normally, I would promise a fair hearing, but when it comes to mates and dragons, things are never handled civilly. My beast's instinct will take over, and I have no guarantees of what will happen. Exile might just save your life."

Most of the murmuring died down. Arabella was so used to Finn's charming and teasing persona that watching him act as clan leader threw her off a little.

Her dragon chimed in. *I like his alpha side. I can't wait until he shows it to us in bed.*

Mentally sighing at her dragon's one-track mind, Arabella's thoughts were cut off by Finn's voice. "Now I've gotten that out of the way and the other males have been warned, tonight is a time to celebrate and get to know the soon-to-be newest member of the clan. The First Kiss ceremony will happen in about an hour. Until then, we'll make our way around the hall before gracing everyone with the gift of our marvelous dancing skills." As some of the crowd cheered, Arabella bit the inside of her lip to keep from scowling. She would give the bastard an earful as soon as she could for volunteering her. Then Finn pointed to a dragonwoman standing amongst a lot of equipment. "Let's get this party started."

As the latest human pop music blared, Arabella turned her face to the side and rolled her eyes. Keeping her voice low, she muttered, "You are a lot less hip than you think you are."

He leaned close, but was careful not to touch her apart from the hand in his. How they were going to dance without even more touching, Arabella had no idea. Finn whispered, "The half-arse jokes help everyone to relax." He winked. "You might find it irritating, but my clan loves it."

"So you're not alpha all the time and they accept that?"

"They don't have a choice. Besides, if they cross my path and act like dicks, then they have to deal with me. After a year, they know what to expect—I'm firm but fair."

Looking to make sure no one was close enough to hear, Arabella whispered, "Then why hasn't it worked with Duncan?"

Finn shook his head. "That male is a special kind of arsehole. Dying doesn't scare him, nor does exile. He'd use the exile to start his own clan of followers and dying would only turn him into a martyr amongst his followers. I don't want either option to come true."

Arabella put it all together. "That's why he's still here, then. You're keeping your enemy close."

"Aye, lass. Although after that warning, I may have to deal with him sooner than I wish, unless I can think of a way to discredit his ideas first." Finn nodded toward the stairs. "But enough about Duncan for now. The clan is waiting to meet you, Arabella. Let's not keep them waiting."

As Finn tugged her toward the stairs, Arabella took a few deep breaths. Some of the clan were bound to ask questions about her past. So far, whenever Finn was near, she'd been able to remain in control. She only hoped that held true for the rest of the evening because if she had a breakdown in front of the clan, it would tarnish Finn's reputation. And she couldn't allow that to happen. While there were many details she didn't know about Duncan or his followers, Arabella knew she could be used as a weakness against her male.

Remember to be the dragonwoman you can be. You are to be a clan leader's mate; act like it.

I'll try, she answered her dragon.

Don't try. Do it.

With one last deep breath, Arabella straightened her shoulders and raised her chin a fraction. It was time to show both Finn and Clan Lochguard what she was capable of and erase the image of her being a timid lamb who ran at the first sign of humans.

~~~

Finn usually didn't mind public events, but after discussing Duncan and seeing a bit more of his female's cleverness, he wanted to discuss other clan issues with her. Maybe Arabella could think of new ways to tackle some long-standing issues on Lochguard.

His dragon grunted. *It can wait. Show her off, dance, and then we can kiss her.*

Usually, you drag your feet when it comes to dancing.

It brings me one step closer to fucking our mate, so I want to dance this time.

Sensing his beast was barely keeping his mating need in check, Finn pushed him to the back of his mind and focused on the Boyd family at the foot of the stairs. They were one of the families who would welcome whomever he chose as a mate; his father and Meg Boyd had been cousins. Smiling at the middle-aged dragonwoman, Finn bowed his head. "If I didn't already have a beauty at my side, I would whisk you away to dance, Meg."

The gray-haired dragonwoman clicked her tongue. "Stop with the flirting, Finlay, or your lass might get jealous." Meg gave Arabella a once-over and nodded. "Aye, you'll do." She put out her hand. "The name is Meg Boyd, hen. Humor an old lady and give me a proper introduction."

When Arabella took Meg's hand without hesitation, Finn wanted to cheer. Arabella answered, "I'm Arabella MacLeod, Mrs. Boyd. Nice to meet you."

Meg leaned closer toward Arabella, but Finn knew the woman wasn't a threat, so he allowed it. Meg replied, "You're all but family, now. Call me Meg." Leaning back, Meg released Arabella's hand and motioned to her sons. "These are my sons, Hamish and Graham. I have another son, Alistair, but he's unmated and didn't want to stir Finn's dragon, so he's off in some corner reading a book."

Sensing Arabella didn't know how to reply to that, Finn jumped in. "At least the lad has developed some sense. Two years ago, he would've tried kissing Arabella just to rile me up."

Meg nodded. "Aye, but he's a changed dragonman these days. If only he'd focus on something besides his work."

Arabella frowned, "Why? What does he do?"

Meg answered, "Some sort of scientist. I don't ask him that many questions."

One of her sons, Hamish, said dryly, "Except if he's found a female yet."

Meg swatted her grown son. "Shush. I can never have too many grandbabies. Eventually, someone has to have a girl."

Concerned the talk of bairns might scare Arabella, Finn stole a quick glance only to find her smiling. His dragon spoke up. *She will carry our young soon.*

Pushing aside the warmth around his heart at the idea of Arabella growing round with his child, he kept his voice stern. *We're not talking about that right now.*

Finn looked to Meg and placed a hand over his heart. "As much as it pains me to leave your shining presence, Meg, the rest of the clan is waiting."

Meg snorted. "The only reason I'm shining is because there are too many people in this room and it's too hot." Meg looked to Arabella. "It's nice to meet you, lass. Stop by sometime and I can show you the proper way to make scones. Finn will do just about anything for a plate of my scones, which might come in handy for you later on."

Arabella grinned and Finn's heart skipped a beat. Seeing his female smiling and interacting with the Boyds made both man and beast happy. His female replied, "I'll try, although Finn might keep me occupied for the foreseeable future."

Meg's eyes twinkled. "Ah, to be young and experience the mate-frenzy for the first time. I have such fond memories."

Hamish shook his head. "Mum, I don't need to think about you in a mate-claim frenzy."

"As my oldest, you wouldn't be here without it," Meg replied.

The quieter Boyd son, Graham, spoke up. "I'm with Hamish on this, Mum. I'm still trying to wash my brain clean of the story of how I was conceived."

As Meg argued with her sons, Finn murmured, "We'll try to catch up with you later," before maneuvering Arabella away. Stopping for a second in an empty spot on the side of the room, he whispered, "Are you ready to bolt now?"

The corner of Arabella's mouth ticked up. "Is there something in the water here that makes everyone crazy? First the MacKenzies, and now the Boyds. If Bram knew the full extent of the zoo you call a clan, he would never have agreed to the alliance in the first place."

Even though Finn knew she was jesting, he frowned. "We're not crazy. We're lovable."

Arabella laughed until she couldn't breathe. Wiping the tears from her eyes, she added, "Sorry, but your pouting was too much to bear. You have a positive spin on everything, don't you?"

"It's not a spin if it's the truth," Finn stated.

Arabella shook her head. "I can't wait for my brother to come visit. Between you, Aunt Lorna, and Meg Boyd, he's going to be more uncomfortable than he's ever been in his life. I should bring popcorn when it happens."

"Before you start planning family visits, we need to get through this evening first. Are you ready to mingle some more? If so, just avoid calling them crazy or Lochguard a zoo. That may not endear them to you."

Arabella tilted her head. "I don't know, it seems to work with you."

With her eyes bright and her posture relaxed, Finn thought she was even more beautiful. He itched to cup her face and kiss her, but he managed to hold back. "Only because it makes you smile and I love to see you smile; it makes you even more gorgeous. My goal is to make you grin so much your face starts to hurt."

Arabella's eyes grew tender. "You're trying to butter me up before the dancing, aren't you?"

He growled and leaned as close as he dare without actually touching her. "Would it kill you to learn to accept a compliment, Arabella MacLeod?"

She stood up straight, the tenderness replaced with something else he couldn't define. "I never had many. But even if I learn to take them, I'm not sure I can just allow you to spout fancy words. You might get the wrong idea."

"Wrong idea about what?" he growled.

A second of silence passed and then another. Finally, Arabella's voice was low as she answered, "That you're the golden darling of Scotland who could charm the pants off any female."

Finn dared to hook his finger under Arabella's chin. The softness of her skin woke his dragon. *If we're to dance, stop touching her. It only makes me want her.*

This is too important.

Finn's steely tone quieted his dragon. He leaned closed to Arabella's lips and whispered, "You're the only female I want to charm out of her pants, Ara. If we weren't in the great hall with both of our dragons on edge, I would show you just how much I want you and only you." Her breath hitched and the soft sound shot straight to his cock. Through gritted teeth, he added, "Are we clear on this?"

"Yes," she answered in a breathy whisper.

"Good." He turned them toward the crowd. "Now, the sooner we mingle, the sooner we can dance and I can kiss you. Try to keep the chatter to a minimum."

Arabella gave a mock salute. "Yes, sir. For once, I won't fight you."

"And why does that make me uneasy?"

"Why, Finlay Stewart, where has your world-renowned self-confidence gone? I thought you knew everything."

He muttered, "I did until I met you."

As Arabella grinned at his admission, he maneuvered them to the next friendly family and introduced his future mate.

CHAPTER SIXTEEN

Twenty minutes later, Arabella's cheeks hurt from smiling so much.

On top of that, the way the Boyds and MacKenzies acted was fairly normal for most families of the clan. The odd loner or obvious Duncan supporter would glare and be curt, but for the most part, everyone was warm.

As much as it felt like a betrayal to her own clan, she was growing to love the people of Lochguard. The choice to come here for a fresh start was the best decision she'd ever made. She only hoped her presence didn't cause too much trouble for Finn or anyone else. After all, it'd only been a few days.

Once word got out she was here, there would be trouble. Both the Dragon Knights and dragon hunters hated her and had vowed revenge for her interview, which had revealed their brutal methods and what dragon hunters would do to an innocent. Even though the knights were a separate entity, her interview had foiled their plan to win support to dismantle the Department of Dragon Affairs.

Even if Finn didn't worry about the local dragon hunters, the Dragon Knights were scarier. Given they had bombed both the Manchester and London DDA offices a few months earlier, nothing was too extreme for them.

Her dragon growled. *If they show up, let me take care of them.*

Right, because you're a trained warrior, Arabella said dryly.

In spirit, yes I am. I won't let them hurt our mate.

He's not our mate yet.

He is to me.

Finn walked up and handed her a cup of water. Since she didn't want to keep talking with her dragon, she was grateful for the distraction. "Thanks."

As she drank, Finn's grin widened and the water in her stomach felt ten times heavier. Lowering the cup, she asked, "What did you do?"

"Who said I did anything?"

She sighed. "Finn, between meeting all of these people and keeping my dragon under control, I'm tired. For once, can you give me a straight answer?" He cocked an eyebrow and she rolled her eyes. "Fine, pretty please?"

"There, now that wasn't so hard, was it?" She growled and he put up his hands. "Okay, okay. The DJ is about to play our song."

"Since when do we have a song?"

He shrugged. "I picked one."

"Finlay Stewart, you had better bloody well start asking me things or I will let my dragon break your penis during the frenzy."

He blinked. "What?"

"You heard me. She has all kinds of ideas to try, and said she may even break your cock. So, if you want me to try and stop that from happening, start bloody asking me what I want instead of just deciding it for me."

Finn unconsciously moved a hand in front of his groin. "I was looking forward to the frenzy, but now, I'm not so sure." When she raised her brows, he cleared his throat. "I will try to ask from now on, provided your life doesn't depend on it. Even if

190

your dragon will break my cock later, I won't ask you if it's okay to save your life before I do it."

She shoved against his chest and ignored the heat that flared. "Now you're just being ridiculous. Of course there will be exceptions in life or death situations. Just tell me about the song. Are we really dancing in front of everyone?"

The twinkled returned to his eyes. "Oh, aye. I hope you remember some of the old dances we all learn during our childhood, because we're doing one of those." She opened her mouth to ask why, but Finn beat her to it. "The reason is because there's very little touching involved. You've done so well with the clan and I don't want to ruin that."

Her dragon broke out of the latest prison Arabella constructed. She really needed to learn how to create a maze.

Stop arguing and dance. It's almost time to kiss him.

You just want to try and break his penis.

Not until the end. Otherwise, he'll never give us young.

Smiling at her beast's logic, she asked, *There will be some touching. Will you be okay?*

Since it means I can kiss our mate and soon after fuck him, then yes. I will last.

Arabella was skeptical, but as the pop music quieted and a female's voice came over the speakers, she pushed aside her doubts to listen to the announcement. "As promised, it's time for Finn and his lovely mate-to-be to dance for us. Please clear the center area of the hall."

As people moved to the sides, Arabella's heart rate increased. She hadn't danced the old, traditional dances in twenty years. Finn would owe her big time later on.

Her dragon huffed. *I remember everything. You will be fine. And then we can kiss him.*

When we're in dragon form, then you can show me your dance moves. It won't help me in human form.

I can show you images. Don't doubt me.

I'm starting to miss you being silent.

Her beast huffed just as Finn put out his hand. Shoving her dragon to the back of her mind, she placed hers on top and discarded her glass on a nearby table. With a wink, he guided them to the empty space in the middle of the hall. Once they reached it, Finn released her hand. Taking two steps back, he bowed.

A slightly upbeat medley of fiddles, a piano, and a few other instruments she couldn't name filled the room. It was time to see if she really had paid attention to her lessons as a child.

After sliding two steps to one side, Arabella moved diagonally toward the center to meet Finn. Pressing her open palm against his, they turned. While the turn was only a few seconds, Finn's gaze burned into hers. Between the desire and slight frenzy in his eyes as well as the roughness of his palm against her, heat flooded her body. Her dragon took notice, but did her best to restrain the frenzy. So far, her beast was keeping her word.

Then the beat required her to drop her hand and brush past Finn's shoulder without touching. Twirling back around, she repeated the steps until her hand touched Finn's again. The jolt of his touch went straight between her legs. Soon, she would have his rough palm caressing her breast, her hip, and the soft spot behind her knee. Suddenly, the thin material of her traditional dress became stifling and Arabella wondered how she would survive the rest of the dance.

Once the twirl was complete, Finn took hold of both her hands and took the lead. As they moved slowly in a circle, she was unable to look away from her dragonman's gaze. Everyone else in the room disappeared; in that moment, it was just her and Finn.

He is ours.

Arabella wasn't sure if the claim was hers or her dragon's.

As she danced, every movement caused her dress to brush against her skin, making her dragon roar. It wouldn't be long before her dragon lost control.

Releasing one of her hands, Finn twirled her out and they moved together, forward and back. Reluctantly, she released his hand and glided back toward where they had started.

The steps familiar again, she didn't hesitate to sway her hands to the left and then to the right before raising them out to her sides. After moving her hips left and then right, she twirled twice to stop with Finn right in front of her. He laced his fingers with hers, and she shivered as his male scent of wind and peat surrounded her.

Raising their arms, he released her hands and outlined her head, torso, and waist without touching her. The act made her dragon snarl. *Hurry up. I want him.*

Ignoring her beast, Arabella focused on the music and outlined Finn's head, shoulders and waist with her own hands. Judging by his slitted eyes, he wasn't the only one on the verge of losing control.

She walked past his shoulder and turned until they were facing each other once again. The music died down and even though the dance wasn't difficult, it was hard to breathe with Finn staring at her as if he couldn't wait to devour her.

After their kiss, he would.

Arabella waited for panic to set in, but all she felt was anticipation. Her nipples were hard and she was already wet from the brief caresses of Finn's skin against her own. One kiss would probably set her off.

Yet she was okay with that. Soon, she would have the gorgeous male across from her naked and hers to claim.

As everyone clapped, her dragon growled. *Make sure he knows that as soon as he kisses us, I won't be able to hold the frenzy off for more than five or ten minutes with him near. We will leave with him or without him. That is the only way to guarantee everyone's safety.*

Understood.

Finn walked up to her and leaned to her ear to whisper, "I love watching your tall, lean body move in time to the music. Promise you'll dance for me again, Ara. Preferably when you're naked and alone with me."

"Maybe, but only if you dance naked for me."

He blinked and she reveled in catching him off guard. However, Finn quickly regained his composure and winked. "Aye, I think I can promise you that. Although one look at my magnificent cock and you'll forget all about the dancing and take me into your own hands."

Shaking her head, Finn looked around the crowd before she could answer and he announced, "And now, Clan Lochguard, it's time for the First Kiss."

As most of the crowd clapped, Finn took Arabella's hand and guided them to the stage. The clapping didn't die down and Arabella didn't have a chance to warn Finn. She only hoped she had a few seconds before the act happened.

Her dragon's snarl told she had better.

Even though Arabella wanted Finn more than anything else she'd wanted in a long time, her heart still beat double-time. Then it hit her—if she and Finn were in the thrall of a mate-frenzy, Duncan could pounce.

194

She needed to talk with Finn.

Once they ascended the stairs, Arabella tugged Finn's hand and stood on her tiptoes to say into his ear, "Finn, I need a second."

~~~

Despite his outward nonchalant appearance, Finn's dragon was clawing to get out of the mental maze he'd created.

From experience, Finn knew he had a few more minutes before his beast would find the exit point. He wanted to kiss Arabella and whisk her out of the great hall before that happened.

Then his lass tugged him to a stop and asked for a second of his time. A bad feeling pooled in the pit of his stomach. He'd meant it before, about never forcing her, but everything about Arabella's actions and demeanor had suggested she was ready for the frenzy. If Finn denied his dragon too much longer, he would have to stay away from Arabella until she could accept him.

Turning his head to look into her eyes, he asked, "What is it, Ara? Tell me quick."

She frowned. "Don't be snappy. I have something important to tell you."

Finn glanced to the crowd. Everyone was watching them, but so far, they probably only thought Arabella was nervous.

Looking back to Arabella, he steeled his voice with dominance and stated, "Then tell me."

When she didn't glare, he knew something was wrong. She replied, "Maybe you should just kiss me on the cheek."

With a growl, he leaned closer. "Are you having second thoughts? Tell me straight, Arabella. The whole clan is waiting."

She shook her head. "No, it's not me, but what about Duncan? In the thrall of the frenzy, you'll be vulnerable. He'll use it against you."

His face softened. "I have safeguards in place. Not only is Faye in charge of security, Bram is sending some reinforcements as we speak."

"When did you do that?"

"While you were getting ready."

She frowned. "Oh. You could've told me."

The corner of his mouth ticked up. "I was too dazzled by your beauty and it slipped my mind."

Searching his eyes, she finally replied, "Well, try harder to resist next time. I don't like being in the dark."

"Right now, I'll promise almost anything if it means you'll kiss me properly. Then I can take you home and treasure you as you deserve."

"Stop it." The blush on her cheeks stoked both man and beast. Clearing her throat, Arabella lifted her chin. "Well, as long as the clan is taken care of, then let's give them a show. I don't want there to be any doubt that you belong to me, Finlay Stewart, and me alone."

Her possessiveness made his dragon roar inside his maze. Finn had better hurry up or he might end up taking the lass in a closet somewhere and she deserved better.

Placing his hand on her back, he guided them toward the stage. "I can't wait to see you claim me properly, Ara. Don't hold back."

Arabella's blushed turned brighter. "It'll have to be soon, too. My dragon gives you five minutes, ten at the most, before she loses control. If you can't get us out of here soon enough, I'll leave without you and you'll just have to catch me."

196

Healed by the Dragon

The thought of chasing Arabella and taking her in a hidden clearing somewhere made his cock throb. "If you run, I'll find you, Arabella. One way or another, I'm claiming you tonight."

She merely bobbed her head and he resisted smiling at her response. Despite the power his dragon goddess had over him, Finn kept forgetting she was a virgin. While her dragon wouldn't be shy, her human half still was.

He turned them toward the crowd. Since his beast was nearing the exit of the maze, he pushed aside all thoughts of him and Arabella naked and scanned his clan members. Faye was supposed to be guarding the main entrance, but she was absent. Shay was there in her stead.

Trusting his cousin had a reason for her absence, Finn started his speech. "Dragon-shifters take their mates very seriously. We protect them with our lives because they are our happiness and light." He turned his head toward Arabella. "Arabella MacLeod, you will be my light and strength through good times and bad. With you at my side, I believe together we can make Lochguard the strongest clan in the United Kingdom." He lowered his voice a tad for effect. "Sorry, but your old clan will lose to us. Only one clan can be the strongest, after all." The crowd chuckled and Arabella did a mini-eye roll. He continued, "I offer you my protection, my home, and my name. I would like to kiss you in front of our clan, as a promise to uphold my offers. What do you say?"

~~~

Arabella hesitated. After all, it had only been two days. Would Finn always want her, even once the novelty wore off?

Arabella's dragon growled. *He is our mate. Of course he will want us. Kiss him. He is ours. Claim him.*

Seeing as this is the most important decision of my life, can I have a bloody second?

No. I will count to ten before I unleash the frenzy lust. One, two…

Arabella mentally scowled at her beast before she finally answered Finn, "Yes."

Cheers rose up as Finn placed his hands on her waist and drew her close. Nuzzling the side of her cheek, he murmured, "I meant every word, Arabella. After this, you're mine and I will do whatever it takes to protect what's mine."

His possessive tone made her stomach flip in a good way. Rather than admit it, she whispered, "Just bloody kiss me, dragonman."

Chuckling, he moved to look into her eyes. "With pleasure."

Finn's lips descended on hers. The second his warm, soft mouth touched hers, her beast roared.

Arabella ignored her to wrap her arms around his neck and parted her lips for his tongue. With each stroke, lust pulsed through her body. When he pulled her up against his hard cock, the strongest desire of her life hit her, causing her nipples to throb, her pussy to pulse, and her skin to burn. Every instinct urged her to toss up Finn's traditional dragon-shifter outfit, wrap her legs around his waist, and ride his cock as if her life depended on it.

Judging by Finn's possessive grip on her arse, he was no less affected as he dominated her with his tongue.

As Arabella tried to fight back and take control, Finn pulled away. She growled, "Not enough. Not nearly enough."

His eyes blazed with heat. "Not here."

Rubbing her body against his, she whispered, "Then hurry."

Finn turned his head toward the crowd. As he spoke, Arabella kissed his throat. "I'm afraid you'll have to enjoy the rest of the evening without us." She nipped his skin. "As you can see, the frenzy is about to start."

Arabella's dragon roared again. *Now. We must claim him. Let's go.*

As if Finn could hear her thoughts, he took her hand and raced down the stairs. The crowd parted, allowing them to pass. Normally, Arabella would study the faces to assess threats, but her eyes were glued to Finn. Both woman and beast wanted him with every cell of their body.

They exited the main entrance and Finn pulled her to the side to kiss her again. The quick, rough brush of lips and tangle of tongues was over before Arabella could blink. Finn whispered, "There's plenty more of that once we reach my cottage."

Digging her nails into his chest, she answered, "There had bloody well better be. My skin is on fire. I need you, Finn."

"Come on."

They all but ran toward his cottage. They were nearly there when Faye jogged in front of Finn and ordered, "Stop, Finn, and listen."

Finn growled. "Not now, Faye. I'm barely holding on as it is."

Arabella leaned into Finn's side, the heat of his body helping to control the pounding need to mate. Somehow, she forced her brain to work. "Tell us, Faye."

Faye nodded and answered quickly, "I was trying to reach you before the kiss. Even though I failed, I need you to listen, Finlay. It's important."

Finn growled. "Tell me what the fuck is going on."

Faye answered, "We're under attack. The Dragon Knights are here for Arabella."

CHAPTER SEVENTEEN

Every inch of Finn's skin pulsed with an uncontrollable need to mate. He needed Arabella naked and under him or he might burst.

As Arabella rubbed against his side, he tightened his grip and turned his head to kiss her when Faye pushed between them and shoved Finn away.

His dragon snarled. *Get rid of her. We need our mate.*

With pleasure.

Blinded by the mate-claim frenzy, Finn jumped and tackled Faye to the ground. They rolled, Faye maneuvering on top at first, but then Finn used his weight to unbalance and move her underneath him. Pressing against her throat with his arm, he hissed, "If you stay, I can't promise what will happen."

Faye narrowed her eyes and shoved against his chest. "Get your bloody dragon under control, Finn. Did you hear me properly? The Dragon Knights are here and *want* Arabella."

His dragon roared. *She's lying. She wants to distract us and allow her brothers to take our mate.*

At the mention of Fergus and Fraser, a ray of reason shone through in his brain. *They would never do that.*

She wants to trick us. Don't believe her.

But what if she's right? Do you really want to chance our mate's safety?

His beast rumbled. *Find out quickly. If you are wrong, I will take control and not let you out until our female is pregnant.*

Easing the pressure against Faye's neck, Finn demanded, "What the hell do you mean we're under attack from the Dragon Knights and they want Arabella? Explain and do it quickly. My dragon views you as a threat right now."

Faye's eyes flashed to dragon slits. "Tell your dragon to fuck off. I'm not about to take his crap."

Finn managed through gritted teeth to say, "Just explain, Faye. You can curse him out later."

Faye huffed. "For the clan's sake, fine. The Dragon Knights are trying to infiltrate through the secret exit points. Since only the clan knows about them, we have a traitor."

Finn growled. "Duncan."

Faye nodded. "Aye, I suspect as much. As for wanting Arabella, they leaked that little demand to the media and I received an alert on my phone." Faye looked to Arabella and back. "What do you want to do?"

Looking over at Arabella, he saw she was standing with her fingers and jaw clenched. The look of concentration on her face told him she was trying to restrain her dragon.

His dragon growled and spoke up again. *She is ours. We must take her to safety. Then we can fuck her and keep everyone away.*

Fucking is the last thing we're doing right now.

His dragon snarled. *I'm done waiting. I want our mate.*

And if we're killed when naked with her under us, what then?

My instincts will protect us, his beast stated.

As much as I trust your instincts, we're doing this my way.

Whatever you do, I will break free.

Try it, dragon. You'll lose.

Healed by the Dragon

Before his beast could take over his mind completely, Finn constructed his most complex maze to date and shoved his dragon inside. His beast roared and threw his body against the walls, but thanks to twenty years of practice and advice from Fergus, the walls held.

At a later time, Finn would need to thank Fergus. His cousin's suggestions might just help him save the clan.

Satisfied the maze should keep his dragon busy for at least an hour, it gave him time enough to deal with the most pressing threats. There was no fucking way he would let Duncan or the Dragon Knights win. He would claim Arabella when this was over, which meant surviving the attack with both his clan leadership and life intact.

He focused back on Faye. "Have they breached any of the entrances yet?"

Faye shook her head. "No. I have my best Protectors holding them off. But that's not the only problem, Finn."

Arabella's scent wafted into his nose and his dragon roared from inside his maze. Gritting his teeth, Finn spat out, "Tell me quickly, Faye. I don't have a lot of time."

Because of the seriousness of the situation, Faye merely answered, "The older Protectors have disappeared."

"Fuck," Finn muttered. "And Bram's reinforcements?"

"They should be here soon but they haven't arrived yet," Faye replied.

Arabella touched his shoulder and his dragon nearly succeeded in breaking free. Her voice strained when she said, "Finn, I can't hold off my dragon much longer. Either leave or fuck me. I'm close to losing control."

Finn released his hold on Faye and stood up to face Arabella. With the faint light highlighting her beautiful face, his need to mate only grew stronger. *Fuck*. If he didn't do something, Finn would end up failing everyone. There was so much he still needed to do to bring peace to Lochguard. If he ever wanted to accomplish any of it, he would have to get his shit together.

Drawing on every protective instinct he held for both Arabella and his clan, Finn blocked out his dragon and ordered, "Give me a second with Arabella, Faye, and then you'll take her to the Protectors' safe room in the command center while I take care of Duncan."

Faye bobbed her head. She was a clever lass, knowing it wasn't the time to challenge him. "A minute is all I can spare, Finlay, so make it quick."

As soon as his cousin was ten feet away, Finn placed his finger under Arabella's chin and stared straight into her slitted pupils. "You are one of the strongest dragon-shifters I know, Arabella MacLeod. I need you to remain in control of your dragon for a little while longer because I need your help. You aren't about to let me down, are you, heather?"

Her pupils turned round as she narrowed her eyes and he knew his lass was slowly gaining control. "At a time like this you're really going to call me heather?"

"Yes. I don't have time to argue. Just listen and imagine the most complex maze of twists, turns, and numerous dead ends. Then stuff your dragon into the middle."

"I've never done that and don't have the time to learn." She rubbed her hand across his chest. "All I can think about is ripping off your clothes and trying not to break your penis."

He threaded every bit of dominance he possessed into his voice. "If you don't help me, then you'll never get my cock." He raised her chin an inch higher. "I need you to call Bram and let him know what's going on."

204

"You want me to lock away my dragon in some kind of maze, control the unstoppable lust pounding through my body, and reach out to Bram? Finn, I can barely have this conversation with you without humping your body. How can I get any of that accomplished without embarrassing myself? I crave an orgasm more than breathing right now."

"You can do it all, Arabella, and you will."

~~~

Every inch of Arabella's body was on fire. Each second she breathed in Finn's scent, her desire pounded harder. All her dragon wanted to do was fuck their mate. How in the bloody hell was she supposed to control her and do what he asked?

Her dragon roared. *You won't. You deny me and you will regret it.*
The threat cut through her lust. *Don't you dare threaten me. I'm stronger and I will win.*

With a growl, she hissed, *We'll see about that, dragon. I'm just as strong as you.*

As her beast rammed against the temporary wall Arabella had constructed, she imagined a labyrinth of stone, shrubs, and even pits of fire. Using circuit board designs as inspiration, she soon had a massive maze-prison inside her head.

Lowering the invisible wall holding her dragon at the new entrance to the maze, her beast rushed forth. Arabella slammed a mental wall at the exit.

Keeping her voice strong, Arabella stated, *I'm stronger, dragon. Now, hush.*

Her beast roared, but Arabella ignored it. She looked back up at Finn and smiled. "I did it, Finn. I constructed a maze."

"Good lass. I would kiss you, but I won't chance it."

She frowned. "I'm going to ignore making a comment for the good of the clan." She glanced to Faye in the distance and back. "I don't know how long I can keep my dragon inside the maze, though. I will call Bram, but you should stay away from me until the threat has passed. I'm not sure I can contain her again. She'll be pissed when she gets out and may take control."

"I believe in you, Ara. Tell your dragon to calm the fuck down."

She raised her eyebrows. "I'm assuming that works with yours?"

"I like to think so." As she rolled her eyes, Finn reached out to touch her, but pulled back. "But don't worry, I'm going to stay clear until I take care of the Dragon Knights."

Arabella's heart squeezed. "Be careful of those bastards. If you get yourself killed before we have sex, then I'll find a way to curse you even in death."

Amusement danced in Finn's eyes. "I'd like to see you try." Finn noticed Faye walking toward them and his face turned serious. "I don't have much time, so I have another request. When you talk to Bram, ask the Stonefire humans if they know of anything that could help with the Dragon Knights. They're crazy bastards and as much as I want to kill them off, I can't anger the DDA if I want any more human sacrifices in the future."

Arabella's dragon roared and threw her body against the roof of the maze. She wasn't going to be happy when she got out.

Still, Finn and her new clan needed her, so Arabella steeled herself against her beast's tantrum and nodded. "I'll see what Evie knows or if she has any contacts that can help us."

"That's my lass."

Finn's belief in her warmed her heart. Her dragon roared again, wanting more than words to warm their body, but testing the walls of the maze, everything was still holding. However, since this was the first time Arabella had tried a mental maze, the process was slowly sapping her energy. She would need to practice more in the future.

Faye walked up to them and held up her mobile phone. "Sorry, Finn. But our defenses are weakening. I need orders and we need to go."

He nodded. "Right, then take Arabella to the safe room inside the Protector's headquarters and have her well-guarded. Bram's reinforcements should be arriving soon to help you." Finn patted the sporran-like pouch over his crouch. "I'll have my mobile, but since I need to take care of Duncan, I'm not sure if I can respond right away."

His cousin replied, "Understood." She motioned for Arabella to follow and then Faye threw over her shoulder, "Be careful, cousin."

"You, too." Finn looked to Arabella. "Show everyone what I already knew you're made of. This is your day to shine, Arabella MacLeod. It's time to save our clan."

Emotion choked her throat. Finn's belief in her was absolute. No one else had believed in her that way since Arabella's mother had died.

Yet she forced her voice to remain even as she replied, "And you don't do anything stupid. I know that's going to be difficult, but try."

Finn winked. "Only because my lovely lass asked me."

Faye placed a hand on Arabella's shoulder. "It's time, Ara. We need to go."

Arabella met Finn's gaze one last time before she turned and walked away. Her dragon clawed to get out of her prison, wanting to hold their mate and never let go. A small part of

Arabella felt the same way, yet she needed to trust in Finn. If she couldn't put her faith in him, then the clan couldn't either. He was Lochguard's leader and it was time to let him shine.

Her dragonman would find a way to make it all work and return to complete the frenzy.

Straightening her shoulders, she focused her energies on containing her dragon. Reaching out to Bram should be doable, but she had no idea how long she could remain in control, let alone knew if she could help Lochguard. She wasn't a warrior; Arabella was only good with computers.

Then an idea hit her. She looked over to Faye. "I'm assuming the safe room has a secure connection and a somewhat powerful computer?"

"Aye," Faye answered. "Why?"

"If you give me access, then after contacting Bram, I have an idea."

~~~

By the time Finn approached the great hall, he was bloody tired of his dragon banging around his head. With a growl, he ordered, *Stop it. I need to take care of Duncan. Do you really want him to take over and possibly kill our mate?*

While his dragon didn't fall completely silent, his roars and snarls were barely audible.

Good. It wasn't as if Finn didn't want to whisk Arabella away to a secret location and let the frenzy claim them. But to do that would endanger his family, his friends, and his clan. He may not like them all equally, but he would keep them together. At least, until he could sort the traitors from the loyal ones.

Finn clenched his fingers at the very idea of someone telling the Dragon Knights how to break into the clan. He'd been too soft up until the present. No more. Finn would find the evidence he needed and punish the traitors.

He was about ten feet away from the entrance when he finally noticed Fergus and Fraser standing off to the side. Good. They'd received his earlier instructions sent via text message.

Walking diagonally away from the hall, the twins moved until they met him under a Scots pine tree. Finn kept his voice low as he asked, "Did you do what I asked?"

Fraser nodded. "Aye. Meg Boyd's younger cousin is flirting with Duncan. He hasn't left the hall, although not for want of trying. Helen is a right tease."

Finn looked to Fergus. "And you?"

Fergus crossed his arms over his chest. "Since most of the Protectors are on the perimeter, Shay ended up calling on the Boyd brothers and the MacAllister siblings. All of them know how to fight and most of them dirty. They're all just waiting for the signal, if needed."

"Good," Finn answered. "Then let's put my plan into action."

Finn took the lead and his twin cousins followed.

Entering the great hall, Finn headed straight for the dais as Fraser and Fergus went the long way around to where Duncan was flirting with the pretty redhead.

Once on stage, Finn checked to see Shay at the main exit with Alistair Boyd, the two other Boyd brothers near the rear exit, and the five MacAllister siblings not too far from where Duncan was sitting. When Fraser and Fergus were in position, Finn raised his hand into the hall and the chatter and music died down. All eyes were on him.

Drawing on every ounce of strength he possessed, Finn addressed the crowd. "You aren't the only one surprised to see me. I had planned to spend the next week with my mate, but all of that has changed. Lochguard is under attack."

Murmurs rose up, but Finn only raised his voice. "If you're thinking of panicking, then stop. We're Clan Lochguard and we're better than that. We survived the attacks during the Sutherland clearances and we can survive this, provided I have your help." Some of the noise died down and more than one set of shoulders straightened. "I need all of you to go home, lock your doors, and guard your families. If you see anything suspicious, make sure to contact the help line and provide as many details as possible.

"As for the intruders, the Protectors are handling them. Stonefire reinforcements will also be here shortly. Barring a nuclear bomb, Faye MacKenzie will have all of this sorted in no time."

Someone shouted from the crowd, "Who are the invaders?"

Finn was always truthful with his clan if he could help it. He saw no reason to lie. "The Dragon Knights."

A few shouts went up and Finn quickly scanned the crowd. Duncan was slowly inching his way toward the rear exit. Since he had yet to find any proof that Duncan was behind the betrayal, he needed to get the bastard out of the room without pointing fingers. Only then could Finn question the older dragon-shifter.

Putting two fingers to his mouth, Finn whistled. Once the noise was at a manageable level, he continued, "Faye and I are taking care of it. Now, I need you to go home and do your part because I can't keep the clan safe without your help." Finn swept the crowd with his eyes. "However, one last thing—anyone who flees the clan's lands before an evacuation alarm is sounded won't be welcomed back. If you won't stand with us under the tough times, we don't want you here during the easy times. To a dragon-shifter, clan and family means everything." More than a few people bobbed their heads. Finn motioned toward the doors, which was also the signal for his people to act. "Now, go home and protect your families. I'll let you know via text or an announcement over the speaker system when it's safe."

Finn clapped and everyone moved toward the exits. At the same time, the MacAllisters, Fraser, and Fergus closed in on Duncan, who was also heading toward the rear exit. The plan was to let him out, but corner him outside so as not to attract notice.

Unfortunately, as much as he itched to leave straight away, Finn had to answer questions and ensure everyone left the great hall. Only then could he check in on Duncan.

He had faith that his loyal clan members would do as asked and stay inside. He only hoped the Dragon Knights didn't start attacking from the sky, because then Finn wasn't sure what to do. Dragon-shifters had always been rulers of the sky. Once all of this was over and he'd claimed Arabella, Finn would think on how to solve that little detail. He wanted to be prepared for the future.

Yet as a family approached him, Finn gave a reassuring smile and focused on the present.

CHAPTER EIGHTEEN

Arabella pulled her hair over one shoulder and twisted it before tossing it back. She was alone in Lochguard's command center, waiting for Bram to establish a video chat connection. It'd taken her fifteen minutes to set up a secure enough line to attempt one.

As she rubbed her hands against her thighs, her dragon banged against the maze walls for the hundredth time. Each time her dragon did it, Arabella's heart rate ticked up a little bit more. Her walls were still holding, but once they finally fell, she would be in a world of trouble. A dragon-shifter in a mate-claim frenzy but without a mate to claim could be dangerous.

Even with her dragon trapped inside the labyrinth, her body was flushed and desire still pulsed between her legs. Until she had Finn naked and inside her, she would never be able to think straight.

She still had most of her brain for the moment. As long as Arabella lasted long enough to help her new clan, she could handle whatever her dragon threw at her. Probably.

Just as she pushed aside her doubt, Bram's frowning face appeared on the screen. He didn't waste any time to say, "What the bloody hell is going on, Arabella? The Dragon Knights have plastered your name and face all over the media and are demanding your blood. Are you safe? Where's the Scottish bastard?"

Arabella's nervousness disappeared at Bram's words. Her voice was strong when she answered, "That bastard is my mate, so be nice."

Evie's head appeared next to Bram's. "I knew it. Is Finn okay? Have our reinforcements arrived?"

Before she could answer, Bram muttered, "I'm clan leader, lass. Let me do my job."

Sensing a couples' argument, Arabella interjected, "No, the Stonefire Protectors haven't arrived, yet. As for Finn, he's handling another clan issue."

Bram's eyes met hers again. "I'm not sure I like the sound of that."

"It doesn't matter if you like it. I trust him to handle it."

Her former clan leader studied her a second before the corner of his mouth ticked up. "As much as I hate to admit it, Scotland has done you good, Ara." His face became serious again. "But Finn must not have everything in hand or you wouldn't be contacting me."

"It's not you so much as Evie and maybe Mel I need to talk to. All I need from you is to ensure you can send more help, if needed."

Bram nodded, but Evie answered before him, "Tell me what you need, Arabella. If it's in my power, I'll help."

A year ago, Arabella never would have thought she'd have a human friend, let alone miss her. She'd have to invite Evie along with Tristan and Mel, provided Bram would allow his pregnant mate to travel.

Arabella leaned forward a fraction. "As much as Finn wants to kill all of the knight bastards, he can't if he ever wants another female sacrifice. Do you know of anyone who could help contain them? Or, of exactly how far we can take it without being called monsters, or worse? Neither he or I want to ruin all of Mel's hard work in building good publicity for the dragon-shifters."

Evie tapped her chin. "If only I knew where Alice was. Give me a second to think. Talk to Bram again while I do that."

Alice was Evie's human friend who knew more than anyone about dragon-shifter and human history. Unfortunately, she'd been missing for the past few months. No one on Stonefire or even their contacts had been able to locate her.

Arabella looked back to Bram. "While Evie figures that out, I have something else to ask. Does that BBC journalist, Jane Hartley, still contact you?"

Bram nodded. "Aye, she occasionally runs pieces, although she usually talks with Melanie about specifics. Why? Do you need to contact her?"

"Yes and quickly. I want to broadcast Lochguard's security feeds and show the world the true colors of the Dragon Knights."

Bram gestured his hand. "Let's say I contact her. The feed will show dragons fighting as well. We don't need the humans thinking of us as monsters."

Arabella hesitated a second as her dragon inched ever closer to the exit point. If Arabella couldn't set things in motion in the next half hour, she might not make it.

Bram was one of the few people she felt comfortable around enough to be herself, so Arabella spit out, "Listen, Bram, there's something I didn't tell you. I'm barely containing the mate-claim frenzy. As much as I wish I could give you two days to plan every detail, I need an answer soon. Consult Melanie and get back to me in ten minutes. I'll set everything up and have it ready, just in case."

Bram cursed. "Why didn't you tell me, Arabella? I'm surprised Finn can put two thoughts together. Maybe I should fly up there."

"No," Arabella answered. "Right now, we have it under control. Just do what I asked and give me an answer. Evie, I know you can hear me, the same for you. I'll patch the connection back through in ten minutes."

Before Bram or Evie could reply, Arabella disconnected.

Letting out a sigh, she closed her eyes and checked on her maze. Her dragon's lust was seeping out from a few cracks in the ceiling, making her body hotter with each breath.

Shit. She needed to think about something else. Opening her eyes, Arabella went to work on setting everything up in case she could broadcast. She only hoped she could last the ten minutes until she called Bram back, and then a few more.

Finn was the only other person she trusted enough who also had the technical know-how to set up the feed to broadcast securely, but her male had his own problems to handle. Arabella had to believe he was faring better than she. Otherwise, Lochguard as she knew it might not survive and she'd lose her new home.

The second the thought crossed her mind, she pushed it aside. Finn was just as stubborn as she; he would use his last dying breath to save his clan.

Arabella only hoped it didn't come to that.

~~~

Finn smiled at the final family before they turned to leave the great hall. Answering questions and placating fears had taken him five minutes, which was longer than he'd planned for.

215

His dragon was currently five minutes closer to escaping.

Growling inside his head for good measure to his beast, Finn exited the rear door of the great hall and jogged toward the small, unoccupied cottage about twenty yards away. He rapped on the door four times and it unlocked. Graham Boyd ushered him inside.

Finn asked, "Any luck so far in extracting information?"

Graham shook his head. "No. Although the techie-half of the MacAllister siblings might have a way of tracing how the Dragon Knights managed to sneak up on us and attack."

Emma and Ian MacAllister had replaced Finn as tech security apprentices after he'd won the clan leadership. "How?"

"After the Dragon Knights bombed the two DDA offices, they mentioned online locations people could offer up information for them to use," Graham explained. "Emma and Ian are checking to see if any sort of tips, or at least access, came from Lochguard or one of the surrounding villages. If they did, they might be able to further pinpoint an IP address and give us a location."

"They've been careful in the past, Graham, so that seems like a long shot," Finn replied.

Graham shrugged. "Part of my job as the clan's analyst has been to pay attention to the Dragon Knights and see what buzz there is online and in the media. Lately, they've been making more mistakes. I think bombing the two DDA offices made them cocky, and that could work to our advantage."

They reached a closed door and Finn paused to look at Graham. "Let's hope so. In the meantime, let's focus on Duncan."

Once the other dragonman grunted his agreement, Finn opened the door to find Duncan surrounded by Alistair Boyd and the remaining three MacAllister siblings. A quick look told him Duncan was relaxed; if he had something to hide, he was doing a good job of not showing it.

Finn studied the older dragon-shifter a second and then stated, "I knew you wanted to be in charge of the clan, but don't you think putting their lives at risk will alienate them?"

Duncan raised an eyebrow. "Who said I did anything? I was in the hall the entire time. Even if you check my mobile phone records, you'll see I'm innocent. A real clan leader wouldn't judge me guilty without proof."

Finn kept his face expressionless, but his dragon roared at the insult. Finn checked his maze, but it would last for a while yet, so he continued, "It seems pretty fucking convenient that an attack would happen right as I'm about to claim my mate. Me being distracted would give you the perfect opportunity to swoop in and take charge. After saving everyone, you could call a leadership retrial."

Duncan smirked. "That sounds like a brilliant plan. Maybe I'll try it next time. It won't be long before you fuck up so badly everyone will call for you to quit, especially with you taking the English dragon-shifter as your mate. She will bring nothing but danger to the clan, and you know it."

Finn resisted clenching his fingers. The man didn't deserve to talk about Arabella, let alone criticize her.

Taking a deep breath through his nose, Finn calmed down a fraction. "What's more dangerous would be to isolate the clan further. At the end of Dougal's eighteen years as leader, his practice of isolation and dragon superiority decimated our clans' number and severed alliances. Even putting aside how we must rely on the DDA for human sacrifices, the humans who once called us friends are starting to turn on us, and as a result, they could start leaking information to the dragon hunters. Returning to those ways would make it worse. Why would you want to do that?"

"Because, dragons have become pawns of the human governments," Duncan answered. "If we unleash our beasts and embrace our animal sides, then the world is ours for the taking. Dragons are the top predators and it's time we start acting like it."

Finn wanted to punch the proud look off Duncan's face, but resisted. He needed to keep the man talking. Not only to give the MacAllister siblings more time to find evidence of the betrayal, but to also see what other threats could be lurking in Europe and elsewhere in the world. If Duncan had been conspiring with other clans, Finn needed to find out.

He crossed his arms over his chest and tried his first tactic. "And one dragon clan, most of whom would be forced into obeying your orders, doesn't stand a chance against the rest of the world. The humans have more alliances than you can imagine when it comes to protecting against rogue dragon-shifters."

Duncan tilted his head. "Yes, that would be a problem for one clan, wouldn't it?"

To prevent from growling, Finn gritted his teeth. A few seconds later, he tried another approach. "You don't seem like the type to come up with this plan yourself. You're clearly not clever enough, so who are you following?"

Duncan's pupils flashed to slits and Finn knew his tactic was working, especially when Duncan growled out, "If I don't want to follow humans, then why would I want to follow another, foreign dragon clan? The British Isles and Ireland are all I care about."

Interesting. Even if Duncan was bluffing about being in charge, his claim about the British Isles and Ireland didn't rule out trouble possibly brewing in Ireland.

Once Finn sorted out the mess with Duncan and the Dragon Knights, he'd have to address Ireland and investigate any threats. He'd always planned to form an alliance with the western Irish clan, the most amicable and open-minded of the Irish clans. His timetable would just have to be sped up a few months.

Finn decided to poke some more at his rival's ego. "The Republic of Ireland's northern clan is stronger than you any day, Duncan. I'm guessing you're taking orders from him."

"Killian is more concerned with how many females he can bed than anything else. Your ignorance only highlights why you're not fit to lead," Duncan hissed.

Finn had one last piece of information he needed to know before he could stop with these games. "That leaves Marcus down south. It must irk you to follow an English dragon-shifter's lead."

Duncan looked to open his mouth but then promptly shut it. *Bingo.* While it was highly likely that Duncan was responsible for the current attack, he was taking orders from Marcus of Clan Skyhunter.

If Finn were a lesser dragonman, he would sigh at the growing list of threats he needed to address. But he wasn't. Once Arabella and Lochguard were safe, he would take on the world with his mate at his side. And while less romantic, he'd need Bram's help as well.

The corner of Finn's mouth ticked up. "Your silence tells me everything." Finn leaned forward a fraction. "You now have a choice—you can either tell me everything and I'll kindly hand you over to the DDA, or I can find out on my own and then I'll claim my clan leader's legal right to give you a just punishment. Which will it be?"

Duncan merely stared at him as the seconds ticked by. Clearly, the dragonman thought he was cleverer than everyone else.

After another minute ticked by, there was a knock on the door. Finn turned from Duncan just in time to see Emma and Ian MacAllister enter the room with triumphant expressions. Since the pair were still both young, he didn't risk inflating their egos. He ordered, "Tell me what you found."

Ian cleared his throat. "I can prove Duncan and some of his supporters are at least partially responsible for the attack."

Finn raised an eyebrow. "Well? I don't have a lot time. Tell me."

Emma jumped in. "As you instructed two months ago, we changed everyone's electronic codes for the secret entrances and kept track of everyone on the list you gave us to see who entered and exited, how often, and with how many people."

The list had been of everyone who had wanted Finn ousted. A quick glance to Duncan's blinking told Finn the older dragonman hadn't known of the secret surveillance.

Finn nodded. "Go on."

Emma continued, "Nothing suspicious had been documented until a little over half an hour ago when the codes issued to Duncan Campbell and about five others were all used along the eastern perimeter." She handed a paper list to Finn. As he scanned the names, she continued, "We voided the codes so no new intruders can use them. Even those who are inside will now be trapped."

Finn looked up from the list. "What did you see on the security feeds?"

Ian's face turned grim. "Ninety-five percent of the fighting is happening along the eastern border with Naver Forest. While no more Dragon Knights can step foot on our land using the codes, we can't see deep enough into the forest to monitor what else they might be doing. It's possible they have a weapon and are waiting to use it."

Fuck. A few illegal weapons could devastate his Protectors.

Careful to keep his expression calm and collected, Finn said to Emma and Ian, "Good work. Now, I want you to locate anyone who provided codes to the knights and send Shay the information to retrieve them. Also, tweak anything else in our security that might be a potential weakness or turned against us. Keep me updated by sending information to my mobile phone. I'll check them on the way to the eastern perimeter."

Ian asked, "What about Arabella MacLeod's project? Should we deny her access as well?"

What the hell was his lass up to? "No, I trust her, but she's the only one outside of you and the usual designated clan members who have full access." He glanced at Duncan and back at Ian and Emma. "Since I have enough proof to lock up the traitor and his followers, I'm going to the eastern perimeter to help Faye and the Protectors. However, I have one last request—I want you two to reach out to Arabella and see if she needs any help. While she's capable, I want her to have backup in case her frenzy breaks loose."

Alistair Boyd's voice rumbled from behind him. "And what about yours, Finn? Is it about to break loose?"

Finn turned and answered truthfully. "Not right now, but it could soon. I need your help, Alistair. The MacAllisters and your brother Graham can look after Duncan."

Alistair and Finn had fought over a lass or two in the past. The version of Alistair from even three years ago would've held it against Finn. The older version, however, merely nodded once and said, "You have it, Finn. I'd do anything to protect Lochguard."

Finn answered, "Right, then let's go. I can fill you in on the way." He looked to the three other MacAllister siblings standing near Duncan. "Tie him up and guard him." Finn moved his gaze to Graham Boyd. "I'm going to leave you in charge of them. If you think the command center is in danger, then put it under lockdown."

Once they all murmured their affirmations, Finn left with Alistair right behind him.

Without his focus on Duncan, his dragon's tantrum was starting to seep out again. Between the shots of lust and the incessant roaring, Finn had the worst headache of his life.

Yet somehow, he pushed on and filled Alistair on what needed to be done. Some things were more important than being at ease. Finn had a future to secure.

CHAPTER NINETEEN

Arabella's dragon jumped and pounded against the roof of the mental maze for the hundredth time. Each time her beast did it, it only made it harder for Arabella to concentrate.

But she was nearly done with her preparations to broadcast the security feed. Any minute Bram and Evie would call her back. Then she could activate the feed and lock herself in a room until Finn could find her.

Part of her hated the fact she needed to hide away from everything, but at least it wasn't because of Arabella's weakness or the past holding sway over her future. No, the mate-claim frenzy was purely instinctual. As strong as she'd become, it still wasn't enough to completely drown out the age-old instinct to mate.

Her beast roared and jumped again. Another crack appeared in the ceiling of the mental maze. Her dragon had no interest in finding the exit point. She would break her way out.

A ringing chime filled the room, signaling an incoming call. Arabella gritted her teeth and hit receive. Bram's face appeared on the screen and instantly turned concerned. He stated, "You're close to losing it, lass."

Clenching her jaw, she muttered, "Tell me something I don't know. What's the verdict?"

Evie's head appeared next to Bram's. "I never thought I'd say this, but you're lucky the Dragon Knights bombed the DDA offices two months ago. They're bloody determined to enact justice."

Hope warmed her heart. "This means they'll help?"

Bram jumped in. "Aye, they already sent reinforcements via helicopter from Inverness and should be there within the next twenty minutes. Although you'd better warn your Scottish dragon-shifters, Ara, because if any of them attack the DDA helicopters, the DDA will take them down and haul them in for questioning and a possible sentencing."

"Send the information to Finn's mobile," Arabella gritted out. Her dragon roared and Arabella only just prevented herself from flinching. Not waiting for a response, she added, "Just tell me if I can switch the feed or not. I can't last much longer."

Evie nodded. "Set it to go live in fifteen minutes and thanks to Jane Hartley, the BBC will pick up the feed." Evie gave the necessary connection details. "The DDA wants to share the publicity. Their taking down the Dragon Knights may help to restore the public's faith in them."

She didn't have time to run the idea by Finn, but Arabella was pretty confident her mate trusted her judgment. "Making the DDA look good is all well and fine, but what did Mel say about how it'll affect the public's opinion regarding dragon-shifters? I'm more worried about that."

Bram answered, "She says it's a gamble, but if Lochguard is shown working with the DDA, then the public will see that the dragon-shifters aren't trying to take over or destroy the human agencies regulating them."

Arabella forced a nod. "Right. Anything else life or death I should know about?"

Bram replied, "Just have someone keep in touch. Once the frenzy clears, call me straightaway, Arabella MacLeod. We need to chat."

Too exhausted from fighting her dragon, Arabella didn't argue. "Fine."

Evie added, "Enjoy the frenzy. Despite all of the crap going on, it's a once in a lifetime event."

Another crack appeared in Arabella's mental maze. "I will. Now sod off so I can do my work."

Bram opened his mouth, but Evie winked and the connection closed.

Arabella brought up another window on her screen and sent a message to everyone she trusted on Lochguard. After that, she set up the connection to go live in fifteen minutes. The BBC could monitor the feed and broadcast once the DDA showed up.

With her dragon banging even harder against her maze, Arabella clicked the final button on the computer. She stood and raced to the room Faye had shown her earlier to use for the frenzy.

She barely made it inside and typed the code that would lock the door until someone typed in the counter-code before her beast broke through the ceiling of Arabella's maze. Lust flooded her body as her beast roared. Wetness rushed between her legs as her nipples turned to hard points.

Laying on the bed, Arabella curled into a ball and placed her hands over her eyes. She needed Finn, and soon. If her male didn't find her within the next day, her dragon could take over and go searching for another male to mate with. Every dragon had a few possible mates in their lifetime. No doubt, her dragon already had a list going.

At the thought of sex with any other male, Arabella curled tighter and used the last of her strength to mentally battle her dragon. She wanted Finn and would use every iota of stubbornness she possessed to wait for him.

The bloody dragonman had better not get himself killed.

~~~

Finn's head was pounding by the time he and Alistair neared the east entrances. According to information sent to his phone by Emma and Ian MacAllister, Lochguard's Protectors were winning against the breach on the eastern perimeter. But neither one knew for how much longer, especially if a powerful weapon were introduced into the fight.

He really needed to talk with Faye.

As they neared the eastern border, dragons roared as they dove and retreated into the sky. To his practiced eye, about half of the flying dragons had slower reactions times than normal—they were tired. Lochguard's Protectors would last another twenty minutes, at most, before exhaustion overtook them and forced a shift back to their human forms.

If only the older Protectors had stayed to help, then he would have one less thing to worry about.

Finn stopped at a high stack of rocks that formed a partial wall. They would provide enough cover to allow him and Alistair to shift. Just thinking of the battle he would have to wage with his dragon to shift gave him a headache. He only hoped his beast would cooperate long enough to warn Faye.

Turning toward the other dragonman, Finn whispered, "Remember what I told you. Use every dirty trick you learned as a young man to win, just make sure you don't kill them."

Alistair nodded as he shed his clothes. "I just hope you're not as daft as you used to be. Being a risk-taker and getting killed isn't an option, Finlay. The clan will fall apart without you."

"I'm sure someone can keep it together."

Alistair growled. "Don't even think about taking a risk that could kill you. Think of your female. If you'd rather do something stupid to show off than be with her, then maybe you don't deserve her."

"She's mine," Finn spat out.

"Then fight for her," Alistair replied.

Finn nodded. Thinking of Arabella set his dragon off. He growled. *Shut it. If we don't stop the attack, we'll never have our mate. Behave a little longer.*

Before his dragon could reply, his mobile vibrated inside his sporran-like pouch.

With a curse, he removed it and saw it was Bram. Pressing receive, Finn barked, "You had better have a bloody good reason for calling me, Bram. I'm about to shift and fight."

The Stonefire leader's voice came over the line. "Then shut the fuck up and listen. Help is on the way."

Finn watched the dragons in the distance. "I already know that. Your Protectors are fighting alongside mine."

"No," Bram answered. "The DDA is sending helicopters from Inverness. Make sure your people don't attack them."

A million questions raced through his head, but Finn pushed them aside. Bram had earned enough of his trust to accept the claim without further questioning. "Fine. Can I go now?"

Bram growled. "Wait a bloody second. Did you get the information that Arabella sent? If you kill any of the Dragon Knights, it won't look good for any of us."

"She must've just sent it because I didn't see it earlier. Even without it, trust me to know killing a human is a bad idea. Anything else? Or, would you like to tell me the color of the sky? I'm sure that's more important than taking care of my people."

"I would call you a bastard, but I'd be just as surly in the same situation." Bram stated. "Give those knights an extra roar from me and scare them shitless."

"Will do," Finn turned off his phone and stripped. He looked to Alistair. "DDA helicopters are coming. I'm going to signal Faye to follow me and shift back to tell her. The others will follow her lead afterward, with the right signals. While I do that, make sure the younger ones don't do anything stupid. Even though you were too stubborn to enter the British armed forces to become a true Protector, you're nearly as good as them."

Alistair grinned. "I'm going to bring that up at a later time."

"Fine, just go do your fucking task," Finn growled.

The second Alistair nodded, Finn reached out to his dragon. *Listen, the sooner we warn Faye, the sooner we can be with Arabella.*

His beast continued to snarl. With a mental sigh, Finn decided to use one of his risky tricks and shift without releasing his dragon.

Finn brushed against the ceiling of his mental maze and his dragon banged his head under his hand. Using the tentative link, Finn imagined his arms and legs turning into forearms and hind legs. After a few seconds' pause, his shift started. He only hoped he could maintain the change. If his dragon retreated into the bowels of the maze, Finn might lose the connection and turn back into a human.

It was risky, but he'd done it several times before. Fergus had discovered the technique and they'd improved it together.

Then wings grew from his back as his nose turned into a snout. By the time he was a seventeen-foot dragon, Alistair was already in his red dragon form, eyeing Finn with suspicion. No doubt, the clever dragonman had theories about how Finn could shift while containing the mate-claim frenzy.

Ignoring Alistair's gaze, Finn grunted, jumped, and beat his wings until he was high above the rock shelter he'd been using. A quick survey told him Faye's blue dragon form was in the thick of the defense line.

Motioning a hind leg toward Alistair to say he was ready, Finn carefully plotted his course toward his cousin.

~~~

Faye MacKenzie swooped down and roared as loud as she could at the group of Dragon Knights working on some sort of tubular weapon.

The sound succeeded in stopping them and making them cover their ears. Reaching out her back talons, she tried to nick the strange device. But just as she was about to take it, one of the Dragon Knights threw his body in the way and she had to draw back. They kept protecting the bloody thing.

Not killing the bastards was taking every bit of her restraint, especially since their actions told her the device was powerful and would probably cause major damage if they ever had enough time to set it off.

Beating her wings, Faye rose into the air and allowed one of her team to swoop down in her stead. Eventually, the humans had to get tired. In the meantime, she and her team would keep trying to steal the device so that they could study it and then destroy it.

Her respite from scaring the damn knights allowed her to monitor the rest of those fighting.

While Stonefire's Protectors were flying and attacking with gusto, most of the Lochguard dragons had slower reaction times than normal. True, most of her team was younger and lacked experience since the older, more seasoned Protectors had sided with Duncan. Not only that, most of the seasoned Protectors had disappeared earlier in the day, leaving her severely understaffed.

If she ever found the deserters, she would teach those old traitors a lesson.

Her dragon spoke up. *Don't waste time on them. Let me eat a few of the invaders and the rest will flee.*

I wish I could let you, but I can't.

I still don't understand why you resist the easiest solution.

Shush. I need to concentrate.

With a grunt, her beast fell silent.

Faye had nearly completed her survey of the situation when a familiar gold dragon caught her eye. Finn was here.

When he opened both of his back talons and closed them two times, she nodded. He wanted to talk with her.

She gave her unique dragon call and her second-in-command, Grant, met her eye. She pointed a wing at him and the green dragon nodded in understanding; he would lead in her absence.

As soon as Grant moved toward the front line and roared an order, Faye dashed left and right to avoid hitting any of her allies.

Finn was landing near a rock outcropping about forty feet away. The spot was closer to the forest and hill on the eastern perimeter than she liked, but none of her scouts so far had reported anything unusual in the section of forest. Still, she studied the trees for any telltale signs of movement or trouble. But nothing seemed out of the ordinary, so Faye headed toward her cousin.

She was about halfway there when a loud crackle sounded. Turning, Faye barely had time to acknowledge the light coming at her before a jolt of pain mixed with burning shot through her body. Her muscles spasmed and she lost control.

She couldn't move her wings.

Her dragon roared inside her head and tried to take control. Faye was weak and allowed her, but not even her beast could make their wings work. Unless someone helped her, there was nothing to break her fall below and the height was too high to survive.

Faye would die.

Using the last of her strength, she tried moving her body toward the trees. They would break her fall and give her the best chance of survival.

While she believed she'd changed her trajectory, she was too tired to keep fighting. Just the air whooshing against her dragon hide sent a thousand needles of pain dancing across her nerves.

Her last thought was she'd been careless and had let Finn down.

As her body barreled toward the ground, the world went black.

~~~

Finn had barely landed when Faye's cry of pain reverberated through the air. Jumping up and beating his wings, he watched some sort of electric charge dance across her body.

231

Then she fell.

The second it took him to recognize what had happened seemed like an eternity. But then Finn's dragon broke out of his maze, roared and urged him not to mate, but to save their family.

Protecting family was the only need more powerful than the mate-claim frenzy.

Finn beat his wings as fast as he could, knowing he had precious seconds to reach Faye before she fell to the ground. If he didn't reach her and help to slow down her speed, she would most likely die.

His dragon growled. *We will save her.*

Finn pushed his muscles to the limit, but then Faye abruptly changed course. *Fuck.* He might not make it in time.

Flapping his wings as fast as he could, Finn was just about to maneuver under her body when something shot through the air. Finn's instinct kicked in and moved just in time to watch a bolt of electricity whiz past him.

Another dragon swooped under Faye, but her speed was too great. She bounced off and crashed through the trees of the nearby forest. The sound of each broken branch was a stab to his heart.

Finn dove down toward Faye as the other dragon, which he recognized as Grant, went back to the front lines. He would thank the other dragon-shifter later; Grant's actions may just have saved Faye's life.

While his heart thumped in his chest, Finn descended carefully, listening for any unusual noises. Faye had fallen outside the perimeter, into the Naver Forest. He had no idea if the area was secure or not.

When Finn was just above the treetops, he heard voices. Landing as quietly as he could on a sturdy branch, he peered through the hole made by Faye's body and spotted two humans touching Faye's tail. When one pulled out a dragon-sized needle, Finn dove down and knocked the humans to the side. Each hit a tree and slumped into unconsciousness.

Going to his cousin's side, he nudged her blue neck. At first, she simply slumped right back down. After three more nudges, there was a small twitching and then a noise in her throat.

She was still alive. But he wasn't a doctor and didn't know how severe her injuries were, let alone if she were dying.

Surveying his surroundings to ensure it was free of any other humans, Finn raised his head and let out the dragon wail used when someone needed help. An answering call told him someone was coming.

Finn lowered his head and rubbed his cheek against Faye's. He wanted to swear at her and tell her not to die, but shifting was too dangerous. He could better protect her in his dragon form.

His dragon spoke up. *I won't let anyone harm our sister.*

Faye may not be his sister by blood, but blood didn't necessarily make a family. He would always think of Faye MacKenzie as his little sister.

Hell. What would he tell his aunt if Faye died on his watch? He nuzzled his cousin's cheek again and willed her to stay alive, and not just because he didn't want to be scolded by his aunt.

After what seemed like an eternity, two dragons descended and landed on Faye's other side. The gold female dragon had a satchel gripped in her right foreleg and a dragon carrying net in the other. It was Layla, the younger of the clan's doctors and one of Faye's oldest friends.

Pain flashed in Layla's eyes right before she dropped her parcels and shifted into her human form. The brown-eyed, black-haired woman went to Faye's head and checked her pulse before opening his cousin's eyelid. Letting it go, she moved to Faye's right wing, the one she had landed on.

Unable to read Layla's expression, Finn waited until the doctor was done with her examination.

About thirty seconds later, Layla looked to Finn and explained, "She's alive, but I need to get her back to my surgery. I'm most concerned about her wing. Forcing a shift may do irreparable damage to it, so Grant and I need to carry her back. There are a few dragons above us, keeping an eye out for trouble, but they could use your help in protecting us as we fly with her."

Glancing to Grant, Finn quickly shifted back. "Grant, you play watch out. I need you to stay with the Protectors. The DDA are sending in helicopters to deal with the Dragon Knights and you need to stop them from attacking the machines." Grant bobbed his head and Finn looked to Layla. "I'll help you carry her back."

Layla answered, "Okay, then help me lay out the net."

She ran to the other side and tossed the net to Finn. Together, they laid it out next to Faye; as he worked, Finn wondered if his dragon would continue to remain in control.

His dragon spoke up. *Stop worrying. We must focus on protecting her and getting her to safety.*

Will you lose control before then?

No. Faye is our sister in all but name. We must protect her.

I wish you'd remember that the entire clan is our family now.

His beast grunted. *Don't push it. I still want our mate.*

With the net and handles laid out, Finn embraced his dragon and shifted back into his golden beast. He looked to Grant and pointed upwards with a talon. The green dragon nodded in understanding—Grant would check the sky before they took off.

Grant jumped into the air as Layla shifted into her dragon form.

As they waited for the temporary leader of the Protectors to check for danger, Finn helped Layla to roll Faye onto the net. His cousin whimpered while remaining unconscious and it squeezed his heart. Even though his cousin couldn't hear him, Finn thought to himself, *I'm sorry, Faye Louise. I'll try to be gentle.*

As soon as Faye was in position, he and Layla both took hold of the carrying handles on their respective sides. Finn looked to the sky. Where the bloody hell was Grant? The sooner Finn got Faye out of here, the better.

The green Protector finally poked his head in the hole above and gave a low dragon call; all was safe.

Taking his cue, Finn jumped up and beat his wings, hovering until Layla was ready. The second the doctor gave him a nod, Finn used all of his muscles to lift Faye upward. While he usually teased Faye about weighing several tons, Finn was glad she was a female and slightly lighter.

They broke free of the trees and Finn was happy to see the fighting had moved a little further away, no doubt thanks to Lochguard and Stonefire's fighters.

Grant and two other dragons moved into position to serve as a type of shield, in case the knights tried to use another electric bolt blast.

Finn and Layla flew as quickly as they could toward a safe area where Layla could set up a tent surgery. Despite Layla being female and slightly smaller, she wasn't straining to keep up. He hated to think she did this often. The not knowing made him realize how he couldn't run the clan without a little help. He would stop thinking he could do everything later, once everyone was safe again.

Focusing on the beat of his wings, Finn blanked his mind and they soon reached one of the safe areas surrounded by high, rock walls, and maneuvered Faye down to the ground. Just as they landed, Finn heard helicopters in the distance. The DDA had arrived.

He needed to ensure his clan behaved. Then maybe Finn would be granted an audience with one of the DDA leaders to discuss securing Lochguard not just for the present, but into the future as well.

Finn nuzzled his cousin's cheek one more time and then looked to Layla. Giving a soft roar, she nodded in understanding—she would do everything in her power to save Faye.

He looked to his cousin one last time and wished he could stay, but Finn remembered his duties. The clan needed him.

Glancing to Layla, he motioned with his head that he was going again. Then Finn jumped into the air and headed back toward the front lines.

He hoped there weren't any more casualties before the DDA contained the situation. As it was, Finn wanted to kill every Dragon Knight on his land as payback for what they'd done to Faye and his clan.

Yet if he did that, he'd never make it back to Arabella.

Increasing his speed, Finn went to see how else he could help.

As he approached the fighting, both the Lochguard and Stonefire dragons swooped and glided around the perimeter. Dragons were diving, snatching up a Dragon Knight in their talons, and dropping them gently into one of the trees.

While the tactic was slowly removing the threats, Finn had his first good look at the hundreds of Dragon Knights inside Lochguard's lands.

There were far more than during the attacks a few months earlier. Hatred and violence really did pull people together, but in a horrible way.

His dragon growled. *Don't watch. Help them so we can claim our mate.*

Give me a second. I need to assess the weak spots in our defense.

His beast huffed and fell silent for the moment, although his dragon's need to protect battled with a pounding lust.

Since he didn't know how long his dragon could contain the frenzy, Finn looked closer at the scene.

Grant had positioned most of the Stonefire dragons in the thickest part of the fighting. The Lochguard dragons were mostly near the edges of the fray, keeping the knights contained within a few hundred feet of the perimeter wall. While Lochguard's fighters were holding the line, some of their actions were sluggish. Whether it was because of exhaustion or Faye's absence, he didn't know. Once the threat was contained, Finn added to his ever-growing list talking with Faye and Grant about a tougher training regimen.

Since Grant was busy with the main defense, Finn glided to the outer edge of the fighting.

Two of his youngest Protectors were about to fall out of the sky, so he moved toward them. They perked up a little when they noticed it was Finn.

Pointing to each with a talon, he then motioned in the direction of the landing area situated deep inside the clan's land. They hesitated, so he gave a low roar and they obeyed. Once they were far enough away to be out of danger, Finn focused back on the remaining dragons in the area.

Noticing Iris, one of the best scouts in the clan, he touched the talons of his front right hand to those of his back right foot and then pointed to the trees along the perimeter. Without a word, the purple dragon left to check the area.

Satisfied Iris would alert him if there were any more of the electric weapons in the nearby forest, Finn took a turn at the knights. Diving down at full speed, he roared and chased the knights in the area toward the wall.

He rounded up a few more before the whir of helicopter blades grew louder. Looking up, one of the DDA choppers was heading straight toward him.

The helicopter flashed a set of extra bright lights a few times and Finn received the message—he needed to get out of the way.

Just as he retreated a little, Grant gave a roar and all of the dragons in the heat of the battle fell back to form two v-shaped formations. Not too soon, either, because the helicopter nearest Finn dropped hundreds of tiny canisters on the ground. No Dragon Knights were in their path, but as soon as they hit the ground, smoked trailed upward.

The human knights moved away from the smoke toward the thick of the fight. If Finn were to hazard a guess, they were some kind of tear gas.

Another helicopter flew in from the distance with a giant cage hanging from the bottom. A few seconds later, it maneuvered the cage on the ground, released it, and rose back into the air.

Ropes were thrown from two of the helicopters and men wearing respirators shimmied down to the ground. Between the smoke and the DDA enforcers, the knights had no choice but to head toward the cage.

Finn's dragon finally spoke up. *Everything is done. The clan is safe. I want our mate. We need to go to her.*

I should check with Grant.

He has things in hand. Let him do his job. I want Arabella. She is probably hurting for us. Do you want to prolong her pain?

Of course not.

Then head back or I will take control.

I'm about ready to toss you into a mental maze again, dragon.

Try it, I dare you. I want sex and I want it now. The maze won't work, anyway. You're tired and I will take advantage.

He didn't want to admit it, but as he hovered in place, his adrenaline high was slowly wearing off. Each beat of his wings felt as if he were lifting rocks instead of delicate dragon wings.

His beast growled. *I am right. Last chance, we go together or I go alone.*

As Finn weighed his options, his bloody dragon released a floodgate of lust. His entire body ached to fuck a female. Since there were two nearby, Finn needed to leave or he would be in trouble.

His crazy dragon had won the upper hand.

Drawing on every ounce of strength he had left, Finn motioned for one of the most senior Protectors in the area to move into the leadership spot. The second the white dragon signaled he understood, Finn turned to the side and glided away from the eastern perimeter.

Another rush of lust surged through his body and Finn headed for the Protectors' command center. He'd have to risk landing in the small area behind it and shift there. He couldn't chance a delay, let alone encounter another female before he met

Arabella. He only hoped he could rush into the building and make it to the room saved for them without being delayed.

Gritting his teeth, Finn beat his wings faster. A little thing such as exhaustion wouldn't keep him from finding and fucking his mate as soon as possible.

Arabella had better be ready. With his dragon in charge, he wouldn't be able to hold back.

His beast spoke up. *She is ready.*

How do you know?

She is part dragon. What her dragon wants, her dragon gets.

Finn wasn't entirely sure of that, but he pushed aside his doubts. His lass wanted him and before much longer, she would be his in all ways.

Chapter Twenty

Arabella rubbed her eye sockets with the heels of her hands as her dragon roared and thrashed about inside her head.

Her beast demanded, *I need sex. Finn is taking too long. He must not want us enough. We need to find someone else.*

I told you, he's taking care of the clan.

He should take care of us.

Arabella removed her hands, sat up, and threw a pillow across the room. *Shut up. If you want a clan to call home, then you'll wait.*

Her dragon roared as loudly as she could. *No. He kissed us. He started it. If he can't finish it, it's his own fault.*

I will wait for him. I want him and only him.

Any cock will do. Find one for me. I'm tired of waiting.

Arabella wasn't sure if she wanted to cry or to punch the wall. Her strength was going fast. If Finn didn't find her soon, she might not be able to control her dragon.

For the first time since reestablishing communication with her beast, Arabella yearned for the previous decade of silence.

She was out of options. Not even wrangling out her own orgasm had helped. If anything, her beast was more impatient.

Where the fuck was Finn?

As her beast started another tantrum, Arabella debated ringing someone for a sedative when the door to her room slid open.

Finn stood naked in the doorway.

His face was drawn. Even though his pupils were slitted, there was a mixture of exhaustion and something else she couldn't define.

She was about to ask what happened when her dragon snarled, *No talking. Fuck him. Now. Or I will push you aside.*

Arabella knew she was close to burning out, so she whispered, "Finn, please."

With a growl, Finn stepped inside, locked the door, and moved to the foot of the bed. "Tell me you're ready, Ara."

The second she answered, "Yes," Finn's body covered hers.

His lips touched hers right before his tongue slid into her mouth. The combined feel of his heat on her skin and his strong strokes helped to calm her dragon a fraction.

But only a fraction. Her beast demanded, *He's here. Fuck him. We must carry his young and claim him.*

Too tired to fight, Arabella grabbed Finn's arse with her hands and rubbed against him. His hard cock pressed against her stomach, which only made her pussy pulse with need. If she didn't fuck him soon, she'd die.

Her dragon hissed. *More. Tell him we're ready or I will.*

Not wanting to break Finn's possessive kiss, she needed another way to tell him because Arabella wanted to be the one in control when she lost her virginity. The frenzy would make everything rushed, but she'd waited a long time for this moment and she would claim it.

Because their bodies were smothered together, Arabella couldn't reach Finn's cock and position him at her entrance.

Instead, she wrapped her legs around his waist and moved. The friction sent a rush of wetness between her legs.

Her dragon growled. *Need him. Now.*

Hearing the thread of insanity in her beast's words, Arabella would soon be too weak to fight off her dragon. A tiny part of her hated the fact she would soon be lost to the mate claim-frenzy. Not just because her dragon would be in charge, but also because Finn was attentive, but she sensed something was wrong.

Then Finn's kiss became even more possessive as their teeth clashed once in the attempt to brand each other. He raised his chest and balanced on one forearm as he reached for her nipple and tugged. Arabella moaned, her instinct taking over her brain.

Reaching down between them, she took his cock in hand and squeezed. Finn broke the kiss and hissed.

Whatever had been in Finn's eyes earlier had been replaced with a burning lust and possessiveness that only made Arabella wetter than she'd ever been in her life. She was ready.

Finn growled, "Mine. Now."

"Yes," she answered and he ran a finger between her pussy lips.

Arabella arched her back. The pounding ache between her legs increased, matching the rapid beat of her heart. As he continued to stroke and tease with light caresses, she growled, "Stop waiting. I need you. Fuck me. Now."

Finn positioned his cock and thrust.

She cried out, the fullness and slight sting easing her itch to mate a little. Somewhere in the back of her mind, she acknowledged the loss of her virginity. But then her mate growled, "Mine," and he moved. The feel of his hard cock made her forget everything but her dragon's instinct to mate.

Arabella reached for his back and scraped her nails. Both human and dragon halves did it again, hoping to draw blood to brand him.

In response, Finn took her breast in his hand and squeezed before rubbing her pointed nipples against his rough palm. She whispered, "Finn."

Even to her own ears, she sounded as if she were begging.

Lowering his head, he took her nipple into his mouth and sucked hard. Digging her nails in his back, he bit her gently and she cried out.

Then the bastard hummed against her sensitive flesh and the vibrations nearly sent her over the edge.

Her dragon roared. *Not enough. He needs to move and fuck us hard, very hard.*

Since Finn seemed intent on sucking and teasing her nipple, she would take matters into her own hands. While Arabella had no bloody idea of what she was doing, she fell back on instinct and moved her hips back and forward.

It wasn't the most graceful of moves, but Finn released her nipple with a pop and met her eyes. Daring him, she moved her hips again.

With a growl, he took her wrists in his hands and pinned them over her head. "I will claim you."

Being held down didn't scare her. If anything, it made her skin flush hotter. "Then claim me."

Finn pulled nearly all the way out and then thrust in hard. Arabella closed her eyes as she moaned and savored the feel of her dragonman's cock inside of her. She waited for him to move again, but Finn stayed still. His gravelly voice filled her eyes. "Eyes open. Now. Or I leave."

Her dragon hissed. *He wouldn't dare. I won't let him.*

Then her beast tried to take control, but Arabella drew on the last of her strength to keep her dragon back. As soon as she opened her eyes and met Finn's gaze, he moved as he growled, "Mine."

"Not yet. Try harder."

Finn thrust in and out, increasing with each movement until the bed shook with his efforts. Every long stroke brought her dragon's lust to the forefront of their mind, but Arabella held on. She was close.

She was so lost in the lust and possessiveness of Finn's eyes that his finger brushing against her clit was a surprise and she arched her back. She'd barely caught her breath when Finn pinched her clit and lights danced across her eyes as pleasure rushed through her body.

Her pussy clenched and released Finn's cock, but he never stopped moving. Each hard thrust deepened the intensity of her orgasm. Maybe Finn would kill her with pleasure.

Finn finally stilled and roared as he came. Because of them being true mates, each spurt of his semen made her orgasm, with each one harder than the last. She wasn't sure if she wanted to moan or cry out.

Then Finn kissed her neck, her jaw, and her lips. As his tongue invaded her mouth, Arabella gripped her dragonman closer. Unlike back in the clearing, when she'd come from his tongue, she wasn't satisfied. Both dragon and human halves demanded more, much more.

Breaking the kiss, Finn met her eyes. "My dragon wants out. Let yours out with me."

Her beast roared. *Yes. We need more sex, much more. Until we carry his young, we haven't claimed him completely. You dawdle. I will claim him properly.*

No penis breaking.

I can't promise anything. I'll do whatever I can to get with child.

Too tired to argue, Arabella lightly brushed her fingers across the back of Finn's neck. "Kiss me first."

With a growl, Finn took her lips again. The taste of Finn in her mouth made her dragon push for control. This time, Arabella let go.

Lust and need filled her body to the point of pain. Only an orgasm would help ease it a fraction.

Then Finn, still hard inside her, broke the kiss and moved. Arabella was slightly aware as her beast controlled her human body. Clawing Finn's back, they both moved.

There was no gentle kisses or light caresses. With the two dragons in charge, it was fucking, pure and simple.

Before Arabella came, Finn did this time. Yet his semen made her come over and over again.

Finn pulled out and her dragon growled, "Why? Not enough. Need more."

His eyes flashed before he flipped her on her stomach and raised her hips. Slapping her arse, he positioned his cock at her pussy. Through gritted teeth, he asked, "Ready for more?"

Wiggling her hips in response, Finn thrust into her pussy hard. Not missing a beat, he started a strong rhythm. Each movement reached deeper, to a place she hadn't known existed.

Arabella moaned as she raised her arse. A pulsing need to have Finn come inside of her again filled her entire body. Until she was pregnant, he wasn't truly theirs. Only carrying his child would embed his scent into her skin.

Moving with him, Arabella's dragon spoke into their mind. *Yes, more, harder. His cock is ours and ours alone. Let's make sure he knows it.*

Her dragon moved their hips in time to Finn's rhythm. The sound of flesh slapping against flesh filled the room. Beyond a series of grunts, there were no voices.

Hovering in the back of her mind, Arabella wished she had the strength to wrestle back control. She missed Finn's human half being in control. She wanted their teasing.

Yet as her dragon roared for more, Arabella knew she wouldn't have Finn or control of her body until she was pregnant.

~~~

Finn was half-dozing in the back of his mind as his dragon stilled in their human form and came inside Arabella for the umpteenth time. He had no idea how many days had past, but his twisting stomach told him it was time to let their mate rest and eat again.

Mustering up the strength to talk with his dragon, his human form collapsed on top of Arabella. Her sweet scent of wild grass and something uniquely hers surrounded him. Yet after a second, he noticed another undercurrent to her scent.

Instantly alert, Finn reached out to his beast. *Is it true? Tell me.*

His dragon paused as he took a few more inhalations and then let out a sigh. *Yes. She carries our child. No one else will try to steal her.*

Happiness shot through his body. He was going to be a father. *Then let me take control. I want to hold our pregnant mate.*

Yawning, his dragon moved to the back of his mind. *Go ahead. My job is done. I want a nap.*

Rather than reply, Finn moved from lying on top of his mate to the side and brushed Arabella's cheek. Her eyes fluttered open. Since her pupils were still slitted, her dragon had no idea the frenzy was over. It wasn't surprising since male dragon-shifters could always tell first.

He smiled. "Tell your dragon to bugger off."

Her eyes flashed and her gravelly voice replied, "More. One more time and then we rest."

"No. It's done. Give Ara back to me."

Arabella's dragon eyes searched his for a second. "If you are in charge, it must be true."

"Of course it's bloody true. Now, give me my mate."

"You get both of us."

He opened his mouth, but then Arabella's pupils turned round and she blinked. Looking up to Finn, she asked, "Are you sure?"

"Why? Are you in need of more sex? I thought days on end would soothe even your appetite."

She frowned. "I'm too tired to argue. Just tell me if it's done."

He placed a hand over her lower belly. "It's done."

A bevy of emotions flashed in Arabella's eyes, although relief and joy were the most prominent. "Thank fuck, because I'm beyond tired. It's going to take days of hot baths to ease the soreness between my legs."

He chuckled and lowered his head to nuzzle her cheek. "You mostly laid there. I'm the one who's tired, and do you hear me complaining?"

"You would be if I hadn't prevented my dragon from breaking you."

Raising an eyebrow, he caressed her cheek. "She wouldn't stand a chance against my dragon."

"Later, when I'm not so bloody tired, we can let the beasts out and settle this."

"No."

"What do you mean no? Are you afraid you'll lose?"

He moved closer, the mixture of his scent and hers reminding him of their child. Leave it to Arabella to turn this moment into a contest instead of a celebration. "No, I'm not allowing my dragon to take you for a long time. I need to test your patience and make you beg without your dragon's need forcing you to do it." He kissed her ear and whispered, "I want to treasure you properly."

He moved back to look at her face. Her frown eased. "You're spouting fancy words. I'm not sure if I should be happy or worried."

"For once, you infuriating dragonwoman, can you let me be sincere?" He rubbed his hand on her belly in slow circles. "You are giving me a child. There is no greater gift to a dragon-shifter."

Arabella's eyes softened. "Finn, I—" she paused and then continued, "It's still sinking in, is all. Right now, I just want to eat and then sleep in your arms. Can you do that without making me fight you for it?"

Brushing the dark smudge under her left eye and then the right one, he murmured, "As long as I get to hold you after we eat, then I'll let you sleep."

He expected a challenge, but Arabella just snuggled into his chest. "On second thought, let's sleep first." She yawned. "I want my wits about me before you try to make deals in exchange for food, which I'm sure you'll do." Looking up, her eyes were tender. "Also, maybe after the nap, everything will sink in and become more concrete. I'm sure then I can guilt trip you into doing whatever I want."

"Oh, aye? Simpering and subservient would be boring."

She snuggled her head into his chest. "As if you would ever be that."

The sight of Arabella curled up against him warmed his heart. While he knew the clan and all of its problems lay outside the door, he wasn't ready to face it just yet. He wanted just a little bit longer with his mate.

Besides, a tired clan leader made mistakes. He needed the rest as much as Arabella.

Settling on his pillow, he hugged Arabella tightly. "A quick nap, then. But don't try to sneak out and eat without me. I could eat a mountain's worth of food right now."

Her voice was sleepy as she patted his chest. "I know you like to talk, but just go to sleep."

Finn closed his eyes and laid his head against Arabella's. Her scent calmed him enough to fall asleep with a smile on his face.

CHAPTER TWENTY-ONE

Finn woke up with Arabella asleep on his chest. He half expected his dragon to demand more sex, but then he remembered the truth—Arabella was pregnant.

Over the last week, his need to mate had battled with sadness. But in that second, every worry vanished as happiness warmed his heart. He would be a father.

Dragon-shifters treasured children, yes, but as Finn smoothed a few strands of hair from Arabella's cheek, he was grateful that Arabella would be the mother of his child. Stronger than almost anyone he knew, as well as clever, she would make a fine mother. Their baby would be a second chance at family for them both.

True, he had the MacKenzies, but being a parent would be entirely different.

Thinking of his second family, sadness squeezed Finn's heart again. As much as he wanted only to focus on the happy, he needed to find out what had happened during his time trapped by the mate-claim frenzy. Was his cousin all right? Were the traitors contained? So many questions, but so few answers; he hated it.

His dragon huffed. *You put good clan members in charge. Stop worrying.*

Kissing Arabella's forehead, Finn moved slowly until his mate was sleeping on the pillow instead of his chest. The circles under her eyes told him she needed more rest. She might hate him later, but he would give her the rest she needed while he checked in with the clan.

His dragon grumbled. *She will be angry.*

I know, but she needs sleep. I will fill her in later.

Don't complain to me later when she yells.

Too tired to argue, Finn quietly snuck out of the safe room. Grant and Aunt Lorna were sitting at a table on the other side of the door.

While Finn didn't usually care about nakedness, he wished his aunt would look away. He was tired and covered in Arabella's scent; he needed a shower.

Aunt Lorna clicked her tongue. "Six days is pretty good, although your uncle only took five and gave me twins to boot."

So, it'd been six days.

He scrutinized his aunt, looking for the slightest sign of worry. Yet her face was relaxed and her smile seemed genuine. "You wouldn't be so calm unless Faye had pulled through."

Lorna's gaze turned soft. "Aye, she's alive although she hasn't been allowed to shift back into her human form yet."

His aunt's tone told him she was hiding something, and Aunt Lorna never held back. "What aren't you telling me?"

When Lorna's eyes turned wet, Grant answered, "Faye will live, but she may never fly again."

Finn felt as if he'd been punched in the stomach. "What?"

Grant embellished more. "When she landed on her wing, Faye broke too many bones. Some are knitting back together strangely, despite the doctors' best efforts. We won't know for sure until Faye's completely healed, but there's always the chance she won't fly again."

Lorna straightened her shoulders. "Aye, but Faye's a fighter. She won't give up easily."

Finn wanted to agree and say everything would be fine, but he wouldn't give false hope. "I need to see her."

He moved toward the bathroom on the far side to clean up and his stomach rumbled at the same time as his step faltered. Lorna's steely voice filled the room. "You will shower, eat, and take care of your pregnant mate first. You put me, Grant, and Meg Boyd in charge. So far, we're doing just fine. That bastard, Duncan, is still in custody, as are several of his lackeys. The DDA is taking care of the Dragon Knights for the time being. And Stonefire still has reinforcements on our land. The clan can wait twenty minutes for you to be more presentable."

Finn looked over his shoulder and frowned. "I lost six days, Auntie. Arabella's sleeping right now, so let me do my job."

Arabella's voice floated from behind him. "Arabella's awake and wants to know what the bloody hell is going on."

Finn turned around. Arabella had her arms crossed over her chest and her left eyebrow quirked. Somewhere in the back of his mind, he registered the fact she was naked, but since she carried his baby and his scent, his dragon didn't worry about other males stealing her away.

Ignoring the rumbling in his stomach, Finn answered, "You should be sleeping. Why are you awake?"

Arabella rolled her eyes. "I'm pregnant, not injured. My brain still works." Her eyes turned serious. "I noticed the sadness in your eyes the very first day you came to me, and judging by Aunt Lorna's still wet eyes, something is going on. Now, tell me what happened."

~~~

Waking up alone had scared Arabella for a second, until she'd heard voices from the other side of the door. Despite her exhaustion and feeling more peckish than she had ever been in her life, she made it to the door and asked Finn to explain.

She didn't falter under his scrutinizing gaze. Arabella knew full well from her time around her brother and his mate how protective male dragon-shifters could be when it came to a pregnant female, but she wasn't about to let Finn coddle her.

Finn's stern expression melted into one of exhaustion and sadness. The sight erased most of her irritation. While she didn't like being in the dark, she liked her mate's sadness even less. She would wrangle the truth from him, but in a rare moment, he needed her support and she would give it.

Knowing touch would help, Arabella walked up to Finn and wrapped her arms around him. "Tell me, Finn. I can't help you if you don't explain what's happening."

Finn hugged her close. "Faye was hurt during the Dragon Knights' attack and landed on her wing. It broke, but it's not healing properly. She might not fly again."

While her heart squeezed, Arabella pushed it away. She needed to be strong not only for Finn, but for Faye as well.

Lifting her head, she narrowed her eyes. "Don't pity her, Finlay Stewart. Believe me, that's the last thing she wants in her situation."

Finn cupped her cheek. "Aye, you're right." The corner of his mouth ticked up. "Although I can't believe I just admitted it."

"I would slap you, but I'm hungry and you need to feed me so I can visit Faye, too."

His eyes turned concerned. "I'm not sure if that's the best idea. Maybe you should sit down. After all, you're still recovering from the frenzy and look exhausted."

"Are you listening? I'm fine."

Finn growled. "The circles under your eyes tell me the truth. If you won't take care of yourself, then I'll have to force you to do it."

Father of her child or not, Arabella was tempted to punch him. Bloody dragon-shifter males and their overprotectiveness. He was going to drive her crazy. She needed to set him straight early.

Her dragon rumbled and her voice was sleepy when she said, *Grab his cock and threaten to bend it in half. He'll stop after that.*

Ignoring her beast, Arabella moved one of her hands to take Finn's chin. "Force me? Are you daft? Let's get this straight right now, Finlay. Coddle me and there will be consequences. If I need help, I'll ask for it. Until then, I won't be contained or isolated as I was for nearly a decade. If that means kicking you in the balls every day to remind you of that, I'll do it."

He frowned. "I'm not coddling. I want to protect you."

"Same difference," she retorted. She looked down at his penis and back again. "Do I need to give you a demonstration?"

He stared at her a second before replying, "No kicking is needed for now, at least. We can iron out the details later, once everything is settled. For the time being, I'll allow you to visit Faye."

Arabella narrowed her eyes. "Allow me? I'll give you ten seconds to rephrase that before I use my knee."

Finn's voice was gravelly when he replied, "Don't push me, lass. I can only rein in my dragon's protective nature so far."

"Then work on it. If you learned how to construct a maze for your beast, you can figure a way to rein him in when it comes to overprotectiveness."

He stared and she stared back. Finally, Finn sighed. "Fine, I'll try, but I can't make any promises. Just promise me you won't go outside of Lochguard's land without telling me. If you can do that, I'll trust you to be sensible."

It was on the tip of her tongue to keep arguing until she had complete freedom, but for a dragon male to give even a little was a huge step. She may not like it, but Arabella knew Finn couldn't completely ignore his dragon's nature.

Of course, that didn't mean she wouldn't fight with him again to obtain more control. For the moment, Faye and the clan were more important.

She nodded. "We can fine tune the agreement later, but for now, I promise to let you know when I plan to leave Lochguard."

Relief flashed in Finn's eyes before he cupped her cheek. "Thank you."

He leaned down to kiss her, but then Arabella remembered about their audience. She patted his chest and looked over to the table. Both Lorna and Grant were unabashedly watching them.

Finn's growl rumbled under her hand on his chest and she resisted rolling her eyes. Maybe this was payback for all the times she'd teased her sister-in-law Melanie about how Tristan had acted during her pregnancy.

Finn's steely voice filled the room. "The show's over." Finn looked to his aunt. "Auntie, can you fetch us something while I'm in the shower?" Lorna raised her brows and Finn sighed. "Please?"

Lorna stood. "Aye, I can. Although it might be more beneficial if I stayed to help keep your foot out of your mouth.

But you're a grown male and you'll learn." She motioned toward Grant. "Besides, Grant is better at clan logistics than I and can give a more complete report."

Arabella acknowledged Grant for the first time. "Um, hi." Grant bobbed his head and Arabella dared to ask, "Did broadcasting the security feed go well?"

Finn growled. "Arabella, not now."

She looked to him. "Hush. This concerns your clan so you should be curious, too."

Finn's tone was dry. "You're going to tell me how to do my job now?"

"When have I stopped?" She looked back to Grant. "Well?"

Grant answered, "For the most part, yes. I have a recording you can watch when you're ready. Just know that the Dragon Knights are contained, at least, for the moment." Grant glanced to Finn and Finn nodded. Grant looked back to her and nodded. "You can listen in while I debrief Finn later."

Arabella smiled. "Good."

Her stomach growled and Finn took her hand. Tugging her toward the bathroom, Finn shouted to Grant, "We'll be out in ten minutes. Have everything ready by then, including a status report on Faye."

Finn didn't even wait for a response before he pulled her inside the bathroom, locked the door and frowned. "I don't care if you order Grant around, but don't do it in front of the clan, Arabella. Understood? Things are still raw and unpredictable."

"The longer you have me hide in the corner, the less likely the clan will accept me as your partner."

Finn blinked. "Partner?"

"Bloody hell, Finn, do you know me at all? Yes, partner. Did you not see my brilliant strategy to help you last week? You were taking care of Duncan, and I found a way to bring the media into it."

"Aye, I vaguely heard about it. Though I have yet to see the footage myself."

"And what about the DDA? They came to help as well," Arabella added.

For one of the only times since arriving on Lochguard, Arabella couldn't read Finn's expression.

Her dragon jumped in. *Does he truly not realize we are brilliant? Maybe we should withhold sex until he does.*

As if you could last that long.

Her dragon grunted. *I could if I tried.*

Finn's stern voice interrupted her conversation. "Make sure you fully understand what you're asking for, Ara. You can't be a full-time IT security person, a mother, and half of a dragon-shifter clan leader." He placed a hand over her lower abdomen. "The mother part you can't give up. Can you really give up computers to help with the clan?"

"Yes," she answered without hesitation. "Although I'm sure I can do a little dabbling for fun in my free time once I've screened the current IT team."

Finn smiled. "I think you just like being in charge."

Arabella placed her hand over Finn's. "No, not in charge, a co-leader. I have a feeling it'll come in handy for our little mini-me once she's born."

"A lass, eh? The odds are against you."

"I'm pretty good at beating the odds."

As they stared at one another, Arabella's heart warmed. There was so much she wanted to say and ask, but there were too many responsibilities to take care of. If she truly wanted to be

Finn's partner, she had to learn how to sacrifice her own desires sometimes. The present was one of those times.

Besides, Faye needed them. Arabella thought of the lively young dragonwoman as her friend. Arabella understood better than anyone what might lay ahead for Faye MacKenzie. Arabella had her own recovery suggestions, ones that lacked smothering, and she planned to implement them as soon as possible.

Her stomach twisted in hunger again, reminding her that the clock was ticking.

Arabella patted Finn's hand and walked toward the shower. Turning the water on, she stepped back and looked at her mate. "The lovey dovey stuff will have to wait, Finn. I want to make our child proud, and that means showering, eating, and sorting out Faye and the clan as best as we can. That's what a clan leader would do, right?"

"Yes, exactly." Finn's gaze turned fierce. He walked to her and whispered, "I love you, Arabella MacLeod," before he kissed her and tugged her into the shower.

Arabella was still trying to think how to respond, when Finn turned her around and scrubbed her back. As he sang a song in the wrong key, she smiled. He was giving her time and space to figure things out for herself.

Jumping on the distraction, Arabella joined him and sang as loudly as she could. Looking over her shoulder, Finn shook his head but never stopped the song.

Finn had claimed her with his body, but he was quickly claiming her heart as well.

~~~

Finn stood with Arabella outside the tent serving as Faye's hospital room.

The shower and plate of sandwiches had helped erase some of his exhaustion. Compared to the three days he'd spent foraging food during the clan leader trials, Aunt Lorna's sandwiches had been heaven and he was ready to tackle his cousin, especially with Arabella at his side.

Glancing at Arabella, he was amazed she looked as refreshed as she did. Some dragonwomen experienced early pregnancy symptoms, such as lethargy and morning sickness.

Not that it should surprise him that Arabella was handling it well. His female could handle anything she put her mind to if she tried.

Arabella frowned and lightly hit his side. "Stop staring. Your gaze only encourages my dragon."

Because of the levity of the minutes to come, Finn jumped on a few minutes of peace with Arabella. "Oh, aye? She's ready for more of my wondrous cock? She never did get her fill, now did she?"

Arabella sighed. "I'm not going to answer that."

He grinned. "I knew there had to be a reason why she didn't break my penis when she had the chance."

Arabella rolled her eyes and looked over at him. "We're here to see your cousin, not discuss your cock."

Layla's voice interrupted them. "As much as Faye needs a bit of normalcy, I don't think she wants to hear about her cousin's penis."

Finn looked to Layla and winked. "Aye, you're right. Although I have other ways to raise my cousin's spirits."

Layla's eyes turned sympathetic and she lowered her voice. "She needs some cheering up, but no one seems to know how. Not even her twin brothers could get a response from her."

Finn's smile died. "Tell me what we need to know, Layla, and the full truth."

Layla nodded, her long, dark braid bouncing behind her. "She's out of danger and will recover. However, I won't know until we take the cast off her wing later this week if she can fly again or not. If the tissue is too knotted or the bones don't mend right, it could throw off her balance."

Arabella asked, "Has she been cooped up inside this tent the whole time?" Layla bobbed her head and Arabella frowned. "Is there any way to remove the outside walls of the tent, even for part of a day? I'd be depressed if I had to stay inside that thing with nothing to do, too."

Layla tapped her chin. "Possibly. It will take some convincing of the more senior doctors, but I'll see what I can do."

Finn jumped in. "As long as it won't endanger her health, make sure the others know I wish it to happen, too. My word may give you the leverage you need."

"I will." Layla turned and parted the slit opening. "Come. You should visit her while she's still awake."

Taking a deep breath, Finn walked into the tent. After blinking to adjust his eyes, he took in the sight before him.

Faye was curled up in a ball, her head tucked under her tail. While the pose wasn't unusual for a sleeping or resting dragon, the dull color of her blue hide alarmed him; the tint was faded, almost as if she were an old dragon-shifter in her twilight years.

The tent was also dim, hiding the last few sunny days of September. Finn squeezed her hip. She looked to him and asked, "What?"

"I think you're right about getting Faye into the sunshine. It should help."

At the mention of her name, Faye raised her head and met his eyes with her own. The despair and pity he saw knocked the wind from him.

But only for a second. Finn raised an eyebrow. "If you're trying to get me to pamper you, it's not going to work, cousin. If it weren't for the frenzy, I would've come sooner and kicked your arse into gear."

Faye lowered her head and closed her eyes.

She'd never had such a lack of spirit in her life.

Arabella moved from his side and went to Faye's ear. She whispered something and then waited. When Faye didn't move, Arabella grabbed a small piece of Faye's ear and twisted.

Faye roared. For a split second, Finn's heart stopped as he worried Faye would knock Arabella across the room. But leave it to his mate to slap Faye's snout and order, "Stop it. Do you really want to hurt Finn's offspring? I have a feeling it might piss him off, not to mention me. You really don't want to anger the pair of us. We'll win against you, even if your brothers jump in to help you."

Faye glanced from Arabella to Finn and back again. She then moved her snout to Arabella's abdomen and inhaled deeply. After a second, the sadness eased a fraction from her eyes. There was still enough there to depress a lesser dragon-shifter, but even lifting a little warmed Finn's heart.

He took a step toward Faye's snout. "Arabella's right. If you want to be an auntie, then you'd better behave. That means stop pitying yourself. If Arabella can survive her ordeal, you can survive yours."

Faye bumped her snout against Finn's stomach, as if to tell him to bugger off. He stroked her hide. "I'm not leaving you alone, so don't waste your energy." Then he steeled his voice and ordered, "Get better as soon as possible so I can hear your brief of what happened. We can't guard against new threats without information."

His cousin looked into his eyes. He couldn't read her expression, but he wanted to believe she was a little better. Maybe her mother and brothers had felt sorry for her; as he'd learned with Arabella that was the exact wrong thing to do with strong, alpha dragonwomen.

Arabella spoke up. "Finn, could you give us a few minutes? I want to talk with Faye alone."

"You're not plotting a clan takeover, are you?"

She scowled. "Be serious for a second. Besides, if I wanted to take over the clan, you wouldn't know about it until it'd already happened."

His dragon chuckled. *I like her.*

Shut it, dragon. You wouldn't be so cheerful if it happened.

I don't know. She likes me.

Finn gave an exaggerated sigh. "I see I'm unwanted. I guess becoming the father of your child didn't earn me any extra brownie points."

Arabella pointed toward the exit. "Out. See about taking the outer wall of the tent down."

Giving his cousin's snout one last pat, he murmured, "Don't make her mad, cousin. The pregnancy is making her bossier and I wouldn't want to be on the receiving end of her temper."

Arabella growled. "You will be unless you leave in the next ten seconds."

Winking at his mate, Finn turned and left the tent. He spotted the doctor in charge and headed toward him. The sooner he made Faye comfortable, the sooner he could go back and hear Grant's updates on the clan. From what he'd seen during his brief visit, Faye should be all right in time, especially with her family behind her. Arabella alone would singlehandedly prod Faye until she gave in and did whatever Arabella asked.

His clan, however, would no doubt be fractured after the recent attack. Finn needed to make things right with them as soon as possible. Both his mate and his future child needed a stable, safe home. He'd do everything in his power to ensure Lochguard would be it.

~~~

Arabella waited about thirty seconds to ensure Finn was gone before she turned back toward Faye. The blue dragon's eyes were closed again, but if Faye was hinting she wanted Arabella gone, she was in for a surprise.

Arabella touched the corner of one eye and poked one of the most sensitive areas on a dragon until Faye blew air out her nose and opened her eyelids. Arabella removed her finger. "Better. Close your eyes again, and I'll just start all over again. You have older brothers, so I'm sure you know that area can get sore pretty quickly." Faye grunted and Arabella continued, "Right. Then listen closely because this is one of the most important periods in your life. You can either choose to hide away from your friends and family to feel sorry for yourself or you can face your tragedy and become a stronger person."

Arabella stared at Faye, waiting for a sign the dragon woman was listening. When the blue dragon turned her head a few inches toward Arabella, she took it as a sign to push on. Arabella crossed her arms over her chest. "My past makes me one of the few people to truly understand you. Yes, we went through different tragedies, but a head Protector maybe losing her ability to fly is traumatic in its own way. I wish I'd had someone to kick my arse into gear ten years ago, but no one stepped up." Arabella leaned a fraction toward Faye. "Just know that I'm here and I'm going to bug you every day until you stop the self-pity and start fighting for what you want." Arabella smiled. "And I should warn you that I'm pretty stubborn when I set my mind to it. I'm sure I can have your brothers, Finn, and half a dozen other people helping me to get you back on your feet.

"So nod if you want to fight for your future or close your eyes if you're going to wallow about life being unfair. Which future do you want, Faye MacKenzie?"

As Faye's giant dragon eyes searched hers, Arabella tightened her grip on her forearms. Maybe she was pushing too far, but Arabella remembered how quickly she'd hid from the world. After all, hiding had been the easiest thing to do.

She wanted Faye to know she could fight before hiding was even an option.

One minute ticked by and then another. Finally, Faye bobbed her head and Arabella clapped her hands. "Fantastic." She moved to pet Faye's snout. "Then spend the rest of the week resting and visualizing yourself flying again. Once the cast comes off, we'll think of how to get you back into the skies."

Faye grunted, sounding as if she didn't believe it would ever happen.

Still, the dragonwoman had admitted to wanting to fight, and that was a huge step. One that had taken Arabella nearly ten years to reach.

Sunlight filtered in and she turned her head from the brightness. After blinking a few times, she watched as one section of the tent opened to reveal Finn and a few other dragon-shifters rolling up the side canvas. Leaning toward the opening, Arabella asked, "Is more coming down? You can barely see the sky with that small opening."

Finn answered, "Well, that depends if you ask me nicely or not."

Arabella growled. "Making your cousin happy should not require irritating me. I'm growing a tiny dragon-shifter inside me, remember? You're the one who's supposed to be nice to me."

Signaling to someone at his side, another section started to come down. "Nice is boring, heather. The baby will only get you so many passes, so choose them wisely."

"Bloody irritating man."

"That's dragonman, love. And don't forget it."

Arabella turned her back on Finn and he laughed. She whispered in Faye's ear, "See what I have to put up with? I need your help to torture him, so get better sooner rather than later."

Something that resembled amusement flashed in Faye's eyes and it warmed Arabella's heart. With time and hard work, Faye would probably avoid Arabella's fate after the dragon hunters tortured her.

Thinking about her past, she placed a hand over her belly. She had yet to tell Finn the whole of it and a part of her wanted to do it as soon as possible. As long as she kept the memories bottled up inside, she couldn't truly focus on her child, let alone Finn and the clan.

Glancing over her shoulder, she decided she would tell him on the walk back toward the command center. Sure, it may not be the best time to do it, but if she put it off, Arabella might lose her nerve. From here on out, there would be a multitude of distractions—mating Finn, sorting out traitors, reestablishing a relationship with the local human villages, and more. She couldn't afford to wait or her baby could be born before she had another chance.

Faye gently butted her shoulder and Arabella looked up into the big dragon's eye. It was almost as if Faye could read her mind.

Arabella patted her snout and murmured, "I have some matters to sort out, but I'll be back. Enjoy the sunshine."

With that, she headed out the door and around the tent to watch Finn help the others take down the last outer panel of canvas. Her dragon was still sleepy and recovering from the frenzy, but she woke up for a second to say, *Ours.*

In that, Arabella agreed.

~~~

Finn felt Arabella's gaze on his back as he helped to take down the walls of the tent.

All he wanted to do was quiz her about her conversation with Faye. Even from the few glimpses he'd stolen here and there during the takedown process, Finn could tell something was different about Faye MacKenzie. Whatever Arabella had told her was helping.

A year ago, he would've resented the fact Arabella had helped his family when he couldn't. In the present, however, he was grateful for having Arabella MacLeod in his life. He would never take her for granted.

Not just because he loved her or the fact she would give him a child; no, his clan would be worse off without her. He was starting to lean on her bit by bit, lessening his own load.

After another week, Arabella would feel right at home giving orders.

The thought made him smile.

The last piece of the outer canvas came down and Finn handed his section to the two younger dragon-shifters helping. He flashed the young dragonwoman a smile and gripped the young dragonman's shoulder. They both blinked a second before mumbling goodbyes and carrying the canvas away.

His dragon spoke up. *You shouldn't flirt with other females.*

I wasn't flirting. I merely smiled.

I don't think our mate will see it that way.

You're tired and grumpy. Go back to sleep.

Before his beast could reply, Finn constructed a complex maze and shoved his dragon inside. Since his beast was still recovering from the frenzy, he would merely go to sleep instead of trying to find the exit.

Finn walked over to Arabella and leaned down to kiss her when she turned her head. For a second, he thought she'd bring up flirting, but she surprised him by saying, "Are you going to stop calling me heather? Now that the frenzy is over, I'm determined to stop the ridiculous nickname."

Taking her chin with his fingers, he forced her head back to look him in the eye. "Deep down, I know you like it. Just think, one day you can regale our child with the tale of how I came up with the clever name."

Arabella rolled her eyes. "More like I can use the story on what not to do when courting a female."

Finn leaned toward his mate. "I think it worked pretty well, don't you think, heather?"

She growled, but he stopped her with a quick, rough kiss. When he pulled away, Arabella's irritated look had been replaced with one of heat. But a second later, she frowned. "We need to head back to the command center, but just know this isn't over."

Finn grinned and hooked his arm around Arabella's shoulders. "Of course not. We have a good seventy years to wage this battle."

Arabella shook her head. "I'm not sure if I should be happy or sad about that."

He growled. "Be happy, Arabella. You're not allowed to be sad." She glanced over at him with an unreadable expression. The sight made him a little uneasy. "Tell me what you're thinking about, love."

The change of endearment eased the tension under his arm. Arabella pointed toward one of the sheltered rock areas not too far away. "Let's go over there and I'll tell you, provided we have ten or fifteen minutes to spare. If not, it can wait."

From her tone, Finn guessed something was weighing her down and she needed to get it off her chest.

Taking out his mobile phone, he checked for any alerts, but there was nothing. He pocketed his phone and started walking. "We have a little time. Besides, you look like you could do with a few minutes of rest."

When Arabella nodded without a retort, his heart rate ticked up. Something serious was on his mate's mind.

As they walked toward the sheltered space in silence, Finn absently rubbed Arabella's arm, wondering what troubled his lass. If it was within his power to fix it, he would.

Arabella MacLeod deserved happiness, and despite his tendency to irritate her on purpose, he would always be the one to give it to her.

His dragon gave a half-hearted rumble from inside the maze, and Finn amended, *Okay, we will be the one to give it to her. Happy?*

A yawn echoed through his head and Finn took that as a yes.

They reached the sheltered space. Once he took off his shirt and laid it over a small boulder, he motioned toward it. "Now, sit down and tell me why you're being so quiet, Arabella. Because, frankly, your silence creeps me out a little."

CHAPTER TWENTY-TWO

Finn's comment snapped Arabella out of her head. "And to think, some people have mates who tell them how beautiful they are. I have one who tells me I'm creepy."

Finn shrugged. "You like honesty."

Arabella's dragon chimed in. *You're stalling. The sooner you tell him, the sooner you can truly put the past behind you. This is the final step to being whole and healthy.*

Final step? Since when are you a psychologist?

I'm a dragon. I know everything.

Not wanting to waste time arguing that point, Arabella looked back up to Finn. "Can you pretend you're a kind, caring mate for a second? What I have to say is serious."

Finn kneeled before her and took her hands. In a dramatic voice, he said, "Tell me, my lady. I am here to do your bidding."

Arabella sighed and decided he would keep being ridiculous to rile her up. Ignoring his statement, she took a deep breath and stated, "I want to tell you about the rest of my time with the dragon hunters."

Finn's exaggerated expression turned sincere. "Then tell me, Arabella. I want to hear it."

She looked away, but Finn squeezed her hands. Looking back, she drew on the strength in Finn's eyes. "If you remember, I was groggy and watching the dragon hunters beat my mother."

Finn nodded and she continued, "Well, I drew on my dragon's strength and managed to break free of my captors long enough to start shifting. My arms had barely started to grow before I was knocked on the head. I went down and my mother yelled my name."

Arabella paused, fighting the memory. Her mother's scream had been full of fear, more so than when her own life had been in danger. To Jocelyn MacLeod, her children's lives had always been more important than her own.

Finn's deep voice brought her back to the present. "And then what happened?"

Blinking her eyes to hold back her tears, she gripped Finn's hands tighter. The next part was the most difficult.

The memory hit her hard and fast. Burning flesh, screams, the stale scent of human males. As long as she lived, she'd never forget them.

"Arabella MacLeod-Stewart, look at me."

She frowned and met Finn's eyes. "I never said I was changing my name."

The corner of his mouth ticked up. "No, but it brought you back to me, love."

Searching her dragonman's brown eyes, a sense of calm came over her. Finn would always be able to bring her back from the memories, and realizing that warmed her heart.

Her dragon spoke up. *Then hurry up and tell him the rest. I can't sleep with all these bad memories coming back.*

Gee, thanks for the support, dragon.

I am supportive. You're just taking too long. Humans make everything complicated.

Arabella sighed and Finn asked, "What did Lady Dragon say now?"

"That humans are too complicated."

He grinned. "She's right, but the complicated makes life fun. If it were up to our dragons, we'd be eating, fucking, and flying all the time."

Her dragon huffed. *What's wrong with that? Life would be better.*

Arabella bit her lip and then said, "Yes, my dragon agrees."

Finn squeezed her hands again. "Now that you're at ease again, tell me the rest. We're not leaving here until you do."

She knew she was stalling, but she couldn't resist asking, "What if I said our little dragon baby wants some steak? You'd let me starve?"

Finn growled. "Don't bloody tease me about that. My dragon is already anxious enough without extra worry."

It was on the tip of her tongue to tease him some more, but her beast growled and Arabella decided to get it over with. "I call peace for the next twenty minutes, but I can't guarantee any more than that."

"Fine, just tell me about the bloody hunters, Ara. I want, no, *need* to know everything about you."

Turning her hands around in Finn's grip, she threaded her fingers through his and squeezed. No matter if she cried or broke down at some point during the retelling, Finn would be her rock.

She could do this and break with her past once and for all.

With a nod, she replied, "Okay." She took a deep breath and then forced the words out. "Once the hunters knocked me down, they flipped me over onto my back and pinned me." Finn moved until his front touched her knees. It helped to ground her. "They said real dragons would breathe fire and maybe I needed a little to calm down."

She moved her hand to touch her neck, but Finn squeezed her fingers and refused to let go. Drawing on his feelings for her, she swallowed and added, "Two of the hunters kept me pinned down when one left. I tried to break free, but with my forearms fractured, each movement sent a thousand pricks of pain coursing through my body. The adrenaline helped, but it still hurt." She closed her eyes. "If only I'd known that was tame compared to what was to come."

The scene with the two dragon hunters putting pressure on her arms to make her scream came rushing back. Despite her best efforts, Arabella had cried out and nearly sobbed. The only good from the situation was that they stopped beating her mother to deal with her.

One of the hunters suggested raping her first, but the other said they wouldn't dirty their dicks with dragon trash; the stench would never wash off.

"Arabella, I'll tape your eyes open if I need to. Look at me."

The steel in Finn's voice struck a chord and she opened her eyes. She nearly hugged him when she saw irritation rather than pity in his expression. "Give a dragonwoman some time, Finlay. This isn't easy for me."

"And you're stalling. Get to it already. I have other stuff to do."

She knew deep down that he would wait all day if she needed the time, but his comment reminded her of not only their clan, but her old one as well.

No more hiding.

She frowned at him. "It would be a lot easier if you stopped interrupting me."

He raised an eyebrow. "Dwell in a memory for too long and it takes over. Remember, lass, I've been where you were.

Watching my parents die in front of my eyes wasn't an easy thing to do."

"You still haven't told me how you survived."

He shook his head. "Until you tell me your story, you're going to keep wondering, too, heather."

Her dragon huffed. *Why aren't you done yet? I'm tired and hungry. Tell him or he'll never feed us.*

We just ate.

It's not nearly enough. Dragon babies take a lot of energy to grow.

Taking a deep breath, Arabella looked to the sky. The slow moving clouds helped to ease some of her anger and fear. Once she finished her duties, she should go for a quick flight and spread her wings to clear her head of the bastard hunters and how they'd destroyed her family.

Looking back to Finn, she forced her voice to work again. "One of the hunters came back with a petrol can. At first, I thought he was bluffing. Dragons were valued for their blood, so why would he want to kill one? If nothing else, I expected them to imprison me until I was an adult.

"Yet as he drew nearer, the smell of petrol grew stronger. Then he took off the cap and splashed a little on the ground. It was then I knew he wasn't bluffing."

The excitement and anticipation dancing in the dragon hunter's eyes haunted her to this day.

Finn moved closer and the memory of petrol was replaced with the mixture of wind and peat she had come to associate with her mate. Not wanting the memories to win, she continued, "The petrol-carrying hunter stopped next to me and then ordered my mother to be brought closer to watch. The hunter guarding her complied, and when my mum stared down at me, I was amazed at the strength in her eyes. Despite everything the hunters had done to her, she hadn't broken."

Finn nuzzled her cheek. "Your mum sounds a little like someone I know."

Arabella shook her head. "She never would've hid from the world like I did. My mother was so much stronger than I."

Moving back to look into her eyes, Finn murmured, "I'm going to argue that point later because you are bloody fantastic, Arabella MacLeod. But for now, you need to tell me the rest."

Even though the worst part of her memories were coming, her stomach was fairly calm. Yes, her palms were a little sweaty and her heart ached at the loss of her mother, but that wasn't that bad compared to her earlier setback when she'd run naked through Lochguard.

And it was all because of her mate, Finlay. Her heart warmed at just how much the dragonman had come to mean to her. She never would be calmly retelling a story about how she was tortured without him.

Never breaking eye contact with Finn, she continued, "As soon as my mum was standing close enough, the hunter standing over me sprinkled petrol on my neck. The instant the liquid hit my skin, dread pooled in my stomach. I tried to be strong like my mum, but when he moved to my arm and continued down my body, I started crying." Arabella looked away, toward the hills in the distance. "I begged for him to stop and asked why he would do this to me. And do you know what the hunter said?"

Finn's voice was steely yet gentle when he asked, "What?"

She looked back to his brown eyes and spat out, "That dragon-shifters only lived to be the play things of humans. Our lives didn't matter and I would learn that lesson."

Finn's pupils flashed to slits and back. "If the bastard isn't dead, I will find him and kill him very slowly."

While Finn's sentiment warmed her heart, she couldn't acknowledge it. Knowing her dragonman, he'd come up with elaborate revenge strategies on how to take down the Carlyle dragon hunters without breaking the law.

Arabella frowned. "The bastard's already dead, but I'm getting to that. If you'd let me finish, you'd know that."

"Staying quiet isn't my strong point, but I'll try harder. Get on with it."

Since her arse was numb, Arabella wiggled until she was more comfortable. She could tell Finn wanted to ask if she was all right, but to his credit, he kept his mouth shut.

Fighting a smile at Finn's clenched jaw, she cleared her throat. "After the hunter put me in my place, he dumped the last of the petrol on my leg and tossed the can aside. When he took out a lighter, I froze. He might be a hunter, but surely he wouldn't burn me alive.

"Then the determined glint in his eye confirmed that yes, he would do it."

Even though she was safe with Finn, her heart rate beat erratically. In that second, she was seventeen again and back on the ground, drenched in petrol, with a lighter a few feet away from her and no way to escape.

Her dragon growled. *I'm here and always will be. We survived. I won't let the memories hurt you.*

They always find a way to hurt me, especially in my dreams.

That's because I wasn't watching over you. Between Finn and I, you'll never have a nightmare again.

Her dragon's tone broke through some of her fear. *You seem quite confident.*

Of course. When am I not?

Arabella smiled at her dragon's words and Finn asked, "Arabella? Please tell me you're smiling at your dragon's words or I might actually start to worry a little."

Meeting Finn's gaze, she shook their joined hands. "Shush. I'm trying to tell a story."

Bowing his head, he murmured, "Then carry on, my lady."

Between Finn and her dragon, Arabella had the strength to continue. "Panic gripped my heart and ignoring the pain in my injured wrists, I struggled until I heard my mum humming an old tune. I met her eyes and she gave an imperceptible nod. She had a plan."

For a brief second, Arabella had believed her and her mum would both find a way home.

How naïve she'd been.

Getting ahead of herself, she forced her voice to work again. "The hunter flicked on a flame and it held since it was one of those fancy lighters that stay lit until you close the lid. He just stared at me with his excited eyes. I was too young to know it at the time, but in retrospect, it was excitement mixed with desire. The bastard got off on torturing dragons.

"The sight made me doubt my mum, and I struggled again. I managed to roll into the hunter above me and he dropped the lighter. While it missed my body, it caught on some of the petrol on the ground. A second later, it reached my arm and covered the right side of my body."

The flames had whooshed up her arm and to her neck, sending indescribable pain shooting through her body. It was as if instead of spilling a cup of boiling water on her hand, someone had dumped boiling water over half of her body.

Adrenaline and shock weren't enough to prevent her from screaming so hard her throat was raw.

Finn released one of her hands to cup her cheek. The gentle strokes of his thumb helped to numb the ghost pain of being burned alive.

Meeting his eyes, he simply nodded. He believed in her.

Clearing her throat, she was reminded that she wasn't trapped in the past. Her burns were healed and her throat was fine. "A few seconds later, my mum screamed. Despite the drugs they'd given her, she managed to shift one of her hands into talons and scraped the man holding her, and jumped on top of my body. I only vaguely remember her rolling me on the ground to douse the flames. At that point, my entire body throbbed and I was barely conscious."

Arabella's eyes prickled with tears and she closed her eyes to keep from crying. Her mother had sealed her fate by saving Arabella.

Finn stroked her cheek some more. "You're nearly there, heather. You're alive today, so tell me how."

Arabella squeezed her eyes tighter and Finn wiped the single tear that rolled down her cheek with his thumb. Then his lips kissed her skin where the tear had been.

Her dragon chimed in. *He cares for us. Tell him the rest. He has earned the full truth.*

It's not as easy as you think. Besides, you're encouraging me to finish so you can eat.

Maybe. I want to hunt. A dragon hunter or Dragon Knight would be tasty.

Sighing, Arabella opened her eyes. "Just to let you know, my dragon wants to eat one of our enemies."

The corner of Finn's mouth ticked up. "You wouldn't hear any complaints from me."

As she searched his eyes, she tried to remember what life had been without Finn. While she would always remember her niece, nephew, and Mel and Tristan, the rest was a blur. Finlay Stewart had not only brought light and laughter into her life, he'd seen the dragonwoman she could be and pried her out inch by inch until Arabella could stand up to the likes of Duncan Campbell without batting an eyelash.

And who knew for what reason, but she was falling for Finn, the cocky bastard.

Drawing on the warmth around her heart, Arabella decided she didn't want her torture to taint their future. It was time to say the rest and start fresh.

Frowning, she replied, "We can debate eating enemies later. Can you keep quiet for a minute more?"

He mouthed the words, "Maybe," and she rolled her eyes. Life with Finn would be anything but easy. Yet she wouldn't trade him for any other male.

Pushing aside thoughts of the future, she focused on finishing her story. "Once my mum extinguished the flames, she slapped the good side of my face and told me to stay awake. One of the hunters came at us, the one who had poured the petrol, and she turned to skewer his heart with her talons. Then she picked me up and ran to the nearby river. Just before she laid me on the water, her voice was stern as she told me she loved me and that I had better bloody well live. Tristan needed me.

"Using what little strength I had, I begged for her to join me, but she shook her head and said she needed to distract the hunters long enough for me to escape."

Her throat closed up. Breathing in and out a few times, she eased the tension in her throat. "Then the sound of the hunters drew closer. She laid me on my back in the water and yelled for me to keep afloat before she pushed me away. I was only half-conscious, but my dragon roared inside my head and kept me awake. Since I grew up in the Lake District, floating on my back was second nature to me."

She paused and her dragon growled. *Finish it.*

Reaching out her free hand, she touched Finn's cheek. The light stubble helped to ground her in the present. "Once I started to float downriver, my mum turned to face the hunters. I was about fifteen-feet down river when I watched my mum attack them. One of the hunters wrapped his arm around her neck while another punched her. Then the man behind her twisted her neck and she dropped to the ground."

Tears rolled down her cheeks and Finn opened his mouth, but Arabella cut him off. "As I watched my mum's murderers kick her lifeless body, I was too exhausted to even cry. My mum died saving me and all I could do was lie there and watch. No one was ever able to find her body, and I never had the chance to say goodbye or tell her one last time that I loved her."

Her voice cracked. She reached to wipe away the tears, but Finn's fingers beat her to it.

For a few seconds, they merely stared into each other's eyes. Arabella conveyed the hurt and sadness she couldn't voice while Finn's eyes held strength and love.

Finally, Arabella moved her free hand to cover Finn's still on her cheek. "I need you right now, Finn. Hold me."

Without a word, Finn pulled her close. Closing her eyes, she reveled in the heat of his skin, the light spattering of his chest hair, and the mixture of peat and wind that was uniquely Finlay's. As long as she had her dragonman, she would always feel safe.

Each second against his chest helped to erase the pain of her mother's death and Arabella's torture. For the first time, she truly believed she could put it behind her and it would stay there.

Finn rubbed her back and after a minute or so, he finally spoke up. "I'm sorry, Ara. As much as I know it won't do anything, I want you to know I truly am sorry."

She gave a sad smile. "I don't mind it coming from you. It's only when someone looks at me with pity that I can't stand it. I'll never forget the look of the dragon-shifters who found me. Their pity and horror set the stage for what would happen once I was home. And without my dragon's strength to draw on, since she'd been scared into the back of my mind and refused to come out, I decided hiding was the best option." She leaned back and searched his gaze. "I won't let Faye do the same."

~~~

Finn's love for Arabella MacLeod tripled at her words and the determination in her eyes. "Here you are, telling me about being tortured, and you're worried about my cousin. You might have hidden it well back on Stonefire, but you have a huge heart, lass."

Arabella wiggled on the rock. She didn't like compliments, but he would fix that eventually.

For the present, however, he rubbed his hands up and down her arms. "Once everything is settled with the DDA, Duncan, and the Dragon Knights, we'll tackle Faye together." Judging from the strength in Arabella's eyes, she was ready to suffer some teasing, so he winked. "I'll even let you boss me around. I'm sure you'll like that."

Arabella gave a half-hearted frown. "Not like you'd follow my orders anyway. I should just start telling you the opposite of what I want done. Things will get done quicker that way."

He grinned. "Then I'd start following them just to irritate you. After all, you're bonny when you're angry."

Arabella shook her head. "I sometimes wonder why I like you at all."

Finn leaned closer until he was a few inches from Arabella's lips and whispered, "Because I'm brilliant, that's why."

Arabella tried to frown but ended up snorting when he waggled his eyebrows. Unable to help himself, Finn kissed her slowly, nibbling and stroking until his lass sighed. Then he pulled away and laid his forehead against hers. "I wish we could spend the rest of our lives like this, just snogging in the open. Sex would be fantastic too. I'd love to see the sun caress your skin as you leaned against a tree and I took you from behind."

She slapped his chest. "Finn, stop it. We don't have time for that. At least, right now."

"Oh, so we can do that later, then? I have the perfect part of the forest to do it, too. It's my secret spot, but I'll share it with you."

"Finlay." Arabella warned. "Your cock should be sore right now, anyway. Besides, there's a crap ton of things to do."

"Aye, I know it," Finn answered. Then Arabella smiled as if she had a secret and he demanded, "Tell me you aren't thinking of a way to break my cock. If you need a rest, just ask. I'm quite fond of having a working penis."

Arabella grinned and the urge to rip off her clothes and take her again coursed through his body. He growled at his dragon.

Stop it. You had six days of almost nonstop sex. Give the lass a break.

It wasn't me. Stop using me as an excuse. You're just a randy bloke.

Not wanting to argue with his beast, Finn added, "You're not going to tell me, are you?"

"Let's just say it's a surprise. You'll just have to figure out how to earn it."

"Do I get a clue?"

Arabella tapped her chin. "I would, but you're so bloody brilliant, you can figure it out on your own."

He was about to growl when his mobile vibrated. Taking his phone from his pocket, Finn checked his messages and cursed.

Arabella asked, "What's wrong?"

Looking up, he answered, "Not wrong so much as bloody bad timing. Bram and Tristan are on their way here. Since they're flying up, they should be here in about an hour."

"What? How do they even know the frenzy is over?"

"My guess is Aunt Lorna. I love her, but she likes to meddle."

"I don't understand. The frenzy is over. We're going to have a child together and I assume a mating ceremony. What need is there to meddle?"

"I don't know, but I'm determined to find out." Finn stood and offered his hand to Arabella. "We need to hurry if we're going to listen to Grant's brief before they arrive. Are you up for it? Or was telling me your past too emotionally draining and you need a rest?"

Arabella placed her hand in his. "Of course I'm up for it. I'm somewhat offended that you even needed to ask."

He pulled her up and turned her to face him. "Promise me you'll tell me if you need a break, something to eat, or whatever you need. Given the frenzy and recent pregnancy, in addition to revisiting your painful memories, you need time to recover." Arabella opened her mouth, but he cut her off. "You're strong, Ara. Bloody hell, you're one of the strongest people I know. But it's okay to ask for help when you need it. If you never do, then my dragon will constantly bother me about your well-being. And you don't want me to go to crazy, do you?"

His dragon grunted. *It's my job to ensure our offspring is born healthy. I will do whatever it takes.*

Yes, and then Arabella will grow to hate you. Do you want that?

She'll never hate me. She likes me. It's you she'll take her anger out on.

Exactly, Finn replied dryly.

Arabella touched his cheek and he met her eyes. "Finn, I don't like to ask for help, but if I'm going to ask anyone, it's going to be you. Is that good enough?"

Placing his hand over hers, he murmured, "That'll do for now. I'm sure we'll continue to renegotiate this as the baby grows." He glanced down to her abdomen and put his other hand there. "Our baby." Looking back up, he added, "It's still sinking in. Is it real to you yet?"

"I'm bloody hungry all the time, so it's hard to forget." Her expression softened. "But yes, it's slowly sinking in. I just hope our baby girl isn't as charming as you, or we're going to have a lot of problems."

"And our baby boy is going to be as stubborn as you, which means I need some reinforcements or I'll go completely gray before I'm forty."

Arabella's expression faltered a second. "You wouldn't want a girl, then?"

Finn rolled his eyes and pulled Arabella close. "I don't care which gender the bairn is as long as it's ours." He moved to her ear and whispered, "But if you could avoid giving me two or three bairns at a time, I'd greatly appreciate it."

Arabella kissed his cheek. "Believe me, I'm with you on that one. A single child is enough for the first time."

Laughing, Finn moved back to Arabella's lips and gently kissed her. "Sounds like a plan." He pulled away and situated Arabella at his side. "Now that's sorted, we only have about twenty more plans to think of for the clan. Are you ready to tackle them?"

They started walking and Arabella replied, "Of course. I'm going to find out what happened with the DDA from Grant and then we're going to face Bram and Tristan together." She paused, and then added, "Just make sure to feed me while we do it. I've never been this hungry in my life."

Finn squeezed her shoulders. "I can order a whole roast pig for your appetizer, love. And then maybe fifteen sandwiches for the main course?"

She punched his side. "Stop being ridiculous."

Glancing at Arabella's expression, Finn grinned. "Never, Arabella MacLeod. You're stuck with me."

She battled a smile and lost. "I suppose it could be worse." He growled and she grinned. "You'll do, Finlay Stewart, you'll do."

He chuckled. "We'll have you talking in Scots in no time, lass. Just you wait and see."

As they continued to banter, both man and beast treasured their time with their mate. Finn only hoped he'd have more time

286

with her in the future. For all he knew, the Dragon Knights would attack again. Or, maybe, the dragon hunters could band together and seek her out.

The first step toward securing a happy future with Arabella was to find out from Grant what had been done and what still needed to be done. As much as he didn't want to, Finn picked up his pace.

CHAPTER TWENTY-THREE

Once Grant switched off the video of the DDA capturing the Dragon Knights, Arabella looked between Finn and Grant as she stated, "Broadcasting the feed was supposed to help us. All it did was make the dragons look subservient to the DDA."

Grant spoke up. "Given the Dragon Knights' message about how dragons want to rule over humans, our looking subservient will help our case."

Finn rubbed the back of her neck. "Aye, Grant's right. I'd rather everyone think we're playing nice than the opposite. Of course, that doesn't mean I won't be thinking of strategies to better protect our clan."

Her dragon chimed in. *Finn is right. Let them think we're weak. Then, when we need to protect the clan, we will overpower them.*

You know nothing about strategies.

Pretending to be weaker than you are to fool someone is a basic idea to a predator. Otherwise, we might never eat.

Her beast had a point, but Arabella decided not to say as much or her dragon would become unbearable.

Yet her dragon chuckled. *I can hear your thoughts. Try harder if you wish to keep a secret.*

Instead of huffing aloud, Arabella looked to Grant. "Has the DDA promised to help further with the Dragon Knights? Or, will helping to restore their reputation be enough for now and they leave us to protect everyone with our hands tied."

Grant raised an eyebrow. "You're a skeptical lass."

"Let's just say the DDA isn't my favorite agency in the world."

Finn gently tugged her hair and she looked to him. He tilted his head. "They gave you your sister-in-law and Bram's mate. I would think that counts for something."

"None of that matters right now. All I want to do is ensure our clan is protected."

Finn gave a lazy smile. "Glad you think of Lochguard as your home, because you belong here."

"You have yet to ask me for a proper mating, I might hint. If you keep me waiting too long, I may just go on a prolonged visit to my brother."

Finn shrugged. "You can try." His eyes turned fierce. "But I'll bring you back and take my time convincing you to stay."

"You still haven't asked."

"It's implied."

Arabella didn't know if she wanted to argue or kiss the bloody man. Thankfully, Grant cleared his throat and garnered their attention. "The Stonefire leader will be here soon. We should finish this meeting before then."

Arabella nodded and Finn jumped in. "Is Duncan still in custody?"

"Yes," Grant answered before handing them each a folder. Opening hers, Arabella scanned the information as Grant continued, "Once we knew to look for connections between Duncan and Marcus from Clan Skyhunter, it was easy to find evidence to convict him. Ian and Emma MacAllister were able to find emails between the two, planning the attack. While Marcus was careful and never gave any indication it was him—no name or identifiable features in the email address—the IP address tells us it had to come from Clan Skyhunter. And as far as I know, there's no one there who would plot behind Marcus King's back."

The Skyhunter leader had a reputation of ruling through fear. She only hoped that one day, someone else would take over the clan leadership. She didn't want to bring her child into a world where an entire dragon clan could turn on Lochguard or the human government and cause chaos, not to mention undo all of Melanie's hard work.

Grant shuffled some papers and placed one in front of her and Finn. "The DDA has granted Finn the authority to determine Duncan's punishment." Grant laid another piece of paper down. "They also said that once you secure Lochguard and can prove its safety, you may have a human sacrifice."

Finn nodded. "Good on both counts."

Arabella knew at a later time, she'd care about choosing a dragon-shifter male to pair with the human sacrifice. After all, she'd seen firsthand how a match could be more than a contract and resulting transaction. Maybe she could help a Lochguard dragonman find love.

Her dragon chuckled. *I never thought you would be talking about helping someone find love.*

Shut it, dragon. I can be romantic at times.

Yeah, right.

She pushed her dragon to the back of her mind. Matchmaking would have to wait anyway. For the present, she was more concerned about the traitor. "So, what are you going to do with Duncan, Finn?"

HEALED BY THE DRAGON

~~~

Finn should be happy about his clan being approved for a sacrifice since it would be Lochguard's first one in nearly four years. Yet to prove Lochguard was safe again would take a lot of work and he didn't have the time to dwell on all that needed to be done.

First, he needed to take care of Duncan Campbell.

Picking up the DDA's approval for Duncan's sentencing, he scanned the wording: *Per the agreement signed in 1984, intra-clan justice can be meted out on a case-by-case basis. The request to try and sentence Duncan Campbell has been approved. Once complete, fill out the necessary paperwork within two weeks of sentencing.*

Just what he wanted—more paperwork.

Laying the paper down, he met Arabella's gaze. "After gathering all of the facts, I'll present them to the clan and they will decide Duncan's fate."

Arabella asked, "You'll let them do just anything? That seems a bit risky."

"Of course not. Some will want to burn him at the stake, or some such rubbish. But their voices deserved to be heard. They know the final decision will be mine." He massaged Arabella's shoulder. "Has Stonefire never had an intra-clan sentencing before?"

Arabella shook her head. "Not since I was a toddler and I was too young to remember. Neil Westhaven probably would've been the first, but you killed him before that could happen."

Finn growled. "The bastard was a few seconds away from killing Evie Marshall. I have no regrets."

Arabella leaned forward a fraction. "I know that. I have zero regrets about you doing it, either. But killing him is the reason I don't know how intra-clan sentencing works."

Finn's dragon spoke up. *Why attack our mate? She will always have our back.*

I know that. I'm tired and grumpy because of your overwhelming protectiveness. It makes me cranky.

Stop using me as an excuse. You're just as protective. You would lock Ara in a room for nine months if you could.

Do I look insane? She would kill me.

You can't lie to me. I know the truth.

Ignoring his beast, Finn took a deep breath and continued to massage Arabella's shoulder. "Well, you'll know soon enough. Until then, Duncan will remain in custody."

She raised an eyebrow. "And what if he escapes?"

Grant grunted. "Unless someone bombs the building he's been put in, there is no bloody way the male will be able to escape."

Arabella pointed a finger. "Cockiness is the quickest way to fuck things up."

As Arabella stared daggers at Grant, Lochguard's Protector merely crossed his arms and almost looked bored. Finn trusted Grant, but Arabella needed to learn how to trust him, too. He'd wait to see how his mate handled the situation before stepping in.

Arabella huffed. "So you're just going to stare? I have a brother who could run circles around your staring, so if that's supposed to frighten me or put me off, you're in for a surprise."

Grant shrugged. "This is me dismissing your words. If I wanted to frighten you, you'd know it."

"It still wouldn't hurt to have a backup plan."

"It's already in place," Grant answered.

Finn battled a smile; Arabella wouldn't appreciate it and considering she had to be tired, he wasn't going to push her.

His dragon chimed in. *For how long? Teasing her is fun.*

Soon enough, dragon, soon enough.

As Arabella and Grant continued to stare at one another, there was a knock on the door.

Without a word, Grant went to the door and opened it. Bram Moore-Llewellyn stood on the other side, with Tristan MacLeod right behind him.

Once Bram and Tristan moved inside the room, Grant nodded and left.

Bram eyed Finn's arm resting on Arabella's shoulders and then met his gaze. "We need to talk, Stewart."

Finn raised an eyebrow. "Really? I never would've guessed considering you're standing here less than three hours after the end of the mate-claim frenzy."

Tristan growled. "Don't remind me of what you've done to my sister."

Finn was about to reply when Arabella stood up and waggled a finger at her brother. "You're not in charge of me, Tristan. Leave Finn alone."

Some males might feel emasculated having their female stand up for them. Finn, on the other hand, sat back and watched. It was time for both Arabella's brother and former clan leader to realize the lass was strong, maybe even stronger than either of them. And she needed to do it on her own.

His dragon stood up at attention. *If they try to take her, I will take control.*

They won't take her. They know she carries our child.

There hasn't been a mating ceremony yet. Bram could order her back. And you really think she'll go?

His beast huffed. *Maybe not.*

Exactly. Now, let Arabella shine. This is her moment. She's earned it.

With that, his dragon fell silent.

~~~

Arabella studied her brother. The fact he would even take a second to think before he spoke was a testament to Melanie's influence on him.

Still, she'd let him boss her around for far too long. He needed to know she wasn't 'poor Arabella' any longer.

However, before she could open her mouth, her brother took a step toward her and growled. "I'm not in charge of you, no. But I'm your family, Ara, and I've been the one to look after you. If the Scottish bastard wants you, he needs to earn you."

Arabella rolled her eyes. "Yes, because that doesn't make me look like a piece of property."

Tristan grunted. "It's a male thing. You wouldn't understand."

Raising an eyebrow, Arabella looked over her shoulder at Finn. "Care to explain this 'male thing' to a poor, witless female like myself?"

The corner of Finn's mouth ticked up. "I would, except I'm not sure I understand it myself."

Arabella smiled and looked back to Tristan. Her brother frowned and replied, "Who are you and what have you done to my sister?"

"Oh, come now, Tristan," Arabella said as she motioned to herself. "I'm the same. You just never bothered to look."

Tristan's eyes looked to Finn and back. He opened his mouth and then shut it.

Arabella's dragon chimed in. *This is the first time, apart from Melanie, that your brother has been speechless.*

I know, isn't it brilliant?

Bram's calm, steely voice filled the room. "Enough, Tristan. I didn't bring you here to scold Arabella. You wanted to see she was all right and she is. Now, behave."

Tristan threw one last glare at Finn before grunting.

Finn moved to stand beside her and wrap his arm around her waist before he addressed Bram. "So, why are you here, Bram? Not that I don't love our wonderful conversations, but between my newly pregnant mate and the recent attack on my clan, tea and scones really should wait until later."

Bram shook his head. "If I hadn't seen you in action myself, I would never have understood how you're clan leader."

Arabella leaned into Finn's side and she jumped in. "Once you get to know the Lochguard clan members, it will make a whole lot more sense."

Finn chuckled as Bram looked between them. Stonefire's leader motioned toward the table. "How about we sit down? The last thing I need is for Finn or his dragon to get huffy about Arabella standing too long."

Arabella sighed. "I am literally days pregnant. Until I look like a giant whale and waddle when I walk, no one gets to fuss about me."

Finn's grip tightened on her waist. "I'll be the judge of that."

Approval flashed in both Bram and Tristan's eyes and she knew she was fighting a losing battle. "Fine, I'll sit. Just know that if anyone tells me to go take a nap or offers me something to eat every three seconds, I will punch that person. You three have been warned and know I'm not bluffing."

Pulling out a chair, Arabella sat down as Bram replied, "Aye, and I'd heed her warning, Stewart. My own mate has already kicked me a few times."

"Aye?" Finn asked. "Your Evie seems tame in comparison. Mine has threatened my bollocks a few times. And my cock." He lowered his voice to a dramatic whisper. "Her dragon is a feisty one, if you know what I mean."

Arabella slapped Finn's side. "She'll carry out her threat, too, if you don't stop it."

Bram smiled. "Threats from her dragon? Handling my Evie is enough. I can't imagine her with an inner dragon."

Regaling Bram with tales of her dragon's behavior, Finn looked to be enjoying himself a little too much.

Arabella resisted a sigh. Bram's mate was six-months pregnant and Tristan had a pair of seven-month-old twins. If she let them, Bram and Tristan might give Finn ideas about the best way to handle her.

And she bloody well wasn't having that.

Kicking Finn under the table, she demanded, "Why are you here, Bram?" Surprise flashed in her former clan leader's eyes and she softened her tone. "Not that I'm not happy to see you, but this isn't the best time for a social call."

"It's not really a social call, Ara," Bram answered. "I contacted Grant the other day with news, but since I didn't have the clearance to tell him, he notified me as soon as you two were done with the frenzy. I have an offer from the Department of Dragon Affairs."

HEALED BY THE DRAGON

~~~

Finn's ease and teasing died at Bram's words. "Tell me the news."

To his credit, Bram didn't waste time asking if Arabella should leave. Bram had enough experience with his mate to guess at their partnership. "In light of the recent attacks, they want to propose a few changes to the agreements the British dragon-shifters have signed over the years. They refuse to give me all of the details until the both of us agree to work together. If we both don't sign, then nothing will change."

Arabella's voice filled the room as she asked, "They must have given you something. No one is daft enough to agree to anything without at least some knowledge."

"Aye," Bram answered dryly. "I see your impatience hasn't changed."

She straightened her shoulders. "You're intruding on my honeymoon period with my mate. Would you be patient if the same had happened right after you claimed Evie?"

Finn's hand moved to her neck and squeezed. Looking to Arabella, he smiled at her and then moved his gaze to Bram. "Well? What do you know?"

Bram crossed his arms over his chest. "They want to work with Lochguard and Stonefire to better contain the Dragon Knights."

"What's in it for us?" Finn asked.

"In addition to regular patrols by the DDA, they promise to focus more on the dragon hunters' illegal activities as well," Bram explained.

Finn drummed his fingers of his free hand on the table. "That hardly seems like a fair exchange."

Tristan finally spoke up. "He wasn't done, Stewart. Impatience for my sister is one thing, but it's bad form for a clan leader."

Finn's voice was like steel. "Until you've done my job, you have no right to criticize. Playing teacher is hardly the same."

Arabella laid her hand on his thigh and squeezed. "What's the rest, Bram? And quick, before they have a fistfight to settle their differences. I'd rather not have Finn with a black eye at my mating ceremony."

Finn tapped his hand against the table. "I wouldn't resort to fighting. It wouldn't be fair."

Tristan growled. "Not fair to you, I agree."

Finn's dragon spoke up. *Challenge him later, in secret. Then we can show him we are faster and stronger.*

I might just do that.

Arabella cleared her throat and everyone looked to her. "Can we focus on what's important for the moment?"

Despite Arabella's bastard brother, Finn was proud of his lass. Judging by the approval in Bram's eyes, he felt the same.

His dragon said, *Of course. Why are people surprised? Our mate has a will of steel.*

Aye, but don't forget she can use it against us as well.

I'm not worried. A few caresses and she will beg us to fuck her.

You and the sex. Now who's the randy one?

His beast harrumphed just as Bram's voice cut through his thoughts. "I'd never thought I'd see a MacLeod as a peacekeeper."

Finn looked over at his mate and Arabella raised an eyebrow.

Bram laughed. "Okay, okay. They also mentioned something about transitioning authority over to the clans who prove themselves."

Finn stilled his fingers. "More autonomy? Somehow that seems like a bad idea given the recent claims by the Dragon Knights, of how we wish to take over Great Britain."

Shrugging, Bram replied, "My guess is that it'll be a slow transition. They'll probably give us boring, crap powers first, such as allowing us to suggest better practices for a DDA inspection or improvements to the sacrifice paperwork process. It'll be a long time before we can do something as powerful as choose our own sacrifices or be allowed to develop our own justice system for all crimes committed within a clan."

Still, the DDA even considering handing over more power was massive. "When do they need an answer by?"

"Soon," Bram said. "They understand your need to clean up the mess here first, as well as the fact you just took a mate. But we need to meet with them in the next three weeks for the remaining details. Any longer, and the offer will expire."

Finn nodded. As if he would pass up a meeting of a lifetime.

His dragon huffed. *I would rather spend the time with Ara.*
Well, one of us has to think of the future.

I think of the future. Politics is just a human invention to make life more complicated.

I won't deny it, but we need to play by their rules, at least, for now.
Why?

Just hush. I need to concentrate.

His beast fell quiet and Finn spoke up. "If nothing else, a meeting couldn't hurt. As Ara mentioned before, no one would agree to anything without enough information. I only hope the DDA understands that."

"Evie is setting it all up," Bram explained. "She'll make sure at least one competent DDA employee attends."

"Good." Finn glanced to Arabella. While his mate would deny it, the circles under her eyes were more pronounced and she was slightly pale; Arabella was exhausted. Finn looked back to Bram. "Send me anything else you can think of, including what little information you received from the DDA, but unless there's anything else pressing you can't share via Grant or my other Protectors, then I need to feed my mate and then call a clan gathering."

"And a mating ceremony," Arabella added.

Staring into Arabella's eyes, he saw tenderness and something he swore was possessiveness. "Afraid I'll change my mind in a few days, love?"

She dug her nails into his leg under the table. "Tease me some more about that, I dare you, Finn." She moved her hand a few inches closer to his crotch and he understood her warning.

Leaning forward, he placed a gentle kiss on her lips. "I'm as anxious as you, but you deserve a proper ceremony, Ara. That takes some time."

Arabella tilted her head. "Knowing your aunt, things are already in full swing. Maybe not for today, but in the next few days, for sure."

Bram's voice interrupted them. "Your aunt wouldn't be the dragonwoman who insisted I call her Aunt Lorna, is she?"

"Aye, that's the one." Finn grinned. "Did you give in?"

"Like I had a choice," Bram muttered. "That bloody woman won't take no for an answer."

"Be careful what you say about my aunt, Bram."

Bram put up his hands. "I meant no disrespect. We don't really have anyone like her in Stonefire, that's all."

Arabella laughed. "Oh, just wait until you meet Meg."

Bram blinked. "Who is Meg?"

Arabella patted Finn's leg. "Oh, you'll know her when you see her." Arabella's voice turned more serious as she looked to Bram and Tristan. "Will you two, Evie, and Mel come to my mating ceremony? I'll postpone it a few days if you can."

Bram answered, "We'll try, lass, we'll try."

Squeezing Arabella's hand under the table, Finn moved it off his leg and stood up. "Next time, I promise to walk you out."

Standing up, Bram put out his hand and Finn shook it. "I understand." Bram looked to Arabella. "And I'll talk with Evie and Mel about the mating ceremony."

Arabella stood up and asked, "You'll let Evie come?"

Bram looked to Finn. "If Finn allows some of Stonefire's Protectors to escort us and an escape plan is devised to my satisfaction, then yes."

Giving Bram's hand one last shake, Finn released it. "I'm sure we can arrange something. Have your head Protector contact Grant and have them work things out."

"Aye, Kai will be in touch," Bram said before moving toward the door.

Tristan stopped in front of Finn and studied him. Even though Finn was an inch taller, it felt as if Tristan were glaring down at him. "Don't hurt my sister. She's had enough pain in her life."

For once, Finn didn't disagree. "Her happiness is my top priority, MacLeod. I would never hurt her."

Arabella mumbled, "Just constantly irritate me."

Finn looked to Arabella and winked. "You know you love it."

From the corner of his eye, Finn saw Tristan put out his hand and he took it. Tristan tightened his grip and looked to Arabella. "If he so much as breathes the wrong way, you tell me. Just because he's clan leader doesn't mean I can't take him."

Arabella sighed. "Fine, yes, I'll tell you. Will you leave now?"

Tristan released Finn's hand and focused on his sister. His tone softened a fraction when he asked, "Is the Scottish bastard what you really want?"

Finn's dragon growled, but he pushed his beast into a mental maze and waited for Arabella's answer.

Arabella moved closer to Finn, wrapped her arm around his waist, and leaned against him. "More than anything."

Her declaration warmed his heart. Even with the frenzy finished, she still wanted him for him.

The only question was did she love him?

Before he could dwell too long in his thoughts, Tristan grunted and went to stand with Bram. After a few more niceties, the door shut behind them and Finn was alone again with Arabella.

CHAPTER TWENTY-FOUR

The instant the door closed behind Bram and Tristan, Arabella shut her eyes and took a deep breath. While her brother had been a bit of an arsehole, the meeting had gone better than expected. The best news was her family would probably be at her mating ceremony. As irritating as her brother and Bram's protectiveness was, she loved them and would miss them.

She'd just have to make sure Grant came up with a good enough plan so Evie could come, too.

Finn's hands rested on her shoulders and he kneaded her muscles. With a sigh, she opened her eyes to look at her mate's upside down face. "My brother is exhausting."

He dug his fingers a little harder as he worked and she moaned. He replied, "Aye, but given he's your brother, I wasn't expecting any less."

"And what's that supposed to mean?"

Finn raised an eyebrow. "Did you really expect your brother to pat me on the back and say well done?"

"No. But if I didn't know any better, I'd say he was brooding."

"His mate will sort him out soon enough."

At the thought of Melanie and the twins, Arabella's heart squeezed. "I hope so. Knowing Mel, she'll succeed in convincing Tristan to bring her up here for the ceremony."

Finn stopped his massage and moved to kneel in front of her. "We can postpone the mating ceremony until later, love. It doesn't need to be so soon. I don't care if I have to fight Aunt Lorna or even Bram. I'll find a way to delay the ceremony to ensure your whole family can attend."

Staring down at her dragonman, Arabella wasn't sure if she wanted to cry or kiss the living shit out of him.

Her dragon rumbled. *Why cry? I don't understand.*

He means so much to me and I can't imagine life without him. This feeling is new.

The feeling has a name.

Arabella knew it, but she wasn't quite ready to say the words.

Her beast grunted. *As I said before, humans make everything complicated.*

Finn looked about ready to ask if she was okay, so Arabella brushed his cheek with her fingers. "Sooner is better. Besides, Bram wouldn't mention the possibility of attending if there wasn't a real chance." She smiled. "And in a few weeks, we can have a big celebration to help the clans mingle."

Her mate's eyes turned heated. "Then we can try some more dancing."

Remembering the feather touches from last week sent a small thrill through her body. "Maybe. You haven't asked properly, yet."

He bowed his head. "Oh lady of Lochguard, would you do the honor of dancing with me at this as-yet unplanned celebration?"

"Well…I don't know. Maybe I should ask you to convince me to say yes."

Finn looked up with slitted pupils. "Even with my schedule, I think that can be arranged."

Arabella's dragon hummed. *I want him, but not until tomorrow. I won't be able to use him properly before then.*

Arabella laughed and Finn asked, "What?"

"My dragon isn't at full power yet. She said to wait until tomorrow."

"Aye, so she can break my cock."

"Probably. But in all seriousness, you have the clan gathering to call. The sooner we deal with Duncan, the sooner we can focus on working with Bram and developing closer relations with Stonefire."

Amusement danced in her mate's eyes. "So you've decided to agree to the DDA's proposal already, then, without me?"

"Don't be silly. I just want to make sure my sister-in-law can come and help with babysitting later. She owes me big time."

Finn laughed and then stood. Pulling her out of her chair, he held her close. "Believe me, we have plenty of prospective babysitters on Lochguard. Ours will be the first for Aunt Lorna. She may technically be my aunt, but she'll be grandma to our baby boy."

"As long as she keeps our baby girl away from your twin cousins, at least until they've been tamed. Fraser, in particular, will give her bad ideas."

Nuzzling her cheek, Finn murmured, "Somehow, I think our boy will come up with enough trouble on his own."

As Finn's comforting scent surrounded her, she murmured, "Girl."

"Boy."

She pulled back to meet Finn's eyes. "Be careful, or I'll have twins just to spite you."

Finn smiled slowly. "You do that, and you're giving yourself double the trouble."

"Damn you, Finlay Stewart."

Chuckling, he laid his forehead against hers as he rubbed her lower back. "I'll love whatever you give me, Arabella MacLeod, because it's a part of you."

"What about a three-headed toad?"

He winked. "Even a three-headed toad."

Love shined out of Finn's eyes. In that moment, she couldn't imagine being anywhere else but with her clever, funny, and slightly irritating dragonman. After so many years of isolation and fear, Arabella finally felt whole again.

All because of Finn.

She wanted to claim him in the proper way, with three words that described the whole bundle of opinions she had about him. Finlay Ian Stewart might be her true mate because of her dragon, but he'd earned his place as the true mate of her heart.

Yet voicing her feelings was hard. Not because Finn would be cocky about it later on purpose, because of course he would, but because it would be a major turning point in her life. Loving Finn and their child would replace the lingering fear and sadness of her past.

Her dragon spoke up. *That's what you want. Do it, already.*

Sometimes, dragon, I wonder about your methods.

I'm a dragon not a human. I don't dance around the issue. We love him. Tell him. Then we can eat, sleep, and fuck our mate again.

I hate to see what pregnancy hormones will do to your crankiness.

I'm not cranky. I'm impatient. There's a difference.

Her beast's words made her smile. And despite her heart hammering away inside her chest, she took a deep breath. Her dragon was right—it was time to stop stalling.

Looking into her dragonman's eyes, she blurted out, "I love you, Finn."

A slow smile took over his face and she waited for a cocky comment.

However, he merely cupped her cheeks and strummed his fingers against her skin. His love shown in his eyes and her heart skipped a beat. Finn was even more gorgeous when he allowed her to see his true feelings.

He murmured, "That's great, but remember, I love you more."

Her warm feelings eased a bit and she frowned. "Really? Here I am, telling you I bloody love you, and you turned it into a contest?"

"Of course. Just saying I love you and then fawning over you would be pretty boring, don't you think?"

Her dragon laughed. *He is right.*

There's no bloody way I'm telling him that.

Her beast laughed some more. Arabella ignored her and moved a hand to the back of Finn's neck. "Just shut up and kiss me already, dragonman." He opened his mouth and she cut him off. "Seriously, for once, just listen to me."

Caressing her cheeks, he moved closer. A whisper from her lips, he murmured, "I just wanted to tell you that this kiss is a down payment for later. Once you've rested, there will be more, much more."

Arabella opened her mouth and Finn's lips descended on hers.

~~~

As Finn nibbled Arabella's lip before moving his tongue between her sweet lips, he battled his dragon's instinct to mate. *Now is not the time. She's tired, hungry, and probably sore.*

She is ours. We need to show her how much we love her until every inch of her body knows it well.

We did that during the frenzy.

It wasn't enough.

Forcing his beast into a mental cage, he pulled Arabella's body flush against his. The second her nipples crushed against his chest, she gasped. He took advantage and stroked deeper.

Yet Arabella recovered and fought back. As their tongues tangled, Finn knew he'd never get enough of his stubborn female.

Moving his hands down her back, he gripped her soft arse. His dragon may have been in control during the frenzy, but Finn remembered everything and would never get enough of taking his female from behind.

Of course, Arabella still had her clothes on. He couldn't do anything until she was at least half naked.

It was time to see if she wanted it, too,

He snaked one hand between them and took her breast in a possessive grip. Arabella moaned and broke the kiss. "Finn."

His name was a plea and he wasn't about to pass it up.

He slowly kissed his way down Arabella's neck until he reached where it met her shoulder. After biting her gently, he licked the sting. Kissing back up her neck, he bit her sensitive skin again.

Arabella threaded her fingers in his hair and arched her back in invitation.

He should stop. A good clan leader would stop and use every second available to heal the rift.

His dragon huffed. *In the time it takes you to decide, we could've fucked our mate already.*

Shut it, dragon.

Stop talking and use your time more wisely.

Fine.

Stealing a few minutes with his mate wouldn't hurt anyone. After all, a few minutes with his mate would help ground him for the possible shitstorm to come.

Leaning back, he put his forefinger under her top and lightly traced her skin. His female was so soft.

Arabella reached out and ran her hand across his chest. Even with a shirt on, her touch left a trail of heat and he yearned to feel her skin against his.

His beast roared in impatience.

Taking the hint, Finn raised her top and pulled it off. Arabella opened her mouth and he stopped her from replying with a kiss. He then scooped her breast from her bra and played with her taut nipple.

The scent of her arousal grew stronger and he moved to her other breast. Just as he twisted her other nipple, Arabella bit his lower lip. The slight sting went straight to his cock.

She broke the kiss and whispered, "Do we have time?"

"I thought earlier you said we had to wait until tomorrow for your dragon."

She raised an eyebrow. "You think I need my dragon to have sex?"

"No, but I'd rather not piss her off."

Arabella reached behind her and unhooked her bra. As the contraption fell to the ground, she took her breasts in her hands.

"If you're so afraid of my dragon, then maybe I can pleasure myself."

As his mate fondled her own breasts, his mouth went dry. Part of him was tempted to watch Arabella make herself come.

His dragon growled. *No. We should make her come.*

A shot of lust rushed through his body. Finn barely prevented himself from moaning out loud. *Bloody hell, dragon. The frenzy is over.*

We will never get enough of her. Fuck her.

Tugging off his shirt, Finn replied, "If you want my cock, then strip and bend over the table."

~~~

Arabella stopped massaging her breasts to ask, "I'm supposed to take orders from you, now?"

Finn's pupils flashed to slits and back. "In this instance, yes." He reached out and his touch was feather light across her breast. "I'll make it worth your while."

Her heart rate kicked up. The frenzy was over and her dragon was present in her mind, but tired. A part of Arabella wanted to cede control in just this situation, but another part recoiled at the thought of giving in to Finn so easily.

Her dragon's sleepy voice filled her head. *Try it once. If he's rubbish, you know for next time.*

Says the beast who controlled the frenzy. From what I remember, he did just fine.

I'm too tired to push you. Make the decision yourself.

Finn watched her with predatory eyes. Since his pupils were round, his human half was in control.

The look shot straight to her pussy. Whatever soreness she'd felt earlier had all but disappeared and had been replaced with a pulsing need.

Even without the frenzy, she wanted Finn's cock.

Arabella undid her jeans and shimmied out of them. "Lock the door and hurry. We have stuff to do."

In the blink of an eye, Finn locked the door and was out of his clothes. Yet all he did was stare at her, then the table, and back at her.

Rolling her eyes, she moved toward the table. "Fine, mister alpha. But if you disappoint me, I'm not going to let you take control again."

Finn's voice was husky when he replied, "It's not just me who will take control, heather. I look forward to you riding my cock and being in charge without your dragon."

The thought of riding Finn and his dick reaching deep inside of her made her even wetter. As she placed her hands on the table, she looked over her shoulder. "Behave, or I'll tie you up and walk away."

In the next second, Finn was behind her. Running one warm, rough hand down her back, he murmured, "You had better never walk away from me, Arabella, or I will tie you up, tease you, and then stop. We'll see how you like it."

Opening her mouth, Finn's hand caressed between her legs and she forgot whatever she was going to say. He thrust a finger inside her and she leaned against her hands.

Finn's breath was hot against her shoulder as he asked, "Are you too sore or do you want my cock?"

Arabella wiggled her hips. "Fuck me, Finn, and quickly."

He chuckled as he fingered her. "Someone sounds like they're about to have another frenzy."

Growling, she met his eye. "At least your dragon gets to the point."

Finn's eyes flashed and he removed his hand. For a second, she thought he'd walk away. But then he leaned over her body and held her in place with his arm around her waist. "Women are supposed to like it slow, but I see my lass wants it hard and fast."

Widening her stance, she leaned forward slightly. "Then get to it, dragonman."

With a growl, Finn released his hold on her waist, positioned his cock, and thrust.

She was so wet he slid in without a problem. The fullness combined with the slight soreness felt good in a delicious way.

Yet he stayed still. Arabella glared and he took her lips in a swift kiss. His breath was hot against her lips as he murmured, "Brace yourself, heather."

Before she could tease him for his ridiculous line, Finn took hold of her hips and moved.

With each hard thrust, her breasts jiggled and she had no choice but to lean on her hands or she would fall onto the table.

Arching her back, one of Finn's hands snaked around to her front and finally gripped her breast tightly, never slowing his rhythm. He changed his angle slightly and Arabella leaned forward with a moan. "Yes, there."

With a grunt, Finn released her breasts and snaked a hand to her clit. He strummed her hard bud with light brushes, but it wasn't enough. It would take forever for her to reach orgasm with such a gentle touch. "Harder, dragonman."

Finn didn't increase the pressure against her clit. Arabella growled, but just before she could glare at him, Finn pressed hard against her nub.

Arabella nearly collapsed on the table.

Somehow she made her arms work and she decided Finn needed a little teasing, too.

Clenching her inner muscles, Finn groaned behind her. Yet the bloody man never slowed his pace.

And damn him, she loved the feel of his cock this way.

Finn's voice was husky as he stated, "Come for me, love."

"As if I can come on demand."

"You will if I do this."

He pinched and lightly twisted her clit and lights started to dance across her eyes. Arabella tried to hold back her orgasm just to spite him, but then he pressed hard and pleasure broke free, spreading throughout her entire body.

She barely registered the growly chuckle behind her before Finn stilled inside of her and roared her name. As he came, he sent her into one orgasm after another.

Only when her pussy had wrung the last drop from his cock did the spasms slow and Arabella came down.

Finn lightly rubbed her back from her shoulders to her arse and back. Arabella tried to put two thoughts together, but before she could say anything, Finn said smugly, "You're welcome."

Somehow she found the strength to turn her head and give a half-hearted glare. "Damn you, Finlay Stewart."

He grinned. "And what are you damning me for now, heather?"

"I was rather hoping you'd be rubbish at something. I'm going to keep searching."

Winking, he continued to rub her back. "That almost sounded like a compliment." He placed his free hand over his heart. "You really must love me."

Shaking her head, she murmured, "Don't worry, I won't let it happen again."

Chuckling, Finn pulled out and turned her into his arms. Too tired to resist, she cuddled into his chest. A dragonwoman could get used to sleeping against a solid, warm chest like Finn's.

Finn's voice rumbled inside his chest. "I'll try to change your mind about that later." Placing his finger under her chin, he forced her to look up. After studying her a second, he asked, "Are you tired? Tell me the truth, Ara. I need to call a clan gathering and I won't be able to think clearly if I'm worrying about you the whole time."

At the mention of being tired, Arabella felt exhaustion settling in. Yet if she told Finn she wanted nothing more than to sleep for twelve hours, he'd order her to go to bed and she wouldn't miss Finn addressing the clan for the first time after the recent attacks for anything.

So, she decided to compromise. "I'm a bit tired, but if I can sit down while we plan the gathering, then I should be all right later."

For a second, she thought he would call her a liar. Then the corner of his mouth ticked up. "Admitting you're tired nearly killed you, didn't it? We're going to have to work on that."

With a sigh, she laid her head back on his chest. "How about you just feed me and get to work?"

He squeezed her tightly. "One roast pig, coming up."

Unable to resist, she smiled. "Make it two. Your little dragon baby needs some energy."

He leaned down to her ear. "I rather thought it was you who needed the energy after experiencing my fantastic cock again."

"Finn."

Chuckling, he murmured, "You know you love me."

She raised her head to meet his eyes. "And I have no idea why, but yes, Finlay Ian, I do love you."

"Good, but remember, I love you more."

She was about to growl when he placed a tender kiss on her lips and Arabella decided she'd rather kiss her dragonman than argue.

She really must love him after all.

CHAPTER TWENTY-FIVE

A few hours later, Finn stood on the dais in the great hall and watched as Grant and two other Protectors escorted Duncan Campbell through a path cleared by the clan. As much as he wanted to be cooking for his mate and pampering her a little, his clan needed him. The sooner the issues with Duncan were resolved, the sooner he could work on healing the rifts in his clan.

Duncan finally met his eyes, but the older dragonman's expression was unreadable. Not that Finn worried. No one from Clan Skyhunter would swoop down to rescue Duncan. The dragonman was expendable.

Grant escorted Duncan up the side stairs to the dais and positioned him a few feet to Finn's left. Finn turned toward the already silent crowd. Meeting Arabella's gaze briefly, he then began. "All of you have received information on what Duncan Campbell is convicted of as well all of the proof of his guilt. The DDA has granted me the power to sentence him. Since the proof was verified by the clan's council, there is no doubt of his part in providing information to the Dragon Knights. He is ultimately responsible for all of the injuries we suffered on that day. All that's left is to determine his punishment. Then we can move on and focus on the future."

He paused to read the crowd. Most of them were glaring at Duncan to his right. A few looked bored, and several more were worried. He mentally catalogued the ones who looked bored and continued, "Now is the time to voice your opinions. A microphone has been provided to the right of the hall. While we realistically don't have enough time to listen to hundreds of suggestions, I will try my best to hear as many as I can. Please form a line now."

When old Archie MacAllister reached the microphone first, Finn braced himself for the old farmer's long-winded rant.

Once the line settled, Finn nodded. "Go ahead, Archie."

The dragonman cleared his throat and stated, "He should be dropped from the skies onto one of the nearby mountains. I say Ben Klibreck will do."

Finn's dragon spoke up. *I like that idea. Can we be the one to do it?*

No, we're not dropping a man from that height. Even if Duncan shifted mid-air, he would crash before he could fly. That mountain is over 3,000 feet tall.

His beast huffed. *I still say we should do it. The clan would appreciate the show.*

Rather than argue with his dragon, Finn replied to Archie, "While I understand wanting to make a public display of Duncan's betrayal, the humans would cast us as monsters. If we're to ever go back to friendly terms with the nearby villages, we shouldn't scare them."

Archie frowned. "In my youth, the locals appreciated a good dragon drop every once in a while."

There had only been one recorded dragon drop in the last hundred years, and it had been an accident. But he wasn't about to embarrass old Archie. Still, Finn threaded his voice with every ounce of dominance he possessed. "Be that as it may, cameras in mobile phones make any public display a risk. We'll punish

Duncan, but not in a way that would damage the clan's reputation."

Archie nodded reluctantly. "Aye, I suppose not. But I still think it's the best idea."

"Your opinion's been noted. Let's give someone else a say, shall we?"

As Archie grumbled and left the microphone, Finn stole a quick glance of Arabella. His mate was biting her lip. The bloody female was fighting a smile.

Another clan member addressed him via the microphone and Finn turned his attention back to the clan. He only hoped there wouldn't be anything more absurd than dropping a man from the sky. Of course, given the imagination of his clan, it would probably happen.

~~~

Arabella was surprised she hadn't bitten her lip hard enough to draw blood.

Watching Finn keep his cool while he listened to ridiculous suggestions was hilarious. As the second clan member suggested tying Duncan's feet to two giant boulders and tossing him into the loch, it took everything she had not to burst out laughing.

Her dragon's voice was bored. *Why does our mate listen to these ideas? Clearly, Finn has a plan already.*

He wants the clan to feel involved. Who knows, maybe someone will have a reasonable suggestion.

This is one of those human ways to make things complicated. Our mate needs to sentence the traitor and then come to us.

Patience, dragon. This is important.

318

With a huff, her dragon curled into a ball and dozed. And just in time for Alistair Boyd's turn at the microphone.

Arabella forced herself to listen. Alistair had helped Finn the night of the Dragon Knights' attack. He might have something reasonable to say.

Alistair's deep voice echoed in the hall. "I don't see why we should try to come up with a creative way to punish Duncan. Do as the DDA does—lock him up and inject him with drugs to keep him from shifting except once every three months. Honestly, we should just hand him over to the DDA since they already have the facilities and resources to complete the task."

Murmurs rose up all around Arabella. A few people cursed the DDA while others seemed to think it was a good idea.

While she rather thought it was a logical choice, she waited to see what Finn would say.

Her mate replied, "Aye, I was leaning toward that choice myself." Some cries of outrage rose up, but Finn merely gave the crowd a cursory glance. Once they were quiet, he continued, "I, more than anyone, know the DDA can fail us." Most of the outrage died down at the reference to the rogue DDA employee who had killed his parents. "But constructing a secure building, positioning guards, and then hiring people to look after Duncan Campbell takes resources away from strengthening the clan as a whole."

Someone shouted, "Then why hold this meeting at all?"

Finn answered, "Because I wanted to hear your thoughts and ensure everyone knows what happens to our clan's traitor." He looked around the room again and met her eyes briefly. "I have plans not just for Lochguard, but all of the dragon clans in Europe. My opinion is we should focus our resources on building alliances and changing the laws to our favor. Am I the only one who wants to someday have full autonomy?" Murmurs of no answered. "Right then, by a show of hands, who wishes to ship Duncan off to the DDA and use all of our resources to focus on the future rather than the past?"

In addition to Arabella and Aunt Lorna at her side, more than three-quarters of the room raised their hands.

Finn's voice boomed again. "Then it's decided. I'll contact the DDA and work out the details." He gave a sweeping stern look. "Any other traitors will face the same fate. My plans are to strengthen relations with both humans and other dragon clans. If you're not with me, then leave within the next twenty-four hours. I won't waste my time dealing with petty plans that could end up endangering our clan as a whole. I'm not the only one with a mate and bairn on the way. I won't risk any more lives over politics. I'm the clan leader. Accept it or leave to form your own clan."

Arabella's heart rate kicked up as the room fell silent. While Duncan's co-conspirators were all locked away, there were more than a few older dragon-shifters who viewed Finn as a weakness. She waited to see if any of them would leave.

One older dragonman turned and exited the door. Four more followed.

She held her breath to see if any more would go.

They didn't.

After two minutes, Finn nodded. "Aye, that's for the best. As for the rest, look for information over the coming weeks. While I have plans for the clan, I won't keep any of you in the dark. My door is always open. Well, unless I'm alone and naked with my mate, of course."

Finn winked and Arabella's cheeks flushed. Deep down, she knew he was doing it to ease the tension, but it didn't mean she wouldn't speak her mind when they were alone. She really needed to establish them handling the clan together soon. She was so much more than a prop.

Her dragon's voice was sleepy. *Don't worry. I will help you get him back.*

As long as it doesn't break his penis, bring it.

I still say we should try.

Finn's voice interrupted her thoughts. "I will start taking questions tomorrow. Tonight, I need to take care of my mate. I'm sure every male in the room understands."

Arabella rolled her eyes as every adult dragonman agreed with him. Maybe she should form a coalition with the other females in the clan to battle some of the males' overprotectiveness.

Her dragon chuckled. *Good luck with that.*

Finn motioned for Duncan to be taken away. Once the traitor was out of the room, Finn headed straight for her.

Lorna elbowed her in the side. "My stint as your guard is over. Take care of my lad, will you?"

Arabella blinked. "Um, of course."

Before Lorna could reply, Finn was right in front of her. He drew her close and whispered into her ear, "You were laughing at me."

"I should have, considering what you just did."

He moved to look into her eyes. "Do you want me to call everyone back so you can make a quip or two?"

She sighed. "Of course not. But from tomorrow, we need to work on handling this clan together. I can be the co-clan leader. Yes, I like the sound of that."

Finn gave her a skeptical look. "I want your help, but I'm afraid the 'co-clan leader' might eventually become 'clan leader.' Promise not to take the clan away from me?"

"It's taking everything I have not to roll my eyes again. You sound bloody ridiculous."

He nuzzled her cheek. "I'm tired, love. All I want to do is hold you close and sleep for twelve hours."

She softened at the exhaustion in his voice. "Then let's do that." Finn pulled away and opened his mouth, but she cut him off. "Everything's done for tonight, right?" He nodded. "And if we put a little note on the door that you'll start seeing people after ten a.m., then we can sleep and take it easy. I think we both deserve it."

Cupping her cheek, Finn smiled. "You're not going to let me say no, are you?"

She raised an eyebrow. "What do you think?"

"I think I'm going to say yes or risk you kicking me in the balls," he answered.

Shaking her head, Arabella murmured, "I wonder half the time why I love you, Finlay Stewart. You're a right pain in my arse."

"Aye, but a good kind of pain." He leaned down and whispered, "Like when I spank you as I take you from behind."

Her dragon yawned. *Not again. I'm too tired. Maybe tomorrow morning.*

Arabella laughed. Finn looked at her funny and she explained, "My dragon says you have to wait until tomorrow morning."

Heat flashed in his eyes. "Then I say we hurry up and go to sleep. That way, when I wake up, I can make you beg for my cock."

It was on the tip of her tongue to scold him, but instead, she said, "Maybe I'll wake up first and tie you to the bed. Then I'll have the chance to make you beg."

"Lass, you can tie me to the bed anytime."

Smiling, Arabella motioned with her head toward the door. "Then I say we go to bed straight away. I have plans for you in the morning."

"Just don't be too rough. After all, you're going to sit with me and listen to any clan grievances."

Her eyes widened. "You finally are going to let me help you?"

Cupping her cheek, his voice was husky when he answered, "You've been helping me all along, Arabella. Before you, I was drowning in clan duties. Now, with you at my side, I feel as if I can tackle anything."

"Finn."

After giving her a gentle kiss, he looped his arm around her waist. "Come, love. I'll introduce to you to a few people as we walk out. It's time for them to know you're much more than the mother of my child. You're my other half and I want to show you off."

"Why does that worry me a little?"

His face turned serious. "Do you think I would embarrass you again?" She raised her brows and a grin spread across his face. "All right, bloody woman, of course I'll do it again. But not when it comes to important matters. Does that sound fair?"

Tapping her chin, she took a second to answer. "For now. But I still say we'll renegotiate as we go."

Finn tickled her side and she laughed. When he finally stopped, he trapped her against his chest and kissed her. He took his time nibbling and sucking her lower lip before stroking inside her mouth.

323

Once he pulled away, he murmured, "As long as you're with me, Ara, I'll renegotiate until we're old and wrinkly. You're worth just about anything, love."

"Just about? I'm not sure I like the sound of that."

He winked. "A man is attached to his cock and I'm not about to give it up."

Linking her hands behind his neck, she rubbed against his hard cock between them. "And you know what? I'm a little attached to it myself, so consider it safe."

Finn laughed and Arabella smiled. She and her dragonman might not be the most conventional couple, but together, they fit.

The only thing left to do was claim him in front of the clan. But for good measure, she stood on her tiptoes and kissed him. After all, it never hurt to cover Finn in her scent. He was hers and she was never letting him go.

EPILOGUE

Six Days Later

Arabella rubbed the silky dark blue material of her dress between her fingers. Any second, Lorna would fetch her. Arabella was almost afraid of what she'd find on the other side of the door.

Her dragon grunted. *It will be fine. Finn won't embarrass us.*

You must have a selective memory. That must be nice.

A dragon never forgets. You are the one forgetting important things, such as last night.

Lochguard tradition dictated that a male and female slept apart the night before a mating ceremony. Why it was still practiced, Arabella didn't know since it seemed rather old-fashioned, but Lorna and Meg had eventually worn her down.

Arabella had been nervous that she'd have a nightmare without Finn at her side. However, a half hour before bed, there was a knock. Even though no one was there, she found a large box. Inside had been two pillows covered in shirts Finn had worn, along with a note: *The all-powerful eau de Finn will keep you safe in your dreams.*

Even with her heart beating double-time for the ceremony, she couldn't resist smiling at the cocky words.

Her dragon added, *Trust him. All will be well.*

Before she could reply, the door opened to reveal Aunt Lorna's smiling face. "There's my lass. Everything's ready if you are."

Arabella straightened her shoulder. "I'm ready."

Her dragon chuckled. *Sure, be strong for everyone but me.*

Oh, shush.

Lorna motioned for them to start walking. Once Arabella was at Lorna's side, she placed a hand on Arabella's lower back and kept pace with her strides. "You look beautiful, Ara. So much so I'm not sure my nephew can keep his wits about him."

Arabella smiled and looked to Lorna. "He would be fine if you hadn't kicked him out of our cottage yesterday evening."

The older dragonwoman shrugged. "Finn knows the traditions. He's already gotten you with child. He can't really make a bigger claim than that."

"Gee, glad to be of service," Arabella answer dryly.

"Oh, come, hen, you know what I mean. Besides, take a dragonman away from his mate for a night and the results can be quite spectacular."

"Do I really want to know the reasons for that statement?"

Lorna clicked her tongue. "Don't be a prude. You wouldn't be here if not for your own parents having sex."

A few weeks ago, a simple statement about her parents would've made Arabella sad and want to hide. However, that was no longer the case.

Instead, Arabella dropped her voice low. "Make sure to mention that to my brother, often and very loudly."

Amusement flashed in Lorna's eyes. "Aye, I have plans for your brother. Just wait."

Healed by the Dragon

Grinning, Arabella noticed they were at the secret side entrance to the great hall. Thanks to Lorna, she'd all but forgotten her nervousness.

Her dragon snorted. *Next time, I can tease you about sex to calm you down. I have lots of fantasies to share.*

I'm sure you do. Just behave for a little while, okay?

Her beast huffed. *If I must.*

Lorna placed her hand on the doorknob and looked to Arabella. "Ready, lass?" She nodded and Lorna added, "Right then, it's time to impress the crowd."

Impress was maybe too strong of a word. All Arabella cared about was finishing the ceremony without any problems. For some reason, things kept happening at clan gatherings, whether here or back on Stonefire.

Her dragon chimed in. *Nothing happened during Duncan's presentation and sentencing.*

Rather than acknowledge her dragon was correct, Arabella created a mental maze and shoved her dragon inside. Her beast roared, but Arabella didn't care. She needed a respite from her dragon's commentary.

Amazing how things had changed over the last year.

Lorna guided her into the room and up the stairs of the dais. Standing in the middle of the stage was Finn, dressed in a deep blue traditional outfit, with material hanging around his hips and a sash thrown over one shoulder. Her eyes fell to his bicep without the dragon-shifter tattoo. Soon, it wouldn't be naked.

Looking back to Finn's eyes, his pupils flashed to slits and back. A mixture of love, appreciation, and desire burned in his gaze.

Even though she knew his body well after the frenzy and a week of exploring him at her pleasure, the mere thought of him covering her with his powerful, broad chest made wetness rush between her legs.

Lorna cleared her throat and whispered, "You two can go at it like rabbits later. Focus for a bit, aye?"

The older dragonwoman's voice snapped Arabella back to the present and she remembered everyone was watching. Straightening her shoulders, she gave a slight nod. "I'm switching to co-clan leader mode."

"Has he accepted that title yet?"

Since Finn was now less than a foot away, he murmured, "Just about, but I'm enjoying how she tries to convince me."

Lorna rolled her eyes and handed Arabella to Finn. "Use the head on your shoulders, nephew."

Finn held out his hand and Arabella placed hers in his. Once he squeezed it, he murmured, "You can go now, Auntie. I can handle Arabella from here."

"Aye, it's the handling I'm afraid will turn into manhandling."

Arabella bit her lip to keep from smiling. "I'll keep him in line, Aunt Lorna."

"Right then, I trust your word over his." Finn opened his mouth and Lorna raised an eyebrow. "I love you, nephew, but I also know how you act where Ara is concerned."

Finn gave a stiff nod and Lorna left. Arabella barely heard the murmuring of the crowd in the hall; all she could see were Finn's warm, brown eyes filled with mischief. Arabella resisted a frown. "I don't want to know what you have planned." Glancing out at the hall, there weren't any decorations; most dragon-shifter mating ceremonies were bare so that the focus was on the couple. She looked back at her dragonman. "Embarrass me and there will be payback."

Placing his hand on her waist, he winked. "You'll just have to wait and find out."

"Fine. Can we start already?"

Worry crossed his expression. "Is the baby giving you trouble?"

She should say yes to get him to focus on getting the ceremony over with as quick as possible, but Arabella wasn't about to lie. "No, but you're killing my patience."

He leaned down to her ear and whispered, "Oh, I know a few ways where testing your patience only makes you scream louder."

She slapped his side. "Finn, focus."

He gave a dramatic sigh. "I suppose. The sooner we're done, the sooner I can have you to myself."

"What about our guests?"

"We'll slip out and come back. No one will notice."

"You do remember that my brother is here, don't you? He'll be watching us like a hawk."

Finn shrugged one shoulder. "Who cares? If he sees us leave, then he'll just have to suffer the knowledge I'm having a go at his sister."

"I'm not sure I need a baby when I have you acting like a ten-year-old."

"Hey now, I resent that. I'm more like an eight-year-old."

She shook her head. "Is there a difference?"

"Of course there is. Eight-year-olds don't have puberty looming over them."

Aware they could keep going back and forth for an hour, Arabella decided to steer them back on topic. "Fine, torture my brother. I might even enjoy it a little. But for now, can we get started? The sooner we're mated, the sooner the celebrations will start, giving the Stonefire visitors a chance to mingle with Lochguard."

Bowing his head, Finn murmured, "As you wish."

~~~

Finn brought Arabella's hand to his lips and his dragon sighed. *Why waste time kissing her hand? There are so many better places to kiss her. And not just her lips.*

Behave, dragon. We can kiss and lick her entire body later.

Fine. Finish the unnecessary ceremony quickly.

Since Finn had argued with his beast before about carrying out clan traditions—his dragon cared about them less each day they were with Arabella—he stood up, smiled at his female, and faced the crowd. Raising his hand, Finn waited for the noise to die down.

Once the hall was quiet, he began. "First, I want to thank everyone for coming, including our small group of guests from Stonefire. Some of you believed I would never claim a mate, but sometimes, the wait is worth it." He glanced to Arabella with love in his eyes and then back to the crowd. "Of course, I know you all are just here for the food and dancing, but give me a few minutes and you can enjoy the party."

Cheers rose up from the crowd. A lesser dragonman would've resented the action, but Finn knew his clan was desperate for a chance at fun after the last few weeks.

His eyes found Faye sitting off to the side in a wheelchair. She needed fun most of all. While she would walk with time, and he hoped fly as well, she wasn't strong enough yet to stand unaided. If that weren't enough, her former spark was barely noticeable these days. Instead, she was more solemn and reserved.

He only hoped it was a phase because if the changes were permanent, it would break his heart.

Faye's eyes met his and his cousin smiled. He took the small gesture as encouragement and focused back on the crowd. "For once, I'm going to spare the dramatics. It's time for me to claim what's mine, so let's begin."

A quick glance told him Arabella wanted to say something, but in a rare occurrence, she kept her opinions to herself.

Reaching to the small box laying on a table behind them, Finn took out the silver arm cuff with "Finn's" engraved in the old dragon language. Most bands were plain, but he'd had a few sprigs of heather engraved to each side of his name. Arabella noticed and gave a mini-eye roll, which made him grin. He spoke loudly so the clan could hear. "Arabella Kathleen MacLeod, you have already claimed my heart, but today I claim you as my mate in front of the clan. You are strong, clever, beautiful, and with a sense of humor to boot. We'll be arguing until we're both gray and wrinkly, but I wouldn't have it any other way. I offer you my mate claim. Will you accept it?"

Arabella smiled. "With an offer like that, I'm tempted to refuse, but then I'd be lonely and bored. So, I accept."

The crowd chuckled as he murmured, "Bloody woman." He took her arm without the dragon-shifter tattoo, the one with the healed burns, and slid the cuff on her upper bicep.

Seeing his name on her arm, covering up her healed burns, seemed fitting. Arabella's past no longer mattered; only her future with him on Lochguard did.

His dragon growled. *Ours.*

Yes, ours.

Arabella reached to the table to take out the larger cuff engraved with "Arabella's" in the old language. He'd barely glanced at it before, but he could see she must have snuck in a request to the silversmith because in addition to her name there were two small dragons playing chase in mid-flight. Just as they'd done right before the first time she'd trusted him with her body.

His heart warmed at the sight. Then Arabella's voice carried in the hall as she spoke, "Finlay Ian Stewart, despite your cockiness and tendency to tease, I will always love you, even when you refuse to admit I'm right." The clan laughed and she continued, "You have made me whole and I plan to keep you always. I offer you my mate-claim in front of our clan and some of my old clan. Will you accept?"

Offering his arm, he growled. "Of course, now hurry the hell up. I want your name on my arm."

The light touch of her fingers as she maneuvered the cuff onto his flesh, combined with the sight of her name on his bicep, sent a jolt straight to his cock. He wanted to claim his mate in all ways.

His dragon huffed. *And yet you chastised me. You're the randy one.*

Ignoring his dragon, Finn took Arabella's hands and kissed the back of each one in turn.

After sharing one glance at his mate, he turned them toward the crowd and hauled her against his side. Everyone clapped and cheered. Even her brother had joined in, albeit half-heartedly.

Finn raised his free hand and the crowd quieted. "Now with the official business out of the way, let's show the Stonefire dragon-shifters how to celebrate!"

As music blared and the majority of the clan started chatting, he noticed Faye sitting with her brothers and mother off to the side. Even Faye was smiling at something her brothers said.

Then he searched out Bram, Tristan, and their mates. It looked like Meg Boyd had found them and was chatting their ears off.

Convinced his clan could handle themselves for a short while, he leaned close to Arabella's ear and whispered, "I think we should have our own private claiming ceremony. While the version where I licked every inch of your body and make you come with my tongue will have to wait, I can claim you hard and rough and be back in time for the dancing." He nibbled her earlobe. "What do you say?"

~~~

Arabella knew the responsible thing would be to deny Finn. Yet her name on his arm wasn't nearly enough—she wanted to claim his body.

Her dragon snorted. *I have been suggesting that all afternoon. Let's find a quiet place and fuck him.*

Arabella glanced toward the secret side entrance and back. "We can sneak off there."

Finn's pupils flashed to dragon slits. "Let's go."

Rather than sneak away quietly, Finn tugged her down the stairs and out the door. Once he shut and locked it, he pinned her against the old wood. "I've always wanted to fuck you against a door."

Warmth surged through her body and her nipples turned hard. "Then stop talking and do it already."

He kissed her as a hand snaked down her body and under her skirt. When his fingers brushed her swollen pussy, she cried out.

Finn broke the kiss. "You're dripping wet already for me, love."

"Why are you still talking?" He plunged two fingers inside her and she moaned. "Not your damn fingers. I want your cock, Finn. Now."

Moving his fingers, she could barely concentrate on his words as he replied, "Telling me to do something is the wrong approach."

He adjusted the angle and she clutched his shoulders for support. She made her voice work to say, "Fuck me, don't fuck me, whatever it takes to get you inside me. I ache, Finn. I want you."

Removing his fingers, Finn nibbled her lower lip. "Tell me what I want to hear."

"If you don't hurry, someone will find us. Do you really want someone to see me with my skirt tossed up?"

Her mate growled. "I'm the only one allowed to see your body naked."

"And me, I hope."

"Bloody woman." Finn positioned his cock and thrust hard into her pussy.

Arabella dug her nails into his shoulders. "Move, already."

"You asked for it." Finn gripped her arse and lifted her off the ground. She had no choice but to wrap her legs around his waist. The second she did, he murmured, "Now, it's time to claim what's mine."

Before she could reply, Finn pulled out and thrust deep. Repeating the process, he increased his pace and Arabella forgot what she wanted to say.

The sound of flesh slapping against flesh filled the small alcove. When he moved just a little to the right, Arabella screamed.

Finn took her lips in a possessive kiss, never slowing his movements. She would probably have impressions left by the wood of the door when they were done, but as the pressure continued to build, she didn't care. She was being claimed by her mate.

He pulled his head back to meet her eyes. While his pupils flashed to slits and back, the human half of Finn was in charge.

Scratching her nails down his shoulder, Finn grunted and adjusted his position. One arm supported her arse as he leveraged her against the door. With his free hand, he snaked it between their bodies to pinch her hard nipple. The mixture of pleasure and pain was nearly enough to send her over the edge, but not quite.

One night apart had been one night too many.

She growled, "More."

Finn pinched and twisted, and lights danced before Arabella's eyes. Pleasure shot through her body as Finn continued to pound her hard, her pussy clenching, and releasing his large cock.

Stilling his body, Finn kissed her as he moaned into her mouth. Each spurt of his semen sent her over the edge again.

Several pleasure-hazed minutes later, Finn nuzzled her cheek as he slowly lowered her down to the floor. The second her feet touched the ground, she was grateful for the door supporting her.

She was the first to break the silence. "That was a good start."

Growling, Finn moved to meet her gaze. "Bloody hell, Ara, that was more than a good start. If I moved away, you'd fall over."

Smiling slowly, Arabella replied, "Maybe. But you're cute when you're angry."

"I am not 'cute.' I'm devilishly handsome."

"Maybe with age, but right now, you're cute."

"I'm this close to finding an abandoned room and convincing you of just how not 'cute' I am."

She brushed her fingers against the back of his neck. "I'm nothing if not open-minded. I can give you five minutes to convince me differently."

Stepping back, Finn pulled out of her. "Give me fifteen minutes."

She raised an eyebrow as she smoothed her dress. "Twelve."

"Deal." With a grunt, Finn scooped her up and carried her down the hall.

Resting her head against the side of his neck, she couldn't help but smile. "You do know how much I love you, right?"

"Sometimes I wonder about that. If you loved me, you'd stop fighting me every step of the way."

"Being complacent is boring. I believe a certain dragonman taught me that."

Finn looked down at her with amusement in his eyes. "Then that dragonman clearly doesn't know what he was talking about."

Arabella laughed. "How about you stop talking about yourself in the third person?"

"Tell this dragonman you love him again, and he just might."

Shaking her head, she murmured, "I love you, Finn, you bloody irritating dragonman."

He grinned. "And I love you, Arabella, you bloody irritating dragonwoman."

As they smiled at one another, Arabella had never been happier in her life. She had a true mate of her heart, her family in the other room, and an inner dragon who was fast becoming one of her best friends.

She may have been hesitant about coming to Lochguard, but Scotland and Finlay Stewart had been just what she needed. There was nothing she couldn't tackle with him at her side.

Dear Reader:

Thanks for reading *Healed by the Dragon*. I hope you enjoyed Finn and Arabella's story. If you're craving more of this couple, then know they feature quite often in my Lochguard Highland Dragons' spinoff series. (The first book is *The Dragon's Dilemma*.) Also, if you liked their story, please leave a review. Thank you!

The next book is about Stonefire's head Protector, Kai Sutherland, and the BBC Reporter from *Revealing the Dragons* named Jane Hartley. Their story is called *Reawakening the Dragon*. Turn the page for the synopsis and an excerpt.

To stay up to date on my latest releases, don't forget to sign-up for my newsletter at www.jessiedonovan.com/newsletter.

With Gratitude,
Jessie Donovan

Reawakening the Dragon
(Stonefire Dragons #5)

Tired of reporting the news but never investigating, Jane Hartley is determined to expose the truth of the Carlisle dragon hunters. While meeting with one of her sources, she spots the tall, blond dragonman she first saw three months ago back on Stonefire. When the dragonman warns her off, Jane becomes more determined than ever to find the truth before he does.

With most of the threats to his clan under control, Kai Sutherland wants to find a way to take down the Carlisle hunters for good. In the beginning of his investigation, he sees the human female his dragon wants. Putting aside his own needs, he tries to scare her away to focus on the hunters, but the female refuses to go.

As they work together to discover the hunters' secrets, the attraction between them threatens the investigation. Kai never expected to find his second chance, yet as the danger amps up, can he find a way to have her while still protecting his clan?

Excerpt from *Reawakening the Dragon*:

CHAPTER ONE

Jane Hartley plumped up her breasts in the low-cut dress and decided it was time to quit stalling. She had a job to do.

As she walked into the Fox and Stag pub, she gave a cursory glance around the crowded room. The bar was wooden and worn. The nicks spoke of more than one pub fight.

A billiards table was at the far back and the rest of the space was dotted with tables and patrons. Most of them were men, although there were a few other women here and there. All of them were dressed in more casual clothes than Jane's tight dress, which was already attracting notice. One or two men gave her lewd glances, but she merely smiled and headed for an empty seat near the bar.

Despite the heavy make-up, tight dress, wig, and heels, Jane wasn't there to pick up a man. According to one of her contacts in Manchester, some of the former Carlisle-based dragon hunters liked to have a few pints there on Fridays. Since the pub was full of somewhat shady-looking men, the hunters should fit right in.

She hoped to find out something useful or she'd have to reevaluate her strategy. She'd already wasted two days of her vacation tracking down the Fox and Stag in Newcastle. The former hunters' hangout in Carlisle had been abandoned after their loss to the Stonefire dragons earlier in the year. Who knew how long they'd use Newcastle and its surroundings as their new base. If she couldn't find the hunters, she couldn't write the story that could change the course of her career. Jane wanted to be more than a pretty face on camera, interviewing passersby. She wanted to be a true journalist.

The thought of never reporting stories that could make a difference in the world made Jane clutch her purse strap tighter. Working with the Stonefire dragon-shifters had reignited her drive to find out the truth and she would find her story even if it killed her. After all, no human had ever revealed the inner workings of the dragon hunters.

If Jane could do it, not only would she have the story of the year, she could also help sway public opinion even more in favor of the dragon-shifters. She knew firsthand from her interactions with Clan Stonefire that they weren't monsters. The trick was proving it with facts and a narrative that would tug at the public's heartstrings and make a lasting impression.

Reaching the bar, Jane slid into an empty seat and smiled at the bartender. It was time to get to work.

After asking for a pint, Jane casually staked out the room from the corners of her eyes. The largest group of men was seated behind her and to the left. Inspecting her nails as she waited for her drink, she listened to the group.

One of the men said, "Check out that bird. She's well fit. I'm going to chat her up."

The man didn't speak with a Geordie accent, but rather a Scouse one, which meant he was from Liverpool. Since Liverpool didn't have a dragon hunter branch, the man could be from the Carlisle group. One of the trademarks of the Carlisle branch was that they recruited from all over Great Britain.

She needed to talk with the men behind her and find out if her hunch was correct.

Jane's lager arrived. Taking a sip, she waited to see if any of the men would approach her. If not, she'd have to take matters into her own hands.

She didn't have to wait long. Less than a minute later, a man of average height, wearing jeans and a button-up shirt with the tails hanging out appeared on her left. His voice matched the Scouser from before. "Hey, beautiful, did you fall from heaven?"

Resisting the urge to roll her eyes, Jane forced herself to smile and change her voice into a flat American accent. "I guess that line works on either side of the pond."

The man smiled. "You're American."

"Yes, I'm here on a little vacation." She leaned forward a fraction and the man's eyes darted to her cleavage. "It's been awesome so far. Everywhere I turn, the men have such sexy accents. I can never get enough."

He met her eyes again and his smile grew wider. "Well, love, this is your lucky day. Me and my mates would love to have you over at our table. We'll say whatever you like."

The glint of desire in the man's blue eyes made her stomach churn. But Jane was prepared. If anything went wrong, she had an illegal can of pepper spray in her purse. Not to mention that ever since the dragon hunter attack on Stonefire earlier in the year, she'd been taking advanced self-defense classes, which would come in handy if needed.

With a nod, she answered, "I'd love to meet your friends. Maybe you can teach me how to sound British."

"Then come with me. My name's Jason."

Jane had long ago picked a fake name similar to her own. "I'm Jenn."

As the man guided her toward a table with about eight blokes, Jane catalogued their faces. While she didn't have an eidetic memory, she had always been good with faces. Even if she didn't find out any information about the dragon hunters from these men, she could later cross-check them with known dragon hunter associates and see if she was on the right track.

Of course, Jane was getting ahead of herself. She had to survive chatting with the slimy men at the table first.

The stench of beer, cigarettes, and stale male sweat hit her as she stopped next to the long table with Jason. This was going to be a long ten or twenty minutes with these men.

Remember, these men can lead me to my next clue. Even as they leered at her breasts before looking back to her face, Jane never stopped smiling. She waved. "Hello."

One of the men whistled. Since she'd spent the last decade focusing on her career, it'd been a long time since she had interacted with men in a pub. If whistling was the way to win a woman these days, Jane would remain single for the rest of her life.

Under normal circumstances, she would probably glare and give him the double finger salute.

However, these weren't normal circumstances, so the mental image of kicking each of the men in the balls would have to do for the present.

Jason placed his hand on her lower back. His touch made her want to take a long, hot shower. "This here is Jenn. She's an American looking for sexy accents. I told her we were it."

A dark-skinned man with black hair and brown eyes spoke up first. "Is that so? Then mine is the best."

A Birmingham accent.

A man with brown eyes and a pale, bald head spoke next. "Don't listen to him. Yorkshire is better. After all, we're the Texas of England."

With three accents identified, Jane's gut said this group of blokes might be the right one.

Keeping up her act as an American, she put her hands up and shrugged. "They all sound the same to me."

"Oi," the bald man said, "sit yourself down and we'll teach you properly. Next thing you know, you'll say we sound Australian."

Putting a finger to her mouth, she tried to look coy. "Well, you kind of do."

The man at her side motioned to some of his friends. "Move your arses and let the lady sit down. I think it's time we teach her the difference between us and the criminals."

Jane's mother was Australian, so she was familiar with how some Brits called Australians criminals—after all, the British had sent a lot of their convicted criminals to Australia and America back in the day.

She couldn't defend her mother, though, so she bit the inside of her cheek to prevent her from saying something out of turn. Playing the part of a clueless American was going to take more concentration than she'd thought.

Once Jane scooted into the booth and Jason slid in next to her, Jane was trapped between two possibly dangerous men. The reminder of exactly where she was and who these men could be calmed her mind. If she fucked up, more than her story would be on the line.

Her life could be, too.

Jane upped her charm and went to work.

JESSIE DONOVAN

~~~

Kai Sutherland tugged the sleeves of his new jumper and exposed his forearms. Unlike most dragon-shifters, Kai had tattoos on both arms. His jagged flame one in black ink helped him to better blend in with the humans and he needed all the blending in he could do given his height and tendency to growl.

Or, at least, that's what the human females of his clan had told him—that he growled too much.

Eyeing the pub across the street, Kai pushed aside thoughts of his growling and focused on his task. Newcastle was a dangerous city for dragon-shifters. While no one remembered the reasons, the Geordies were the most afraid of his kind in the entire United Kingdom and they did everything in their power to keep their cities clean of dragon-shifters. He couldn't fuck up or he could end up in the hands of the DDA, or worse.

However, their hatred was why Kai was here.

Because of it, the city welcomed dragon hunters without a second glance, believing the hunters could help protect them. According to his contacts, the pub across the street should be one of the usual hangouts for the hunters in the area.

Kai's dragon grunted. *Lure them out and we can eat them.*

No eating humans. That's one of the rules.

But rules are meant to be broken.

Not this time. Remember what they did to Charlie? Eating one or two isn't enough; we need to bring the bastards down.

Charlie had been Stonefire's first female Protector. Seven months ago, she'd been captured and drained of blood.

Clenching his fingers, Kai forced his anger to the back of his mind. Strong emotions would cloud his judgement and risk what might be the only chance he had to try to capture and

348

interrogate one or two hunters at his leisure. To protect his clan, he needed to take down Simon Bourne, Carlisle's leader. But he couldn't do that without more information.

His dragon replied, *The DDA will punish you if they find out what you're doing.*

Fuck the DDA. They always let us down.

Except Evie.

Evie Marshall was the human female mated to Kai's clan leader. *Of course, not Evie. That female proved herself.*

Just hurry up. I hate being in the crowded streets of cities.

In this, Kai agreed. *Then stay quiet and let me do my job.*

Fine, but you owe me a hunt later.

With that, his dragon retreated to the back of his mind and Kai crossed the street to the pub.

Upon entering, he took in his surroundings as he made it to the bar. Most of the patrons were working class males celebrating the end of the work week. A few human females drank with them or watched as some men played billiards on the far side of the room.

Then he looked toward the left and saw the back of a dark blonde-haired female sitting with a group of males. Her hair was swept up, exposing the delicate skin of her neck.

His beast growled out, *Ours.*

Don't be daft. No one is ours.

She is. Get her away from those humans.

Her biceps are bare, free of material and tattoos. She's human too.

That doesn't matter. Those human males aren't worthy.

Kai wanted to sigh. His dragon had always been a little dramatic. *You're not being quiet, so I will make you quiet.*

Wrestling his dragon into a mental prison before he could reply, Kai took the last few steps to the bar. While he waited for the bartender, he looked over his shoulder so he could see the woman's face.

The second he saw the blue eyes, long face, and bright smile, he felt as if he'd been punched in the gut.

The woman might be wearing too much make-up and had blonde hair instead of black, but it was Jane Hartley, the BBC reporter who'd been working with Stonefire over the last few months.

He wondered why the hell she was in Newcastle. He highly doubted it was a coincidence.

———————

Want to read the rest?
Reawakening the Dragon is available in paperback

For exclusive content and updates, sign up for my newsletter at:

http://www.jessiedonovan.com

AUTHOR'S NOTE

I'm both relieved and sad that Finn and Arabella's story is over. This has been one of the hardest stories I've written, but I hope I did it justice. Arabella very much deserved her happy ending!

I didn't do this alone. There are some people I'd like to thank for their help:

- Clarissa Yeo of Yocla Designs is an amazing cover artist and I'm lucky to have her. The attention to detail on my covers is just mind-blowing. I'm not sure how many other cover artists would be able to portray Arabella so well, with her scars and all.

- Becky Johnson and her team at Hot Tree Editing. Becky really pushed me on this one and I'm grateful. She doesn't allow me to be lazy. I'm sure my readers appreciate that!

- Iliana, Donna, and Alyson are my beta-readers and their input has been vital to this series. These ladies catch typos missed by five other sets of eyes. Not to mention they point out when something is off. I'm extremely grateful to have them.

- My readers. The support and enthusiasm from you all is amazing. You help make writing that much more awesome.

Thanks again for reading and I can't wait to for you to see what I'm cooking up in my next dragon story. It's about Kai, Stonefire's head Protector, and Jane Hartley, the reporter from *Revealing the Dragons*. After their story is the first book in my Lochguard Highland Dragons series, *The Dragon's Dilemma*. To keep up to date on news for that book, make sure to sign up for my newsletter on my website.

See you around! :)

ABOUT THE AUTHOR

Jessie Donovan wrote her first story at age five, and after discovering *The Dragonriders of Pern* series by Anne McCaffrey in junior high, she realized people actually wanted to read stories like those floating around inside her head. From there on out, she was determined to tap into her over-active imagination and write a book someday.

After living abroad for five years and earning degrees in Japanese, Anthropology, and Secondary Education, she buckled down and finally wrote her first full-length book. While that story will never see the light of day, it laid the world-building groundwork of what would become her debut paranormal romance, *Blaze of Secrets*. In late 2014 she officially became a *New York Times* and *USA Today* bestselling author.

Jessie loves to interact with readers, and when not reading a book or traipsing around some foreign country on a shoestring, can often be found on Facebook:

http://www.facebook.com/JessieDonovanAuthor

And don't forget to sign-up for her newsletter to receive sneak peeks and inside information. You can sign-up on her website:

http:///www.jessiedonovan.com

19760497R00207

Printed in Great Britain
by Amazon